The window was painted shut, so I grabbed a $100,000 chair and threw it through the glass. My adrenaline was pumping, because it went far enough to hit the next building. I went out first and was reaching up to help Archer when she suddenly froze, a look of stark terror on her face. I turned. Standing on the first steel landing below us were two figures aiming Kalashnikovs directly at our faces.

CIWAR

By Neil Russell

CITY OF WAR

NEIL RUSSELL

CITY OF WAR

HARPER

An Imprint of HarperCollinsPublishers

"Christmas Always Breaks My Heart." Lyrics by Neil Russell. Music by Chris Lang and Cesar Benitez. Copyright Russell/Lang/Benitez. All Rights Reserved. Used by Permission.

HARPER

An Imprint of HarperCollins*Publishers*
10 East 53rd Street
New York, New York 10022-5299

Copyright © 2010 by Neil Russell
ISBN 978-0-06-172168-7

First Harper paperback printing: March 2010

HarperCollins ® and Harper ® are registered trademarks of Harper-Collins Publishers.

Printed in the United States of America

Visit Harper paperbacks on the World Wide Web at
www.harpercollins.com

10 9 8 7 6 5 4 3 2

For Rick and Jim . . .
You're playing two-handed now,
but one day, we'll all be together again.
There'll be a lot of laughing and lying and remembering.
Then somebody will yell, "Shut up and deal."
Until then, play on.
I miss you more than words can tell.

God, give us men . . .
Men of honor, who will not lie . . .
Tall men, who live above the fog.

JOSIAH GILBERT HOLLAND

CITY
OF
WAR

1

Marcus Aurelius and the 405

A naked woman running full tilt through ankle-deep water in a freeway carpool lane isn't something you see every day. But if you happen to stumble across it, your eyes could do a lot worse than Kimberly York.

Sometime around 167 AD, Marcus Aurelius said that life unfolds exactly like it's supposed to—that neither gods nor man can change a thing. And over the years, as I've watched the pleas of good men go unanswered while scoundrels prospered, it's become clear to me that Marcus stumbled onto something. But looking back on that Saturday night last August, if the Man Upstairs Himself had told me that what was about to unfold was preordained, I'd have asked Him to take a breathalyzer.

The earthquake wasn't much by California standards. Only a 3.6. But the guy with the funny hair on the 11 o'clock news said it started a fire on my block in Beverly Hills, so I ushered ashore my dinner guests, Rhonda Champion and Bert and Brittany Rixon, and buttoned up my boat, the *Sanrevelle*.

It was a quiet night at the Dolphin Bay Yacht Club, and the parking valet wasn't at his post. I eventually located him behind the kitchen sharing a smoke with Emilio, the club's chef, I tipped him generously for hustling up my Rolls Phantom and started the fifty-five-mile trek north from Newport Beach.

As I crossed into Long Beach in the heavy, but fast, late-night traffic, the first aftershock hit, setting off burglar alarms in the surrounding neighborhoods and undulating the grooved concrete of the 405 under my tires. Fifteen miles ahead, it also ruptured one of the City of Inglewood's prehistoric water mains, creating half a dozen thirty-foot geysers along the freeway and sending hundreds of thousands of gallons of water pouring onto the northbound lanes. As the torrent rushed south, channeled by the solid concrete center divider and an unnatural inward tilt of the freeway's right shoulder—compliments of stellar Cal-Trans engineering—it was turning my side of the highway into a six-lane trout stream. I just didn't know it yet.

Ten minutes later, I noticed the pavement was wet, the water was getting deeper, and there wasn't a drop of rain in sight. Anywhere else, drivers might have taken a beat. Maybe even considered it slightly distracting, feeling their vehicles hydroplaning under them while they tried to see through sheets of spray butterflying skyward off big-rigs slamming along at seventy miles an hour. But this is L.A., where we get on the freeway to watch a DVD, so in unison, several thousand would-be Mario Andrettis dialed their wipers up to Warp-3 and pushed their accelerators down a little further to compensate for the resistance.

I was in the fast lane approaching El Segundo Boulevard, and it was all I could do to see through the billowing cascades and still keep up enough speed so the red Lamborghini tailgating me didn't drive up my exhaust. And thanks to the Phantom's twelve cylinders and six thousand pounds of British steel, I was doing a pretty good job plowing a path for both of us until the 18-wheel Budweiser truck a quarter mile ahead saw the forest of geysers, hit his brakes and turned everything to shit.

Ten tons of metal, glass and beer sliding sideways with fast, bumper-to-bumper traffic bearing down on it isn't missionary position driving—even in Southern California—and the first two rows of cars had no chance. They rammed into the truck without so much as tapping their brakes.

By the time the rear-ending got back to me, I'd swung my black and silver behemoth into the carpool lane and gotten it down to zero a few feet from the rear door of a sideways Mercedes. The guy behind me in the Lamborghini wasn't so lucky. He tried veering into the carpool lane too, but there wasn't any room left, and he hit the center divider at just the right angle, went airborne and tumbled end over end into the southbound lanes.

I stopped counting after I heard six cars hit him. And a few seconds later, all twelve lanes in both directions of the busiest freeway in the world came to a standstill. I was just about to get out to see if there was anything I could do for the guy in the Italian sandwich when Kimberly York entered my life.

Stopped dead in the southbound carpool lane, directly across the concrete barrier, was a midnight blue Ford van with the windows blacked out—like the ones you see in presidential motorcades. The driver's side glass was down, and the guy behind the wheel looked nervous. He had a deeply pockmarked face and was wearing a thin black tie and a white shirt with the sleeves rolled up, revealing a large spider tattoo with red highlights on his left forearm. I noticed the spider was missing a leg.

More intriguing was the bloodred cloth headband tied tightly around his forehead, its loose ends trailing down his back. There was someone else in the front seat smoking a short cigar, but from where I sat, I could only tell he was solidly built and had on a dark baseball cap.

Suddenly one rear cargo door of the van burst open, and a tall, stark-naked woman leaped out. Before either guy in the van could react, she had climbed across the divider in front of my car and taken off running north like a track star, splashing through the six inches of water like it wasn't there.

By the time Headband-man realized what had happened and got his door open, the girl had twenty yards on him. He climbed onto the divider, but I turned the Rolls's wheels and pulled forward the few inches I had left, leaving him no room to get down. Angry at the intrusion into his affairs and wobbling awkwardly on the narrow ledge of concrete, he kicked at me through my window. I caught his foot, twisted it and pushed it back out.

He fell backward against his van and slid down between it and the center divider. When he came up, his eyes were murderous. Just then, the southbound carpool lane opened, and the traffic ahead of the van shot forward. In courteous L.A. fashion, the driver of the white Caddie behind the van leaned on his horn and yelled out the window, "Hey, asshole, get that fuckin' piece of shit moving!"

Headband-man never took his eyes off me. He reached into his hip pocket and came out with a long switchblade, which he flipped open like he'd been born doing it. Finding new respect for his fellow motorist, Caddie-guy stopped yelling and got off his horn.

Just then, the van's passenger shouted, "Tino, get the fuck back in here and drive. We'll swing around and get her on the other side."

The guy had some kind of accent, but I couldn't quite place it. Tino didn't move. He continued staring at me and waving the knife. So I said, "Hey, Cochise, why don't you hustle on back to Universal before you miss the next tour bus. The girl voted with her feet."

Tino lunged forward, reaching over the divider and swiping the knife at me. He didn't really come close, but enough was enough.

"You know, Tino," I said, "you're the Babe fucking Ruth of bad decisions." And I climbed across the front seat and got out on the passenger side. Seeing that Headband-man was preoccupied with me, Caddie-guy regained his gonads and leaned on his horn again.

It's always interesting to watch people's reactions when they see me unfold. I'm what you would call really tall, and even if you're used to being around big people, I get your attention. I'm also lucky enough to have been born with enough definition to look like I spend more time in the gym than I do. It's a combination that usually ends disagreements before they get up a head of steam.

I felt my Top-Siders grip the wet pavement, and I was glad I wasn't wearing that slippery pair of Nikes I'd been too lazy to take back. Tino took a long look at me, and I could see him doing the math. But while he was deciding whether to go for it anyway, Caddie-guy broke the spell. He jammed his car in gear and rammed into the back of the blue van. Out of the corner of my eye, I saw Tino's passenger fly forward and almost hit his forehead on the dash.

Cigar-guy's voice tremored with rage. "Goddamn it, Tino, get back in here, or I swear to God, I'll take that fuckin' knife and cut you a new asshole myself."

Without taking his eyes off me or lowering the knife, Tino climbed back in the van and roared away while the white Caddie leaned on his horn and tailgated him at breakneck speed.

The northbound lanes weren't going to open anytime soon, and my feet were already wet, so I locked up the Rolls and went after the girl. I'm not really a runner, but I move pretty well, and my long stride was an advantage in the rushing water.

When I got to the Budweiser truck, smoke was coming out of the cab. I could see the driver slumped over the wheel, unconscious. Three men were taking turns standing on the truck's top step trying to wrench him out without success. Suddenly, flames leaped up out of the dash and set the truck's ceiling on fire. The acrid black smoke of burning plastic surged out the door and drove the rescuers back. The driver opened his eyes and moaned.

* * *

Suddenly, I was three thousand miles away. Treading water in a wreckage-strewn, gasoline-slick sea. Then the fire came, searing my face and blistering my hands. I heard her scream, and I dove and swam in the direction I thought it was coming from. But when I surfaced, gasping for air, there was only more fire. I called her name. Then came the second explosion . . . and then nothing.

"Hey, buddy, you okay?"

I turned. A well-dressed man in horn-rimmed glasses had hold of my arm. I looked at my hands, but there were no burns. I saw the smoke-engulfed Budweiser truck.

I ran to the cab, held my breath and with my height and reach, felt around the driver's waist. He was still belted in. Just as I found the seat-belt release, he screamed that his legs were on fire. I grabbed his shirt and pulled—hard. He came tumbling out into my arms as flames erupted through the cab.

I threw the driver over my shoulder and, with the searing heat pushing me along like a blast of wind, I ran clear of the flames, then sat him down in the rushing water, where his legs stopped smoldering. As other motorists came over to help, I heard sirens in the distance. I left the driver with a couple of guys who seemed to know what they were doing and continued after the girl.

I'd gone about thirty yards past the wreck when I saw her. She'd crossed the empty northbound lanes and was picking her way through a patch of freeway forest trying to find a path past the geysers. But the water was so deep here, and pounding down so hard that, all of a sudden, she lost her footing and went down.

When I got to her, she was spitting mud and leaves and swearing like an angry rapper. I reached down and pulled her up, but instead of being grateful, she took a swing at me. I caught her fist in my palm and held it. So she kicked me. Even though she was barefoot, it stung, so I squeezed her fist until she got control of herself.

I was still wearing my hanging-around-the-boat clothes—

a beat-up pair of khaki bush shorts and a blue denim work shirt over a navy Tee. I took the denim shirt off and put it on her. She was pretty tall herself, but even so, my 17 x 40 extra-long was like a dress on her. She buttoned a couple of buttons to keep it from flying open, then started back into the underbrush.

Rather than fight with her again, I opted for fear. Shouting to be heard above the pounding water, I said, "Tino and his friend are circling around on the side streets. They figure you'll be easy to spot."

At the sound of the name Tino, her head shot up like she'd been slapped. I could see she was teetering on the edge of hysteria. She started to sob. I went over and put my arm around her and felt her go limp. Doing most of the walking for us both, I waded her back across the freeway and headed toward the Rolls. To try to ease her anxiety, I said, "You're safe now," and she seemed to relax a little.

When we got to my car, she looked at it, started to say something, then didn't. I saw her working to compose herself as she dried off with one of the towels I handed her, then she got herself situated in the passenger seat with a blanket over her legs. I took off my wet shoes, threw another towel on the floor and got behind the wheel barefoot.

I saw her fingering the lettering on the blanket.

"What's *Sanrevelle*?" she asked.

"The name of my boat."

"And it's big boat, right?"

"Pretty big."

She looked at me, and I caught a little bit of a glint in her eye—a good sign. "So you're either married or gay or live with your mother."

"Mind telling me where you're going with this?"

"I'm in a Rolls with a terrific-looking guy who owns a boat with monogrammed blankets. Things like that just don't happen to me, so I'm looking for the punch line."

"Sorry to disappoint," I said. "No wife, no boyfriend, and the only person at home is my valet."

"Oh, this is just great," she said with mock sarcasm. "Now there's a fucking valet! And here I sit. Drowned Rat Cinderella. Well, my luck's holding."

We both laughed, and I felt the mood in the car change.

"You wouldn't happen to have a Big Mac lying around this crate, would you?" she asked. "I'm fucking starving. The least those assholes could have done was feed me."

If you can swear with that kind of conviction, you're probably going to live. "There's a picnic basket in the backseat. See what you can come up with. I'm a little hungry myself."

She managed to stretch far enough to reach the basket with only a slight loss of modesty, and when she got the cover off, she smiled in genuine delight. And it was a good smile. Lots of teeth and a faint wrinkling around the temples that gave her eyes a Christie Brinkley look.

Pawing through the goodies like a hungry cat, she took inventory. "Sandwiches, cheese, crackers, caviar, a pair of wineglasses . . . and this . . ." She held up a bottle of cabernet sauvignon and scrunched her eyes at the label. "What's PlumpJack Reserve?"

"Something Shakespeare could have only dreamed of."

"Really? And is '95 a good year?"

"Well, it's before the company started putting screw caps on a great wine, but you be the judge. There should be a corkscrew in the glove compartment."

"You always travel like a Ruth's Chris?"

"Only during earthquake season."

"Is *that* where all this fucking water came from?"

"That and Flintstones-era plumbing."

"Well, thank God for good timing."

"Ruined Tino's plan for a big night?"

"Kept me from being fish food." She shuddered involuntarily.

I looked at her, but she wasn't acting. I reached for my cell phone.

"What are you doing?" she asked with an edge in her voice.

"Calling the cops."

Her sarcasm was palpable. "What, so I can spend the next several hours being asked questions I don't know the answers to? Thanks just the same, but I think enough of L.A. has already seen my ass."

I put the phone down. "You want to talk?"

"Maybe later," she said. "You have a name?"

"Rail."

"First or last?"

"First. The last is Black."

"Rail Black. You do anything like . . . ordinary?"

"Actually, it's Rail Sheridan Black—after my grandfather, but without the 'Lord' in front of it."

"You some kind of royalty or something?"

"Mostly the 'or something.' "

"And you are?"

"Kimberly York."

"Okay to call you Kim?"

"Ordinarily, no, but I make an exception when I'm wearing the guy's clothes. So who's Rhonda?"

I saw that she was looking at the gift card she found in the wine basket. "A friend. Rhonda Champion. Tomorrow's my birthday. We were planning to go bonito fishing. That was lunch."

"From the tone of this, I think Rhonda was expecting to be dessert."

"Could be."

"You and Rhonda serious?"

"Well, I couldn't just sit around waiting for you."

That got a laugh, and it was as nice as I'd expected it would be. So we sipped our PlumpJack, and she ravaged the rest of the basket while tow trucks and ambulances came and went up ahead of us. There's something I've always liked about watching a very pretty, extremely ravenous, young lady eat. And this was a tall, healthy girl who went at it with both fists and talked with her mouth full.

After a while, the emergency workers had a couple of

lanes clear, and the geysers shut down, so the highway patrol started waving people through.

"Where can I drop you?" I asked.

"Where do you live?"

"Beverly Hills."

"Then your place will be fine."

2

Sexy Elevators and Killer Pastrami

Beverly Hills is a city of 35,000 halfway between downtown L.A. and the Santa Monica pier. But it's not your ordinary town. It's not even your ordinary rich people's town. From its beginnings as a Native American spiritual site called "The Gathering of the Waters" through its cattle ranching days and finally as home to some of the wealthiest people on the planet, it's a place of boom, bust and mythmaking.

It's also as Balkanized as any city in America, but not by race, ethnicity or bloodlines. All that matters here is money and celebrity. Pick the first, and regardless of how many banks your family robbed back in Dubuque, presto, you're a leading citizen. Pick the second, and your white-trash in-laws can hang their tattooed asses out the window of your twenty-million-dollar mansion and get applause from appreciative tourists.

I've got a friend, Richie Catcavage, who's a brilliant screenwriter and a brilliant drunk—and not necessarily in that order, which is why he keeps turning up on my doorstep. In one of his many unproduced scripts, he wrote a piece of dialog.

*"Beverly Hills is a place where nobody runs for president
because they don't want to move to a smaller house."*

A drunk or not, he's probably right.

I turned north off Sunset and wound my way up the hill to
Dove Way. A fire engine sat at the corner, but its emergency
lights were off, and the crew was busy rolling up hoses.
About a dozen people were standing outside my neighbor's
house, which had its gate open and lights on. I recognized
one of the men as the owner, and when he saw me, he smiled
and waved. A television truck sat nearby, its crew taking
shots of mostly nothing. But that's Beverly Hills. A movie
star burns his toast, stop the presses.

My place sits on two landscaped acres hugging a hillside, but the ten-foot ivied walls, thick privacy foliage and
screened gate keep it from being seen from the street. It's
a 17,000-square-foot Spanish hacienda with a little Hollywood eccentricity thrown in.

Elevators in private homes were pretty rare in 1922, especially ones between the master suite and an underground
sixteen-car garage—with both entrances hidden. But whoever had needed this kind of egress had also been particular
about lift aesthetics. On the ceiling, there's a painting of a
bare-chested, gold-helmeted conquistador astride a rearing,
fire-snorting stallion. And clutching him from behind is a
Vargas-inspired, exceptionally buxom, mostly unclad young
lady, head thrown back in ecstasy, a rose clenched between
her teeth. Add in the extra-thick tapestries on the walls, and
the effect is apparently to render the conveyance both erotic
and soundproof—a design nuance I have yet to see fully ex-
plored on HGTV.

1001 Dove Way is one of the original "North of Sunset"
properties, and over the years, it's had a litany of owners,
including some fairly famous ones. But to me, none of the
prior inhabitants is as intriguing as J. C. Stinson, Howard
Hughes's personal attorney.

Legend has it that during Howard's early paranoid stage, to avoid subpoenas, he lived in Stinson's pool house. And since it doubled as a screening room, he spent months lying naked on one of the couches, watching *Citizen Kane* over and over.

Personally, I think if he was watching anything, it was a picture of his own, like *The Outlaw*, instead of one done by a guy he hated—but *Kane* makes a better metaphor. That's what I mean about Beverly Hills mythmaking. When was the last time anybody cared what John D. Rockefeller watched and what he wasn't wearing while he watched it? And even if they did care, where else would it be bold-printed in the real estate listing?

I bought the house—furnishings and all—six years ago. The previous owner had had a little problem with the tax man and was going to be spending the next decade as a federal guest if he didn't get out of town—fast. He'd kept the house in his secretary's name, and I was a cash buyer, so there wasn't much haggling. The last I heard, he was living in Belize with a Norwegian underwear model.

Little by little I've brought the place back to its past glory. I say little by little, because it's nearly impossible to find craftsmen who can duplicate the original work. If I were counseling young people, I'd tell the ones who weren't headed for college to forget everything they've been told about technology and learn the old trades. The supply of talent that can work with hardwoods, stained glass, hand-made fabric and countless other one-of-a-kinds you can't buy at Home Depot is practically nonexistent.

Anyone with any skill at all has a backlog of projects that runs into years. And because clients almost always have heavy money, you can charge whatever you like, and people will line up to pay it. Not a bad way to earn a living and get some creative satisfaction in the process. And woe be it unto the billionaire who gives his craftsmen a hard time. They simply walk out and leave him with a half-restored terra-cotta fresco or a marble staircase to nowhere. The rich generally aren't very careful about the way they treat people, but believe me, they kiss artisan ass.

As I passed through my gate and wheeled up the tree-lined drive, I saw Mallory coming out the front door. He's my houseman, valet, confidant and friend. He's been with me almost from the day I was born, and his power to antici-pate my needs is uncanny. I have no idea how I'd get along without him, and I try never to think about it.

As soon as I stopped, he was already unloading my week-end gear from the Rolls, and in typical British fashion, he didn't register so much as an arched eyebrow at the young lady who climbed out of the car wearing my shirt and noth-ing else.

"Kim York, this is Mallory," I said.

Kim stuck out her hand, and Mallory took it as if he were greeting a *marquesa*—not a half-dressed young lady with mud on her feet.

His clipped accent is as impeccable as his manners. "Wel-come to the Black home, Ms. York. I knew some Yorks once. Sir Elliot and his lovely wife, Margaret."

"I don't believe I know El and M," Kim answered, "but we Yorks are a reserved lot, so it's possible we were just never properly introduced."

I think Mallory was amused, because as he turned to go inside, he winked at me.

Kim had gaped at the house when we'd arrived, but once inside, she stopped dead in her tracks. She took in the oval foyer's marble and murals, then looked up the thirty feet or so at the massive crystal and wrought iron chandelier sus-pended from a long, thick chain. After a moment, she said, "There's dust on the bulbs."

I laughed and said to Mallory, "Put Ms. York in the Toledo Room and see if you can scare up something for her to wear. Then let's attend to that dust."

"Toledo Room? Pray tell?" Kim asked.

"The previous owner had a real thing for Spanish steel.

You'll understand when you see it. Why don't you grab a shower and come down for a snack and a nightcap."

As the two of them mounted the stairs, I stole another look at Kim's long, tanned legs, and for the second time that night, I was impressed. When Mallory returned, I asked him if there was anything to eat.

"I'll set something up in the kitchen. If I may say so, it's good to have you back, sir. It's never quite the same when you're gone."

"I take it the quake didn't cause any damage."

"Not unless you count the jar of pickles I dropped when I grabbed onto the counter. Other than the food, will you be needing me for anything else?"

"No, Mallory, I don't believe so. Thank you."

"Then good night, sir."

I went upstairs and grabbed a quick shower and a change of clothes, then slipped some Wynton Marsalis onto the house sound system. The best jazz artist of today was just easing into something low and slow when Kim reappeared. She was wearing a long, teal silk robe with a pair of matching slippers. I hadn't seen those clothes in a long time, and I felt the sadness well up. It always came when I least expected it. Turning a corner and catching a glimpse of copper hair. Seeing a profile in a passing car.

Kim turned to model her outfit. "You must have quite a budget for drop-ins. It only took Mallory about five minutes to come up with an entire wardrobe."

I tried to keep my voice light. "He's resourceful."

Kim had pulled her still-damp hair back and gathered it with a strand of white lace. There was a matching strand tied around her neck, its trailing ends hanging down her back. I recognized the lace as the tiebacks from the draperies in the Toledo Room.

"Nice touch, the lace," I commented.

She fingered the strand at her neck. "I couldn't resist. It's Alençon."

The blank I drew must have shown, and she shook her

head again. "Made by French nuns and almost priceless. I thought the robe needed a little something."

Looking at the way the silk clung to her, I said, "Groucho wouldn't have been able to resist that line—especially when you threw in nuns. But I'd probably get my face slapped." Shifting gears, I said, "The accommodations up to your standards?"

"That room is just flat-out magnificent. All those swords hanging on the walls. Very Ali Baba." She paused. "I think everyone should have a completely unexpected place in their home, don't you?"

"What's yours?"

"I don't know you well enough yet."

It didn't sound like she was being coy, so I dropped it. "Well, if the Mongol hordes try to take Rodeo Drive, we'll mount our Ferraris and drive them back to Malibu."

She laughed and saluted. "Aye, aye, Captain. By the way, I was impressed with the Vettriano over the fireplace, too. *The Letter*, isn't it? I'm sure you know that the last time one of his originals was offered, it brought well over a million."

"I bought it for a friend. It was her favorite."

"Not Rhonda." It wasn't a question.

"No, not Rhonda."

"Then it must have been the one in the photograph Mallory was hustling out of the room when I wasn't supposed to be looking."

"I'll have to tell him he's slipping," I said with as much lightness as I could muster. I knew which picture it was.

We'd gone riding along the beach that morning. Mallory had packed a picnic lunch, and we stopped under a copse of trees. But each time we began a conversation, a large blue macaw above us would interrupt with loud, maniacal chatter. Eventually, we got to laughing so hard we couldn't eat.

Figuring it was looking for a handout, she kicked off her shoes and stood on her saddle to offer it a banana chip. Our antagonist wolfed it down and squawked for more. I snapped the picture just as she looked back at me. The cop-per-haired girl and the blue macaw. Two hours later, she would be dead.

"French lace and Scottish artists. You're full of surprises," I said to change the subject.

"I just read a lot, that's all. Is that it? Just plain Mallory?"

"No, but I've never heard anyone call him anything else."

"It's appropriate somehow. Subject change. If you don't mind my asking, just how the hell tall are you?"

"You have any questions you get tired of?"

She grinned, "Like, Can I borrow twenty till payday? That bad, huh?"

"Worse."

"Let me guess, hoops."

"You only say that because I have a good jump shot."

That made her laugh again, and I decided it was a sound I could get used to.

"Actually, I swim."

"Ah, a contrarian."

"I was just better at it, that's all. But you can't be my size and not have had someone stick a basketball in your hands, so once upon a time, I did play. It's a terrific sport played by some of the best athletes in the world, but the shoe jack-als have seduced an entire generation of gullible kids into believing that the ticket out of desperation is through a play-ground instead of a library."

"And what do you *really* think?"

I smiled. "You asked, you got."

"Remind me not to ask if I look fat in this robe. Hey, what have you got to eat in this palace? I'm ravenous again. And I could use another glass of that Plump stuff. It was almost as good as sex."

"Mallory said there'd be something in the kitchen. Take a left through the dining room, and I'll fetch another bottle of orgasms."

3

PlumpJack Gets You to Toledo

Mallory had done his usual stellar job: Jerry's Deli pastrami on onion rolls with sides of coleslaw and potato salad. The only thing people in laid-back L.A. tend to be passionately myopic about—other than the interminable Lakers/Clippers debate—is their deli. Factors, Nate & Al's, Junior's. Pick one, get an argument. Jerry's may not be the Carnegie or the Stage, but for my money, it's as close as you're going to get on this coast. And the one on Beverly Boulevard across from Cedars-Sinai is open until 4:00 a.m., which in itself is cause for celebration in a city that rolls up the sidewalks after *Wheel of Fortune*.

While we ate, we small-talked, and after a couple of glasses of wine, I saw Kim start to relax. When we'd wiped the last dabs of mustard off our mouths, she said, "I'd kill for a cigarette, but as you may have noticed, Capt. Black, I came aboard without pockets. Is it too much to hope for that amid all this wretched excess there might be a Benson & Hedges? Or are you one of those California assholes who starts coughing and yelling cop if they see something being fired up that isn't a joint?"

"Actually, I'd like a cigarette too. And my position on

tobacco is pretty much my position on everything that's legal—and a few things that aren't. It's none of my business what you do. I only smoke two or three times a month, but if I wanted to go through four packs a day, as long as I'm not doing it in a nursery school, it's between me and my butane salesman. I can't help you with Benson & Hedges, though. When I want a cigarette, I want to taste it. So it's English Ovals or nothing."

"Bring 'em on."

"I should warn you, they're not filtered."

"Then it'll be like when I used to sneak my stepfather's Camels."

"Okay, let's sit outside. I'll turn on the pool lights."

It was a beautiful night. Warm and full of stars. We sat, had another glass of wine and smoked. I let her get back to the events of the evening on her own.

"Dante and Tino," she said. "Who the fuck ever figures you're going to be kidnapped at Ralphs?"

"When did it happen?"

"About 5:30 this afternoon. The one on Olympic behind the Fox studios. Instead of doing what I usually do, which is park in the open lot in front, the sun was still really hot, so I pulled into the parking garage underneath and took the elevator up. I was in the salad aisle when this woman walked up and said, 'Excuse me, miss, but is that your silver Mustang downstairs?' "

Kim stopped, seemed to falter. "Jesus, it's like I'm watching a movie in my head."

"Sometimes that happens. It's why it's usually better to tell a story instead of just answer questions. Now close your eyes and freeze-frame on the woman. Tell me about her."

She swallowed a couple of times, seemed to work up her nerve, then closed her eyes. "Slender, maybe five-five. Attractive, but not drop dead. Black pantsuit, lime green blouse. Silk, I think."

"How about her hair?"

"Shoulder-length. And she's wearing a scarf. Designer.

Also lime with red geometrics. Jesus, it's too fucking hot for a scarf."

"Don't get sidetracked. Concentrate on her face."

"Sunglasses. Those ugly-as-shit Valentinos with the creepy butterflies on the temples. I call them the M. Night Shyamalan Collection." She hesitated. "Terrible makeup choice too. She's got olive skin, so her lipstick should be dark. Especially with the lime. But it's bright pink."

"Jewelry? Birthmarks?"

"Her ears are pierced, but there's nothing in them. And her breath smells like cigarettes. Strong ones." Suddenly, without warning, Kim burst into tears. After a moment, she got herself back under control. "I don't know why I did that."

"Emotional release. Healthy."

She took a sip of wine. "After I told her I did have a silver Mustang, she said, 'I thought I saw you get out of it. It's none of my business, but some guy in a van ran into it, and he's down there now leaving a note.' "

"What about her voice?" I said.

"Accented. French, but lower class. Inconsistent with her outfit." She stopped again and looked at me. "My panties were in a bunch because I'd just gotten my car back from the body shop. Some old fart in Westwood thought the word 'yield' meant close your eyes and go for it and almost tore off my bumper."

Kim was one of those people—mostly women and CIA directors—who can't tell a story in a straight line. "What did you do?" I prodded.

"I left my cart in the salad aisle and made a beeline."

"How long were you in the store before she came up to you?"

"Ten minutes, maybe fifteen. I was. . ."

I interrupted her. "Did she follow you out?"

Kim furrowed her brow, took another sip of wine and finally said, "Yes, she did. When I was getting in the parking elevator, she was walking across the front lot. Hey, her shoes were lime green too. Low heels."

"But she didn't get in the elevator."

Then it hit her. "Shit, she couldn't have seen anybody hit my car. She was parked on the upper level. What a freaking fucking idiot I am."

"Okay, now we've established that there were at least three of them. Had you ever seen this woman before?"

"She looked kind of familiar, but not like I know her. More like when you see your Starbucks clerk at the dry cleaners. The face rings a bell, but it's out of context."

"Like someone who might have been following you earlier, but it didn't register."

Kim looked at me strangely. "How do you know so much about this stuff?"

I ignored her question. "Go on."

"No, I want to know how you know what to ask. Are you a cop?"

"You've found me out. And this is the Beverly Hills PD safe house. But we have to be out by noon tomorrow because the chief has it reserved for a lunchtime quickie."

She got a little irritated at my response, but that was okay. Emotion can help jog memory. I let her stew for a moment, then she calmed down and apologized. "Look, this has been the most traumatic experience of my life, and I know I'm not handling it very well. I appreciate everything you've done, but I haven't got a clue who you are."

"You're handling it just fine. And for the record, I'm just a private citizen who sometimes helps his friends. Besides, you're the one who invited herself home with me."

She lit another English Oval. "These are strong, but good. I need a break. Give me an example of how you help people."

I gave it some thought. "Okay, last year, a good friend of mine, Shane Davis, a successful home builder, got a very aggressive form of leukemia. The last time we had dinner, he'd just finished running a marathon. Three months later, I was standing beside his hospital bed, and he weighed sixty-six pounds. He died the next day.

"Shane had a wife, Joanne, and four small daughters. He also had a business partner, Merle Street. When Merle realized Shane was dying, he hired a slippery law firm to rewrite the corporate records, then he looted the bank accounts, stopped paying creditors and let them force the place into bankruptcy.

"By the time Joanne called me, she'd lost her house, and she and the girls were living in a transient hotel near LAX, subsisting on food stamps. It didn't take a genius to figure out what happened, but it was going to take years and hundreds of thousands of dollars to get it through the courts. And even after she won, what was she going to get? A judgment she'd have to try to collect on?"

Kim's face took on a look of distress. "Are you going to tell me you killed this guy, Merle, because if you are, I salute you, because it sounds like the prick deserved it, but I don't want to know."

I shook my head. "What good would that have done? Another corpse, and there still wouldn't have been any money for Joanne. Besides, it wasn't equitable. Street was a jerk and a thief, but he didn't kill Shane. Leukemia did. So I went to see him and asked him to do the right thing."

"Let me take a wild stab. He told you to go fuck yourself."

"You must have seen the movie."

"So what did you do?"

"I called in some watchers."

"Watchers?"

"People who watch people for a living. They followed Merle everywhere. Took his picture, sent over drinks when he was at a bar, waved to him in church, rode the same planes, went to the movies and sat next to him. They even got a guest membership to his country club so they could play golf and take saunas with him. The only time Merle was alone was when he was home in bed—and then he wasn't sure."

"God, that would be creepy having someone invade your space like that."

"After a while it makes you jumpy. Your mind conjures up things."

"Is it even legal?"

"Merle didn't think so, and he tried to convince a judge. So I brought the watchers into court. All twenty-two of them, and they sat there smiling, well-dressed and polite as you please. But there wasn't a single incidence of blackmail or intimidation Merle could point to. And when the judge asked me how long I expected to continue the 'watching,' I told him I'd set up a fund to cover it for five years, then I'd reevaluate. I think he was secretly amused. He told Merle not to waste the court's time again unless he had something actionable."

"So Merle figured out you were rich—and powerful."

"I don't know about the power part, but yes, by then Merle knew I had considerably more money than he did, which always makes a wealthy man nervous because he knows that nine times out of ten the biggest bankroll wins. About a month later, I got word that Merle was looking for someone to take me out of the picture."

"Like kill you?"

"Preferably painfully. And though Merle was operating out of his league, every now and then even a blind pig finds an acorn. So rather than risk his stumbling into something stupid, I ratcheted things up. The watchers had learned that his wife, Eve, was on Merle's case to buy her a Jaguar. She was a regular at the showroom, brought home brochures, and once, she and Merle had had a shouting match in a restaurant where he'd stomped out yelling, 'If you want a goddamn Jag, get off your goddamn ass and get a goddamn job!' "

"Classy guy."

"It gets better. Merle had a girlfriend . . . Babette."

"Of course, what else could a girlfriend be called."

"One day while Merle's at work, Eve answers the door and finds a brand-new British Racing Green Jaguar XK convertible sitting in her driveway, complete with a giant bow and gift card. Unfortunately, it read. . ."

My Sweet Babette,
For all your patient understanding and warm comfort.
One day we'll be together forever.
In the meantime, as the ads say, Purrrrrrrrrrrrrr
Love, Merle.

"Oh, Jesus."

"Things moved pretty quickly after that. When Merle called, his voice was trembling. 'What the fuck do you want?' I told him that if he ever happened to come across anybody in need of something other than a Jag, maybe he'd be a good citizen."

"This is fucking great. How much did he send her?"

"Three hundred thousand."

"What a cocksucker."

"I thought so too, so the watchers stayed on the job, and Babette got tickets to Paris—again care of Eve. The second check was more generous. One million. But the third, which came right after Eve and Babette got into a hair-pulling contest in Merle's office lobby, was just right—an additional one and a half million, bringing the total to exactly what he'd stolen from Shane."

Kim whistled softly. "Two point eight mil. So it was over."

"Not quite, there was still the matter of the house."

"Don't tell me he bought *that* back?"

"No, another family was living there. So he bought her a bigger one across the street."

Kim burst out laughing. "And how much of this windfall did you get, if you don't mind my asking?"

I looked at her and just kept looking. She must have seen it in my eyes. Finally, she got so uncomfortable that her lip started to tremble.

"I'm sorry," she whispered. "He was your friend, of course." After a moment, she asked softly, "Do I qualify? As a friend, that is?"

"You're getting there, but you need to know that I only

help those who tell me the truth. Bullshit can get people hurt—or worse."

I watched as she took that in, turned it over in her head a couple of times and made a decision. "Okay, where was I?"

"The elevator at Ralphs."

"Right. When I got down to where I'd parked, I saw a dark blue van sitting behind my car and the guy called Tino standing beside it. I didn't see anyone else, but I really wasn't looking. I was just supremely pissed that in a big garage with maybe six or seven cars in it, this clown had managed to hit mine. As I approached him, he looked up with this great fucking concern. 'Is ziss your car, miss?'

"It was such a half-assed French accent I actually thought he was putting it on . . . like some goddamn Westwood waiter. So I gave him my best 'Yes, it's my car, asshole. And you better have fucking insurance.'

"'I so sorry,' he said. 'I talk on zee phone. And before I know, zee goes crunch.' "

I interrupted her. "'Zee goes crunch?' Are you sure those were his exact words?"

"Who the hell would make that up? Is it significant?"

"I don't know," I replied, "but it's distinctive, and distinctive is always good." I'd heard Dante speak, and I'd thought I'd heard a slight accent, so it didn't seem logical that Tino would be putting on a heavier one. It was probably legitimate.

Kim continued. "So I walked around the van to get a look, and sure enough, there was a long scrape on the driver side door. I bent down and ran my finger along it, and as I did, someone came up behind me, slapped an adhesive patch over my mouth and threw a pillowcase over my head. Then another pair of hands grabbed me, and pretty soon, my wrists and ankles were taped so tight I couldn't move. They put me in the back of the van, and one of them got in with me. Tino, I'm pretty sure. I could hear him breathing."

She hesitated, and I let her sit for a moment, collecting her thoughts.

"He cut off my clothes," she said finally. "And he touched me. God, I wanted to scream. But even if my mouth hadn't been taped, I think I was too afraid. It didn't go on too long before the other guy said something, and he stopped. Then he rolled me up in some kind of carpet and got back out. The pillowcase smelled like gasoline, so I was trying my best not to vomit when they got in a shouting match. That's when I heard their names. It was 'Fuck you, Tino,' and 'Fuck you, Dante,' like some kind of bizarre comedy act."

"What was the argument about?"

She looked uncomfortable. "About Tino's molesting me."

"What exactly did they say?"

"Dante told him to act like a professional. That if he tried anything like that again, he'd kill him. He might have even hit him because Tino went crazy-mad. He screamed, 'Maybe you watch, you learn zee man way!' "

She fumbled for another sip of wine, hands and glass shaking.

I said, "I know it's difficult, but the sooner you get it out, the more you'll remember. And in the for-what-it's-worth department, most people who've gone through a terrifying experience feel better after they've told someone."

She nodded, then blurted, "Wait a minute! And another car came in the garage! I remember praying somebody would see what was happening. But then it faded away."

"And. . . ," I said, trying to keep her going.

"Something hit the ground."

"Loud?"

"No, just . . . shit, it was my car keys! There's this big ring on them—you know, one of those gaudy pieces of crap from the car wash that says, 'Grab Your Brass.' I got it in a gift exchange. It's ugly and it's too big, but it made so much noise whenever I dropped my keys that I left it on."

"So since Dante and Tino ended up in the van, somebody had probably arrived to drive the Mustang away. What do you want to bet she was wearing lime green and the wrong lipstick."

"Like I said. I'm a freaking fucking idiot."

"Nope, you're like everybody else, completely unsuspecting. It's why Americans are what we are, but it sure does cost us sometimes. Every cop knows that serial killers, kidnappers, child molesters and all sorts of other bad guys love vans. So they tell their wives to never, ever park beside—or even walk next to—one. Go around the block, go to another store, go home. But stay the fuck away. And if you come out of a place, and there's one parked next to you, get a security guard or call a cab, but *don't get near a van—ever.* And with 95 percent of them, it goes in one ear and out the other. It's just more husband blah, blah, blah. So if a cop's wife, who's had it drummed into her, isn't paying attention, what do you think everybody else is doing?"

"It gives me the creeps." Then she exploded. "Fuck, I had everything in there. My phone . . . my datebook . . . like maybe fifty CDs . . . my goddamn dry cleaning."

"But you're alive."

She cooled off immediately. "You're right. I gotta stop worrying about the pain-in-the-ass stuff."

I switched subjects. "I know this is a difficult question, but were you—"

"Raped?" she said. "No. Except for Tino's handjob, it was just like I was a package they picked up. They didn't even talk to me. We drove for a long time, maybe a couple of hours, mostly on freeway, I think, because we were going fast. When we finally stopped, there was no more light coming through the pillowcase, so the sun must have set. We sat for a while, and I heard planes landing not too far away."

"Props or jets?"

She thought for a moment. "Both. Smaller ones, not 747s. A little while later, the back door opened, and somebody—Dante, I think—got in with me. He pulled the pillowcase off my head and shined a flashlight in my eyes. Before I could stop blinking, the pillowcase was back on. I heard another voice—a man—say, 'Okay,' then the door closed, and I was alone again."

I looked at her. "So they needed to prove to somebody they had you . . . or they were making sure they had the right person."

Kim looked shocked. "You mean somebody paid them to do this?"

I ignored the question. "When you said earlier that you were going to be fish food, what did you mean?"

"As soon as the van started up again, Dante asked Tino if he'd gassed up the boat. Tino said he didn't have to because there was half a tank left. When Dante heard that, he went ballistic. He started yelling that half a tank would only get them out twenty-five miles, and they needed to go at least fifty to be sure the current wouldn't pull my body back to shore. He said that they'd have to stop in Catalina and fill up, and he didn't think he had enough room on his credit card.

"When I heard that, I panicked and started thrashing around. I don't know why, but I have this almost sickening fear of drowning. And I'm terrified of boats—especially small ones. I must have been making quite a racket, because Dante climbed over the seat and told me to lie still or he'd have to knock me out. I knew it was Dante because he didn't have that stupid accent. Then he slapped me—hard. It hurt even through the pillowcase."

"So you went to work on the tape."

"My hands were in front of me, and during the struggle at Ralphs, I'd broken off four nails on my right hand. The stubs were jagged enough so that if I twisted my hands just a little, I could scratch at the tape on my left wrist."

I looked at her hand. She'd obviously found a file upstairs, but four of her nails were ground down to her fingertips. She saw me looking and covered her right hand with her left. It was a small thing, but it was the kind of modesty you can't fake, and I was moved.

She went on, "It was completely dark, and Tino drove with his window open, which let in enough noise so they didn't hear me when I finally got loose. I was going to jump out right then, but a big semi came up behind us, and all I could think about was being sucked under it and dragged."

"And then you got lucky, the traffic stopped."

Kim nodded and burst into tears, and I knew it wasn't going to be productive to continue. So I said, "How about if we pick this up tomorrow when we're both a little fresher."

She bit her lip and nodded.

I walked her upstairs, but when we got to the door of the Toledo Room, she suddenly turned and lunged into my arms. "I don't want to be alone tonight," she sobbed quietly. "Please."

I let her cry for a few moments until she had gotten through the worst of it, then I led her gently to my room. I put her under the covers, silk robe and all, turned out the lights and lay down on top of the bedspread next to her. I reached over and stroked her hair.

"No," she said. "Not like that. I want you to hold me . . . I *need* you to hold me."

So I got up, slipped out of my shorts and shirt and got into bed next to her. I'm not a prude, but I've got this thing about making love to women who are in a fragile emotional state. It can lead to complications and bitter feelings later, and I have the scars to prove it. But like a lot of things, my philosophy looks better on paper than it plays after you've had several glasses of wine and you're naked.

As she came into my arms, I realized that she'd shed the robe and the lace in her hair. She'd left the strand around her neck. So it was just me, Kim York and her tears—and several inches of nuns' handiwork.

She clung to me for a long time, but gradually her muscles relaxed. I thought she'd fallen asleep, but then she started to move against me. I'm a gentleman, but I'm not a saint, and I responded.

At some point, she turned over and pushed her tight rear end into me. "Do you mind?" she asked. "I want you to work my nipples while you fuck me."

"You get right to the point."

"It saves time."

I had to agree. If people would spend a little more time talking in bed and a little less pretending it's the Olympics, there'd be a lot more smiling faces and a lot fewer women masturbating after the guy falls asleep. I never quite figured it out. You're not wearing any clothes, and you're headed into the most intimate act a man and woman can perform, but somehow you can't bring yourself to say, "Here, do this."

She was a lot of girl, and she fit against me perfectly. I kissed her and caressed her and rolled her nipples between my fingers until she was groaning for me to get inside her. I must have done my job, because she had her first orgasm on my way in. Her second came a few moments before my own, and if it was half as intense as the sounds she made, we had done well together.

Afterward, as we lay in each other's arms, she said, "I've never been made love to by this much man before."

To which I naturally replied, "Shucks, ma'am, it's not *that* big."

Benny Joe and the Dobermans

When I awakened, sun was streaming through the windows. I glanced at the clock. 8:46. Kim was still dead to the world, so I eased out of bed, slipped into a pair of swim trunks and went out to the pool.

I start every morning swimming a mile—fast. For me it's the best workout and the greatest high you can get. Every time I see a jogger struggling up a hill, I'm happy he's exercising, but I'll put my endorphins up against his any day. In college, I swam butterfly and the IM, and there was a moment in time when I was almost world-class. But there was that tenth of a percent of talent that wasn't in my chromosomes, and no matter how hard you work, you can't train into it.

For years, I did my morning swims in the ocean because it's a harder workout, but I got tired of plowing through things I didn't recognize—or worse, did. Put an ordinary person on a body of water, and he can't wait to start heaving shit over the rail. So when I bought this house, I had a lap pool added to one end of the main pool, creating a fat blue T that never fails to elicit comments from my houseguests.

When I climbed out, Mallory asked me if he should get

breakfast started, but I told him to wait a while. I went into
the pool house, which doubles as my office, took a long hot
shower, shaved and dressed in some cutoffs and a Polo shirt.
Then I sat down at my desk.

I'm not a genius with a computer, but I can make it do
what it's supposed to. More importantly, I've got friends
around town who seem to like me enough to take my calls
and answer a question or two. After some cruising around
the Internet and working the phone, I went back to the main
house. Mallory met me on the patio with the Sunday *L.A.
Times* and a strong cup of coffee. I told him I was starving,
and he headed for the kitchen while I sat down at the big outdoor table under the bougainvillea-draped trellis and started
through the paper.

It didn't take long to find the account of the accident. A
picture of the now-deceased driver of the red Lamborghini
—a semi-famous music producer—was on the front page
under the headline

EARTHQUAKE CLAIMS MUSIC LEGEND

I supposed the earthquake part was technically correct,
but it would seem that reckless driving and the cocaine dust
they found on his upper lip might have been contributing
factors. As for being a legend . . . well, I'm not sure one
Top 40 hit is enough for me, but in a town where Pee-wee
Herman has a star on the Hollywood Walk of Fame, and
Harvey Keitel, the second-best actor of the twentieth century, doesn't, the legend label probably now applies to my
dry cleaner. Ten years, and he's never lost a pair of pants.

Inside, on page twelve, there was a shot of the Lamborghini
lying on its top like a dead turtle. Whoever had taken it had
been standing on the opposite side of the freeway, and sure
enough, there were the blue van, the white Caddie and the
hood and windshield of my Rolls. The rest was obscured by
the center divider and the back of the van.

I went into the kitchen, rummaged around in a drawer until I found a magnifying glass and went back outside. I was studying the picture when Kim came up behind me.

"Happy birthday."

As I turned, she put her arms around me and gave me a kiss. I noticed she was still wearing the strand of lace around her neck. "So where's my present?" I asked.

"You got it last night."

"I hate it when they come unwrapped."

She wriggled tight against me, and I felt myself respond.

She fingered the lace. "I happen to have a little time right now." Her breathing was shallow, and her eyes had a faraway look.

I held her at arm's length. "I have a rule. Never when there's bacon on the wind."

She sniffed the air. "I've got to admit, that does smell wonderful. Okay, you've got a rain check. By the way, was I as good as Rhonda?"

In the big book of life, these are the kinds of questions where the answer is so obvious that you wonder why any guy ever gets it wrong. But the cemeteries and alimony lines are full of guys who do. "Rhonda? Who's Rhonda?"

Kim gave me a mock punch, but she liked it. "You know, when I woke up, it took me five minutes to figure out you weren't there. That's the biggest goddamn bed I've ever seen—*or* been laid in. Who knew sheets even came in that size."

"The Martha Stewart Big and Tall Collection."

"And I didn't even have to shave you."

"That one of your hidden talents?"

Suddenly, she seemed flustered, as if she'd said something she hadn't intended to. "Just a figure of speech," she stammered, then looked at the newspaper on the table. "What have you got there?"

I handed her the magnifying glass. "You tell me."

While she bent over the newspaper and adjusted her eyes,

I admired the fit of the familiar jeans, the white sleeveless blouse and sandals. And once again, it took a couple of deep breaths to get my emotions back in their cage.

After a long moment, Kim stood up. "My God, that's me," she said.

"And your best side too." Under magnification, you could make out Kim's bare back climbing over the center divider. I made a mental note of the name of the guy who was credited for the picture—Walter Kempthorn.

While Mallory served us cheese omelets and thick slices of slab bacon, Kim and I made light conversation. Finally, I said, "You want me to run you home later?"

She looked away, seemed to gather herself. "Hey, it's Sunday anyway. Why don't we just lie around this little ol' place of yours and soak up some sun. Maybe catch a nap this afternoon." The last line was delivered with a seductive lowering of her voice that I read as genuine, but it could have just been wistful thinking.

"Sounds fine. Especially the nap part. But I've got to run an errand first."

"Need company?"

"Why don't you stay here and get started on that sun. I won't be long."

"Okay, but if you want to win my heart, stop and pick up a pack of smokes. I promise to pay you back."

"I'll hold you to it."

I took the Rolls down the hill and turned east on Sunset. Drove through West Hollywood and on the far side hung a left on one of the winding streets up into the hills. Almost at the top, there was a narrow drive marked by a couple of reflectors on a metal pole over a KEEP OUT sign. I turned in and immediately heard Benny Joe's dogs barking.

I like dogs, but there's nothing warm and cuddly about four aggressive Dobermans that don't obey their owner all that well. Having been chased back to my car more than once after they'd slipped through an unlatched gate, I sat in the Rolls and leaned on the horn. That set the dogs off even more.

A minute or two later, Benny Joe Willis came out wearing a pair of old sweatpants and a wife-beater. As usual, he was shoeless and unshaven. Also as usual, he was carrying a can of Pabst Blue Ribbon in one hand and a .357 Magnum in the other.

I opened the door. "You can put the peashooter away, Benny Joe. I shook the FBI tail coming through town."

"You're a fuckin' riot, Rail. It ain't the cops I'm worried about. It's that fuckin' ex-wife of mine. She's got a fuckin' hit out on me. Says I implanted a listening device in her. That I get my rocks off sittin' up here listenin' to her fuck other guys. Jesus Christ, I couldn't stand hearin' that when we were married."

Benny Joe uses "fuck" at least once every time he opens his mouth, and I've had entire conversations with him where that was the only word he uttered.

"Sorry, I didn't get the newsletter. Last I knew, it was some UFO guy on the radio you were obsessed with. Heard you had a picture of the Roswell crash and ratted you out to the Men in Black."

"Fuckin' cocksucker. I'm never gonna call that Commie fuck's show again. Let's get the fuck inside in case the bitch hired a sniper."

In contrast to Benny Joe's appearance and mouth, his house is extremely well-decorated in excellent taste. Lots of rich leather furniture, black stone tables and an entertainment center he says cost him a hundred grand, which I believe. He's also compulsively neat. Not even a book out of place. The only thing that isn't super-clean is the outside glass because the Dobermans put their faces right up against the windows and snarl and slobber the whole time there's a stranger inside. Makes you feel welcome.

But it's the walls that make the place unique. There isn't the standard framed Normandie poster or Guernica print anywhere. Instead, the entire house is covered with 48 x 36 blowups of the Kennedy assassination, tacked up with red pushpins—the only color Benny Joe uses. Says the other colors don't hold.

Benny Joe's quirky, but he's a photographic genius. A fuckin' genius, if I can be excused for plagiarizing. He doesn't have much of an eye as a picture-taker, but he's the best restorer of film and video on the planet, and he can coax things out of an image no one has seen before. He makes a handsome living analyzing security camera tape for business and law enforcement. But he makes more money than God doing exactly the same thing for news organizations— who never met a consultant they couldn't overpay.

Benny Joe made his reputation as an analyst at the National Reconnaissance Office, the people who operate our spy satellites. He was something of a legend there, but it all came to a screeching halt one day in the Oval Office. Benny Joe's boss had been summoned to brief the president about Middle East satellite imagery after some mindless act of terrorism had killed half a dozen Americans. But the boss was a bureaucrat, not an analyst, so to avoid looking like a schmuck in case there were questions, he decided to take along the guy who had actually done the work.

Knowing that Benny Joe had a proclivity for offering his opinion on just about everything and a compulsion to do it X-rated, the boss warned him that if anybody asked a question, he was to stick to the technical stuff and not go into some rant about Jerry Jones or the ozone layer or the high cover charge at strip clubs or whatever it was that he was exercised about that week.

But as fate would have it, after the Q&A, the president complimented Benny Joe on his work, then asked him what he thought about the current crisis. Benny Joe looked at his boss, who gave him a reluctant nod, and Benny Joe went with it.

"Well, shit, Mr. President, if you really want my advice, when you get your hands on the motherfuckers who drew this up, you should fuck them in the ass until their goats die." Word is the prez laughed like hell, but nobody else did. Two weeks later, Benny Joe got his ticket punched to early retirement.

Apparently they've had a little trouble replacing him, though, because they keep sending guys around trying to lure him back. He says that's one of the reasons for the .357. The other reasons come and go.

"You get that new enlarger you've been waiting for?" I asked.

Benny Joe's second floor is filled with lenses, snoots, vacuum chambers, strobes and a lot of things he invented himself. He's even designed software that does things I didn't think were possible. Like being able to distinguish temperature gradations on the skin of aircraft from regular photographs.

"Fuck no. The manufacturer's got some real attitude. Says I cost him a fuckin' million-dollar sale on some bullshit machine I wrote an online review about. Wait'll I crack the fuckin' JFK case. He'll chase me down to kiss my fuckin' ass."

As anyone who's been in his house or talked to him for five minutes has discovered, Benny Joe is obsessed with the Kennedy assassination. He's convinced that the bullets fired in Dealey Plaza that day are actually captured on the Zapruder film, and that it's just a matter of time before he comes up with the technology to tease them out.

He reminds skeptics that twenty-five years ago, they'd have sent you into therapy if you'd suggested DNA would eventually put criminals in prison. That it's the same with photography. Everything's there, you just have to have the right equipment to see it.

I'm not smart enough to know one way or another, but Benny Joe's got his supporters, one of whom from his former government life sneaked him a first-generation copy of Abraham Zapruder's 8mm contribution to history.

I do know I've seen him work magic. Like the pictures I bought a couple of months ago. I like estate sales. I don't buy much, but it's fascinating to look at what people accumulate over a lifetime and a lot more interesting than walking around a mall.

I was in Pittsburgh when I saw an ad for a sale in Point Breeze, one of the city's ritzy old neighborhoods. The home had belonged to a member of the Thaw steel family, who'd lived there in grandeur for over a century before they'd finally died out.

When I showed up, the place was jammed, and the auctioneer was hawking in orgiastic delight as dealers and speculators tried to outbid each other for Tiffany lamps and Chippendale furniture. Nobody, however, was interested in four boxes of old photographs evidently taken by a succession of family members.

I don't know why I bought them either. Maybe it was intuition, or more likely, I was just bored. Either way, the whole thing only set me back seventy-five bucks, which was less than I'd paid for dinner the night before.

When the boxes arrived at Dove Way, they sat in the dining room until Mallory got tired of stepping around them and started leaving clumps of pictures all over the house. I got the message and sat down one afternoon and went through them.

Mostly they were what families usually leave behind— shots of long-forgotten birthday parties, picnics and vacations. The difference in these, however, was that the Thaws had taken the time to jot notations on them, giving the year, place and names of the people. A photographic family history, as it were, and the voyeur in me enjoyed the tour for an hour or so.

I'd pretty much made up my mind to send them anonymously to the Pittsburgh Historical Society when I came across an old Islay's Ice Cream bag in the bottom of one of the boxes. Inside were half a dozen square negatives of a baseball game. They were in pretty bad shape, and I couldn't make out much, so I called Benny Joe, whom I've known since he came west.

They turned out to be pictures of Babe Ruth batting at Forbes Field. And he was in a Boston Braves uniform, which meant it was May 1935, the last week of his career and possibly the day he hit his final three home runs, including Number 714.

Benny Joe was just about coming out of his skin when he called me. "These fuckers were taken on a Rolleiflex, which means once I get them restored, they'll be fuckin' sharp. And I'm just finishing a new program that'll make them look almost digital. You have any idea what the fuck these are worth if there's a home run on one?"

I didn't, and I didn't think he did either, but I was glad he was enthusiastic.

Now, as we stood in his living room, he said with an edge in his voice, "If you're here about the Babe Ruth shit, I told you it's gonna take a couple of fuckin' months. And I don't like people pushing me."

"Like I said before, take as long as you like. I'm here about this."

I handed Benny Joe the photograph from the morning paper. The one showing the crash.

"You think you can improve it?" I asked.

He set his beer and gun on an end table, took the picture and looked at it. Then, with thinly veiled irritation, he said, "What the fuck are you? Some kind of clown? I can't do shit with a newspaper picture. You get me an actual print, and I'll win the guy a fuckin' Pulitzer. Get me the negative, and fuckin' museums will call."

"That's the answer I was expecting, but I'd like you to look at it anyway."

He took a swig of Pabst, rolled his eyes. "Which fuckin' part?"

"Anything that might help identify the two guys in the van or its plate."

Benny Joe said something rude, then went upstairs. I

watched the dogs for a while, and they watched me back. Pretty soon, I heard him coming back down.

"It was taken on film. Good fuckin' camera too. Probably a Nikon. The answer to your question is who the fuck knows. Get me the fuckin neg, man."

5

And Along Came Dana

My friend at the *Times* who could tell me how to find the guy who'd taken the accident picture wouldn't be around until Monday, so I headed home. Remembering the Benson & Hedges, I stopped at a liquor store on Sunset. I also had the manager dig out another couple of bottles of PlumpJack and grabbed a six-pack of Stella Artois. Then I stood in line behind a shirtless guy with a tattoo of a giraffe covering his back, who kept his hand on his purple-haired girlfriend's ass while he glanced over his shoulder and grinned toothlessly.

Late for a Mensa meeting.

The clerk put my purchases in a bag with the cigarettes, but before ringing me up, he said, "Hey, man, it's none of my business, but that Belgian beer is shit-fuck expensive. We're runnin' a special on Keystone Light. You could get you a 12-pack for almost the same price."

I thanked him and passed. So he asked if I needed ice for the wine. Benny Joe came to mind. Fuck!

Kim was sitting in the solarium talking to Mallory.

She looked up when I came in. "I've put on all my best moves, but Mallory won't tell me anything about you. Just that you're kind and generous."

"I'll have to slip an extra hundred grand in his pay envelope."

Mallory stood. "At the risk of losing the bonus, might I say that dinner is timed precisely for eight and that you have an unnerving habit of not looking at clocks."

Kim spoke up. "We'll be there. I guarantee it. Whatever you're cooking has been in the air all day, and I'm already fantasizing."

I took the Benson & Hedges out of the bag, threw them to her and handed the beer and wine to Mallory. "Get the Stella on ice, would you. I've been at Benny Joe's, and I'm going to need one."

"Stella, yum. Who's Benny Joe?" asked Kim as she tore open the cigarettes.

Mallory frowned. "A perfectly dreadful little man," he said.

Then he headed toward the kitchen, and I changed the subject. "So what did you get into while I was gone?"

"Oh, I poked around a little. Found a big pool table in the billiard room, which is probably where it belongs. You any good?"

"I know which end of a cue to use."

"I'll take that as a warning. There's also a hell of an accumulation of vehicles in that unbelievable basement garage. Jesus, what a place. But why are they all either red or black?"

"I'm not exactly sure. Seems like every time I like something, that's what it is. Think I should see a shrink?"

She laughed. "If they were Mary Kay pink, I'd say run, don't walk, but I think red and black check out okay with Freud. By the way, your car wash guy, Angelo, was here."

I raised an eyebrow. "Is that what he called himself, 'my car wash guy'?"

"Not exactly, I hung that on him when he started soaping up your Morgan. What year is it?"

"1968."

"I was close. I guessed '70. Great-looking car, but Angelo said your legs are too long to drive it."

"He was being charitable. I can't even get my ass down in the seat."

"So why buy it?"

"Because it's beautiful."

Kim thought for a moment. "Like not having room to hang a Calder but not being able to resist it."

"Bingo."

"So who's Angelo?"

"He used to be chief mechanic for Ford Racing."

"That's a big deal, right?"

"Right."

"And he's another friend. Somebody you did a favor for who stops by now and then. And he probably washes your cars because . . . he can't keep his hands off them."

"Give the lady a cigar."

"I'd rather have one of those Stellas."

We had dinner on the patio. Mallory's world-famous Sicilian pot roast with a side of porcini risotto washed down with PlumpJack—no ice. It was magnificent.

Kim didn't offer any more details about the night before, so I kept the conversation loose. Mostly talked about what a pain in the ass it is to own a big house, especially an old one, and how I'd kill for a really good terra-cotta guy.

Later, we went into the screening room, and I threw *Papillon* on the DVD. If there's something better than a good meal, a great-looking woman and Steve McQueen, I don't know what it is. Well, actually, I do, and we found ourselves doing it on one of the sofas sometime after Steve's first escape. Then we toddled off to the bedroom for Round Two.

Next morning, I was up first again and done with my laps before Kim found her way outside.

"You ready to go home yet?"

"You throwing me out?" She laughed.

"Nope, just that it's Monday, and I figured you'd have to go to work." I saw her flush, then recover quickly.

"I'm between jobs."

I didn't say anything, but after breakfast, I got up and went to the phone.

"Who're you calling?" she asked.

"Beverly Hills Taxi."

"I thought you were going to ask me some more questions."

"I was, but your end of the deal was to tell the truth."

She flashed angry. "What are you talking about?"

"Well, the name you gave me is almost right. Actually, it's Dana Kimberly York, and you live at 429 Princeton St. in Santa Monica. You're current with your bills, have never been arrested and earned undergraduate and graduate degrees in art history from Penn and a PhD in European masters from the University of Paris. But here's where the story gets interesting.

"First, 429 Princeton St. is titled to an Alexander Connor Cayne, whose Social Security number indicates he's been dead since 1975. Further, you've got a restraining order out against somebody named Brandi Sue Parsons, who coincidentally is also on the Pasadena Police Department's missing persons list. And finally, you *do* have a job—a serious one. You're the editor-in-chief of the Getty Museum's art journal—and P.S., you called in sick about an hour ago."

Kim looked like she'd been slapped.

I gave her a minute, then said, "So you tell me, *Doctor* York, where do we go from here?"

She took a long moment, then she said tightly, "Well, for starters, I hate the name Dana, so I never use it. And Alexander Cayne was my father, a navy commander flying off the *Enterprise*. A month after I was born, he was shot down over North Vietnam and captured alive. We know because his name and picture were in a Hanoi newspaper. But like two thousand other dads, brothers and sons, he never came home.

"After the war, the navy declared him dead, but my mother didn't believe them—not even after she remarried, and her new husband, Truman York, adopted me. So she never filed the paperwork to have Dad's name taken off the house. No one cares anyway, as long as the taxes are paid, and I think she was always half-expecting that one day, he'd come up the walk, and everything would be like it was. And later, after my mom and stepfather died in a crash, I couldn't bear to change it either."

"The POW/MIA debacle is a national stain," I said. "And it's on every president who didn't force the Vietnamese and the Defense Department to come clean."

Kim bowed her head, and I could tell her eyes were wet. "There are no words to describe what the families went through—the same people who were so loyal to their country that they absorbed the lies in silence. You know, I never even knew my dad, but I always felt connected. I think my mother's love for him was so great and her grief so profound that it became part of me too."

Kim took a deep breath and went on. "Now, Brandi Sue Parsons. You can starve on what museums and galleries pay, so I took the journalism route. I was always good at getting people to talk, and I got lucky and picked up regular free-lance pieces for some of the more prestigious art publications. I was doing pretty well too—at least I was eating—but like a lot of people with my degrees, I was dead certain I could find undervalued works and resell them for a fat profit. So when I wasn't writing about lost Caravaggios or forged Warhols, I hung out a shingle as a consultant.

"Mrs. Parsons, who is two years younger than me, was a former Miss Universe runner-up and the brand-new trophy wife of a wealthy Pasadena developer. She hired me to locate something outstanding for the new mansion her husband was building her. And I did—a wonderful pair of Kubicek watercolors. But the owner would only sell them as a package, and the price was $400,000, twice what Mrs. Parsons had authorized.

"When I explained it to Brandi Sue, she went to see the paintings—a still life and a landscape—and fell in love with the landscape, which was valued at $180,000. So I told her I'd scout around and see what I could do. I got lucky. I found an investor willing to put up $200,000 in return for an eighty percent share of what the still life might eventually bring. I borrowed against my credit cards for the balance. Case closed. That is, until I sent the still life to Sotheby's to be auctioned."

"Let me guess, somebody bought it for half a million."

"Not even close. One million, six hundred sixty-five thousand, five hundred. It turned out to be one of the artist's lost works. It had disappeared from the Spanish royal family in 1808, probably looted by one of Napoleon's officers. Mrs. Parsons read about the sale in the paper and came looking for what she considered her share of the money—which by her logic was all of it.

"Her opening line was, 'You thieving fucking bitch. You set me up!' Then she hired a lawyer and accused me of pushing her to buy the landscape when it was the still life she wanted all along."

"Naturally."

"The judge threw the case out, but she kept at it with harassing phone calls and poison e-mails. Then one day, as I was crossing the street in front of my apartment, she tried to run me down with her Mercedes. I managed to dive out of the way, but I felt the bumper graze my skirt."

"Hence the restraining order," I said.

Kim nodded. "I was really scared. The funny thing was, a few months later, her husband came to see me. He was beside himself. He said Brandi Sue had taken all the money she could lay her hands on, pawned her jewelry and left town with the foreman who'd been overseeing the construction of their new house. She'd also taken the Kubicek landscape, and he wanted to know if maybe she'd contacted me about selling it."

"I guess he didn't know the history," I said.

"I think he was so hung up on her, he wasn't thinking clearly. He was absolutely sure his foreman had coerced her, maybe even used force. So sure, in fact, he'd made a police report."

"I'm sure the Pasadena cops jumped right on it."

"They called me about three weeks later, but there wasn't much urgency in their questions. I think they figured it for what it was."

"Gotta watch those Ms. Universes," I said.

"I think it's just the runner-ups," she smiled. "And finally, I do work at the Getty. My Kubicek find—lucky as it was— got me noticed, and they asked me to start a journal for them. And because I'd had a windfall, I could afford to take the job. I also edit their catalogues and write most of the captions for the exhibits. And for the record, I just couldn't face going to work today. I don't even know why I lied about that."

She looked drained.

I said, "Well, Dr. York, now that the truth serum has taken effect, and you have the day off anyway, why don't we run over to Ralphs and have a look at the scene of the crime."

As we rode down the hill into the relative civilization of the 90210, the radio in the Rolls was on. Steve Hartman and Petros Papadakis—the Jimmy Neutron and Jack E. Leonard of Los Angeles sports talk—were, as usual, making intelligent, insightful points. Unfortunately, they were doing it at the same time. Hartman and Papadakis are the two heavyweights in town and have separate shows, mostly because you can't shoehorn that much IQ, ego and certitude into one studio. But management apparently thinks it's good radio to jam them together every once in a while, step back and watch the ignition. I wonder if they'll feel the same way the day their two biggest stars go fists, teeth and key man policies over the desk at each other. In the meantime, though, while the bosses smile, the audience listens . . . and waits.

When I couldn't decipher what they were shouting about, I turned it off. Kim was quiet, which elevated her another notch in my book. People who have to fill every silence with conversation make my ass tired, so it was nice to just ride along with my own thoughts.

I kept turning her story over in my head, but it didn't quite mesh. Like what was the real reason she hadn't wanted to call the cops last night? Naked or not, most people's reaction is to scream for a police officer if a dog is barking three blocks over, let alone if they've just escaped a kidnapping.

I was pretty sure that if her car was eventually found, the clothes she'd been wearing would be in it. But why take the car at all if you were just going to dump her in the drink? Why chance getting picked up in a vehicle that isn't yours? Unless somebody wanted to go through it first, thoroughly.

Kim said she hadn't been raped, and after her reaction in bed, I believed her. Women who've been sexually abused aren't usually interested in making love a couple of hours later. But bad guys holding a woman they're going to kill anyway generally aren't paragons of restraint. Usually only pros have that kind of self-control. Or men who've been sent to do a job by someone they deeply fear.

And why did Tino get out of the van? You have to figure if you've botched an abduction, you'd want to get as far away as possible as fast as possible. Why let half of the drivers on the 405 get a look at you?

I concluded she was holding something back. Maybe without even knowing it—but that's not what my gut said.

I turned off Santa Monica into Century City and honked my horn as we passed my law firm's offices. Miguel, the parking valet, saw my Rolls, gave a big grin and waved. Where else but L.A. can you valet park to visit your lawyer.

"Somebody else you've helped?"

I smiled. "Miguel does just fine on his own. He and his cousin, Jorge, have the Century City valet parking and car washing concession. They probably make more than half the people working in the offices. My attorney did the negotiations for them. No charge, providing he got free valet service and clean cars for life. That's his building."

Jake Praxis has been my attorney and friend for a while now. He started life as a navy aviator, but that ended during a night carrier landing when a cable snapped and flipped his F-14 into the South China Sea. When they fished him out, he had a broken back, and his flying days were over. And in Jake's words, "Once you've flown a shit-hot jet, you can't bear watching somebody else doing it."

So with that career plan gone, he tried law school and discovered it was a lot like being a pilot. You get to call the shots, and if your passengers don't like it, they can get the fuck off your plane.

And if there are two things Jake's good at, it's calling the shots and firing clients who try to tell him how to do his job. You've got to respect that. He's the best, and if you don't want to listen, get yourself another lawyer. According to the *L.A. Times*, he represents eight of the top ten box office stars, five of the biggest earners in sports and all of the studio heads. Not bad for a ranch rat from East Jesus, New Mexico.

Jake represents so many Hollywood players that he sometimes finds himself on both sides of a negotiation. Anywhere else, that would be a conflict of interest, and one of the parties would have to get another lawyer. But if Jake represents you, you sure as hell don't want some Number Two going up against him. So when it happens, everybody signs conflict waivers, and Jake goes into a room and makes the deal with himself. He says he likes representing both sides. It's easier to sort out the overreaching.

He's also the first call for reporters when something big breaks in show business or sports. But except for his pet environmental causes, you can't drag a quote out of him. Talking to the press is not how you end up owning a Century City high-rise and homes from Sun Valley to Sorrento. Neither does having your face plastered across television screens.

"Why would I do that?" he asks. "To get more fuckin' pain-in-the-ass clients?"

So, unless you're an insider, you wouldn't recognize him—even in his courtside seats at Lakers games.

"That was Jake Praxis's building, wasn't it?" said Kim a block and a half later. "Is he your attorney?"

I nodded.

"No shit."

"You know him?"

"Hardly. But he's on the board of the Getty, and I shook his hand once at a cocktail party. He had an Italian actress on his arm who could have stood next to a Ferrari and nobody would have noticed the car."

"Only one?"

Kim grinned. "I've heard he's quite the man. How'd you meet him?"

"Did a favor for one of his clients."

"Back to the favors. You must be quite the fucking guy to know. What was it? Another 'watcher' operation?"

I smiled. "I wish it'd been that easy. The client is a big action star who coincidentally happens to live up the street from me. The guy had a bad case of couldn't-keep-it-in-his-pants and liked living on the edge. Jake warned him more than once about fooling around with women he didn't know, but like a lot of people—especially actors—when his boxers bowed, his brain went out for a smoke.

"Then he got himself paparazzied in a Brentwood bar licking the face of a Colombian drug lord's seventeen-year-old daughter who was in town visiting colleges. The photographer was a whole lot smarter than the actor. He followed the happy couple to a poolside suite at the Four Seasons and got more shots of them playing lap trampoline in a hot Jacuzzi."

Kim whistled. "Colombians don't send warnings. They just kill everything that breathes, including your goldfish."

"Actually, when it comes to their daughters, they like to torture the goldfish first."

"Seventeen-year-old *chocho*. At least it was a piece of ass the guy was going to remember."

"Yep, but not in old age. The actor got my name from a friend, and by the time he called, he was nearly hysterical, holed up and surrounded by more security than an Israeli ambassador. He swore up and down the girl told him she was twenty-three and an illegal from Guatemala. I believed him, but so what? Guys who use the phrase 'Swiss bank' in the same sentence as 'remote landing strip' don't much care about the pure of heart. I wanted to tell the schmuck he didn't need me, he needed a priest.

"But the guy was crying so hard I felt sorry for him. He was supposed to start a picture in a month, but he was too terrified to leave the house. Eventually, I said I'd make a couple of calls—mostly so I could just get the hell out of there."

"You're not going to tell me the actor's name, are you?"

"Nope."

"That's okay. There's a big star who's got such an attitude that I'm just going to pretend it's him. Go ahead."

"I got in touch with a friend in the DEA who told me this particular bad guy, Wilson Garza, liked to straighten out personal problems by strapping offenders to a drum of gasoline and shooting it with a grenade. Probably fitting for an actor who couldn't keep his dick under control, but tough on the studio that was paying him thirty mil. But my DEA guy also told me that Garza was in the middle of a power struggle he was probably going to lose. It might take six months or so, but sooner or later, he was going to be taking a MAC-10 nap."

"So the actor just had to wait him out."

"Yeah, but the studio wouldn't. If he didn't show up for work, they'd recast and sue for damages. So I got myself invited down to Medellín to meet with Garza."

"How?"

"The DEA guy called him."

"They can do that?" She sounded incredulous.

"It isn't like TV. These guys all live in the same world. They know each other. They have each other's private numbers. It's business, even with the Colombians.

"I'd already determined Garza was a big movie fan, so

while he was showing me around his hacienda, I told him that the wayward and now-penitent actor had always wanted to shoot a picture in Colombia but didn't have the right contacts. And just like the old saying—everybody's got two businesses, their own and show business—Garza got a Hollywood erection. He even had a story he 'just knew' would be a worldwide sensation."

"Let me guess. The Wilson Garza Story."

I nodded. "And who better to play Garza than the real deal. So the actor hired a Spanish-speaking screenwriter, Carlos Goldstein, who, in return for twice his usual fee, agreed to log a lot of overseas phone hours with Señor Garza, talking character arc, motivation and act breaks.

"Motion picture development makes cancer research look fast, and if you've got a slow writer, it's like waiting for the Academy to honor Reagan. And just about the time Garza started wondering if he'd been had, somebody put an RPG up the ass of his Escalade. Problem solved."

Kim was laughing out loud. "I know you don't take money, but this guy owes you big time."

"Well, sometimes, if the situation warrants, I come up with something that reinforces a lesson or has a positive impact somewhere. In the Garza matter, I told the actor I would appreciate his taking a hundred thousand of his tax-deductible dollars and giving them to Sister Vonetta, the head of St. Regis Catholic School in South Central L.A.

"A product of hood herself, Sister V. is one of my all-time favorite people. Imposing in every way—physically, spiritually and vocally. And over the objections of the archdiocese—and maybe even the Vatican—through sheer force of will, intimidation and a lot of shouting, she has single-handedly created the most rigorous learning institution in the city.

"South Central is as rough a place as there is, but once you enter the gates of St. Regis, you wear a uniform, you don't speak street, you have to buy all of your own materials and the discipline is unforgiving. Parents sleep in line for a week to apply."

"Sounds like she should be on Oprah."

"Wouldn't work. Oprah wouldn't get a chance to talk."

"And Jake Praxis was grateful."

"Loved the whole thing—especially the hundred grand to Sister V., which he told the star, was about ten times too light considering his stupidity. So Jake and I became friends, and every now and then, he calls me when he has a delicate situation. Most of the time I give him some advice and move on, but sometimes something comes along that's intriguing, and I get involved."

"So he's not really your lawyer, he's more like a colleague."

"We do things for each other. He's on the board of my foundation too."

"That would be the Black Foundation?"

"Catchy name, don't you think?"

Kim was looking at me strangely. Finally, she said, "Just who in the fuck are you?"

6

A Torn ACL and Russian Women

I eased the Rolls off Olympic and into Ralphs underground parking garage. We'd driven by the outside lot upstairs, and it had been packed, but down here, there were only three cars, all grouped near the elevator. Kim directed me to where she'd parked the night of the kidnapping. I pulled in a few spaces beyond, and we both got out.

"What are you expecting to find?" she asked.

I stood in Kim's parking space. "You were here, and the van was behind you, facing the building."

"Yes."

I pointed to the ground, and Kim saw the four broken fingernails lying on the pavement. She took an involuntary step backward, then came forward and bent over them. "My God, it really did happen."

With Kim trailing me, I wandered off in the direction the van would probably have come from. In the farthest corner of the garage, I found three unfiltered cigarette butts that had burned themselves out rather than being stepped on. I bent down and picked one up. The blue lettering was intact—Gauloises.

"What's that?" asked Kim.

"Confirmation of Tino's bad taste." I threw the butt back down and walked a few steps further. I found what I expected. The distinctive ash from a cigar. I pointed to the parking space between the two ash piles and gestured with my hands. "Tino backed the van in here, then he and Dante waited until the woman sent you down. I thought you said you were only gone ten or fifteen minutes. Tino got through three cigarettes."

"Maybe he was nervous," she shot back. Then she reconsidered. "It could have been a little longer. I did browse the deli section for a while. So they were following me."

"All the way from work, I expect."

"And I made it easy by going into a deserted garage. Some price to pay for a little shade."

"They were probably going to take you from home, but when you pulled in here, they improvised." I made a full circuit of the garage. In the corner near the elevator was a surveillance camera mounted in the ceiling. If it had the right lens, it could see the entire garage, but someone had spray-painted its eye with black enamel.

"Let's go upstairs," I said.

When we entered the store, Kim took hold of my arm. I looked down at her, and she shivered. "It gives me the creeps being back in here."

We walked over to the manager's desk at the front of the store. It sat up on a platform and was being manned by a handsome young guy wearing a name tag that read Arkadios. As we approached, I saw him look up and try to figure out if I was a Laker. It's a look I'm familiar with.

"Excuse me, sir," I said. "Yesterday my wife parked her car downstairs while she was shopping, and it got scratched. I noticed you have a surveillance camera down there, and I was wondering if maybe there's a tape I could look at."

"We don't assume liability for our customers' cars, sir."

"And I'm not claiming any. I just want to see if there's a license number I can take down to give to my insurance company."

Arkadios furrowed his brow. "I couldn't do that, sir. What if you tracked the guy down and beat him up or something? Ralphs could get sued, and I'd lose my job."

A woman walked up and asked Arkadios where she could find the ricotta cheese. After he directed her, he turned back to me. I leaned over his desk so our faces were almost touching. It made him uncomfortable.

"Arkadios," I said, looking at his name tag. "Greek?"

He drew himself up proudly. "Yes."

"Athens?"

"No, Santorini."

"Ah, the Cyclades Islands. Paradise. Tell me, does Nick Pouliasis still make his famous lamb with rosé sauce?"

A smile came across Arkadios's face. "I was a waiter at Koukoumavlos," he said with pride. "Nick hired me when I was sixteen."

"Then you are a responsible young man. Nick is a very demanding boss."

"He said I was one of the best."

"Arkadios, are you married?"

"Yes, sir, I am."

"Then I hope you'll understand my problem." I lowered my voice. "You see, I caught my wife sleeping with this guy she works with." I heard Kim suck in her breath, but she stayed silent. "I told her I was taking the kids and leaving. But she begged, and she cried. Said she'd been crazy and stupid. That she'd never do anything like that again. So for the sake of the kids, I decided to give her another chance."

Arkadios looked up at Kim, who must have looked properly shocked. I continued, "Then two nights ago, she comes home with alcohol on her breath and a big fucking scratch on the new Mustang I busted my ass to buy her. She says she stopped off to have a glass of wine with a girlfriend, then came here, where the car got scratched in the garage. I want to believe her, but I think you'll understand I need to be sure. "

I saw Arkadios look over at Kim again, then back at me.

When he did, the apprehension was gone from his eyes. We had just become coconspirators. "I'll get the key to the security room."

It was more like a closet wedged between the meat cooler and the employee lockers, and there was barely enough room for the three of us to stand. But the technology was up to date—Panasonic Digital with almost unlimited memory.

"When were you here, ma'am?"

"Saturday, between five thirty and six."

Arkadios expertly manipulated the equipment, and in seconds, he had the right scene. The camera was fitted with a good lens, and after a moment or two, the Mustang came into view at the entrance ramp. As Kim parked, the dark blue van entered the garage and stopped just inside the entrance.

Unfortunately, the camera was positioned so that only the van's right side was visible, and it was too far away and the garage too dimly lit for me to make out any details. After a few seconds, an arm extended out the passenger window and pointed toward the camera. Immediately, the van backed out of the garage and disappeared.

We watched Kim walk to the elevator, enter it and the doors close. Then, from out of nowhere, a hand holding a can of spray paint came around from behind the camera. A finger depressed the valve, and everything went black. But not before I saw the seven-legged spider tattoo on the spray painter's forearm.

"People are assholes," said Arkadios. "If they're not stealing carts or drinking a carton of milk while they shop, they're vandalizing the parking lot. I'm afraid this isn't going to tell us who scratched your car, but it does prove your wife was here." He looked at Kim and smiled.

"Yes, it does," I said. I nodded to the Mac on the small desk in the corner and said to Arkadios, "Do you think you could burn me a copy of that scene we just watched?"

"No problem."

A few minutes later, Kim and I were back in the car.

"Thanks for making it so I can never go in there again," she said tartly.

"You'll be a celebrity."

"Yeah, and next time I stop for a head of lettuce, Arkadios'll check my cart for Trojans." Kim lit up a Benson & Hedges. Exhaling, she said, "And what was with that Santorini business?"

"It's one of the most beautiful—"

Kim rolled her eyes. "Save the travelogue. You're not the only one with a passport. I was just wondering what you'd have done if he'd been from Helsinki."

"I'd have asked him about the sautéed reindeer at Kappeli—and if Ari still sings the Love Song from *Carmen* at midnight." While Kim chewed on that, I let a FedEx truck go by, then turned west on Olympic and accelerated into traffic.

Princeton Street is in a fashionably run-down Santa Monica neighborhood about two miles from the beach. The aging one-story bungalows sit on postage stamp lawns, and broken-down Dusters and RVs drip oil on driveways hand-poured by the original owners when they came home from Iwo Jima. During Rose Bowl week, when rubberneckers from Iowa and Michigan cruise SoCal streets in their rental cars, the color drains out of their faces when someone mentions that these places go for over a million.

Chez York was a cute little place with green shutters and a front yard full of cactus. Unlike most of its neighbors, the paint was fresh and the awnings new. I pulled to the curb in front of 429 and told Kim to wait in the car. Picking my way past a couple of dwarf saguaros, I peered through the front window. It was dark inside, but not so dark that I couldn't see that the place had been trashed.

I went around back, past more cactus and a blue tile fountain, and found the back door jimmied. I pushed it open. The kitchen was a mess. Not only had the drawers been pulled out and dumped and the cabinets trashed, but whoever had been here had also taken everything out of the refrigerator and thrown it against the wall.

Further in, they'd shoved the china cabinet over onto the dining room table and hacked at the furniture in the living room with a knife. They'd even cracked the television screen with the fireplace poker.

The master bed and bath hadn't fared any better. Drawers were smashed, the bedposts broken off, and every mirror and even the shower door were shattered. The guy with the knife had been busy here too, slashing Kim's clothes and the drapes. Same with the second bedroom.

But whatever this was, it was by design. Vandals usually aren't thorough. They lay waste to a couple of rooms, then get tired. This was pros covering up a sophisticated search, and it confirmed my suspicion about why they'd taken her car. They'd been looking for something. I needed an inventory, so I started back toward the front to get Kim.

I heard the guy coming behind me, but the hall was too narrow to get completely out of the way. I didn't know where he'd come from, only that he had a clear shot at my back. At the last second, I flattened myself against the wall, and the shovel he was swinging missed my head by inches. Instead, it hit me on the top of my left shoulder, clipping my ear as it went by and numbing my arm all the way down.

The force of the blow drove me to the floor, and the guy moved in for the kill. But instead of trying to get away like he expected, I rolled toward him, and his second swing whanged off the hardwood floor.

I aimed my foot at the front of his left knee and connected. The guy was wearing shorts, and I saw his leg bend too far in the wrong direction. The ligaments popped audibly. He screamed in pain, but instead of collapsing, he turned the shovel on its edge and brought it down savagely, like an axe. Fortunately, he missed, but the floor didn't fare so well. The shovel hit a seam in the hardwood, splintered it and got wedged in the gash. It was all I needed.

I kicked upward into his crotch and felt the heel of my

shoe mash soft flesh. This time, the guy went down. Taking no chances, I rolled on top of him and hit him in the chin with two short, powerful shots. His eyes glazed, then closed. He was out.

"Gary! Jesus Christ, what are you doing in here?" I looked up and saw Kim. But Gary wasn't going to be answering her anytime soon.

Shakily, I got to my feet and took inventory. There was no telling how big the bruise was going to be where the shovel had hit my shoulder, but nothing was broken. Kim was bending over the unconscious man, pushing his hair off his forehead. I finally noticed how big the guy was. Linebacker size.

"If you don't mind my asking, who the hell is Gary?"

"Gary Wainwright. He lives next door. He's got a landscaping business and takes care of my yard when he does his own. Do you think he needs an ambulance?"

Just then Gary rolled onto his side and began to snore, a common reaction when people are knocked unconscious. I looked at him, then at Kim, and shook my head. "What he's really going to need is an orthopedic surgeon, but that can wait."

Kim looked at Gary's knee, which was already swollen to twice its previous size. I thought she was going to be sick, but she managed to keep it together.

We walked back to the living room, and Kim looked around, really seeing the mess for the first time. She started toward the kitchen, but I stopped her. "It's just as bad in there. Everywhere, actually."

Fumbling out a cigarette and clumsily lighting it, she sank down on her sofa with the stuffing hanging out and took a deep drag. "Why would Gary do something like this? I've always been nice to him."

"Gary didn't do anything. My guess is he saw the mess and came in to check on you. Then I walked in."

"How do you know he didn't do it?"

I explained why and asked her what she had that somebody

would want badly enough to risk a noisy, time-consuming break-in in a quiet neighborhood. "Let's not kid each other, okay. You know, and I know, it was Tino and Dante—or somebody working for them. It may not be why they grabbed you, but it's a loose end they wanted tied up."

I watched her carefully. For a split second, I saw something in her eyes, then it disappeared. She pretended to run through a mental checklist. "I can't think of anything, but let me look in the bedroom. See if my jewelry is still there."

She was buying time. She returned shortly, shaking her head. "What a fucking disaster, but nothing's missing."

She was acting like a schoolgirl, so I pushed. I didn't expect an answer, but I wanted to see her reaction again. "Cut the crap, Kim. Tino and Dante weren't looking for a drug score. You have something they want. What is it?"

Again her eyes flashed, but she covered it more quickly this time. Now, though, I knew it was fear, not calculated deception. She shook her head. "I have no idea."

I wasn't finished. "If they found it before they grabbed you, it was probably in the van."

She got angry. "I told you, I don't know. And I didn't see anything. Maybe you forgot, but I was a little fucking busy trying to save my life."

There was a moan from the hallway. Kim got up, and I followed her.

Gary's face was pale, and when he got to his feet, he was trembling from the pain in his knee and elsewhere. But I had to give him credit, he sucked it up and didn't complain. He even apologized to me. "I was so pissed I just didn't think," he said.

"When did you notice the break-in?" I asked him.

"Only about fifteen minutes before you got here." Looking at Kim, he said, "I was going to plant you a new cactus I had left over from a job in Brentwood, and when I came through the backyard, your door was standing open."

We got Gary to the sofa, and he sat down heavily. Kim brought him a glass of water.

"Did you notice anything unusual the last couple of days?" I asked.

He nodded. "Yesterday. I had a Sunday re-sod over in Culver City, and when I left about 8:00 a.m., there was a dark blue van out front. Two guys. The driver flicked a cigarette out the window as I drove by. It hit my truck, and I stopped. The guy gave me the finger, and I gave it back. Smarmy-looking weasel, but I didn't have time to stop and kick his ass."

"So it really was them," Kim said, not really to anyone.

"Then you know who did this?" said Gary.

Kim looked at me, so I answered him. "Yes, the question is why."

"So you gonna call the cops?" asked Gary.

Kim shook her head. "What are they going to do? Paw through my stuff then make a report nobody will read. Waste of time. Theirs and mine, but mostly mine."

That made twice she'd passed on calling the authorities.

A friend, Melvin Rose, runs a business that cleans up after fires and violent crimes. It can be revolting work, but people will pay a lot to get the smoke smell out of a house or not have to wipe up the viscera of a loved one. I never asked Melvin how he prices out a job, but he lives on the beach in Malibu, so he must not be bashful.

I got hold of him on my cell, and an hour later, there was a team of Russian women putting the house back together. Melvin hires only women and only ones from the old East Bloc. Says nothing bothers them, and they don't steal.

"The men, they're a different fuckin' breed," he told me once. "Loot a cathedral and get the cardinal to help carry out the altar. One showed up in drag once and snuck through. Broads on his crew almost beat the fucker to death when they caught him shovin' a clock down his skirt. Now I make the new hires strip. Had a couple run out the door."

Gary got up to limp home, and I told Kim to pack a bag so she could stay at my place. Besides the mess, the back door wouldn't lock, so there was no point tempting fate.

I saw Gary look at her, and I realized he had a crush. Women always know that kind of thing, but the vibe from Kim was that, for whatever reason, Gary hadn't gotten anywhere. Now, not only was his knee wrecked, but he also had to watch the guy who did it leave with the girl. I felt bad for him.

I called Mallory on the way, and by the time we arrived, he had the Toledo Room brightened up and the closets empty. I reminded myself to tell him to donate the clothes to charity. But I'd made that note before, and somehow it hadn't happened. My failure, not his.

Kim wanted to take a nap—a real one—so I went out to my office to make a few calls and try to locate a photographer named Walter Kempthorn.

7

Skycaps and a Walk on the Beach

LAX is never fun, but Monday afternoons are usually lighter than normal. I was driving my Dodge Ram, and I pulled into the parking garage opposite the Delta terminal. Surprisingly, I found a space on the street level. I crossed to the terminal and took up a position along an iron fence about thirty feet down from passenger drop-off. Traffic was moving easily, and the skycaps were handling people as quickly as they arrived.

After ten minutes, I had what I wanted and approached a heavyset skycap in his late fifties whom I had seen the other men deferring to. He was wearing an ID that gave his name as Mitchell Adams.

"Excuse me, sir," I said. "May I have a word with you?"

He sized me up and said, "I saw you standing down there. You was figuring out who was running this shift."

It wasn't a question, and I didn't answer.

"I know all the cops, and you ain't one a them or TSA neither, or the airline, so if you want something, you'll have to talk to my supervisor, and he ain't here."

"Mr. Adams, my name is Rail Black." I didn't offer my hand. "And I'm trying to find someone."

"Like I said, you'll have to talk to my supervisor."

Most people don't know it, but skycap service in many large domestic airports is the exclusive province of African-Americans. I don't mean the airlines only hire blacks. They don't hire anyone. It's contracted out, and the real power is a group of smart, hardworking, African-American men who run a patronage system as tight as Chicago aldermen. And since a hustling skycap can make $125,000 a year, there's no shortage of people showing up on bended knee.

"I think you're the supervisor. But even if you're not, you call your own shots."

He looked at me expressionlessly for a moment, then smiled. "You're a pretty smart fella. Who you looking for?"

"Walter Kempthorn."

"This is about the picture he took, ain't it?"

"Yes."

"You with some insurance company?"

"No, just a civilian with a couple of questions."

"No sworn statements? No testifying?"

"Nothing."

He looked bemused. "Walter's always taking goddamn pictures. Drives a lot of guys around here nuts. Especially when they're out having a few drinks, unwinding. Had to step in a couple of times to keep him from getting his ass kicked. But he's my nephew, and blood is blood."

"He here today?"

"No, he's home. Layin' low."

"Why's that?"

"Somebody called this morning and said they wanted the negatives. That they'd be sending someone around tomorrow. And if he didn't hand them over, they'd burn down his house—with him in it."

"You believe that?"

Mitchell Adams shook his head. "I figure if it was real, they wouldn't have said nothin'. They'd have just showed up."

"That what you told Walter?"

"I told him the negatives might be the best friend he had.

That he should give them to a lawyer and sit tight. See what happens."

"You're a pretty smart fella yourself, Mr. Adams."

"Call me Mitchell. You want to talk to Walter?"

"If it's possible."

"You got somebody I can call? Check you out?"

"You know Sister Vonetta? Runs the St. Regis school?"

"I heard of her."

I borrowed Mitchell's pen and a piece of paper and wrote Sister V's phone number on it.

He looked at the number then at me. "My shift's over in an hour. You check out, I'll be at Roxy's Diner on Imperial Highway. You think you can find it?"

"We're both smart fellas, remember?"

He seemed to like that.

Walter Kempthorn's house was on a neatly kept street just off Artesia Boulevard. I parked behind Mitchell and followed him up the walk. The windows were closed and the blinds drawn, giving the place a we're-not-home look, but Mitchell didn't bother to knock. He produced a fistful of keys, selected one and opened the front door.

"One of my places," he said by way of explanation. "When it comes to the rent, Walter's a slow pay, but he keeps the place up, and he watches over his mother."

The house was as neat inside as out.

"Paula?" Mitchell called out. "It's me."

"She ain't here," a voice answered, and then a good-sized man in his twenties stepped into the room. He was dressed like a lot of young black men: loose-fitting jeans, oversized white T-shirt and an Oakland Raiders cap with the ultra-flat brim pushed off-center.

Mitchell said, "Walter, this is Mr. Black."

Walter said nothing and didn't move.

So I said, "Pretty good camera work the other night on the freeway. You really know what you're doing."

"What the fuck's it to you?" Walter spit back. "You got

one blood Uncle Tommin' for you today; you ain't gettin' a second."

Without warning, Mitchell Adams reached out and slapped his nephew across the face, hard. The Raiders cap flew off, and Walter's eyes went wide. He rubbed his cheek and started to pick up his hat.

"Leave it," said Mitchell, and Walter did. Then Mitchell locked eyes with his nephew, and in one of the coldest voices I've ever heard, he said, "You and me will deal with the disrespect later. Right now, we're on manners. Man's invited to your home, you smile and say, 'Glad to meet you.' "

Walter's tone went from confrontational to petulant, but he wasn't ready to back down all the way. He looked at Mitchell warily. "I didn't invite him. You did. So you tell him how glad you are."

Mitchell held his gaze level, and Walter blinked a couple of times, but he kept himself together. After a moment of watching them stare at each other, I said, "What I'd like, Walter, is to borrow your negatives. I promise you'll get them back in pristine condition, and I'll pay you for the accommodation."

Walter didn't say anything, so I went on. "If I could, I'd look at them here, but I'm not an expert, and the guy who is needs his own equipment."

"A hundred grand," Walter said suddenly.

"Excuse me?"

"I said a hundred grand. I got one guy says he's willin' to kill me for them, and now you show up. Must be mighty valuable pictures. So you want them, it'll cost you a hundred large."

I saw some nervousness in Walter Kempthorn's eyes, but there was something else there too. Deeper, more feral. The slap across the face had brought it closer to the surface. I spoke softly. "If you'll look closely, at least one of your shots shows a young lady getting out of the back of a van. You won't be able to miss her. She's not wearing any clothes. She was escaping a kidnapping."

If Walter had been teetering on the edge, now he went over. "What the fuck do I care about some white bitch I never met? Here's the way it is, man. I carry your fuckin' bags at the airport 'cause people hear a black man say, 'Yes sir, right away, sir,' and they reach deep. That, and my uncle here is such an important fuckin' guy that when I take a day off, nobody says boo. But when I'm on my own time— which is right now, motherfucker—I'd just as soon shoot you as look at you. So it's a hundred grand, or get the fuck out of my house."

I don't get angry often, but I almost grabbed Walter Kempthorn and choked the fucking life out of him. It would have been a fool's errand.

I believe in life force. That some people are more alive than others. You can feel it when they enter a room. It's sometimes confused with star quality or charisma, but it's more. Charisma can get men to follow you into battle. Life force can make them volunteer to die.

The strongest I've ever witnessed was JFK's, and he was killed before I was born, so I've only seen it on film. It must have been overpowering in person. I've heard people say that the moment he died the sun dimmed. I believe them.

The second strongest was my father's. It didn't matter who was in a room. The only person anyone noticed was him.

But there's also negative life force. People whose spirit is so dead that it's already begun slipping into the next life. I had it happen on a plane once. A guy sat down next to me, and without looking up, I knew there was something wrong. I didn't even want to hear his voice. I got off. Took another flight.

Mitchell Adams was a man who'd seen a lot, but he radiated life. His eyes twinkled, and his movements were confident. But at Walter Kempthorn's core was something that sucked out any warmth or light he might have once had. He occupied space but offered only despair.

I said, "You know something, Walter, if I thought you were worth the trouble, I'd negotiate with you, and you'd probably end up with ten grand for just doing a good deed. But anyone who can be so disrespectful to a member of his family in front of a stranger is nothing but a punk, and I don't waste my time with punks."

Then I really bore down. "The great thing about being an owner is that you can set your price. And the great thing about being a buyer is that I can decide to pay it—or not. And right now, I wouldn't take your fucking pictures if *you* gave *me* ten grand. Because then I might have to see you again, and that's something I hope never to do."

I turned to Mitchell. "I know you said there's some good in there, but it's close to flickering out."

I could see the pain in Mitchell Adams's eyes. "We got a good-sized chunk of a whole generation like this," he said sadly. "Those of us who fought the last century's indignities so these guys wouldn't have to now find ourselves shedding more tears for them than we ever did for ourselves. The good news is Walter's got a real job, and he's got his cameras. Maybe one day he'll get something else to go along with them."

I didn't think so, but I left it unsaid. Instead, I went outside and was never so glad to breathe fresh air. As I was starting my truck, I saw Mitchell come out, but he didn't look my way. He just headed for his car.

You can't think constructively when you're angry. You have a tendency to forget the problem and just keep drawing a straight line between the guy who pissed you off and putting his head in a vise. I needed a little thinking time, so instead of heading home, I turned west toward the beach.

Playa del Rey is a short stretch of oceanfront and low hills just south of LAX. Because there's very little parking and a constant river of jets taking off overhead, it doesn't get much love. But despite being able to count the rivets in a 747's belly when you're there, it's not as loud as you might think, and you can still watch a sunset without being assaulted by humanity.

I parked at a meter along Vista del Mar, left my shoes in the car and took the stairs down to the beach. It was quiet except for a few dozen sunbathers and a skinny, white-haired guy in a dirty U.S. Navy captain's hat and WWII desert shorts working the sand with a metal detector. I crossed the thirty yards to the water and turned south, the late afternoon sun off to my right. The surf was coming in hard, and I had to pay attention to avoid getting swept off my feet by the tail end of some of the larger breakers. I put my head down and walked hard.

By the time I got back to the Ram, my anger was gone, and the sun was going down. I rinsed my feet with a bottle of Arrowhead and slipped back into my shoes. I suddenly realized I wanted hot food, and plenty of it. The first place I saw was a Del Taco, and I inhaled a Macho Combo Burrito and a Jumbo Coke. I'm not usually a fast-food guy, but it was almost as good as getting laid.

While I ate, I thought about Walter Kempthorn, and when I finished, I turned the truck back toward Artesia Boulevard. I didn't know exactly what I was going to say because it wasn't a conversation you could rehearse. But I did know that, photographs or no photographs, I didn't want to leave it the way it was.

Walter's house was dark, but I rang the bell anyway. A young kid walking by saw me and called out, "Nobody home, mister. Walter and his mom, they left."

So I got back in the truck and headed home. I promised myself I'd drive out to the airport the next day.

8

Dinner and Roses

I didn't tell Kim about Walter Kempthorn. What was there to say, anyway? That I'd let some kid get under my skin when I didn't have a backup plan? Not smart, and definitely not professional.

Despite the Del Taco, I was hungry again, so we went down the hill for a belated birthday celebration at my favorite restaurant, Tacitus. It was a gorgeous night, and we sat outside on the front patio alongside some movie people and a young couple who were so into each other, I don't think they knew where they were, or cared.

Tacitus Gambelli runs the best Tuscan kitchen this side of Florence, and it's always at the top of L.A.'s most romantic restaurants list. I'm sure that makes Tacitus proud, but it doesn't give enough credit to the lovingly prepared dishes and personal service that are increasingly rare since corporate stores started elbowing their way into the high-end dining experience. Don't get me wrong, I love a good Morton's porterhouse as much as anyone, but as sexy as it is, it's still assembly-line food.

After bruschetta and a pair of Morettis, I had the lamb, and Kim the lobster ravioli. While we ate, Tacitus came by with a bottle of something from his private stock. A rare Tignanello. After a sip, Kim declared it as good as Plump-Jack, which was high praise, I guess, considering it was about seven times the price, and something thieves break into warehouses to steal.

But Tacitus didn't bat an eye and thanked her in the way men from the Continent have that Americans can't seem to master. While Kim beamed, I wondered if the Tignanello would have the same effect as my cheaper grape juice had. I hoped so.

As the three of us chatted, a young Hispanic teenager carrying a basket of individually cellophane-wrapped roses came into the restaurant. He was working a foursome in the corner when Tacitus saw him and excused himself. We watched him hustle the boy out.

When he returned, I joked, "So much for capitalism."

Tacitus shook his head. "I feel sorry for the kid. He's just trying to make a buck. I used to let them in, but then one of my customers' purses disappeared. There's always one jerk who screws it up for everyone else." At that moment, Tacitus spotted the 20-something star of a hot sitcom arriving with his entourage and hustled off to kiss some actor's ass.

As Kim and I headed into our second bottle of wine over shared chocolate truffle cake with a candle in it, she gave me a mock serious look. "You know, it'd be nice if I knew something about the man I'm fucking."

"How romantic."

"When it feels that good, there's no other word for it."

"So what's your pleasure? You still wondering how tall I am?"

Kim flicked her hair. "Couldn't care less. I want to know about your women. What kind do you like?"

"I may not look too bright, but I know better than to answer a question like that. Unless you describe the lady you're with down to her pedicure, you're on your way to sleeping alone—and maybe wearing dessert."

Kim laughed. "Spoken like a man who's been there. That's not what I meant."

"That's exactly what you meant."

She laughed again. "Okay, okay, I surrender. So humor me. Pretend I'm Barbara Walters, and you're a big star. Skip past the kind of tree you'd be."

"Carly Fiorina," I said.

I saw her eyes go blank, then it came to her. "The computer company broad?"

"Ex-computer company. But yes, I think she's one of the most desirable women I've ever seen."

She thought I was putting her on. "Isn't she a little . . ." She seemed stuck for a word.

I tried to help. "Off the radar?"

"Old," she said.

"Isn't that a bit catty, Ms. Walters?"

"This is like unbelievable. I'll admit, she's attractive . . . in a boardroom kind of way. But what in the hell—"

"I'll help you along. She's a complete woman. Smart, feminine, self-assured, and most importantly, she has character."

"Character? You know her?"

"Never been in the same room. But you can always tell by the way a person speaks. Ask a question, get an answer. No long pauses while she runs down the PR checklist. No eyes wandering around the room searching for just the right ring of truth to the lie she's about to tell. No ten-sentence paragraphs that don't say anything but that you know you can get away with because the media will dutifully report anything that comes out of your mouth. And for good measure, she doesn't talk down to people or lose her temper. Oh, I'm sure her husband has seen her in a splendid red rage, and she's probably bullshitted him a time or two, probably even stepped on his ego. But that's what husbands are for."

Kim sat back in her chair. "I don't even know what to say. You're by far the most unusual man I've ever met. Carly fucking Fiorina. I'd love to tell somebody, but I don't know anyone who would get it."

"You did."

"Thanks," she said after a moment. "I think that's a compliment."

"It is."

She regarded her wine for a moment, then asked, "You do anything besides help people and fantasize about chicks in business suits? Collect stamps? Maybe some hog calling?"

"A little this and that," I answered.

"Is that what you keep in the locked room off the library? Your this and that?"

I studied her before answering. "Locked room?" I said evenly.

"Your eyes just turned to stone. Now I'm really intrigued. The room where if you go outside and look, it's as big as the library, but the shutters are closed tight, and you can't see in. The room Mallory doesn't answer questions about."

"Remind me not to leave you alone so long. Your imagination gets stuck in overdrive."

"I'm not imagining anything. Just asking, that's all."

I said nothing.

"Not going to tell me, right?" she said finally.

"Nothing to tell. Just storage."

She rolled her eyes. "Got it," she said in a tone that meant she didn't get it. "Okay, I'll worm it out of you later. Right now, we'll go for something easy. How about your mother."

I'd have to ask Mallory to fill me in on her wanderings. I took a sip of wine. "She was from Brazil. Rio," I answered.

"A Carioca. How exotic. How'd you end up in Beverly Hills?"

"The long way around."

Putting her chin on her fist and leaning forward, Kim said, "So pour me another glass of wine and tell me a story."

I did a healthy pour for both of us and began. "Her name then was Amarante Grasciosa. She was a singer and songwriter, and she'd gotten all she could out of Rio, so she borrowed some money from an uncle and headed north."

"Amarante," Kim said. "Wow. What I wouldn't give for a name like that."

"Hey, you got Dana."

"Watch it," she warned, but she was smiling.

"She landed some chorus work on Broadway and sang backup on a couple of albums, but the big break always seemed to elude her. To make ends meet, she worked at a club in Spanish Harlem, where she met a Puerto Rican bartender with the unlikely name of Jerry Green. And in a moment of extreme loneliness, Amarante married him, not knowing that after a few drinks, Jerry'd hit anything or anybody. Eventually, she got tired of being slapped around and moved out, but not before she'd locked down her citizenship."

"You've got to give the girl credit for making the most of a bad situation," said Kim.

"That's what she used to say, but I think it was revisionist history. And then she met Gabriel Navarro."

"The Formula One driver?"

"Yes, and it was the love match she'd been waiting for all her life. They were inseparable."

"Oh, my God, didn't he. . . ?"

I nodded. "At Monaco. While she watched."

I waited until Kim finished processing. "She walled herself up in her New York apartment and cried for three months, finally deciding it was time to go home."

"But she didn't."

"Like a lot of exceptionally beautiful women, Amarante was routinely asked to be an arm decoration for wealthy men. And before Gabriel, she'd occasionally done it. But she wouldn't accept money or gifts."

"So no sex. Just a good time."

"Correct. She was hoping to make a music connection, plus it was a way to see things she never would have. A few days before she was supposed to leave for Rio, she got a call from a closeted gay banker whom she'd bearded for at business functions. He asked if she'd like to go to a Christmas housewarming party."

"How very suburban," Kim quipped.

"Well, it wasn't exactly your drop-by-in-a-Santa-hat affair. Limousines deposited the invitees at a private hangar at JFK, where a chartered 727 flew them to Miami. Breaking into smaller groups, they boarded shuttles to a private Bahamian Island. You might have heard of it. Clarissima."

"Vaguely. Didn't some really rich guy develop it way, way back?"

"A Dutch rubber baron. Built himself a forty-thousand-square-foot tropical hideaway called Heaven's Wind, complete with a village for his staff. But after he died, the place ran through a succession of owners until it finally fell into disrepair. Then one day, a British newspaper and shipping chap, Lord James Black, rode in."

"Ah, Lord Black. I see a picture emerging here."

"My father-to-be bargained the price down to almost nothing, then poured in millions renovating the main house and dredging the harbor so he could dock his private ship at the front door. When the work was completed, he threw open the gates and invited the world's rich and famous to spend the holidays. *A Heaven's Wind Christmas* was the must-have ticket for the jet set that year. Yachts backed up miles into the Caribbean, and there wasn't enough tarmac to park all the planes."

Kim pointed to her glass and smiled. "And here came the beautiful Amarante hanging with a gay guy."

I hadn't told this story for a long time, and I was actually enjoying it. I poured while I talked. "Lord Black had recently divorced his first wife, a Windsor cousin, and his dating exploits were the talk of the London scandal sheets—even the ones he owned. As the story goes, the moment he laid eyes on Amarante, he was entranced. And when he found out she was a singer, he sent a plane to Miami to fetch an arranger.

"The second night, she performed six songs, the finale

something she had composed after Gabriel's death. It was called "Christmas Always Breaks My Heart." And as the story goes, it brought down the house. It also brought down the walls of Lord Black's heart."

Kim's face was flushed. I assumed it was the wine, but it wasn't. Her voice was husky. "That's the most sensuous story I've ever heard. And that name. Amarante. It's so perfect. My God, I just came."

"Wait'll I get to the part about my toy train collection."

"Don't make fun of me. I mean it; it's never happened to me like that before."

"So it's true. All little girls like princess stories."

She took another sip of wine. "Please don't stop now."

Tacitus broke the mood by showing up with a box of cigars. He wanted me to try one. So while Kim went off to the ladies' room, I fired up an Arturo Fuente Opus X. Very nice.

When Kim returned, she lit a Benson & Hedges, and we sat for a moment as she blew her smoke into mine. Then I got back to my story.

"Lord Black wasn't interested in Amarante's singing career. He wanted her all to himself. So two months later, he threw one of the most lavish weddings outside the royal family. It was a tongue-wagging marriage. Wealthy British lords traditionally kept their working-class lovers in gilded cages out of sight. They didn't bring them to the Queen's Tea at the Derby.

"But Amarante was so beautiful and James so unforgiving of anyone who slighted her that, eventually, she won over enough of the upper crust that she began being invited to a few events on her own. They divided their time among homes in London, Hong Kong and, of course, Clarissima, where I was born. And where for the first six years of my life I ran wild, chasing parrots and lizards and swimming and fishing and riding my horse in the surf."

Kim sighed longingly. "Sounds like a kid's dream. Hell, anybody's dream."

"It was, but then the real world came calling. They called it school. So we packed up and moved permanently to Strathmoor Hall, our country house in Derbyshire."

Kim looked at me with skepticism. "I've been to Derbyshire, and anything called a hall ain't a country house. That's nobility country. Let me guess, forty rooms?"

"One hundred and thirty-six."

"Oh, my fucking God."

I laughed. "It gets worse. I was eight before I realized not everyone owned an island."

Kim started to giggle and couldn't seem to stop. Finally, she got control of herself. "Wake me when this is over, will you? Where's the goddamn wine?"

"Frankly, it took the kind of money my father had to maintain the place. A lot of dukes and earls with front-page names but street sweeper incomes have to take in tourists just to keep a turreted roof over their heads."

"That's why every year I contribute a little something to down-on-their-luck gentry," Kim said, straight-faced.

I raised my glass in a toast. "And here's a heartfelt thanks for those who can't be here to speak for themselves. Anyway, as grand as it was, I hated Strathmoor. There was always some servant ratting you out for something. I hated school even more. Some stiff-collared headmaster whacking you with a stick if your homework was late or if you farted during morning prayers. I went into full-scale rebellion. Did you know you can herd Arabian horses with a Bentley?"

"You didn't."

"Oh, I did. But I wasn't stupid enough to use my father's car. I swiped a neighbor's. Took three tractors to pull that baby out of the mud."

Kim was laughing again, and I joined her. It was a good memory. "Right after that, they shipped me to the States."

"Eastern, private and very fancy."

"Nope, my father decided to try something different. Discipline. The Army and Navy Academy."

"Yikes."

"And then some," I joked. "But you know, it didn't take me long to get with the program. I took a page from David Copperfield and became the hero of my own life—or at least the architect. And besides, I might have been marching, but I was doing it on the California coast. It wasn't Clarissima, but it wasn't cold, rainy England either."

"I think you turned out great."

"Tall, anyway."

"So where's the accent? If I had your upbringing, I'd be working overtime to talk like Audrey Hepburn."

"Right, and my classmates wouldn't have kicked my ass three times a day. That was the first thing I got rid of. But I can slide back into it when I need to."

"At my house, while I was packing, I thought I heard you speaking Russian to those women."

"I'm lucky, I've got an ear for languages, but I've never been able to get that one really down. I think it's the moroseness I'm missing. I told them you were a big movie star and wanted them to have a generous tip. It was my deal with Melvin for getting them out there so fast."

"How generous was I?"

"Let's just say there's caviar with the borscht tonight."

"I'm running up quite a tab."

"I'll take it out in trade."

She smiled over her glass. "Not so fast, you've got a story to finish."

I took a sip of wine. I'd come this far, so I plowed ahead. "By the time I was a senior in high school, James and Amarante's marriage was coming apart. Her dream had been to become an entertainer, not the lady of Strathmoor Hall. She was indulged and spoiled, but hopelessly trapped. So she got a friend—vodka.

"And then one day, she told my father she was moving to Los Angeles. She'd found somebody new—a record producer—who, surprise, was going to make her a star. And besides, she said, she'd be closer to her son, which looked nice on the label but didn't play out so well in practice. And that was that."

"Storybook romance, dime novel ending," said Kim.

"The good news was that my father took a renewed interest in me. He was satisfied I was becoming a gentleman, but he also wanted to make sure I became a man. So on school breaks, he took me on the road and showed me the intricacies of life—the ones that don't come in a book.

"I played poker against men three times my age in London clubs, baccarat against sheikhs in Cairo and roulette against the house in Monte Carlo. I sat through tough business negotiations, then held up the bar with him while he celebrated or stewed. My father was also big, which is a magnet for the occasional drunken loudmouth, so more than once, we bareknuckled our way out of a place. Gave the place a 'Black and Black,' we called it. It was an extraordinary life, and I loved it—and him."

"So what happened to Amarante and the record producer?"

"Their relationship was shorter than the flight over. So were most of the dozen that followed. Then she seemed to get her bearings and married a mining magnate named Charlie Fear. But once again, she'd bet wrong. The only thing I can say about him is that they got the name right. He was an abusive prick, but Amarante never got the chance to divorce him. And I never got the chance to take him out in an alley.

"On New Year's Eve, the year I turned eighteen, they were gunned down coming out of a party in Miami Beach. Lots of witnesses, but no arrests, so you had your pick between one of Charlie's legion of enemies or just a bad night on Collins Avenue. Six months later, my father was skiing the Himalayas when he got caught in an avalanche. And all of a sudden, a Black and Black was down to one Black."

"My God, how dreadful."

"In some ways, yes. But in another, I wasn't going to witness my mother drinking herself to death. And my father, well, one could argue he had fifty-six terrific years and five bad minutes."

Kim looked away. "I like that way of looking at it. *Relief* is the only word I could come up with when Mom passed away. She was so sad all the time. I promised myself that no matter how much I hurt, I'd never wear it on my sleeve."

I nodded. "The bonus was that I fell in love with America—and everything it stood for. I couldn't imagine living anywhere else. Legally, I'm a dual citizen, but there is no other country in my heart."

Kim took the last sip of her wine. "So you went to college, and now you run your father's empire."

I shook my head. "I couldn't work up much enthusiasm for college. After what I'd seen and done, a frat party seemed inconsequential. So I went into the army. As for Part Two, I run the 'empire' only in the sense that I make the decisions who does."

"So you're a man of leisure who helps people. I like that."

"It keeps me off the streets," I said.

"Only I think there's more to it."

"Why?"

"I've felt your arms around me. You don't hold a woman like a dilettante. You're lean and hard, but not just because you work out. You know exactly what you're doing every time you move. And there's that little bit of tension in your body, even when you're asleep, that tells me you're never completely relaxed, always on alert. Listening. Anticipating. You're a very mysterious man, Rail Black, and I aim to find out everything about you."

"I'll keep an eye out for truth serum and cattle prods."

She laughed. "Did you inherit Clarissima too?"

I wasn't prepared for the question.

And suddenly, there it was again. The flash of sun-glinted hair . . . her face. Sanrevelle Adriana Marcelino Carvalho. Then the explosion . . . and the fire. And her scream.

When I managed to speak, my voice rasped. "Yes, but I don't go there anymore."

Kim opened her mouth, then seemed to realize something

had entered our space. "Whatever happened to your mother's songs?"

I looked away until she had to ask me again. "I had them recorded once, but just for me."

"You know what I want, Mr. Strathmoor Hall, Proud American? I want to go home, get into that big bed of yours, and listen to 'Christmas Always Breaks My Heart' with you inside me."

"In that case, you'll have to be a fast listener."

She reached across the table and put her hand over mine. "Rail, I want you to know that wherever we end up, or if we don't end up at all, I'll always remember tonight." She paused, then said, "And if I ever have a daughter, I'm going to name her Amarante."

I put my other hand over hers. "It has been a terrific night. So I want you to promise me that, a little while from now, when we get into your favorite position, you'll drop the evasion and tell me what you've been holding back."

She looked down, bit her lip and nodded. Her voice was almost a whisper. "Okay. I promise."

"So I know you're serious, how about a preview."

Kim looked off into the trees around the patio. After several moments, she lit a cigarette. "Sooner or later, I've got to start trusting someone." Still looking away, she said softly, "City of War."

"Should I know what that is?"

She started to answer, when out of the corner of my eye, I saw someone coming toward us. I turned. It was the kid with the flower basket. I looked around for Tacitus, but the place was almost empty, so he must have been inside.

Kim smiled as the kid approached. "Hey, birthday boy," she said, "how about springing for a rose for the lady?"

As I reached for my money clip, the kid was about ten feet away. He smiled and put his hand in the basket. He came out with a 9mm Beretta.

And everything went into slow motion.

He shot Kim in the face. I watched the hole appear, then

fill with blood. I started to get up, and the kid casually pivoted and shot me in the chest. Then again . . . and again. And I was falling, and dishes were breaking. Somewhere, somebody screamed.

Kim just sat there, her head lolled back, her open eyes staring, but seeing nothing.

Just as I lost consciousness, something slipped through the fog, forcing me to remember. Like Tino, the kid had a spider tattoo on his forearm, but this one only had one leg.

9

Pain and Memories

Cedars-Sinai is a very good hospital. And it was close. It had to be. I was mostly dead when they got me there.

I regained consciousness long enough to see the Code Blue team scissoring off my clothes and jamming needles into my arms and legs. Then a pretty, young Asian lady wearing a tiny jade Buddha around her neck loomed over me with a long hypodermic. There were drops of sweat running down her forehead, and one of them started to fall. Suddenly, the sound of my heart pounding in my ears slowed and began to fade. I closed my eyes. From someplace far away, I think I heard a Marlboro-tuned voice growl, "Hit him! Now!" Then the darkness came, and I rushed into it.

In the movies, the hero gets shot, pulls himself off the operating table and goes after the bad guys. It doesn't work that way. The pain is beyond excruciating, and there aren't any he-men. Everyone asks for drugs—lots of them. Especially after they hack off a rib that looks like a pack of wolves have been fighting over it, reassemble a lung and dig half a dozen furrows through your upper body, chasing fragments.

One of the shots had gone through my left hand, chipping off pieces of bone along the way. The doctor said it was probably the bullet that had been meant for my head, but I'd instinctively raised my hand, and the slight trajectory change had been enough. You don't usually say thanks for more pain, but this time I did.

Mallory moved into the Sofitel Hotel down the street and was with me every minute. Ordering a special bed to accommodate my size, feeding me when I could eat and listening to me babble in delirium. I know I said some things to him that were cruel. But that's why he's the valet. He's the better man.

Men who've been on the cover of *Forbes* and pretty young women don't get gunned down in Beverly Hills without a media firestorm. Because they deal with so many celebrities, Cedars is used to stiff-arming the paparazzi, but this was beyond even their capabilities.

Mallory asked my friends not to visit so they wouldn't get caught in the frenzy. He also hired round-the-clock security. Even then, some parasites still squeezed through. And I even had to admire the guy who bribed his way onto the window washing detail and took my picture from the rig.

I was half-in, half-out for a week, and all I really remember is that I kept getting Kim's and Sanrevelle's faces mixed up. Sometimes, I would be trying to save Sanrevelle again, only she looked like Kim. And once, I was on fire, and Kim and Sanrevelle were just watching me burn. Watching like I had when both of them died.

Two special women. Two dead women. Both only an arm's length away. And I had done nothing for either of them. Nothing. Hospitals give you time to remember things you don't want to.

But sometimes, they also spring the lock on the place you store memories that should be visited more often. The ones you can't talk about but that help define you.

"Hey, Mister, wake up. Hey, Mister . . . Mister . . ."

The small voice penetrated the fog in my head, but I couldn't seem to turn to see who it was. Strange. I'd never had that trouble before. Okay, let's try something easier. Just open your eyes.

I sent the command, but nothing happened. It stayed dark, even though I was sure there was light out there. Then I felt something running down the side of my face, pooling under my cheek. Something wet . . . warm.

I heard heavy surf. Very close. I listened for seagulls, but the waves were too loud. Then from very far away, a deep-throated engine. A motorcycle maybe? As it came closer, it wasn't a motorcycle. It didn't rumble, it pounded like a giant pair of wings. Whumph! Whumph! Whumph!

The ground began to shake, and suddenly, all other sound and sensation were lost. Then there was a terrible wind, blasting sand into my nostrils, and I couldn't breathe.

I came awake in the chopper. A medic was holding a chunk of white nylon the size of a pencil stub under my nose. He pulled it away, rolled it between his fingers, then pushed it under my nostrils again. Something stung all the way to my brain, and I started to cough, violently.

Over the thundering rotors, I heard the small voice again. "Is Mister gonna be A-okay?"

I recognized the accent, and the voice. It was the same one I'd heard when I'd grabbed the kid and started running. Then the fire had rained down, and I'd dropped and pulled him close, curling myself around him. I remember thinking I was a lousy shield, but I was all there was.

Then nothing.

The hospital was old but clean. Sunlight splashed across the ceiling, and through the open windows I could hear exotic birds calling to one another and an occasional monkey chattering at some unseen irritant. The lone nurse attending to the ten of us in the ward was stiffly starched and dressed in a long white dress. Her winged hat made her seem larger than she was. A nun. She was young and darkly attractive. When I tried to speak, she put her finger on my lips and shook her head.

My bed had been made for much smaller patients, and my feet hung over the end past my ankles. I wiggled them, and they worked. A relief. The only pain I felt was a dull headache and a slight burning under the bandage on my left arm. Otherwise, nothing.

I took my time and worked my legs around to the side of the bed. I rolled onto my right shoulder, pushed up with my elbow and, with leverage from the steel headboard, struggled to a sitting position. I breathed heavily, gathered my strength and stood.

The room spun wildly, and I found myself draped over the nun's shoulder. I wondered how she could hold me. Then I was lying down again.

I slept.

Later, the rest of J-Team came to see me. Six of them. Snake Gonzales hadn't made it. They sat around my bed, and we talked. Made some bad jokes. Got wet eyes. When they were gone, I slept again.

The name patch over the left pocket of the 3-star's jungle camos said Starkweather. We were sitting in a tin-roofed shack, where, during the day, it would have been too hot to draw a breath. But in the dark, with the door propped open and a sea breeze, it was comfortable enough.

There wasn't much furniture. A couple of folding chairs in front of a field desk, but in keeping with the scrounging ability of enlisted men when it comes to commanding officers, somebody had rustled up an executive chair for the lieutenant general. A couple of flies the size of bumblebees lazed languidly under the battery-powered desk lamp that threw a jaundice-colored light over everything.

The general reclined in his chair and put a well-shined canvas boot on the desk. "How you coming along, Sergeant?"

"Fine, sir," I answered. "I'd like to rejoin my team."

"Mind telling me what you were doing running after that goddamn kid when you knew the F-16s were coming in to pound the beach?"

"Protecting an asset, sir. And my team. He was our translator, and he knew where we were headed." I hesitated.

"Something else, Sergeant?"

"Sir, I don't believe he was trying to run away. I think he just got disoriented."

"Scared, you mean."

"Almost as much as I was."

The general smiled, and it was an easy one, creasing his face pleasantly. "Well, I hope he lives a long happy life and names his firstborn after you."

"That should be interesting. All he ever called me was Mister."

Starkweather reached for a pack of cigarettes, offered me one. I took it, then his lighter. We smoked in silence. Finally, he said, "What the hell is a guy your size doing in Delta Force, anyway? They like them tough, but they don't like them over 6-3."

"They were desperate to beat Airborne at basketball."

He laughed again. "How'd it work out?"

"Another well-planned, well-executed Delta mission."

"Congratulations, the only thing they usually win is the fight after the game."

"We did okay there too." I ground out my cigarette on the dirt floor. "Sir, I'm J-Team's Number 2, and I do the underwater work. I'd really like to get back."

Starkweather leaned forward in his chair. "Why didn't you tell somebody who the fuck you were when you joined the army?"

"At the risk of sounding out of line, General, who am I?"

"From what I'm told, some kind of British royalty."

"That was my father, sir. He was titled, but not royal. I'm just a sergeant."

"But you're also a Brit—even though you don't talk like one. And heir to some kind of goddamned business empire."

"Technically correct, sir. But the business is in the hands

of professional managers. I do have dual citizenship, but I think of myself only as an American."

"Well, some very high-placed folks in London seem to have a problem with that kind of simplicity. And when word reached them that you'd almost been killed, they demanded we put you on the next available flight."

"Begging the general's pardon, sir, but I have no interest in going to the UK. I'm a Delta operator."

"So now you're a Delta operator attached to an ally. The decision was made way the hell up the chain of command, Sergeant, and it's not open for debate. Draw your travel orders from my aide. That's all."

I arrived at 10 Downing Street in civilian clothes accompanied by a Mr. Vickers, who had lectured me in his office beforehand. "The prime minister is extremely busy, and though he's asked to see you, it's only perfunctory. So you'll listen, say nothing, and we'll be out of there in ten minutes. Do you understand?"

I looked at Vickers, a dour gent with some vague title in the Home Office. He had graying hair and an ill-fitted glass eye that maintained a position looking off to the right. And so far, he'd shown no indication he knew how to smile.

"Perhaps I could answer his hello. You know, just so he'll realize I'm not deaf."

Vickers's sense of humor must have resided in his missing orb, because he gave me a look that would have chilled stone.

We were ushered into the PM's study, a tightly organized room down the main hallway to the left. Number 10 is a rambling warren of niches, passageways and offices stretching two blocks and housing a maze of staff and electronics. To thwart a bomb blast, none of the rooms in front is used except for formal occasions, making the already jammed facility mostly windowless and claustrophobic.

As Vickers and I waited, I admired a portrait of Cromwell over the fireplace and the hand-bound collection of Sir Winston's books behind glass an arm's length from the desk. When the prime minister appeared, he was taller than on television. His rugged face housed a pair of bright, insightful eyes and a good smile. It was the kind of face people instinctively liked. A politician's face.

He crossed the room and took my extended hand in both of his. "Mr. Black. I'm so pleased to meet you. You're taller than your father, but you look just like him. He was one of my role models."

"Thank you, sir. Mine too."

"Something not easily said about a newspaper publisher," he laughed.

The PM suddenly noticed my companion. "Ah, Vickers. No need for you to stay. I'll send Mr. Black home in my car." He turned back to me. "You're staying at Strathmoor Hall, I assume?"

"I didn't know how long I'd be here, so I booked a room at the Lanesborough."

Vickers cleared his throat. "Excuse me, Mr. Prime Minister, but I know how busy you are. I could just wait."

There's something about power. When it speaks, no matter how softly, the words take on weight. The PM's were like blocks of concrete. "Mr. Black and I have a great deal to discuss, and I'm certain you have pressing issues of your own. You're dismissed, Vickers."

Vickers disappeared like a puff of smoke in a gale.

The PM led me further down the hall to a comfortable sitting room. A valet brought us tea, and as he was leaving, the PM told him we weren't to be interrupted.

"May I call you Rail?"

"Of course, sir."

"I know you're unhappy about being sent here."

"It's just that I would have preferred not leaving my team. And, sir, I've cross-trained with British Special Forces, and there is no skill I have that they don't."

He took a sip of tea. "Except that none of them is named

Black. And none of them is the controlling shareholder of several of our largest companies."

We'd each said our piece, so it was time for me to listen. "Sir, if I can be of any assistance, of course I'm ready to serve."

"Thank you, Rail. I know you mean it, and I'm deeply appreciative. You remember the Ravensheart family, don't you?"

"If you mean Stanley, I was an altar boy at his wedding, and if I'm not mistaken, he and his father visited us once on Clarissima."

"Stanley is Lord Ravensheart now. His father passed on several years ago. I wonder if you wouldn't mind picking up your acquaintanceship again. He's managed to get himself into a bit of unpleasantness that could be embarrassing to a great many people."

"Can you tell me what kind of unpleasantness?"

He hesitated. "I'd rather not."

"Then may I speak frankly, sir?"

"By all means."

"Presumably, there are others you could have asked to pal around with the new Lord Ravensheart who could do a much better job of collecting gossip among the idle rich than I."

I had made my point, and I could seem him wrestling with what he wanted to tell me. Finally, he took a deep breath and said, "Stanley's fallen in with some folks who want to assassinate me."

I don't think I could have been more surprised. "Well, he was always a horse's ass, but assassination? Are you sure?"

"Quite sure. They've even hired a shooter. A very competent one, I'm told. From somewhere on the Continent. And they've given him a timetable."

"For God sakes, why?"

"Back at Cambridge, I wrote my thesis on the inevitability of independence for Northern Ireland."

"True independence, not reunification?"

"It's the only thing that makes sense. In the short term, there would be political turmoil and perhaps even some bloodshed, but the oil wealth of the country would eventually force the factions to sort it out, and we could all get on with business. No more military drain on our economy and a trading partner of real importance."

"But you haven't advocated such a position as prime minister."

"No, and I'm not certain I will. Timing is everything. However, Lord Ravensheart and his coconspirators, all of whom have significant portions of their wealth tied up in the status quo, have convinced themselves it's imminent."

"That's the problem with going through your whole life never having heard the word no. You can start to think like a Menendez brother."

"I like that," the PM smiled. "But let's hope Stanley's chap is a better shot. I'd prefer not to roll around on the floor while someone pours birdshot into me."

The man had a sense of humor.

"Isn't this something for the police?" I asked.

"It was one of their informants who provided what I've told you. But Stanley's little club is made up exclusively of members of the Derbyshire crowd, meaning they speak only among themselves. So we don't know everything—or even everyone who is involved. Besides, I don't want them in jail. That would mean trials, and nobody's served by that . . . except, of course, the press."

He stopped and looked at me, and I could see that he knew how vulnerable he'd made himself by saying what he'd just said to someone who owned several hundred newspapers. He didn't need to worry, and I told him so.

"What do you want to happen to them?"

"I just want them to get back to fox hunting and fucking each other's wives."

* * *

I must have dozed off again, because all of sudden Mallory was standing over me with a breakfast tray from the Sofitel. I told him what I'd been remembering.

He gave me a wry smile. "I've never been sure saving the life of that particular prime minister was all that admirable, but from my standpoint, it's been a lot more interesting living in California than rambling around Strathmoor Hall with no one to talk to but a flatulent cook."

A Couple of Cops and a Tiger

The cops came, of course. In the early going, the place was swarming with Beverly Hills detectives who looked and dressed like the citizens they served, meaning lots of gym work and very sharp clothes. The Colombo look doesn't fly at BHPD, which occasionally earns them static from other law enforcement types. But when you're dealing with people who think fast food is a brisk sushi chef, you get a lot farther if you don't show up sporting three shades of plaid. The chief once told me that being a good cop *and* knowing which tie goes with which shirt aren't incompatible skills. I agree.

But well-dressed or not, they'd all been warned by Jake Praxis, who'd somehow shown up at the hospital an hour after I'd been shot, to not even breathe in my direction unless he was present. And when one captain tried an end-around, Jake buttonholed him and said that if he did it again, he'd drop the chief as a client.

So when the medical staff finally okayed an interview, Jake, attired in his jury-best, sat in my green La-Z-Boy, dangling an Italian loafer, while Detective Sergeant Dion Manarca, a stocky guy with a prematurely gray crew cut, opened the session. His partner, a piranha-eyed skeleton named Pantiagua, stood off to the side, one hand in his pocket, absentmindedly clicking a Zippo.

But Manarca and Pantiagua weren't from Beverly Hills. They were from the Major Crimes unit of the LAPD, and they didn't open the conversation by explaining why they were involved.

Earlier, Mallory had brought me a quart bottle of Broguiere's milk and an egg salad sandwich from Jerry's, but I'd only eaten half the sandwich and had one glass of milk. Sgt. Manarca eyed what was left. "You gonna finish that?"

When I said I wasn't, he took the sandwich in one big paw and the bottle of milk in the other and got both down in a few seconds. As he wiped his face with the back of his hand, he said, "Fuckin' ulcer needs to be fed like six times a day."

He took me through the two days I'd spent with Kim like the pro he was, covering everything in minute detail, sometimes going over a point several times. While he talked, he jotted an occasional note in a small, black leather notebook, but I couldn't tell what seemed to matter to him and what didn't.

As we were reliving the evening at Tacitus for the second time, I suddenly remembered the spider on the shooter's arm. But just as I was about to mention it, Manarca closed his notebook, reached into his breast pocket and came out with two photographs. He handed one to me, and I took it with my good hand. Staring back at me was a mug shot of a good-looking, dark-haired kid in his early teens.

"That the shooter?" asked Manarca.

"Could be, but I'd need to see him in person to be sure."

"Would it help if I told you Tacitus Gambelli and two of his waiters have already made a positive ID?"

"From this?"

"Yep."

"I'd still like to see him."

Manarca took a breath like an exasperated teacher talking to a thick third-grader. "I'm afraid that's not going to be possible. One of our black and whites found his body early this morning—in the back end of a stolen pickup."

"Where?"

"East L.A. Behind a dry cleaner's. Name's Jacinto "Kiki" Videz. Age fifteen. Guatemalan. Came in by coyote six years ago with his parents and four brothers. Father died of a drug overdose. Mother works as a domestic in Los Feliz. Two brothers are vacationing at San Quentin, and the other, Fernando, is a fugitive. Wanted for boosting about a hundred cars. Another fuckin' tribute to Homeland Security."

Now I understood why the Armani cops had stepped aside. They'd want to be kept informed, but this wasn't their beat. "So what's Kiki's story?"

"Known associate of Los Tigres. His juvie record is sealed, but the gang detail has him in the system. Drug trafficking, strong-arm robbery, extortion and arson. A solid citizen."

"A gangbanger doing a hit in Beverly Hills. I don't buy it."

Pantiagua spoke for the first time, spitting out his words. "Fuckin' Westside gringos. You live in your big fuckin' houses behind those big fuckin' walls and don't know shit."

Jake coolly looked at Manarca. "Sergeant, why don't you tell Jimmy Smits here that if he wants to play whose dick is bigger, we'll call downtown before you ask your next question."

Pantiagua's eyes narrowed, and he took a step toward Jake, fists clenched. "What's with the Jimmy Smitts bullshit, you Jew motherfucker? You don't have the balls to say 'beaner'?"

Jake was on his feet and into a boxer's crouch faster than I thought any man could move, let alone a millionaire lawyer with a bulge around his middle. "For the record, my mother's name was DaSilva, so I suggest you grab yourself a fistful of 'lo siento' before I kick your cock up between your ears. And you so much as breathe the word half-breed, your skinny ass goes down the elevator shaft."

Now, this was a new side of Jake Praxis, and I've got to say I was rooting for Pantiagua to test him. But the cooler head of Manarca prevailed. "Manny, you can't afford another write-up, so stand over there and shut the fuck up."

Everybody went back to their respective corners, and Manarca got on with it. "Los Tigres force an associate to murder somebody to become a full member. It's the way they bond, and how they make it difficult to cultivate a snitch. Not much incentive to turn state's evidence if you know you're gonna have to do twenty-five to life anyway. Usually, these guys just whack a rival banger, but Mr. Videz must have had a little showboat in him. You and Ms. York were just in the wrong place at the wrong time."

"They get bonus points for shooting two?"

"My guess is he decided he had no choice. Guy your size."

"Then why isn't Kiki nursing a tequila hangover from his initiation party instead of lying in a meat locker downtown?"

"Because what he did was stupid. Bangers are like cockroaches. They hate the fuckin' light. It brings out the politicians and the task forces. And there ain't no brighter light than being the lead story on CNN five straight nights. Videz was a liability, so they served him up."

I thought about it for a moment, then shook my head. "Too many leaps."

"Mr. Black, you ever put together jigsaw puzzles when you were a kid?"

"What's your point?"

"Ninety percent of the pieces could be missing, but if you had the right ones, you'd still be able to recognize the Eiffel Tower."

"That line usually close a reluctant witness?" I said with not-very-well-disguised sarcasm.

So Manarca handed me the second photograph he'd taken out of his pocket. It was a shot of a blue-jeaned knee, bent at an odd angle, and next to it was an empty flower basket. Well, not completely empty. A 9mm Beretta lay in the bottom.

"I suppose you've already got a ballistics match, or we wouldn't be going through this charade?"

"Unequivocal," said the detective.

Jake stood up. "Then I take it you're finished with my client."

I handed Manarca back his pictures. He took them and put both back in his pocket. "The good news is that as soon as the story breaks, the media's gonna beat feet outta here and give you some peace." Turning to Jake, he said, "If it's all right with you, Mr. Praxis, I'll have a statement typed up and sent to your office. Mr. Black can review it at his convenience and make any changes he feels necessary. Just get it back to me as soon as you can so I can close this out."

Pantiagua was already heading toward the door.

"Sorry about Ms. York," said Manarca. "Beautiful lady. I'm glad you pulled through."

But I wasn't finished. "So that's it? No follow-through on Tino or Dante?"

Manarca gave me his best tired-cop look. "Even if what she told you was true, it was unrelated to her death. And since I don't have a complaining witness, the kidnapping, or whatever it was, is history."

He was right, and I knew it, but that didn't make it any easier to swallow. As Manarca turned to leave, I said, "Humor me for a minute, Sergeant. Did Kiki Videz have any tattoos? Maybe one on his right arm?"

I thought I saw a flicker of something in Manarca's eyes, then it was gone. "Funny thing. The ME said somebody took a machete to the body after the guy was dead—hacked both arms off at the elbow. They weren't in the truck, so my guess is Los Tigres had a little show-and-tell with the troops to smarten up anybody else who might have a wild idea."

I took a long look at the detective, who was suddenly perspiring. "Starting to look a lot more like a steaming turd than Paris, isn't it, Sergeant?"

Manarca didn't answer.

"Who claimed Dr. York's body?"

"So far, no one."

When the cops had gone, I said to Jake, "You think he'll work it on the quiet?"

"Right. Because he's got that big incentive clause in his contract."

I looked out the window. There was a crane across the street swinging an I-beam into the frame of an unfinished building. I watched the two guys on the receiving end expertly get a rope around it and pull it in.

Suddenly, I felt very tired. I closed my eyes, and when I opened them again, it was dark, and Jake was gone. I heard the dinner cart in the hallway, then someone knocked on my door. "I'm not hungry," I called out.

But the door pushed open anyway, and Mitchell Adams came in, wearing a Delta Airlines Windbreaker over his uniform. He looked old and very, very tired. "I read about you in the paper," he said. "The girl? Was she the one in Walter's picture?"

I nodded.

"Walter's dead too," he said wearily.

I looked at him. "Why don't you sit down, Mitchell. You look like you're out on your feet."

He sat on the edge of the green La-Z-Boy. I let him get to it in his own way.

"The night after you got shot." Mitchell's voice cracked, and he took out a handkerchief and dabbed at his eyes. "Walter had a nice little darkroom out in the garage. Somebody surprised him. Opened him up with a knife. So much blood, it came up over the soles of my shoes. Had to identify him from his clothes. Thank God my sister didn't find him."

"Tino," I said under my breath.

"What?"

"I'm sorry, I didn't know," I said.

Mitchell shook his head. "No way you could. Didn't make the papers. Detective they sent around was a brother, and he didn't want to fuck around with what he figured was just one more dead hustler."

I didn't answer. I'd met black cops who had nothing but contempt for their own.

Mitchell went on. "This guy, Davis, when he saw the house had been torn to hell—furniture sliced open, carpet pulled up—he asks was Walter dealing or using or both? I told him Walter didn't even take fucking aspirin. Like he didn't hear me, he asks what gang he was in."

I watched Mitchell. There was a quiet anger on his face now.

"So I says to him, he was a member of the skycaps. And the guy starts to write it down. Then he gets it, and I can tell he's done with me and Walter. Unless the killer shows up with a confession hanging around his neck, he ain't even gonna think about it anymore."

Mitchell reached into his Windbreaker and pulled out a manila envelope. He threw it on the bed.

I looked at it. "Walter's negatives?"

He nodded. "Found them in his locker at work. Figured you was the only one might put them to good use. Wasn't gonna be Detective Davis."

Mitchell looked out the window. "And I'm the one told him to hang onto them. You think I helped kill my nephew?"

"I don't think it would have made any difference. Whatever this is about, they aren't leaving any loose ends."

He thought about that for a moment. "All I want is one favor."

"Name it."

"If you find the guy, you call me, and I'll come do the job. That's not possible, you promise me you'll make him suffer."

Amazing Grace and the Executioner

On the three-week anniversary of the day I was shot, I went home. I'd had to negotiate hard with my surgeon, Dr. Ted Goldman, a lanky, ponytailed genius with a Hoboken accent like a Mafia hit man and the same reverence for profanity as Benny Joe Willis. He wanted to keep me another week, but I made promises up the ass that I would follow his instructions to the letter, which consisted mostly of putting a no in front of everything I normally have to do, like to do and can't live without. But I'd have flown in a planeload of Scandinavian supermodels to give him backrubs if that's what it would have taken to get me out.

Dove Way had never looked so good. Mallory had turned the downstairs library into a convalescence center, complete with hospital bed, exercise equipment, and a television the size of a drive-in theatre. My meals he prepared precisely to the doctor's specifications, which meant that after two days of stuff that could only be described as warm and wet, I threatened him with bodily harm if he didn't come up with a greasy burger and some heart attack fries.

Fortunately, they'd invented Carney's for that eventuality,

so Mallory made a run down Sunset for double cheeseburgers and a trough of chili fries, complaining all the way. Tacitus did his part too, sending up dinner the next night. After what I'd done to his restaurant, I was grateful there wasn't a grenade tucked under the fusilli.

But it was a hollow existence. I couldn't get rid of the image of Kim, her head hanging over the back of her chair, one hand touching the floor, the other still demurely in her lap. I tried Ambien, then something stronger, and though both put me to sleep, neither kept me from dreaming. I was taking Vicodin, so I couldn't even drink myself into a stupor. After a while, I just let the night sweats come. And when in doubt, abuse those closest to you. I moved upstairs and shouted at Mallory to get the goddamn hospital smell and all that goddamn equipment out of the library.

Later that week, we buried Kim on one of the few rainy days we get in Southern California. It came down in sheets all the way to Westwood Memorial Park, a cemetery incongruously tucked in behind some high-rises on Wilshire Boulevard. Not many people even know it's there, but it's a popular final resting place for Hollywood celebrities, and we passed the graves of Natalie Wood and Roy Orbison on our way to the tented gravesite.

I saw a producer friend, David Permut, bareheaded and wet, heading across the lawn with some flowers, which I assumed were for Rodney Dangerfield, since they'd been close friends. He stopped and said he'd read about the shooting and wished me a quick recovery. I thanked him, then we went on with our respective duties.

Mallory had done the legwork and discovered that Kim's mother had bought three plots twenty-five years ago, probably hoping her missing husband would someday join her, and there'd be one left for Kim if she wanted it. Kim's mother and Truman York now occupied two of the graves, and we put Kim in the last. He wasn't there to speak for himself, but I thought Commander Cayne would have been okay with that.

I didn't know what kind of service Kim might have wanted, so I told Pierce Brothers, the owners of the cemetery, to select something appropriate. They brought in a Presbyterian minister to read from the Song of Solomon and a talented soprano to sing a quiet rendition of "Amazing Grace." I chose "Flight One" by the tragically talented poet Gwendolyn MacEwen to be inscribed on her headstone, and I asked the minister to read it at the end. I think Kim would have approved.

During the service, I watched the mourners, but other than Gary Wainwright, who was now on crutches, I didn't recognize anyone. Most appeared to be coworkers, along with some neighbors who stood with Gary.

Halfway through the service, I saw a large silver BMW pull up and double-park outside the 8-ft. iron fence along Malcom Avenue. But the rain plus the distance and angle made it impossible to see inside. After a moment, the driver's side window went down, and a pair of binoculars extended out a few inches.

Tourists and paparazzi routinely lurk around L.A. cemeteries, hoping to catch a celebrity attending a funeral or visiting a grave, so it could have been something that simple. But the binoculars held on our little group longer than I thought was necessary to determine we weren't front page.

Then a yellow DHL truck pulled up behind the BMW and honked, but the car didn't move. The DHL guy used some loud profanity and gave a New Jersey salute as he navigated the narrow space around the car, but the binoculars remained in place. Shortly after the minister finished the poem, people began to leave, the binoculars disappeared, and the BMW drove away.

On the way out, I asked the funeral director to let me know if anyone called about Kim. I really didn't expect anything, but I wanted to cover every base.

As Mallory and I were making our way to the car, Gary came up and asked if I knew what was going to happen to Kim's house. I told him my attorney was checking to see if there was a will, and I'd let him know. He said he'd fixed the back door and would keep up the lawn. I thanked him.

But I wasn't ready to go yet. I sent Mallory on to the car, turned and went back to Kim's grave. I stood over it and read MacEwen's poem again.

> *Good afternoon, ladies and gentlemen*
> *This is your Captain speaking.*
> *We are flying at an unknown altitude*
> *And an incalculable speed*
> *The temperature outside is beyond words.*
> *If you look out your windows, you will see*
> *Many ruined cities and enduring seas*
> *But if you wish to sleep please close the blinds.*
> *My navigator has been ill for many years*
> *And now we are on Automatic Pilot: regrettably*
> *I cannot foresee our ultimate destination.*
> *Have a pleasant trip.*
> *You may smoke, you may drink, you may dance.*
> *You may die.*
> *We might even land someday.*

Then I said good-bye and went home, leaving Dana Kimberly York alone with Gwendolyn's words, the comics, the singers and the stars.

One of the promises I'd made Dr. Goldman was that I wouldn't drive, but I was going stir-crazy. So the day after the funeral, I grabbed Walter Kempthorn's negatives and the security DVD from Ralphs and eased myself into my truck. I managed to get to Benny Joe's driving with one good hand and wincing at the pain in my chest every time I hit a bump. Why I didn't take the more comfortable Rolls suggests that getting shot lowers your IQ.

Benny Joe isn't much for anybody else's pain when he could be talking about his own. "You shoulda seen me when I went for that midnight swim after my fuckin' wife drained the pool." I wanted to laugh, but it hurt to even smile.

"Actually, I was praying you'd check the fuck out," he continued. "Then those Babe Ruth pictures woulda been mine."

"Probably not with Jake Praxis around."

"You still friends with that fuckin' throat slitter? Jesus, get some fuckin' taste."

"Spoken like somebody on the wrong end of a negotiation."

"Fuck you."

While the Dobermans slobbered on the living room windows, we went upstairs, and Benny Joe got to work with his equipment. It was like watching Jerry Rice catch passes. Effortless. An hour later, he was printing enhanced blowups of two photos—the one in the paper, and another from a more severe forward angle that Walter had probably taken when he'd first gotten out of the car.

Even working through the van's windshield, Benny Joe's magic had been able to enhance Tino and Dante's faces to the clarity of a mug shot—red headband on Tino and Denver Broncos baseball cap on his partner.

"Give me a couple of days, and I'll tell you what fuckin' brand of cigar the stocky asshole is smoking," Benny Joe said.

The second photo wasn't as important as I'd hoped. Only a tiny sliver of the first letter of the van's front license plate. Benny Joe and I agreed it could be B, D, P, or R. Not enough for a DMV run.

Then Benny Joe projected the four and a half seconds of Ralphs footage onto a fifty-inch monitor and went through it one millimeter at a time. He zoomed and corrected and sifted, and when he was finished, the spider on Tino's forearm was as clear as a National Geo shot. Oval-shaped thorax, seven delicate legs with a space for an eighth and thirteen comma-shaped marks on its abdomen.

"Fuckin' Bonifacio Executioner," said Benny Joe matter-of-factly. "A deformed one, but I'd know it anywhere."

"What?"

"The fuckin' spider, man. Think black widow on acid. Venom'll eat the fuckin' lungs out of a German shepherd."

"How do you know?" I asked.

He lifted his right pant leg, revealing an ugly red scar running halfway up his shin. "What the fuck do you think?" he said. "They wheel you in, and nobody even fuckin' asks. They just cut you open and drain the fucker before they have to take off your leg."

"Bonifacio? As in Corsica?"

"Fuckin' A. Took a ferry over from Nice on my fuckin' honeymoon. Good views and great food, somebody said. But I didn't give a fuck cause I was followin' a tip about a Marseilles shooter in the JFK hit."

I rolled my eyes. "How'd that work out?"

"Don't ask. Guy I went to see washed up onshore with his tongue cut out a couple a days before I got there. All I got was this fuckin' scar. I'll tell you one thing, though. The next time one of those Corsican motherfuckers smiles, it'll be the first."

After a moment, I asked him, "You got a safe in the house?"

"Better. A fuckin' underground vault out in the yard."

I thought about that and came up with a mental picture of Tino getting his face eaten off by the dogs. I liked it. "Okay, anything happens to me, you take all of this out to LAX and give it to a guy named Mitchell Adams. He's a skycap at Delta. And you do it personally. Got it?"

"Jesus, you know I'm fuckin' afraid to fly. Airports give me the fuckin' willies."

"Take a pill. And remember. Personally. Give me your word."

"Fuck."

"Good enough."

12

A Fortress on a Hill and A.A.

By the time I got back to Dove Way, I was close to passing out. Mallory helped me into bed while giving me a lecture. Fortunately, I was asleep before he finished.

The next morning, fortified with French toast and more Vicodin, I toured the Internet looking for anything called City of War. The first hit I got was War, West Virginia, and even though a 700-person burg in the Appalachians didn't seem a likely connection for a kidnapping and murder in L.A., I scanned the business listings, then used my good hand to dial Rixie and Dixie Quantrill's Beauty Parlor and Bridal Shop, figuring that between those two disciplines there wouldn't be much in War they didn't know.

I couldn't have been more right. The charming and effervescent Quantrill sisters got on separate extensions and chatted away nonstop for twenty minutes. They even invited me to a home-cooked dinner if I ever wandered through the Mountain State. When we finished, I knew which War citizens could use a few more Sundays in church and the number of kittens born behind the gas station the night before. Unfortunately, nothing they'd said even remotely coalesced with my problem, and I thanked them and promised

I wouldn't forget the dinner. And I wouldn't. Small-town America. It's why we're a great nation.

After an hour of drawing zero with Google, I went back to the phone. Art dealers, auctioneers, book collectors, horse breeders, even a couple of historians, but no one had ever heard of anything with that name. The same with three university librarians and an archivist at the Smithsonian.

I even persuaded Jake Praxis's secretary, Stella, to use the firm's databases to check ship registries, copyright filings and trademark applications. But after my third call to her with more suggestions, I could tell by her tone that it wouldn't be long before she complained to Jake that a raving lunatic was harassing her.

Toward noon, to avoid Mallory, I went upstairs and used the private elevator to the garage. Not that he wouldn't eventually notice I was gone, but I wanted to forgo the disapproving look. This time, I took the Rolls, and on my way west, I called Jake again.

"What now?" he asked in a long-suffering tone. "I can't get even get a letter out because Stella's too busy working for you."

"I need a pass into the executive parking lot at the Getty."

"You feeling culturally deprived?"

"I want to talk to Kim's boss."

"What's wrong with riding the tram up the hill like everybody else?"

When I didn't answer, he sighed and said, "Okay, what day are you going?"

"If traffic holds, I'll be there in fifteen minutes."

"You're a fucking asshole," he said, but I think I heard some love in there too.

"Thanks," I said. "How you doing locating a will?"

"So far nothing. Tell you what, though. I find something out, you'll be the first to know. In the meantime, don't ever fucking ask me for a progress report again."

I smiled. "That's the kind of attitude that keeps you from being able to hang with Benny Joe Willis."

"Christ, is that jackass a friend of yours? I'll let you know tomorrow if I can continue to represent a guy with such shit taste." The phone went dead.

The Getty Museum sits on the most visible piece of real estate on the Westside, a promontory capped by a marble monolith that would have awed Ramses. More than one architecture critic has suggested that its grandeur is the modern equivalent of a European Castle Hill, also designed to send a shiver up peasants' spines should they get restless. A second museum, the Getty Villa in Malibu, only adds to the metaphor.

J. Paul Getty wasn't much of a human being, but he sure knew how to turn a buck. And in the end, he was more generous to the arts than any other man in history. J. P. Morgan runs a distant second. Maybe it's in the initials.

Unfortunately, the museum built with Getty's fortune came late to the acquisitions party. After centuries of plunder and shady transactions, most countries now have laws protecting their national treasures and have even begun unwinding some of the past's larceny.

So when the Getty arrived on the scene, it was in the odd position of having more money than God and nothing to buy. Terrified that this new museum would drive prices into the stratosphere for the few important pieces that might come on the market, or that the Getty would begin offering large sums for works owned by financially strapped institutions and screw up their cozy little world, the major museums called a sit-down with the Getty trustees and coerced them into becoming "a good member of the community." This was like letting the United Nations set American foreign policy. In other words, if you promise not to create an open market, we'll like you. We really will.

The result was the Getty got the privilege of remaining a second-tier museum while coughing up money to help financially strapped places like the Louvre. In return, they were given a spot on the traveling exhibit circuit and a heartfelt thanks in small print on the last page of catalogues. Oh, the big guys throw the Getty a bone every now and then. Let them buy something the others would have to sell off holdings to afford, but it's rarely something incredibly important. Meanwhile, in Paris and Rome, they laugh. But that's socialists for you. They'd skip the Super Bowl to take a tour of the post office.

A lot of people think the Getty should have just taken their chips and gone for it. Started a bidding war only they could have won. That in a generation, they would have built the finest museum ever—one the others would have come on bended knee to *borrow from* instead of reluctantly *lending to*. This strategy would have also raised the value of everyone else's collections, not to mention what it would have done for the private market.

That's what old J. Paul, the capitalist, would have done. He didn't build the largest fortune of his time asking what he could do for others. But once you become an appeaser, you might still have your weapons, but you never get your nerve back. As a result, what's left is one of the world's truly magnificent buildings where you can get in out of the sun and have a pretty good salade Niçoise.

A security guard at the museum's private entrance questioned me with the same attitude he would have used on an Al-Qaeda suspect, then made copies of my driver's license and registration while his partner went through my car with a metal detector and some kind of wand I presumed registered chemical signatures. Neither man was openly rude, but they weren't friendly either. It was the same mentality as the TSA people at the airport. Show Joe Citizen who's in charge by keeping everything humorless and curt.

The experts will tell you that a smile gets you a lot farther, because unless somebody shows up shirtless with a bomb strapped to his chest, the best chance you have of nailing a bad guy is when his demeanor is out of step with everyone else's. And if you're a badge-heavy asshole, you make everyone tense, so there's no differentiation.

The tough-guy attitude also intimidates people who might otherwise come forward with information you desperately need or who could rat out somebody with mayhem on his mind. It's why cops with good dispositions almost always rise faster and go farther in their departments than hard-asses. But that memo hadn't gotten down to my interrogators, so when they finished, and I wished them a nice morning, they didn't answer. Big surprise.

On my way up the tree-lined drive, I was suddenly seized by searing pain through my patchwork lung and where my missing rib should have been. It was so intense that sweat burst from every pore, and I had to stop the car to get my breath and gulp some Vicodin. After a few moments, the pain receded, and I was able to continue.

Kim's boss, Dr. A. A. Abernathy, the executive vice president of the museum, kept me waiting only a few minutes. We recognized each other from the funeral. He was a long, lean, tweedy Londoner in his sixties, with a David Niven moustache and the yellowed teeth of a confirmed smoker, who projected that distinctly British academic manner that can't be imitated, except badly. It wasn't difficult to picture him in a well-worn Cambridge pub puffing Rothmans, sipping Guinness and holding court among adoring students.

He also had only one arm, his left, and wore no prosthesis, tucking his empty sleeve into the pocket of his suit jacket. We shook cross-handed and went into his office.

"Call me A.A.," he said as we took seats.

We were surrounded by tiny soldiers—hundreds of them on every available surface. They were Wellington-era miniatures in perfect regimental regalia, exquisitely painted, and arranged in what I had to assume were correct battle groups.

A.A. chuckled. "A damned addiction, I'm afraid. And as with all fine addictions, what's the point if it's not overdone."

My eyes wandered to his empty right sleeve.

"Bit hard to believe, isn't it?" he asked good-naturedly. "But actually, the only impediment is getting the tops off those blasted little jars of paint."

"I have a friend in the prosthesis business who'd be broke if there were a lot like you. Accident?"

"No, I was born with one good arm and a withered one. About half-length and only two fingers. Today, nobody'd blink, and you'd go on about your business. But the doctor told my parents I'd be marked a freak and tormented unmercifully. Suggested amputation. Said people'd take note of a single arm then forget it, but if they left me with a flipper it'd be like wearing a curse every day of my life."

"How do you feel about that?"

He looked thoughtful. "Hard to hold people accountable for making tough choices."

I nodded and told him a little bit about my background, which immediately put us on comrade footing.

"So they took my arm and your accent. I think I got the better deal."

We both laughed.

"May I offer you something to drink?" he asked.

"Water would be terrific."

He reached behind his desk and opened a small refrigerator, coming out with two bottles of Fiji water. It was ice cold and felt very, very good going down.

Nodding at the bandage on my hand, he said, "I take it you're the gentleman who was with Dr. York when she was murdered."

"I am."

"Had you been seeing each other for some time?"

I listened for any nuance in his voice, but it seemed to be a straightforward question. "Actually, we'd only recently met."

"A genuinely nice lady with a wonderful sense of humor. Had I been a bit younger, I might have tried for something more than a professional relationship myself. A terrible tragedy. I must say, I was quite surprised when the police didn't call me or come around."

"They've closed the case," I answered, but I was surprised too. I thought Sergeant Manarca might have wanted to cover all the bases—if only out of habit.

A.A. said, "I take it you're not so easily fooled."

"Why do you say that?"

He leaned forward slightly. "I live just around the corner from Tacitus, and it's one of my few extravagances. Pricy, but wonderful. If one simply needed a dead body to join a gang, why in the world would he go through those creaky, hard-to-open iron gates, chance being stopped by the maitre d', then thread his way through a maze of closely set tables when all he had to do was just stand outside and shoot someone getting into his car? Heaven knows, the valet wouldn't have stopped him. No, in my opinion, the young man who shot you and Dr. York did exactly what he'd been sent to do. And he was damned good, and, if you'll forgive me, damned ballsy too."

I sat without saying anything. This ivory-tower type had reasoned it out the same way I had. Why hadn't the cops? "You obviously read a lot of Doyle," I said, only half-joking.

He enjoyed the compliment. "I came up through the authentication side of the house, where art can be as much the product of good detective work as it is beauty. Value and provenance often rest on one's ability to reason things through from incomplete evidence—then convince others we're right. It's the same process a talented police officer uses. Part science, part logic and part intuition. And generally speaking, in both disciplines, the more complicated or illogical the explanation, the less likely it is to have occurred."

I nodded, and Abernathy continued. "In this case, to agree with the police, one is asked to believe that a Hispanic street kid carrying a gun traveled seventeen miles from East L.A. into Beverly Hills, where the constabulary are so aggressive they check the IDs of residents out walking their Lab-radoodles.

"And then, *camouflaged* with a basket of roses in a town where it's illegal to sell a bag of peanuts without a storefront, he made not one but two trips into Tacitus to shoot some-body at *random*. My Lord, if this story were a painting, I'd report the dealer to the FBI."

He was absolutely right.

"Convenience and laziness," he said. "Afflictions without prejudice. And just as common in cops as anyone else."

"Was Kim . . . Dr. York . . . a good employee?"

"Marvelous. I hired her six years ago to put us on the publishing map with our own journal, and she exceeded all expectations. And the creative flair she brought to our cata-logues was the envy of our competitors, though they'd be loathe to admit it." He paused. "However . . ."

I waited.

After a long moment, he said, "Unfortunately, I was about to let her go."

A.A. Abernathy was full of surprises.

"May I ask why?"

"She just wasn't cut out for museum work. The world of institutional art moves at a glacial pace. Often slower. One might be involved in something of real importance only once in an entire career. Perhaps never. Dr. York was a doer. She wanted to make her mark. Right away. Yesterday, even. Admirable in real life, but impossible here. And intolerably irritating . . . in a good way, of course."

I could tell by the affection in his voice that he meant it. I said, "In other words, she would have been perfect had the Getty chosen competition over socialism."

He looked at me, and a wry smile crossed his face. "I can't speak to that, because had it occurred, I might not be here."

I thought about what Abernathy had just said, but it didn't ring true. "Forgive my bad manners, A.A., but it's difficult to believe that in these litigious times an institution as high-profile as the Getty would terminate an extremely bright, highly educated woman on nothing stronger than your opinion that her gut wasn't in her work."

He looked at me, then out the window, then took a sip of water. "Personnel matters are supposed to be confidential, but since Dr. York is deceased, I'm going to make an exception.

"She'd become preoccupied with something outside the museum. No, that's not the right word—obsessed is more like it. After being a model employee, she suddenly began taking days off without permission. A couple of times, an entire week. And when she'd finally show up, she wouldn't even offer a lame excuse. She'd just say, 'Sorry,' and that was it. I tried to get her to talk about it, but she just said she'd do better."

"Was there any pattern to her absences?"

"Every one began on a Friday. Then she wouldn't come in until Tuesday, or Wednesday, or whenever. A couple of times I tried calling her at home, but no one answered. You'll forgive me, but at first, I assumed she was shacking up."

"But you changed your mind."

He nodded. "One day accounting called and said they were concerned about excessive personal charges on her corporate American Express card. Employees are encouraged to use the card for personal travel then reimburse the museum, but she'd been using it remarkably often and for very large amounts."

"Seems like an odd policy."

"Actually, it's not. This is a paranoid business, and it allows the watchdogs on the second floor to chart your movements. Dr. York had charged almost fifty thousand dollars in airfare and hotel rooms, and though she had paid off every dime, the red flags had gone up."

"Where was she going?" I asked.

"Paris and Nice mostly. But she also traveled the former East Bloc too, and, of all places, three or four jaunts to Odessa. Not a place for the faint of heart."

"What did she say when you confronted her?"

"That it was none of my business. Oh, she was polite, but she made it abundantly clear that she wasn't going to tell me anything."

"Had you told her she was being terminated?"

"No, but she knew it. In this business, we work too closely with one another to have many secrets. I even got the sense she was relieved. Like she'd already mentally moved on. It's a shame we'll never know what she might have accomplished with all of that energy."

I finished the last of my water and noticed that in spite of the air-conditioning, I was perspiring again. I didn't feel any pain yet, but the room was starting to close in.

"Let me shift gears for a moment. Have you ever heard of something called the City of War?"

Abernathy leaned back in his chair, thinking. "I don't believe so," he said finally. "Is it important?"

"It might be connected to Kim's death."

"I'll do some checking."

I wrote my number on one of his notepads, and he gave me a business card.

"My cell is on there, and that's usually the best way to reach me," he said.

I stood up to leave, and as we shook hands, I asked if it would be possible to get a look at Kim's office. He shook his head. "I'm sorry, it's already been redecorated. I know that seems cold, but once I realized the police weren't going to be coming around, I wanted to give the staff some closure."

"What about her computer?"

"Tech security purged the hard drives on both of them— the Getty's desktop and her personal laptop. Company policy dictated by our insurer. We are a careful and suspicious lot, aren't we?"

I had to agree. This brave new world is still sorting itself out, but society lost a little something when people stopped jotting things down and sticking them in their pockets. Today, if you want to get a phone number in a bar, instead of lipstick on a napkin, everybody takes out their BlackBerry. Not the same.

A.A. went on. "All of her personal things I boxed up and sent to her home."

We reached the stairway, and I felt the dull ache beginning in my chest again, but I had one more question. "Can you tell me what Kim was working on?"

"Yes, she was writing captions for an upcoming exhibit."

"Something important?"

"A departure for us: Napoleon and the Middle East. A subject that gets very little attention but that is vitally important to understanding the history of preservation."

"In other words, looting," I said.

A.A. smiled.

I said, "Since the Louvre was founded on the plunder from his conquests, won't that be a fairly sensitive subject for the French?"

His eyes twinkled. "Oh, I do hope so."

13

Veronica Lake and a Son
of a Bitch Named Truman

By the time I got to my car, I was really struggling. Between another burst of pain and three more Vicodin, my vision was starting to blur, and I felt detached from reality. Like I was watching myself through the wrong end of a pair of binoculars.

I wanted to go home and climb into bed, but first I wanted to get a look at the things from Kim's office—even though I had no idea what I was looking for.

Princeton Street was quiet. Two gardeners were packing up to leave a neighboring house, and a plumbing truck sat across the street. Otherwise, nothing. Gary's pickup was gone, so he must have been able to work in spite of the crutches. I hoped so.

I drove past Kim's, made a U-turn at the next intersection and parked in front of Gary's. As I walked up her driveway, I noticed some remnants of police tape on the front porch, but otherwise the place looked normal.

The single-car garage was padlocked. I went around to

the side and found a door that had been painted shut. I put my shoulder into it, and it popped. From the sound, it hadn't been opened in a long time. Inside was the usual clutter of magazines, paint cans, garden tools and old license plates nailed to the wall. The centerpiece was a tarp, and when I flipped up a corner, I found a red '63 Corvette. I suspected that at one time it had been Alex Cayne's pride and joy.

There was a fine layer of dust over everything, so it appeared that Tino and Dante had confined their search to the house. I pulled the door closed behind me and walked into the backyard, where there were three pieces of patio furniture around a Mexican chiminea.

I knelt and looked inside the chiminea. The melted remains of something lay on top of some partially burned briquettes. I fished out the blob. I wasn't sure, but it could have been a digital picture card.

I stood and dusted off my hands. For the first time, I noticed another structure behind the garage. A greenhouse, situated so that it was not visible from the house. It was about the size of the garage, and one side was engulfed in a wild, thorned creeper that had been allowed to grow unchecked until it had covered more than half the glass. An old wheelbarrow was tilted against the door. I moved it to the side and pulled the door open. It creaked loudly, and a pair of field mice ran out and over my shoes, disappearing into the undergrowth between the greenhouse and the property next door.

I stepped inside but was immediately stopped by wall-to-wall, floor-to-ceiling cactus. In pots, on shelves, growing out of wooden boxes, hanging from the rafters, jammed into every conceivable space, creating an impenetrable forest of stems and spines. Albuquerque on steroids. I couldn't even see across the room. I remembered reading that there are two thousand varieties of cactus. It looked like Kim was going for a clean sweep.

"You a realtor?" The voice startled me. I turned and saw an attractive, 20-something woman in a tight black leotard and high heels peering at me through some overgrown birds of paradise between Kim's house and the one behind. "If so, I hope you're gonna set a real high price, 'cause if you get it, you can sell mine next."

She was smiling broadly and didn't seem even a little bit suspicious, so I went with it. "Just trying to get an idea," I said. "How's the neighborhood?"

"Other than some biker jackass who keeps his motorcycle in his living room and fires it up whenever he gets a snoot full, it might as well be a morgue."

She suddenly realized what she'd said. "Sorry, that was disrespectful. I really liked Kim. She was an angel."

"Were you and she friends, Miss . . . ?"

"Laura," she said, shaking her head, "Laura Kennedy, and no, we didn't hang. My old man thinks I should be working 24/7 so he can watch soap operas and fart. Kim and I just yammered over the backyard fence, so to speak. But every Christmas, she got all kinds of food baskets at work, and she'd give me some. My old man just loves those Mrs. Beasley's muffins."

"Did she have a lot of friends?"

"No, I always wondered about that. Sometimes she'd sit out back and drink a beer with Gary—the guy next door who does her lawn—but I never saw anybody else. I just figured she was a lez."

She stopped and looked me up and down, lingering for a moment on my bandaged hand. Then she glanced at her watch. "You're one big, good-looking son of a bitch. What's your position on sex with married chicks? Especially ones who scream? Afterward, we could talk multiple listings."

"I've got to get home to catch *Days of our Lives*."

She laughed. "Don't worry about him. He's down picking up his unemployment check. After that, he'll stop for a few beers. We're good till midnight, minimum."

"Any other time, but I really do have work to do."

"Can't blame a girl for trying. You got a card?"

"Fresh out, but I'll be by again tomorrow. I'll drop one off."

She looked at me and licked her lips seductively. "Don't knock, just put it under the mat. I'll call you."

I changed the subject. "I take it Kim liked cactus."

"She lived in that greenhouse. Never could figure it out. Not much you can do with a cactus, and not much they need."

I thought about it. Maybe that was the point. I closed the door and turned to go.

"Don't forget that card," Laura said.

Gary had fixed the back door, but he hadn't put on a new lock. It pushed open. The air was musty inside, like all houses after they've been shut up for a while. I contemplated opening some windows but decided against it. I didn't need an enterprising neighbor who wasn't as friendly as Ms. Kennedy calling the cops. I wasn't sure what explanation I could give them that wouldn't cost me a ride to the station.

I let the water in the sink run until it got cool then put my head under it to get rid of the cobwebs. It seemed to work, and afterward I dried off with a dishtowel. The box containing Kim's things from the museum was on the kitchen table. I decided to have a look at the rest of the house again before going through it.

The Russian ladies had done a thorough job straightening up. Even the drawers were neatly arranged, which made looking through them easy. I found the usual things. A collection of matchbooks, old photographs, a sewing kit, two unused tickets to a Dodgers game.

Her bookshelves strained under the weight of art histories and photographic studies of artists, some famous, some I'd never heard of. On a shelf near the top was a framed picture of a ruggedly handsome naval officer in dress whites standing beside a beaming, attractive young woman. Commander and Mrs. Alexander Cayne, I presumed. I glanced around for a photograph of Truman York but didn't see one. It probably didn't mean anything, but it's a good idea to never presuppose family dynamics.

Alongside the shelves, I found a large leather art portfolio full of charcoal prints, watercolors and pencil sketches, none signed. I had no idea if any were valuable, but since the back door was still open to anyone who wanted to walk in, I zipped the portfolio closed and slid it behind the bookcase. It wouldn't slow down a serious thief, but it might deter a casual intruder.

I'd saved Kim's bedroom for last, and as I systematically went though her things, I was conscious of the smell of her perfume. With the house closed, it was still in the air, and it held a kind of sadness. Taped behind the headboard, I found a Walther .22 with a full clip of ammunition. I put it in my pocket and was once again baffled by the police work. How had the cops missed this? The only answer was that they'd been so focused on the gang angle that their search had been cursory.

All of a sudden, I felt flushed, and I was conscious of the pain welling up in my chest again. I slammed three more Vicodin. I needed some fresh air.

I was on my way through the living room back to the kitchen when I saw the silver BMW from the cemetery pull up out front. I stood in the shadows and watched as a tall woman got out. She was wearing an exquisite green and black designer dress, black heels and large, dark sunglasses. The most striking thing about her, though, was her hair. It was shoulder-length platinum and styled dramatically over her right eye and cheek, like the 1940s actress Veronica Lake. She looked up and down the street, then opened her purse and extracted a key. I watched her come up the walk, then I melted back down the hall.

The key turning in the lock was loud in the empty house, and when she entered, I could hear her hesitate for a moment before she closed the door. I had no idea who she was, but since she was obviously going to stay for a while, I didn't want to scare her witless. I called out, "I'm in the bedroom. I'm coming out."

Her reply showed no trepidation. "I should hope so. I can smell you from here."

I suddenly realized I'd been sweating on and off for several hours, and with no ventilation in the place, I must have been pretty gamey. I walked into the living room. "Sorry, it's been a rough day."

I'm not usually overcome by physical beauty, but this woman was truly dazzling. And she had a presence that filled the room. Heat, musk and sex.

She looked me up and down. "Mind telling me what you're doing in my house?"

"Your house?" I managed.

"Yes, I'm Archer Cayne. I grew up here."

Suddenly, my cell phone rang. I answered it.

It was Jake. "I just talked to some lawyer in Santa Monica. A Virgil Bateman. There's no will, but there's a sister."

"I know, she just caught me breaking and entering."

"What?"

"I'll explain later." I clicked off.

"You're the boyfriend," she said. "I saw you at the funeral. There any coffee in this place?"

"Sorry to disappoint. I was a friend, that's all. And the only other time I was here, I was too busy trying to keep my head from being caved in to check the cupboards."

"I won't ask. You have a name?"

"I'm sorry, Miss Cayne, I'm Rail Black." I extended my hand, and she took it. Her grip was warm and strong. Sure of herself.

"Call me Archer." Then, as if she were tired of answering the question, she added, "My father was a naval aviator. 'Archer' was his call sign."

I was about to say something when the room began to spin. I staggered and felt myself starting to go. Too many painkillers, no food. "I need to lie down," I managed, and I felt her strong hands helping me toward the bedroom.

When I awakened, it was pitch black. The clock across the

room read 9:48. I'd been out almost eight hours. I was aware of the pain in my chest again, but it was duller. Bearable. I took stock. I was undressed, and I couldn't smell my sweat any more, just soap. Evidently she'd cleaned me up. It was like being back in the hospital.

Then I realized I wasn't alone. She came into my arms, and it was like someone had thrown a switch. She moved against me with the kind of hunger that is both electrifying and unsettling. While my body reacted, my conscious mind tried to detach, analyze what was happening. But she was skilled and voracious, and I couldn't hang onto a thought.

She started to roll onto me, and I winced involuntarily as she pressed against my chest. Immediately, she sat up, straddled my hips and forced me inside her. As she plunged down with all her weight, she gasped, and I felt her body convulse in a violent orgasm.

And then she began thrusting against me with such force that I realized whatever trip she was on, it had nothing to do with me. It wasn't even really sex. It was primal—no, savage. I reached up to caress her breasts, but she pushed my hands away, hard.

I felt myself rushing to climax, and when I came, she crashed again. And still she wasn't finished, and I felt myself responding again as she continued driving her hips against mine unrelentingly.

Somebody's porch light went on next door, sending a sliver of light through the curtains and bathing the room in a blue glow. She was too much into whatever moment she had found to notice. Her head was bent forward, the long, blonde hair obscuring her face as she grunted and moaned from somewhere deep in her throat. Her breasts weren't large, but they were perfectly formed, the aureoles wide and brown. And this time, when I touched them, she didn't object.

I raised one hand to her cheek, and she twisted her head away. But I persisted and pushed her hair back, taking her face between my hands. She sat straight up, and now I could see what she was trying to hide. A deep, ugly knife scar running from her forehead, down through her right eye and halfway down her cheek. The eye itself was dead, sewn shut by the doctor who had performed this grim surgery.

"Go ahead," she spit out as her hips moved even more wildly. "Go ahead, fuck the scar! That's what all of you want! So go ahead, fuck it! Fuck the scar!"

She threw her head back and came again, and so did I. It was a release void of passion, care or even much awareness. It was simply over.

But she continued to thrust, beginning the process again. I grabbed her hips and held them still. She convulsed a couple more times, then her breathing began to ease, and after a couple of moments, she rolled onto the bed beside me.

I put my arm around her and pulled her close. Moments later, I felt the warm wetness of tears against my neck. What they were for, I couldn't guess. Just before she fell asleep, she murmured, "Was I as good as my sister?"

When I awoke a second time, she was still sleeping soundly. I got up, every muscle stiff, found a towel and stood under a very hot shower for a very long time.

I made coffee, and the sun was beginning to break through the curtains in the kitchen when I heard the shower go on again. I checked my phone and saw there were two messages.

One was from Mallory, concerned he hadn't heard from me. The second was from Stephen Bennett, a friend who lives in Los Feliz. I'd called him a few days earlier, and his message said he'd located Marta Videz—the mother of the dead kid, Kiki.

I turned my attention to the box from the museum. Kim's computer was on top. If it's not done in a certain way, data can still be recovered from a wiped hard drive, but my guess was the Getty's security experts were good, so I set the laptop aside.

I took out a small cactus with a tiny brass tag hanging around it that read, HUG ME—I'M LONELY. Next came a red file folder with some old credit card statements and two letters from a guy named Lew, the most recent of which, dated eighteen months ago, said he was sorry, but he was getting married and moving back to Boise to start an organic farm. It seemed Lew didn't use e-mail. I immediately like the guy.

Further down, I found a ticket for a shoe repair shop, a pair of grinning alligator bookends, an assortment of pens and pencils, twelve dollars in ones—probably for the Coke machine I'd seen in the museum hallway—an eyeglass screwdriver, a scrimshaw-handled letter opener, a cell phone charger and her passport.

I put the rest of the items back in the box and opened the passport. The immigration stamps confirmed what Abernathy had said. I looked at the France trips first. There was a calendar taped to the refrigerator. I moved the box to the kitchen counter and compared the dates.

For each trip, she was stamped into the country on a Friday and back into L.A. later the next week. I knew the route. Thursday overnight to Paris, two-hour connection, commuter flight to Nice, arriving in time for dinner. Depending on the airline, sometimes you can do it an hour faster through London.

Giving her two hours at LAX on the outbound, another two at Nice returning and an hour of leeway, that totaled thirty-five hours of travel time. On her shortest trip, that left her fifty-five to sixty hours on the ground. Enough time for almost anything. Eyeballing the other trips, they looked similar.

Archer came into the kitchen wearing one of Kim's nightgowns, her wet hair combed over the right side of her face. I slipped the passport into my pocket.

"That coffee any good?" she asked.

"Not prime, but hot and strong."

She poured herself a cup and sat down across from me. "Surprised to find you still here."

"Why's that?"

"Once the mystery's gone, the guy usually is too."

"You need to start hanging out with a better class of people."

She looked at me, started to say something, then decided not to.

I said, "Give me your cell phone."

"What for?"

"Just give it to me."

She went into the living room and came back with her purse. She fished the phone out and handed it over. I programmed my number into it. "In case you ever need anything . . . or just want to talk."

For the second time, she opened her mouth then closed it without speaking.

"City of War," I said without any lead-in and watched her reaction.

She smiled nonchalantly. "That would be anywhere I ever lived. Which guy do you want to hear about?"

I'd found out what I wanted to. "Another time." I smiled. "When did you leave here?"

"At fourteen. Went to live with a cousin in Boston. Then dropped out of high school a month before graduation and bolted for New York."

"Where you became a model," I said.

"Kim tell you that?" she asked accusatorily.

"I wasn't kidding when I said I never knew you existed. I saw you walk, that's all."

She relaxed a little. "A blessing or a curse, I don't know. But once you learn to move on a runway, you can't get rid of it."

"And you want to?"

"Sometimes. It's like a subliminal message to every jerk with a hard-on. Pretty soon, they're sniffing and snorting and rubbing their cock on your leg."

"I don't suppose you've ever considered you might be giving off other signals."

She flashed. "And like every girlfriend I've ever known hasn't told me the same thing. Whoever was handing this shit out should have had to get a consent form signed."

I didn't think she needed to hear that, in my opinion, she was working it for all it was worth, so I said gently, "Someday I'd like to hear what happened."

"What happened to what?"

She knew what I meant, so I let her decide on her own.

It took a minute, then she sighed. "It ain't a fucking cliffhanger. The model's curse—a rich guy who's going to take care of you the rest of your life. Most of the time you know it's over when your Christmas gift goes from a four-carat emerald to a magazine subscription. But that's not the way it works with Russians. They figure they fuck you, they own you. And besides, they're so good in the rack, they've ruined you for anybody else. Jesus, where do they come up with this shit?

"Well, this guy, Marko, explained the rules a couple of times—with his fists—but I was a slow learner and thought the police would help." She looked away, and her voice dropped. "Marko spent the night drinking wine with the *Sureté* captain, then they drove him home. I wasn't finished packing, but I was finished getting my picture taken."

"Where's Marko now?"

"He went back to Moscow, and somebody threw him in prison for not paying off. I read he's out now and running for Parliament. Think I should write?"

"I'm sorry about your sister," I said to break the moment.

"Stepsister," she said.

I was confused. "But your name's Cayne."

"And here I thought I'd fucked your brains out."

"So Commander Cayne *wasn't* Kim's father?"

"I was pretty self-absorbed in those days, but I probably would have noticed her at dinner. No, J. Edgar, she and that asshole old man of hers, Truman, didn't show up until four years after Dad had been declared dead."

Suddenly, things were more complicated. I said, "Mothers don't usually let their daughters leave home at fourteen. But if there's a stepfather, nine times out of ten, that's the reason."

"Pretty ordinary shit, I know."

"Unless you're the one it's happening to."

Archer's voice took on a sardonic tone. "Mom just couldn't seem to shake loose from those crazy, madcap flyboys. Grew up a Pensacola girl, where the career choices were being a pilot or marrying one. That's where she bagged my father— her word, not mine. I never met the guy. Disappeared before I took my first breath. Truman York was just one more in a long line of tall, clear-eyed gents with one hand on their dick and the other on the doorknob. A KC-130 jockey out of Nellis. Three wives long gone and stuck with a snot-nosed brat from one of them. Mom met him in some Vegas saloon, so for Christmas that year, she got her itch scratched, and I got a kid sister. Thanks, Santa."

"You and Kim didn't get along?"

"Truth is, she was probably okay, but I was so pissed at inheriting a new father over a Miller Lite I never gave her a chance. We probably had a lot in common. Pilots are the same wherever you find them. Forget management by committee; learn to duck."

"So you were odd girl out."

"You could say that. That is, until Captain York decided to sample some fine teen pussy. Then I got real popular."

"When did your mother find out?"

"Pretty quick, but she didn't do anything except start drinking a little earlier in the day. So I worked it out myself and never looked back."

"Except every day."

She looked at me, and I thought she was going to get angry, but instead she nodded. "I've watched Oprah and Dr. Phil out the ass, and I've heard all the excuses, but I've never quite understood not protecting your kid."

I had no answer for that either.

"I used to lie awake at night and hope my real dad died in

a lot of pain. Makes a lot of sense, doesn't it? You know why we hurt the ones we love?"

"Maybe because we can."

"No, because they deserve it."

She got up and poured herself another cup of coffee. "I'd kill for a fucking cigarette. I quit, but sometimes . . ."

I ignored her. "Did Kim have any idea what her father was doing to you?"

"I don't know. It wasn't the kind of girl talk you get into over pizza and a sitcom. For all I knew, he was doing her too."

"And you never spoke to her again after you left?"

Archer shook her head. "I stayed in touch with Mom. I don't know why, but I called her every month no matter where I was. Usually on a Sunday when I knew she wouldn't be at work. We just yakked about small stuff for half an hour or so. Where I was, what I was doing. That kind of crap."

She hesitated, as if remembering something. "Come to think of it, I did talk to Kim a couple of times. Once, when she was graduating from high school and wanted to come live with me. Go to Columbia or NYU or something. Shit, I could barely feed myself. The other time was when she called to tell me the happy couple was dead."

The picture was beginning to clear. Kim had been as lonely as Archer, except that she didn't have an escape option. So she assumed her stepsister's history. It probably made explanations easier too. And who was going to care? She didn't have to swear to any affidavits or make a court declaration. It was just between her and her God.

I was now certain Truman York had been molesting his daughter too. That's why she took Alex Cayne as her fantasy dad. While Alex's actual daughter was lying awake nights wishing him pain, Kim was pretending big, strong Commander Cayne was watching over her. Twisted, but that's the kind of thing that happens when a child's innocence is stolen. But now something else was bothering me.

"Archer, your mother had three burial plots."

She nodded. "She bought them right after the navy men came and told her the Pentagon was declaring Dad dead. I was in second grade, and when I saw the uniforms coming up the walk, I yelled, 'Daddy's home.' Not a good moment."

"I'm sorry. So when Truman and your mother were killed—"

"Bess. We keep talking about her, but we never use her name. It was Bess. She was weak, but she still had a name."

I knew because I'd seen it engraved on the marker at the cemetery, but now that Archer mentioned it, Kim had never used Bess's name either. Unconscious anger, I guessed.

I began again. "What I'm trying to say is that I'm not sure Kim would want to spend eternity lying next to them, certainly not her father."

"You're fucking kidding, right?"

It wasn't the reaction I was expecting. "I realize they're dead, but it's still symbolic."

"Jesus, you really don't know, do you?"

"Know what?"

"Bess and Truman's graves are empty."

"They didn't die in a car crash?"

"Is that what Kim told you?"

"That was the implication."

"This is like the fucking Twilight Zone. There's symbolism in the graves, all right. And it certainly was a crash. But not the kind you're talking about. Bess and Truman went down on Egypt Air 990, and their bodies, like most everybody else's, were never recovered."

Crimes and Tears

At exactly 1:20 a.m. on Halloween morning, 1999, Ahmed El-Habashy, captain of Egypt Air 990, gently eased the nose of his Boeing 767 into the night sky. Seconds later, the last of JFK Runway 22-Right dropped behind him. He retracted his landing gear and felt the bonds of earth loosen, experiencing the familiar and exhilarating rush of raw power as the massive, twin Pratt & Whitney turbines pulled his craft steadily upward.

As the 767 climbed through seven thousand feet, El-Habashy banked the aircraft slightly, turning east. The light fog at ground level was now well beneath him, and he could see lights poking through the low-lying mist along the left side of the aircraft, outlining the southern shore of Long Island. It was the same path followed by hundreds of flights each day, including one three years earlier that was still steeped in controversy—TWA 800.

In the darkened cabin sat a full planeload of tourists, students, businessmen and deadheading crew, along with the two relief pilots and flight engineer who would take over the cockpit sometime during the ten-hour flight to Cairo.

*Also aboard were thirty-four Egyptian Air Force officers,
a dozen of them generals, returning home from training in
California. A total of 217 men, women and children.*

They had thirty-two minutes left to live.

*El-Habashy keyed the intercom and asked a flight atten-
dant to bring him a cup of coffee—one sugar, two creams.
His first officer, Adel Anwar, thirty-six, ordered nothing.*

*The night ahead was clear, the ride smooth, and like co-
workers do, El-Habashy and Anwar engaged in easy banter
about their bosses and their company. During the conversation, seemingly apropos of nothing, El-Habashy suddenly
raised the issue of a passenger, possibly one of the military
officers, who had boarded the flight without some required
paperwork.*

*Whether this man had come aboard at LAX, where the
flight had originated, or at JFK, where El-Habashy had assumed command, is not clear. Nor is the passenger's identity. But El-Habashy indicated that he had been pushed into
turning a blind eye to the violation of regulations by others
traveling with the man.*

*What is clear is that Captain El-Habashy, fifty-seven, an
organized, meticulous officer with more than thirty years'
flying experience, was perturbed enough by the anomaly to
raise it again with his copilot twice in the next few minutes.*

*Twenty minutes after takeoff, Flight 990 was approach-
ing its cruise altitude of 33,000 feet when the reserve first
officer, Gameel Al-Batouti, fifty-nine, nicknamed "Jimmy,"
entered the cockpit. Al-Batouti was not due to assume the
copilot's seat for several more hours, when the entire reserve crew would take over, and when he told Anwar that
he intended to fly now, Anwar said that he had already slept
and wanted to continue.*

*Words were exchanged, and the disagreement ended only
when Al-Batouti invoked his considerable seniority and told
Anwar unconditionally that he would be taking over as first
officer. It is unknown why El-Habashy did not intervene on*

behalf of his friend and first officer, but it appears he did not. Al-Batouti then left the cockpit for a few moments and returned, taking the right seat as Anwar departed.

Captain El-Habashy then also left the cockpit to use the restroom.

Twenty-one seconds later, Al-Batouti, now alone at the controls, uttered the phrase, "I rely on God," and disengaged the autopilot. He then moved the throttles to idle, thereby cutting off all engine thrust.

As the nose of the plane tilted down, it rolled slightly to the left, and Al-Batouti again said, "I rely on God." He then shut off the engines.

Captain El-Habashy bolted back into the cockpit, struggled into his seat and began trying to wrestle the nose of the plane up, imploring Al-Batouti to help. "Pull with me! Pull with me!" he screamed.

But in the right seat, Al-Batouti repeated, "I rely on God" several more times and fought to keep the nose of the aircraft down.

During the next ninety seconds, the men struggled for supremacy. Then suddenly, the plane lurched upward again. Whether this was an aerodynamic reaction to the speed brakes applied by El-Habashy or whether it was because he had regained momentary physical superiority is unclear. One can only wonder how those in the back felt as they experienced unimaginable g-forces and perhaps sensed reprieve.

But the captain was no match for the combination of Al-Batouti and gravity, and when he could no longer hold them both off, the 767's nose once again turned down.

On the cockpit voice recorder, the terrified screams of the passengers can be heard for more than a minute and a half. Finally, 400,000 pounds of aircraft, traveling at six hundred miles per hour, hit the water, and all sound ended.

At 1:52 a.m., Egypt Air Flight 990 ceased to exist.

Despite the usual conspiracy whack-jobs and the spin put on the investigation by the Egyptian government—owing

to both economic and cultural concerns—aviation experts,
law enforcement and the intelligence community have no
doubt what caused Flight 990 to plunge into the sea. Nor
is there any dispute that Gameel Al-Batouti had numerous
personal problems that most likely contributed to his ac-
tions.

The unanswered question is whether this was the last,
lone act of a desperate man or the termination point of a
conspiracy. And if it was the latter, who was the target? The
Egyptian government? The airline? The military officers?
Or perhaps another passenger?

One might think that since 9/11, this would be a seri-
ous concern worthy of further investigation. One would be
wrong.

Though I had showered at Kim's, I was still wearing the
same gamey clothes. I had also taken my last Vicodin, and
the pain was returning. But now that I knew where Marta
Videz worked, I wanted to talk to her. As I drove toward
Los Feliz, I replayed what Archer had told me about Truman
York.

After his military career ended, he bounced from airline
to airline but couldn't manage to hold a job. Unauthorized
absences, insubordination, heavy drinking—the common
themes of a man with no direction and no plan. Eventually,
he ended up flying freight in Canada, but when that didn't
last, he took a job as an air courier, and an old air force contact helped get him certified as a "Special."

It's not a job many people know exists. They're not supposed to. Special couriers are authorized to carry a loaded
firearm aboard an aircraft, and they get absolute priority,
meaning they can bump almost anybody—CEOs, senior
government officials, even celebrities.

They used to travel with a case handcuffed to their wrists,
but that was a walking billboard for someone to lop off their
hand and walk away with the goods. If a professional wants
to steal something, he's not squeamish about a quick ampu-

tation with a sharp cleaver and a little blood. Or, as occurred in Lagos, Nigeria, where the thief walked into the outdoor baggage claim area, fired up a chainsaw and removed a CIA courier's entire arm.

In response, courier cases now have high-tensile steel cable molded into their handles which are then run up the courier's sleeve and down his back and locked around his waist. This refinement has saved hands, but if the bad guys manage to kidnap the courier, he no longer comes back simply needing a hook to eat his cereal.

Since Lagos, special couriers on assignment for the government usually travel by military aircraft. Otherwise, they travel by charter or in one of the half dozen passenger seats fitted into FedEx, UPS and DHL planes. When it is absolutely necessary to fly commercial, they sit in the first row of first class with the seat next to them paid for and unoccupied. No one, not even a flight crew member, is permitted to sit down next to a "Special." They are escorted onto the aircraft by security personnel well before anyone else and are the first to deplane.

Being a "Special" was the perfect job for Truman York. He traveled well and lived on an expense account. And he was away from home often. By contrast, according to Archer, Bess hated flying and had no interest in visiting any city she couldn't reach by car in a day. She was on Flight 990 supposedly because she and Truman were going to celebrate their wedding anniversary in Marseilles. Bess told Archer that she would board the flight in Los Angeles, and Truman, who had a job originating in Washington, would get on at JFK. They couldn't sit together because he was working, so she would be riding in coach while he was in first class. Once they got to Cairo, and he was relieved of his obligation, they would fly on to France together.

I asked Archer what she'd thought about that.

"You ever been to Marseilles?"

"I have."

"How many people do you think go there to celebrate anything—except maybe escaping prison? I didn't buy it then, and I don't buy it now. My mom thought the best meal on the planet was the Admiral's Feast at Red Lobster, and she was claustrophobic in the extreme. The idea that she would cram herself into a narrow seat and fly half-way around the world to a place she couldn't pronounce is absurd."

"So why take her?"

Her eyes hardened. "I've thought about it a lot, and there's only one conclusion that works. Truman was going for what the French call a Marseilles divorce—a thump on the head and midnight swim in the Med. There were almost certainly other women in Truman's life, and it was time to move on."

I agreed. Truman York wasn't a guy whose best friend was his wife. And unless Bess was an aficionado of freight terminals, smokestacks and street crime, Marseilles isn't an-niversary material. It is, however, just down the road from Nice, where Benny Joe caught his ferry to Corsica. And it now seemed that Kim had developed a fondness for the South of France as well.

I didn't think this was about another woman, but whatever it was, it wasn't going to be pretty.

Los Feliz is "Old Hollywood."

Occupying the high ground north of downtown L.A., it's where the early movie legends like DeMille, Jolson and Lugosi built their mansions, and where the next generation—Gable, Grant and Garbo—unwound at a branch of the Brown Derby. It's also where the Manson Family scrawled "Healter Skelter" (Tex Watson couldn't spell) in blood on a refrigerator door.

Recently, Los Feliz has been rediscovered, and an ener-getic new crop of homeowners has started buying up the old estates and bringing them back to their former glory. The rebirth has attracted some current stars too—the ones who want to be able to fish the morning paper out of the shrub-bery wearing a ratty old bathrobe without having to check the tour bus schedule.

A couple of friends of mine—Stephen Bennett, owner of a chain of hair salons in the Valley, and Warren Van Meter, an Academy Award-winning set designer—bought the old Valentino villa, the one Rudy lived in before he built Falcon Lair, and turned it into a showplace that's become the back-drop for some of the town's most talked-about parties.

Redoing the gardens alone cost "The Valentino Boys," as they call themselves, half a million. But it got them the cover of *California Design*. And when some sultan saw it and sent his lawyer to offer them so much for the place that they could have bought a small country, they slammed the door in his face and threw a "Take Your Cash and Shove It Party" that went on for two days.

So after having heard Manarca say that Kiki Videz's mother worked as a domestic in Los Feliz, finding her hadn't been difficult; Stephen and Warren's housekeeper just tapped into the neighborhood network, and now I was sitting in the kitchen of a big house on Chislehurst Drive while sunlight streamed through a large bay window and a pair of Siamese cats lolled on the white tile floor.

Marta was a slight woman with large brown eyes, but de-spite having borne five children, she was still trim and attrac-tive. She hadn't made eye contact with me since I'd arrived, and as I spoke to her in quiet Spanish, she kept glancing at the bandage on my hand and crossing herself nervously.

I finally said, "Mrs. Videz, I don't think Kiki is the one who shot me."

Her voice was so soft that, as close as I was, I still had to strain to hear her. She spoke with a peasant accent, but there was an articulateness to it that indicated she had attended school for at least a while.

"I brought my family to this country so they could have a better life. My husband didn't want to come. He was afraid. But I insisted, and now he is dead. In Guatemala, the narcotraficantes make you carry drugs, then they kill you. In America, you take the drugs and kill yourself."

Silent tears rolled down her cheeks, and she dabbed them with the back of her hand. "Kiki was such a good boy. When he was little, he used to sit on my lap and just hold onto me. And when he went off to school, he cried so much the teacher asked me to come and sit in the class. The other children made fun of him, but Kiki would just look at me and smile."

"Mrs. Videz . . ."

But she wasn't finished. "Kiki didn't want to join a gang, but they beat him so many times that he finally gave in." Then, with an anguish that sent a chill through me, she looked into my eyes for the first time. "Why did they cut off my baby's arms? Why?" Now her tears spilled with no sign of slackening. I gave her my handkerchief.

I had no words of comfort for this kind of pain, so I simply reached out and put my hand on her shoulder. She wept for a few more moments, and then struggled and got control. "But you did not come here to listen to a mother's heartache. I am glad you do not think Kiki shot you or that woman. How can I help you?"

Here was the strength that had carried Marta Videz and her family from the dirt streets of the tropics to the barrio of East Los Angeles. "Mrs. Videz, I need to know if Kiki had a tattoo on his right arm."

She nodded. "Yes, so many tattoos, so awful. It was like he was trying to show the world how much he hated himself." She gestured to her left forearm. "Here, he had a knife, a dagger, dripping blood down to his hand." Then, gesturing to her right, "And here, he had a leaping tiger. Very large with many colors. Los Tigres."

"No spiders?"

She shook her head. "Kiki was very afraid of spiders. He would never have let anybody draw one on his skin."

"Mrs. Videz, did you ever hear Kiki mention someone named Tino?"

"No."

"Or Dante?"

Her face took on a fierceness I could not have imagined. "Oh, I know him. Dante with the marks on his face." She pointed to both cheeks, and I was sure she meant acne scars. "I saw him twice. He came to our house to pick up Kiki. While my son was out of the room, he put his hand here." She pointed to her breast and blushed deep red. "He didn't say anything, he just . . . how do you say it . . . pinched the . . . the tip . . . until the pain made me so weak I couldn't move. It was not the touch of a man who knows women. It was a touch of evil—and a warning."

"What was Kiki doing with him?"

"He only told me he was doing some work. And he was being paid a lot of money. If I had just told Kiki what this Dante did to me, he would never have gone with him, and my son would be alive. But I was too ashamed." I thought she was going to cry again, but she didn't.

"Did you find anything unusual in Kiki's car?"

"Kiki didn't have a car. When he went someplace with Dante, he picked him up. In a truck."

"You mean a van. Dark blue."

"Yes, very clean and shiny. He always parked it in the middle of the street, so nobody could get past. One day, a man got out of his car to yell, and Dante put a gun in his face. Then he laughed. But not a funny laugh."

"Did your son tell you where they met?"

"At the Home Depot. In the back, where the men wait for work. Sometimes, on Saturdays, Kiki would go there to make extra money. He was good with his hands, and my husband taught him how to put down cement."

"You said you saw Dante twice. Was the other time at your house too?"

She shook her head but didn't offer anything.

"Can you tell me?" I asked gently. "It might be important."

She looked at me, and I could see real fear. She thought for a moment, then made a decision. "On Sunday, my day off, I get up early and help my cousin, Rita, clean the bar at the Biltmore Hotel. We ride the train downtown, and that way we can finish in time to walk to eleven o'clock mass at Our Lady of Angels. It's such a beautiful place, and there are so many people. It makes God feel very close. Do you go to church, Mr. Black?"

"Not as often as I should."

"I will say a prayer for you."

"Thank you, I'd like that."

"The Sunday before Kiki was . . . was killed, Rita and I were finished with our work and getting ready to leave for church, when Dante came into the hotel. He was dressed in a suit—very expensive."

"Was he alone?"

"No, there were other men there."

"In the lobby?"

She nodded. "Five or six. All young, dressed very nice. They were with a man with much white hair. A very, very big man, but not so old like you would expect with such hair."

"When you say big, do you mean tall? Like me?"

"Tall, yes, but also very . . ." She used her hands to demonstrate a thick torso. "Very *anchuro*."

"Wide?" I said.

She nodded. "Yes, wide. But graceful. Like a dancer. Like he was big all his life. And his mouth. Much teeth . . . much teeth. Not a nice man to look at."

She stopped, looked at me. "I also saw the woman."

"The woman?"

Marta nodded. "The woman who was shot . . . with you. Dr. York. She was standing on the balcony that looks down over the lobby. Watching the men."

I was taken completely off guard. "Are you sure?"

Marta's voice turned firm. "Her picture was on television. I am sure."

"How long did you watch?"

"Not very long. At first, they just stood there, like they were waiting for somebody else. Then Dante said something that made the big man angry, because he slapped him—hard."

"What did Dante do?"

"Nothing, he didn't even put his hand on his face. Then all of sudden, more men came into the hotel, some of them from across the other ocean. Many men, maybe ten, twelve, and they had things in their ears, like when you are deaf. They went to different places in the lobby and stood. One of them was right next to me."

Somebody's private security, I thought. Wearing earbuds, like the Secret Service. "When you say from across the 'other ocean,' do you mean they were Asian?"

"Yes, Asian. But I cannot tell the difference between Japanese and Chinese and the others." She seemed embarrassed. "I have a friend who is Korean, and she looks like them too. I'm sorry."

I reassured her. "It's okay, Marta. What happened next?"

"A man wearing sunglasses came in. He was not Asian, like the ones who were protecting him. He went to the man in the white hair, and they shook hands. Like they were old friends."

Old friends don't bring security. And somebody had insisted on meeting in a public place. It was the kind of show reticent people participate in only when they think there is real danger.

Marta had started speaking again, and I had to stop her and ask her to start over.

"The elevator opened, and everybody got very nervous. Like it wasn't supposed to open. The man standing next to me took out a gun. Then from the elevator, a man got out . . . an American."

"An American?"

She nodded. "No matter how hard they try, people who live in other countries cannot dress like Americans. And they cannot walk like them. This man had on jeans and one of those shirts with a horse on it, here." She indicated her left chest. "The shirt was white and the horse was blue, and he was wearing a leather jacket. An old one. Brown, very neat. And cowboy boots. Not like a Guatemala vaquero. Very expensive."

"What did he do?"

"He walked right through all of those men with things in their ears like they were not even there. Smiling. That is what Americans do. They are not afraid of anything."

She was right. It gets us killed sometimes, but it's also what makes us . . . us.

"The man in the white hair was angry, and he said something, but the American didn't seem to care. Then . . ."

She stopped, and I could see she was clasping and unclasping her hands.

"Go on, Marta," I said softly.

She nodded, but her hands were still busy. "The woman. Dr. York. She had a camera. One of those little ones you hold out like this." She extended both arms. "One of the men saw her and pointed. The white-haired man started shouting, and Dante and some of the others went after her. There was much yelling and running, and I was afraid. So I took Rita's arm and we left."

"What did your cousin say?"

"That she didn't see anything."

"But she did."

"Of course. She was standing right beside me."

"Do you think she had ever seen any of them before?"

Marta shook her head. "I waited until she wasn't expecting it, and I asked her."

"And you believe she was telling the truth?"

"Yes, Rita would never lie twice. And never on the way to church." Marta smiled for the first time.

"Marta, I want you to take a moment and think back. Get a mental picture of the scene. Then I want you to describe the man wearing sunglasses."

Marta thought for a moment. "He was not tall, but not

short either. And his suit was tight across his chest, like those men on TV who tell you to buy their machines, and you will become strong."

"A weight lifter?" I said.

She nodded. "His arms were thick too. Like they were almost too big for his clothes. He had a square face, and his hair was very dark, but it had a white streak in it. Right here." She pointed at the front of her own hair.

"Did you hear him speak?"

"Yes, and he did not come from America. He talked like Mr. Nik."

"Mr. Nik?"

"Yes, the man who owns this house."

She pointed to a framed movie poster on the wall across the room. It was an art film I had never heard of, but as I read through the credits, the composer's name stopped me. Nikita Kuchin.

I looked at Marta. "Is Mr. Nik Russian?"

She nodded. "He says most people leave Russia because of politics. He just wanted to get warm."

The Siamese cats suddenly heard something and bolted out of the room. Marta smiled and shook her head. "Loco."

I got up to leave. "One more question, Marta. Have you ever heard of something called City of War?"

She thought for a moment. "In Guatemala there is a large cemetery called City of the Souls. I have never heard of one for war . . . but maybe there should be such a place . . . where we could put the men who start them."

The wisdom of the unlettered. Once again confirming Buckley's observation that he'd rather be governed by the first two thousand names in the Boston phone book than by two thousand Harvard professors.

I handed Marta my card. "If you need anything, or if Dante contacts you . . ."

She took the card, looked at it, then at me. "Thank you, Mr. Black. You're the first person who has been kind. And your Spanish is beautiful."

At the front door, I stopped and turned. "Marta, you are a very strong person."

"I am trying," she answered. "For Kiki."

As I went down the front walk to my truck, I knew more than when I'd gone in, but, unlike Sgt. Manarca, I was a long way from making out the Eiffel Tower. One thing was clear, however. Kim was batting 100 percent in the bullshit department. And not only had she seen Dante before, it wasn't in the hot fudge line at Baskin-Robbins.

In the car, I replayed my conversations with her. She'd talked about losing her cell phone, datebook, even her dry cleaning, but she'd never mentioned a camera. And there hadn't been one in the house or in the box sent over by Dr. Abernathy. I dialed the Getty.

"Everyone in the art world carries a digital camera," said A.A. "It's one of the wonderful things technology has brought us. Even a lox like myself can take a picture that it used to take an entire crew to get."

"Do you know what kind of camera Kim had?"

"The museum issues us each a top-of-the-line Olympus. Nikon be damned. It's just marvelous."

"And you didn't find it in her things?"

He thought for a moment. "No, and I actually thought about it, because it's supposed to be turned in when an employee leaves. But I didn't know who to ask, and it seemed unseemly to start calling around. I take it you didn't find it either."

"No, but if it shows up, I'll be sure to send it to tech security."

He laughed. "You do that."

15

Big Boats and Bigger Bullshit

As the gates on Dove Way slid back, I saw the silver Lexus. I recognized it right away. Instead of driving down into the garage, I parked alongside. When I walked into the house, Rhonda Champion and Mallory were sitting in the living room.

Rhonda got up, gently put her arms around me and pressed her lips against mine. Her long, raven hair smelled of lilac as it brushed my face. I held her a little longer. When she stepped back, she let out a short whistle. "Whew, you need a bar of soap."

"You're the second person in two days to comment on my hygiene."

"Why did it take two of us? Go directly upstairs and leave those clothes in the hall."

I did as I was told, and a few minutes after I stepped into the shower, Rhonda came into the bathroom and leaned against the sink. She was holding a couple of tall Arnold Palmers, and I extended a hand through the steam so she could hand me one. I realized I hadn't spoken to her since the shooting, and now the guilt set in.

Noting the nasty scar on my chest, she said, "When they were rummaging around in there, did they happen to find a heart?"

"I'm sorry. I should have called."

"Damn right you should have. Fortunately, Mallory isn't as civility-challenged."

"So what are you doing this far from Orange County? Not that I'm not happy to see you."

"I've come to take you away from all this."

"I'm sorry," I said, "but I can't leave right now."

"That's what Mallory said you'd say. So he called your doctor."

"Ted Goldman? What's he got to do with this?"

"He said you either go with me and rest, or you're fired as a patient."

"Doctors don't fire patients, and especially not Ted."

She took out her cell phone and dialed. When she handed me the phone, Ted was already on the other end. He didn't wait for me to plead my case.

"Listen, you fucker, you gave me your word, and I bought it. You've got an appointment a week from tomorrow, and if Rhonda doesn't call here every goddamned day and tell me you're on that big-ass boat of yours resting and recuperating, don't bother to show up. Don't even call. I'll mail a referral."

"Ted . . ."

"Wake the fuck up, Rail. This isn't a hollow threat. I don't waste my time on assholes. You do what I say, or you're out of my practice. *Capice*?"

When I started to answer, he'd already hung up.

Rhonda saw me looking at the dead phone. "How great is that? Somebody who doesn't give a fat rat's ass how much money you have."

This didn't happen to me very often. When you're rich, you always get to be the magnanimous one—or the jerk. Everyone laughs at your bad jokes and tells you you're incredibly smart when you're really a fucking dunce. And they hang on every word of your bullshit stories that they've heard a hundred times before and that weren't interesting from the get-go. For the first time in a long time, I was just like the rest of the world. A guy who had to yield to a higher power. And I didn't like it. But Ted Goldman didn't seem to give a shit what I liked.

To Rhonda I said, "Okay, what do you have in mind?"

She cut me some slack. "No heavy lifting, but you could end up sweating a lot. We never got to celebrate your birthday, remember?"

While I dressed, Rhonda sat on the bedroom patio and made phone calls. When I was ready, she came back in. Standing on her toes, she kissed me again.

"What was that one for?" I asked, smiling.

"I missed you."

"I missed you too."

She took my hand. "I'm not going to ask now, but one of these days, I want to know who Kim York was."

We walked hand in hand downstairs. Her skin felt terrific. I'd forgotten how much I liked her company.

In the foyer, Mallory was standing with the front door open, holding a small valise. He handed it to Rhonda and said, "The pharmacy. His bags are in the boot. I'll come down in a couple of days with fresh things."

"You don't have to look so pleased with yourself," I said to him.

Mallory gave me that grave look Brits must go to a special camp to learn. "No, I could have taken a fireplace poker to your self-destructive highness, but that would have cost me my paycheck. For the record, however, Dr. Goldman isn't the only one who thinks you're a schmuck."

Rhonda and I laughed. Mallory didn't.

Rhonda's an interior designer who specializes in yachts. She also drives like she's taken a wrong turn off Le Mans. I'm not sure we could have flown to Newport Beach any faster, which was good, because I hate holding my breath that long.

The *Sanrevelle* is a black, 102-foot Benetti with red trim on the superstructure and an interior of polished mahogany. The combination of the black and red hull against the rich wood makes it stand out even when surrounded by larger boats. Rare is the Friday I'm not headed south for a couple of days away from the endless cacophony and barely controlled chaos of L.A. I love the city, but it can be unrelenting, and a two-day change of pace refreshes me more than a week at a fancy resort. A lot of weekends, I don't even leave the dock.

When Rhonda handed her Lexus over to the yacht club valet, brakes smoking, and I saw the *Sanrevelle* sitting there in the sun, clean, unbuttoned, flags flapping, I felt better than I had in a long time. And when Bert and Brittany Rixon appeared on the forward deck and Bert leaned over to drop me an ice-cold Corona, the moment was complete. The Vicodin would have to move over. Mexican brew coming through.

People ask why I keep a boat fifty miles away rather than at Marina del Rey. Those are the same people who think Orange County is just something they have to pass through to get to San Diego. It's only the next province south, but if L.A. is hip-hop, OC is Sinatra. It's not an age thing, it's an attitude.

With her auxiliary tanks full, the *Sanrevelle* can cruise more than fifteen hundred miles on her twin Volvos. I usually hire crew when I'm going on an extended trip, but if Mallory's aboard, he's twice the sailor of anyone else I've ever met, and the two of us have taken her to Mexico several times.

She's really too big to be operated by one person, but if I stay focused, I can manage. It doesn't matter how discreet a crew is, private conversations simply aren't as private, and I dislike having security determined by the weakest link in a chain of employees.

When I bought her, I'd been looking for a boat, but not one this big. She'd been built for an NBA All-Star—one of those guys you would know even if you don't follow basketball. Tired of bumping his head on doorways, he'd had everything designed to his specifications. Vaulted ceilings, oversized furniture, a massive bed half again the size of a king, and forty-five-inch-high counters instead of the standard thirty-six.

Then his career took a turn for the worse, and he was forced to take a gig in the European league for a fraction of his NBA pay. Adding to his troubles were a couple of ex-wives. When the broker—an old friend, Gil Huppy—called me and said he had a two-year-old, 102-footer available, I almost hung up on him. I wanted to get back on the water—needed to get back—but I'd had in mind something half that size.

Then Gil explained that because of her interior scale, she was unappealing to most buyers, and the owner would take just about anything—as long as it was cash. So, like the house on Dove Way, everybody got something out of the deal. And I quickly discovered that this particular yacht fit both my size and my lifestyle. I've also made great friends at the club, and, in the reverse of my friends in L.A., the OC people can't understand why anyone would live anywhere near Los Angeles, even Beverly Hills.

Rhonda had to go to her office for a while, and Bert and Brittany always take a nap in the afternoon—at least that's what they call it—so we agreed to meet back on the *Sanrevelle* at seven for dinner.

After they'd gone, I hiked up the hill to Hoag Hospital, which sits on a cliff overlooking Newport Beach. It wasn't built as a lighthouse, but you can see its rooftop beacon ten miles out, and every boater I know gets his bearings from it.

I went into the small chapel off the main lobby and sat down. It's a place I like to go to think. Today there was only one other person there, an older gentleman who seemed to be carrying the weight of the world.

I was raised in the Church of England—although my mother used to sneak me out to Catholic mass when she didn't think anyone was looking. But as I got older, I ended up like my father. He believed in God, he just didn't want an intermediary.

A number of years ago, after a particularly unpleasant operation in Portugal, where the people who put it together ignored the intelligence and a couple of good men died who shouldn't have, I found myself walking by a small church in Lisbon. On a whim, I went in. Mass was going on, but I didn't care, I just wanted to collect my thoughts. Later, after the congregation had gone, the priest saw me sitting alone and asked if he could be of any help. With my English-accented Brazilian Portuguese, I managed to tell him I was fine.

His reply has stuck with me. "That's why we're here, *senhor.* For when you're *favoravelmente.* And when you're not so *favoravelmente.*"

Today, I was both.

The four of us brought in Chinese and spread it out on the circular rosewood table in the salon. Bert always orders for everyone because he insists on at least two dishes per person to assuage his prodigious appetite. When he had his business, he spent a lot of time in China and learned Mandarin, so he relishes conspiring with Marty Wong, the owner of Jade Pavilion, to sneak in something none of us recognizes.

This time it was pickled eel, which I didn't tell him I'd been eating for years, and while we sampled, he regaled us with stories about sautéed chicken hearts in Shanghai and beef tendons up the Yangtze. We'd heard the stories before—many times—but we laughed in the right places anyway, like good friends do. Bert, Brittany and Rhonda tapped into my cabernet rack, but I had gone to iced tea and stayed there. I'd drunk the one Corona earlier, and even though I hadn't taken any more Vicodin, I didn't want to end up drooling in a corner.

Bert's only forty-five, but he's retired—sort of. He's an engineer, and he got very rich inventing a prosthetic leg that's so good, amputees can run marathons. When he sold his company, the buyers forked over $300 million with two caveats: don't come to the office and stay out of the prosthesis business.

So Bert bought himself a 212-foot Italian Codecasa, the *Once More With Feeling,* where he and Brittany live, and a small warehouse nearby where he can tinker. I've never been invited to the warehouse, but Brittany—they've been married eighteen months after ten years of dating—says that Bert is working on something that will advance prostheses twenty-five years. I told her I hope he's saved some of that $300 million for the lawsuit.

Rhonda had just finished redecorating the Rixons' boat, and the owners were raving about how much they loved what she'd done. But when I saw Rhonda roll her eyes and pour herself a third glass of wine—a rarity—I suspected she was just glad the job was over. Like every engineer I've ever met, Bert doesn't do anything that he's not involved in up to his elbows. And that he doesn't think he's a genius at.

The *Once More With Feeling,* in keeping with Bert's personality, is the most magnificent assemblage of steel and mahogany in the marina. Nine cabins, a crew of seven and a helicopter pad make it just slightly less comfortable than the Palace of Versailles. The previous owner, an Argentine cattle rancher, had decorated it like a Polish cathedral, but Rhonda took a fire axe to the brocade and broadloom and turned the interior into a showplace for Bert's Charles Russell sculptures.

Bert's favorite topic of conversation is politics, which, frankly, bores me. Since twenty-four-hour news, no matter what people tell pollsters, nobody is undecided about anything. So why break a sweat arguing that the other side is uninformed or boneheaded or criminal. Nobody's changing.

But Bert does it for exactly that reason. He loves an argument. I have no idea how he votes, because I've heard him advocate both sides of every issue, sometimes in the same conversation, especially if he's getting a rise out of somebody. And Rhonda, the ultimate cynic, always takes the bait. Add wine, and she takes it loudly.

I heard her saying, "I go with the long view. Every few years, the clowns in power end up just like the clowns who came before them—gone. The only thing that changes are the names on the payoff checks."

I'd been here before, and it had always ended in a death spiral, so I tried to head it off. "It's my first night back, let's find another topic, okay?"

But Bert was ready for me. "I've heard when somebody gets shot, they get philosophical. I've never quite figured out where you stand on the death penalty, Rail. How about now?"

Pascal, the seventeenth-century mathematician, said that all of man's troubles are caused by his inability to sit quietly in a room alone. They ought to put Bert's picture next to Pascal's in Wikipedia as the guy who won't stop practicing it.

I replied, "Bert, I'm not going down this road."

"So you're saying you're undecided."

"Read any good books lately?" I answered.

Then Rhonda rode in. "I'm with Bert on this. I have no idea where you stand either."

"And it matters because . . . ?"

"How about, you're a fascinating guy, and I want to know more about you. Here, I'll help you get started. I think Texas has it right. Kill 'em all, let God sort 'em out."

Bert was smiling. "So, Rail, let's pretend they've caught the guy who killed that young lady and shot you, and it's your call what happens to him. What does?"

Rhonda turned in her chair. "Yeah, what does, Big Guy?"

"That's why we have cops and prosecutors. So it's not personal."

Rhonda rolled her eyes. "Jesus, what a wimpy answer. This isn't civics class. It's a liquored-up bull session."

"All the more reason," I said evenly.

These kinds of confrontations are never about conversation, they're about control. About getting someone to say something he didn't set out to say. In an amateurish, ham-handed way, it's Chapter 1, Paragraph 1 of interrogation. Establish a dialog—even if it's hostile. Ordinary folks don't realize that if somebody knows what he's doing, he can manipulate other people's emotions to the point where they will always relent—always. And afterward, if they have any IQ at all, they feel violated. There's a clear winner, and a clear loser, and everybody knows which is which. I've seen these kinds of situations end in near murder.

Done by a professional, and for keeps, the interrogator stays engaged with his subject; never lets him have that down moment. Uses positive reinforcement. Food. A cigarette. Maybe tells him something about himself to develop the bond further. I've suffered through enough mock interrogations and conducted enough real ones to know what my weaknesses are. And wanting to please isn't one of them. I never tell anyone anything I don't intend to tell them. And I never discuss my personal views on a host of things. Ever.

"Answer the question, Rail, goddamn it." Rhonda's voice had taken on an edge I'd never heard before. An ugliness. I looked at her without smiling. But she rolled on. "Or is this the kind of thing you only discussed with your dead piece of ass."

Sometimes a relationship ends in a heartbeat. They say that at those times, in your mind's eye, you can see the skin tighten against the bones of the person's face and picture them in death. That didn't happen, but at that moment, whatever Rhonda and I had was over.

I'm not sure Bert even heard her, but Brittany did, and her face said it all. Women are always harder on other women.

I don't believe a bellyful of hootch unlocks some secret place and lets the demons out. Anyone with reasonable intelligence knows all the forbidden words and where the dagger will do the most damage. Alcohol simply hands your mouth a permission slip. What gets selected is a function of circumstance and emotion. But even then it takes a second or two to get it out, plenty of time to check the process. So whiskey talk is mostly laziness.

To Bert, I finally said, "I'd turn the guy over to Ted Goldman. He's the scariest person I know."

Rhonda let out an exasperated moan.

Bert looked at her. "Who the hell is Ted Goldman?"

Brittany answered, "It's time for us to go home."

16

A Jogger and a Best Friend

At 11:30, I was sitting in my favorite place—the captain's chair of the flybridge. I like to finish my days there. Few things are more pleasant to look at or listen to than a marina at night. Hundreds of boats, flickering lights, creaking docks, distant laughter, a tinkling wind chime, muffled love-making, the occasional horn far out to sea. It always reminds me of a seagoing *Rear Window*.

I lit a cigar. My favorite, an AF 858 Maduro. Like English Ovals, if you're going to smoke, taste should be a priority. I keep a bottle of Macallan 25 in the bin under the life jackets, and I had it open in my other hand. I could guess what Amy Vanderbilt would say about drinking an expensive single-malt out of the bottle, but she wasn't there.

When Bert and Brittany left to go back to their boat, I sent Rhonda home to her condo, which is just a short walk outside the yacht club gate. I told her I wanted to get a good night's sleep, and I wouldn't be able to with her aboard. Her vanity wanted to go with the lie, but the wine was persistent.

"I'll come by tomorrow to check on you."

"That won't be necessary."

I saw her lower lip tremble, but she got control. "It was what I said, wasn't it? About that woman, Kim."

Her words had just been a shortcut to what would have happened anyway. But there wasn't any reason to go there. I kissed her cheek gently. "Goodnight."

"When they kiss you on the cheek, they might as well be sticking a knife between your ribs. I'll call Dr. Goldman and tell him I won't be checking in."

"I'd appreciate that," I said. I didn't care what she did, but indifference at that moment would have made it uncomfortable for her to ever be in the same room with me again. I watched her walk up the dock with purpose. Silently, I wished her luck.

Now, from where I sat, I watched a guy one dock over, who'd obviously had too much to drink, try to get his forty-foot Bertram into its slip. It was laughing-out-loud funny, and he thought so too, because he was doing more of that than driving.

Just as I was contemplating going down to help him, my phone rang. Before I could say anything, an out-of-breath female voice said, "Rail? It's me, Archer. Archer Cayne."

Said like I knew a dozen Archers. "How are you?"

"Scared."

"What's wrong?"

"I just got back from my evening run, and the paperboy had thrown the *Times* into the cactus patch under the front window. I went up to get it, and a car across the street pulled out. His lights hit the house, and there were two men in my living room. Just sitting there . . . in the dark."

"Did they see you?"

"I don't think so. I dropped and crawled around the side. Nobody came out, and no lights came on."

"Where are you now?"

"Up the street a block."

I was standing now. "Okay, the first thing we're going to do is get you out of the neighborhood. Think you can run another couple of miles?"

"Shit, with this much adrenaline, I can run to fucking Miami. That is, if I don't pee myself first."

"Okay, here's what I want you to do. Go west two blocks, then down to Santa Monica Boulevard and head toward the ocean. You know the Fairmont Miramar Hotel?"

"Haven't got a clue."

"It'll be on your right. Northeast corner of Santa Monica and Ocean Avenue. You go too far, you'll run off a cliff."

"So either way, I'm gonna be okay."

I liked this girl's moxie, but I guess if you've lived with a Russian thug who blinded you, you're not going to fold up easily. "No matter what happens, don't get off Santa Monica. Somebody pulls up alongside, cross the street. But do it behind the vehicle, got it?"

"Yes."

"You're actually going to run past the main gate and turn right on Ocean. About half a block up you'll see a side entrance. There's a ladies' room straight back on your right."

"I really appreciate the plan, but I hope there's a bigger finish than a john."

I laughed. "When you're ready, go out the main entrance. You can't miss it. There's a long driveway facing Santa Monica Boulevard. Then dial my number and hand the phone to the doorman."

"What the fuck for?" she spit.

"I lost my wallet, and I want to see if he found it."

That stopped her for a moment. Then she laughed. "Okay, boss, whatever you say. But is there some reason I can't just go *in* the front door?"

I could tell by her breathing that she was already jogging. "Because if there's a chance you're being followed, I don't want you entering and leaving the same way. You get lonely, buzz me back, I'll be here." I hung up.

I dialed the home number of D. J. Kaplan, owner of Symphony Limousine, and a member of my board. Five minutes later, I was talking to a guy who identified himself as Billy

Mack Tulafono, doorman at the Fairmont. Then I called the yacht club.

My next call was to Mallory, but as I started to dial, I saw Bert coming back along the dock, walking purposefully. He saw me topside and waved, and I heard him mount the wooden stairs to the *Sanrevelle*. It was late, so if we were going to talk and not disturb anyone, it needed to be inside.

I met him in the salon. He was already at the bar pouring himself a glass of cognac. He asked if I wanted one. I shook my head and got myself a bottle of water.

"Brittany explained what happened with Rhonda. I gotta tell you, I missed the whole thing."

"I know."

Bert shook his head. "Sometimes when I'm wound up, I don't pay attention to anything except the sound of my own voice."

"It's one of the keys to your success. Single-mindedness of purpose. If you came over to apologize, it's not necessary. Just do me a favor and don't try dragging me into any more of your bullshit hypotheticals."

"I noticed you don't drag." He sipped at his cognac. "Deal, no more bullshit hypotheticals. Sorry about Rhonda."

"Don't be. It would have happened anyway."

"That's what Brittany said."

"Smart girl. You should listen to her more often."

"I'm beginning to realize that."

"So are we done?"

"You expecting somebody?"

"Yes."

"You don't beat around the bush."

I looked at him. His hands were shaking. "What is it, Bert?"

"Goddamn it, Rail. I'm fucking dying."

I thought for a moment he meant in the conversation, and I was about to agree, but then I realized he meant for real. "What's wrong?"

"I've been real clumsy lately. Fell on the boat a couple of times. Again coming out of Ruth's Chris. Brittany kept telling me to go to the doctor, but I figured I just needed to be more careful, maybe cut back on the booze. Then all of a sudden, I noticed I had muscle spasms. Little ones, like after you work out real hard. But they were all over. Back, arms, everywhere."

He raised his leg, and I saw a muscle twitch in his calf, then another in his thigh. "See what I mean?"

I did, and I knew exactly where this conversation was going.

"Lou Gehrig's disease," I said.

He looked at me hard. "Fuck, do you believe it? I sure fucking don't."

"When did you find out?"

"Two weeks ago."

"And, of course, you haven't told Brittany."

"I don't know what to say. She's everything to me."

"And what? You think she'll leave?"

"The doctor says I'm pretty far along. I got eighteen months, maybe less. And the end's gonna be ugly. She's ten years younger than I am and pretty as hell. What if she doesn't want to sit around spooning baby food into a vegetable?"

"Pardon me for saying this to a guy who's sick, but, Bert, you're a fucking jerk."

"Huh?"

"Jerk. Capital J, capital E, capital R . . ."

I could see his face flush. "What the fuck's wrong with you? Jesus, I thought you were my friend."

"Bert, she already knows."

He was reeling. "What do you mean, she knows?"

"She came to see me a month ago. Worried sick it was ALS. Couldn't get you to a doctor. Wanted my advice. Jesus Christ, Bert, she's got a computer. All she had to do was type in the symptoms."

He sat back in his seat, his cognac forgotten. Finally, he said, "What did you tell her?"

"Same thing I'm going to tell you. Go home and make love. Hold each other every chance you get. Don't miss a moment together."

Tears started to roll down his cheeks, but they weren't tears of self-pity, they were tears of relief. "Rail . . ."

I held up my hand. "Every minute you spend fumbling around with me is a minute you're not spending with her. Read my lips, go home."

Just then my phone rang. I answered it. "Billy Mack, is that you?" I listened. "How's she look . . . besides scared?"

Billy Mack, the doorman at the Miramar, said that Archer was shaking, so he'd put a blanket around her. That would be the adrenaline wearing off.

"Thanks," I said. "You can do me one more favor. Anybody looks like they're trying to follow her, jot down the license number. Maybe impede their progress a little too, if you can. Thanks, Billy Mack."

I turned back to Bert, who was getting unsteadily to his feet. "I'm taking your advice, Rail. Going home."

When he had trouble going down the stairs, I decided I better walk him to his boat. We didn't talk, just moseyed along, like a couple of guys with nothing but time. The *Once More With Feeling* loomed up over the dock like a small hotel. We shook hands, and Bert got onto the electric lift that would take him up to the deck. A few seconds later, when he stepped off, he looked down and waved.

I waved back and turned away. Of one thing I was sure. It wasn't going to take eighteen months.

With my binoculars, I saw the limo come down Newport Boulevard and turn onto Pacific Coast Highway. A few minutes later, the parking valet was leading Archer down the dock, a blanket draped over her shoulders.

"Permission to come aboard, Captain," she called out.

"Only if you're willing to take a shower. I recall being insulted along those lines once upon a time."

She laughed. "Can't wait. That poor limo driver."

After she'd used up most of the hot water, she slipped into the white terrycloth Dolphin Bay bathrobe the club had sent down along with a basket of women's toiletries and a new pair of snow white Uggs.

As she looked around the salon, she let her eyes linger on some of the more interesting furnishings. "This is Kelly Wearstler, isn't it?"

"That obvious, huh? The broker must have dropped her name thirty times before I finally figured out he wasn't talking about a Dallas wide receiver."

"You're kidding, right?" She shook her head like she couldn't believe anyone could be so obtuse. "Did your broker also happen to mention that something designed by her probably doubles its value?"

"It wasn't that kind of transaction."

She had found a pair of Ray-Bans somewhere and put them on to cover her eye. I thought about the similarities of this arrival with her sister's but didn't say anything. "If you're hungry, there's some leftover Chinese."

"Thanks, but all I really want is a beer."

"Those we have plenty of, and they're icy."

I got her one of the Coronas, and we went up top. She sat next to me in the other captain's chair and sipped her beer.

"So how did it go at the hotel?"

"Do you know that doorman?"

"Who, Billy Mack? No, we've never met, but his accent sounded Samoan."

She held her arms all the way open. "His shoulders must have been a yard across. He saw me shivering and sent some underling for a blanket. And when the limo showed, he almost threw a cabdriver across the lawn to get him out of the way. Then he stood in the middle of the drive, blocking traffic until we turned onto Santa Monica Boulevard. I saw the limo driver hand him an envelope. Just curious, how much?"

"A couple of C-notes."

"Nicely done."

"At your house, did you happen to see any unfamiliar cars?"

"I was a little busy trying to get my heart out of my throat."

"Perfectly natural."

"I did notice one thing, though. One of the guys in my living room was wearing some kind of headband. Red, I think."

"Headband-man," I nodded. That's what I expected.

"You know him?"

"Name's Tino. The other guy is Dante. But that's the extent of my book."

"They had something to do with Kim's death, didn't they?"

"Yes, but they're only a part of it."

She looked off toward the channel. "Gives me a chill. It's like my stepsister and I are finally connected."

Suddenly, I remembered. Mallory. I had been about to call him when Bert had shown up.

He answered on the third ring.

"Sorry if I woke you, Sleeping Beauty."

"I wasn't asleep. Is something the matter?"

I heard another voice behind him. A woman's. Mallory has a Danish girlfriend, Jannicke Thorsen, who's in her fifties and drop-dead stunning. She runs a fur import business, which has earned her a prominent position on PETA's blood-splash list, but she just shrugs and goes on with her life.

Her primary office is in Copenhagen, but when she's in L.A., she stays with us. It's a big house, and I'm glad for Mallory. I also like having her around. She doesn't get jokes, but she's a wonderful conversationalist, and she always brings Danish sausages. None better.

I said to Mallory, "Tell Jannicke I'm thinking about a full-length sable for après shower."

I heard Mallory talking to her. "She says to call her next time you're bathing, and she'll come up and do the measuring herself."

I laughed. "Sorry to interrupt your evening, Don Juan, but I want you to leave the house."

"Tonight?"

"As soon as you can throw a few things in a suitcase."

"May I ask why?"

Suddenly I heard Jannicke's lilting Danish accent. "There it is again."

I said to Mallory, "There's *what* again?"

"We heard a noise out by the gate. I was just on my way outside to check when you called."

I felt a chill run down my spine. I almost shouted, "Don't go outside!"

"What's wrong?"

"Where are you?"

"In the den, playing the new Grand Theft Auto. The graphics are incred . . ."

I cut him off. "Listen to me. Take Jannicke and go upstairs right now. Use the back stairway. And bolt yourself in my bedroom."

"I don't under . . ."

I heard the sound of crashing glass. Then Jannicke screamed. I yelled into the phone, "Mallory!"

Through the open line, there was shouting, then running feet on wooden stairs. Jannicke screamed again. More shouts, then a door slammed, and a loud click. A dead bolt flying home.

"Mallory, are you there?"

He was out of breath, but he answered. "We're here. Who the devil are these people?"

I could hear them beating on the bedroom door.

"How many are there?"

"Two, sir."

From the sound through the phone, Tino and Dante were using something heavy and metal to try to get in. I guessed sabers from the Toledo Room. The door was four inches of solid oak reinforced with steel, but it wasn't impregnable.

"Mallory, listen. The elevator. Go to the garage. How's your driving, Sport?"

"If I take the Morgan, it'll be as good as when I was sixteen."

"Be sure to activate the front gate before you open the garage."

I heard the elevator door close and the motor begin to whir. I said, "The good news is that if they were going to shoot you, they already would have."

"How comforting," Mallory answered as only a British retainer could.

"Get out of L.A. Go to San Diego, San Francisco, Vegas. Park the car in a downtown garage, and take a cab to the airport. Does your sister still live in Florida?"

"Yes, Palm Beach."

"Then go there. Take Jannicke."

"After the last few minutes, I'm not so sure she'll . . ."

I listened as he got into the Morgan and revved it. I heard the garage door slide open. Then shouts, followed by the sound of screeching tires. I got a mental picture of the Englishman hunched over the wheel, Jannicke, beside him, blonde hair flying.

A few moments later, I heard Mallory shout over the wind, "We're out, sir. Haven't had this much excitement in years. And Jannicke says she's never been to Florida."

Just before he clicked off, he said, "And Mr. Black, I don't really think you're a schmuck."

17

State Department on the Pacific

The next morning, Brittany came over to take Archer shopping. Archer had gotten up early and laundered her jogging gear. When she put it back on, it showed off her long, athletic body, and I told her so.

"Thanks," she said. "You don't get that many compliments when you run at night." She pointed to her bad eye behind the Ray-Bans. "I like to keep from scaring kids."

She'd slept in one of the two spare staterooms and looked completely rested. "I never knew I could sleep so soundly."

"Sea air," I said.

"Gotta take a bottle home."

I told Brittany to get Archer whatever she wanted, and we'd settle up later. By the time they left, they were chatting away like they'd known each other all their lives. Another thing women are better at than men.

After Brittany started down the stairs, she stopped and came back. She stood on her tiptoes and pulled my face down to hers. Then she kissed me on the cheek. "Bert told me about your conversation. Thanks, Rail."

"You're welcome."

"He's with a real estate guy right now putting the warehouse on the market. Afterward, we're never going to be apart again." There were tears in her eyes.

I made some phone calls, then went up to the club. I found Emilio Rodeo in the kitchen ordering his underlings around like a Prussian drill sergeant with a Spanish accent. He used to cook at Horchow in Madrid, the survivor of the old Berlin eatery, so Emilio's menu sometimes looks like he can't decide whether to flamenco or invade France. When he saw me, he came over, and we walked into the empty dining room.

"I need some provisions."

"Ingredients or prepared meals?"

"Prepared. I'm dangerous around fire."

"So I've heard. Mallory mentioned you ruined an entire set of cookware trying to make a grilled cheese sandwich. Too bad he didn't get film."

"Good luck to him if he asks for another vacation."

Emilio chuckled. "What do you need?"

"Say, breakfast and lunch for five days. Dinner we can have out."

"How many people?"

"Two."

He smiled. "A little cruise to nowhere?"

"Who knows, maybe we won't leave the dock."

Emilio liked that. "Consider it done. This afternoon okay?"

"Sure."

As I climbed back aboard the boat, my phone rang. It was Benny Joe. "I got your voice mail. The guy you want is Jacques Benveniste. He was born on that fuckin' island you're so interested in. But when I was talkin' to him he called it somethin' else."

"Corse," I offered.

"Yeah, that's it. Corse. What the fuck? Either speak American, or shut the fuck up. Jackie used to be the State Department's organized crime guy in the Med. Smart as they come but not one a them fuckin' Ivy League dorks who tells you where he went to school before you're done shakin' hands. Ole Miss guy. So he won't be lecturin' you about how Karl Fuckin' Marx had some good ideas, but there just aren't enough Harvard PhD's to get the word out. Goes by Jackie. No fuckin' shit, I would too if my parents had laid Jacques on me. Fuckin' frogs."

"Benveniste? Small book. Corsican Jews."

"Whoa, what's that you're always fuckin' preachin' about stereotypin'?"

"You mean like Ivy League dorks? Not the same thing, but nice try. How do I reach him?"

"Happens he's retired some fuckin' place out here. Dana Point. You know it?"

"Just down the road."

"Then get a fuckin' pen."

I parked the silver Escalade I'd rented at the end of the cul-de-sac on Mercator Isle Drive. A sixtyish Jackie Benveniste sporting a salt-and-pepper ponytail opened the door of his gated, 1950s bungalow. He was dressed in yellow swim trunks and a purple Lakers jacket, sleeves pushed up. Jackie was linebacker-sized and going paunchy, but it looked like under the layer of good living, there was still some steel. Peeking out from behind him was a good-sized fawn boxer with four white paws.

"Meet Annie," he smiled. "Seventy pounds of please-love-me."

I bent down and the dog came to me, head down, wriggling everything at once. I scratched her behind the ears, and we were friends for life. Except for Benny Joe's Dobermans, animals and kids always seem to like me. The rest of society . . . spotty.

Jackie said he was just hosing down the back patio, and I followed him and Annie through the house, which was crammed with stuff accumulated from a career spent overseas. Jackie, barefoot, walked with a slight side-to-side motion, which he explained over his shoulder as, "Paratrooper knees and maybe crawling out of one too many bars." I liked the guy immediately.

The back of the house was solid glass, and when we stepped onto the patio, the view of the Pacific was so spectacular that it took me a second before I noticed the small, sunken spa off to the right, where a very buxom, very naked young lady lounged unself-consciously.

"Meet Nancy," Jackie said, and Nancy smiled and waved. "This retirement shit should start when you're seventeen," he said and laughed.

Niguel Shores, a half-moon, terraced cove rising along the Pacific, was once the playground for aerospace engineers working at firms along the Orange Coast. They built their modest weekend retreats on this remote stretch of beach, partied hard and talked shop. In their backyards, over burgers and Pabst and sometimes a little wife-swapping, they planned space missions and invented breakthrough aircraft.

If you were a Soviet spy in those days, the very best duty on the planet was being asked to infiltrate this community of SoCal engineers. It was one of America's finest hours, and one nobody took the time to record.

The few remaining pioneers, now heading into the sunset, have watched their five-thousand-dollar lots appreciate to $3 million or more, which means the biggest thing they have to worry about is wiping up the drool when their heirs come to visit. Some of the homes that have been torn down and replaced reach into eight figures.

Jackie's was one of the unimproved ones. He said it was owned by a Lockheed Skunk Works widow who had recently gone into assisted living but wouldn't let the place be sold until she was dead. "Said she needed to be able to dream about coming home, even if she wasn't going to be able to. You'd fall over if you knew the rent I was paying. She thought I reminded her of her husband."

I looked out at the 180° view of the ocean, broken only by three palm trees further down the hill, and asked if he'd gotten an option to buy.

"On State Department retirement pay? Shit, why break my own heart. I'm just hoping she has a long, happy stay in the home."

He turned off the hose, and we sat in a couple of comfortable deck chairs on either side of a teak table facing the water. Two hundred yards in the distance and seventy-five feet down, breakers thundered against the wide, deserted beach. Annie curled up next to her master and went to sleep. There was an icy pitcher of lemonade on the table, and Jackie poured us each a glass. I took a sip. Good.

"Benny Joe said you need some info. Want me to send Nancy inside?"

I looked over at the young lady, oblivious to us, playing with a water jet. "I don't think she's much of a security risk."

Jackie chuckled. "I sure as hell hope not. No telling what I've said."

I went through everything that had happened, leaving out nothing. When I finished, he pointed to a long one-story house further down the cliff. "See that place?"

I nodded.

"They were on Egypt Air 990. Lifetime dream to see the Pyramids. Everybody says they were wonderful people. Yet here I sit, a guy with no right to be alive, enjoying the view they should be. No fuckin' order in the universe."

"Marcus Aurelius would say you're here because you're supposed to be."

"Then let's go with Mr. Aurelius." He laughed. "Benny Joe tell you I was born on Corse, and I'm a hard case?"

"Pisses him off you don't say Corsica."

"I can go either way on that, but I like jerking his chain. Where do you want to start?"

"I've visited a couple of times, and it didn't seem like a hotbed of Jewish culture."

"That's an understatement. A hundred families and one

synagogue on the whole fuckin' island, and not one grave-stone that doesn't have a swastika painted on it. There've been Jews there since the beginning of recorded history, and through most of it, somebody's been trying to run us out. My, but we are a stubborn people."

"Lot of ignorance in the world."

"Fuckin-A. That's State Department talk for, 'If I didn't get weekends off, I'd cash out.' "

A phone rang in the house, and Jackie held up his hand so he could listen to the message machine. It was somebody named Doris inviting him and Nancy for drinks and hors d'oeuvres at seven.

"Nance, you want to go over there and get groped by that dame's husband again?"

"Sure, why not. Long as I come home with you. You love those little shrimp things they serve," she called back cheerily.

Jackie looked back at me. "Is this fuckin' great or what?"

I was happy for the guy.

"Okay," he said, "let me give you in a few sentences what it takes diplomats and presidents years to figure out. On Corsica, whether it's separatists, terrorists, nationalists, revolutionaries . . . whatever . . . sooner or later everything intersects with the Mafia. Not the fat guys at the big tables on Mott Street in Manhattan. They're dangerous, but they're one-at-a-time killers. Corsica's run by the originals, the Si-cilians. Guys who a lot of times can't get on the same page long enough to steal because they're too busy whacking cops, mayors, prosecutors and each other. As many as pos-sible, as often as possible. Those of us who made our living keeping track of them used to say that 'Go along, get along' can't even be translated into Sicilian."

"Who runs the show?"

Jackie poured himself another glass of lemonade.

"Guy by the name of Gaetano Bruzzi. They call him *Il Iena Bianco*."

" 'The White Hyena'?"

He nodded. "Huge fucking guy. Long mane of curly white hair. Not old man's hair. Just white. And a mouthful of over-sized teeth that push back his lips in a perpetual grin. Like those Chupacabra pictures that scare the shit out of Mexicans. If you hung Bruzzi's mug shot at the border you'd probably end illegal immigration."

I thought back to Marta Videz. A very tall, very *anchuro* man. Long white hair. *Much teeth.*

Jackie continued, "And just like Chupie, when he bites, it's for keeps—in more ways than one. A few years ago, one of his crew smuggled in a pair of hyenas for his birthday—real ones. Bruzzi thought it was the best gift he'd ever gotten. Just the idea of it gave people the shits."

"If that catches on, what'll we do with all the unemployed Rottweilers?"

Jackie laughed. "The guy had some regrets, though. Bruzzi caught him with his hand in the till. Tied a couple of dead chickens around his neck and put him out with his gift. Told him to see how fast he could run. The answer was, not very."

"Hyenas can really fuck up an apartment, so where does Ghandi of the Med live?"

"Ghandi of the Med. You woulda fit right in at State. We liked to put shit like that in open cables to drive the political guys crazy. He's got five thousand acres of vineyards up near Apollonica. North of Bonifacio. Rumor has it he's added more hyenas too. Probably up to a pack now, though I think officially it's called a cackle."

"You're kidding. The guy's a vintner?"

"He'll tell you he makes the best wines on the island. But that's on the Bruzzi scale. There is some okay stuff around, but it's on the west coast. Bruzzi's . . . well, you can wash your feet in it. But that doesn't keep restaurants from stocking it once they consider the alternative."

"Hyenas," I said. "The gift that keeps on giving." I thought I knew the answer to my next question, but I asked it anyway. "Would it be unusual for him to be in the United States?"

"Never happen."

"Why?"

"First off, even though Bruzzi loves a party, and let's face it, Corsica isn't on anybody's hot list, he never leaves Europe. Doesn't trust his lieutenants enough to be too far away. He also knows that if we got our hands on him, we'd take him someplace nice and quiet and waterboard him until his asshole bled. And after we'd drained him dry of intelligence, we'd forget where we put the key."

"But if he *was* here?"

"Money. That's the only reason. Colossal money."

"Sorry," I said, "I interrupted your class on Corsica."

He chuckled. "So you did. The white headband, or *tortil*, is associated with the FLNC, an organization that officially began in the 1970s but whose roots go back to the thirteenth century. It's one of dozens of quasi-political factions that merge, reorganize, splinter, sometimes even disappear for years—but always come back.

"A red *tortil* and a spider tattoo identify members of Les Executeurs, a group of criminals known as much for their violence as their politics. They imprint their made members with the head and body of a local black widow, *U Malmignattu*, nicknamed the Bonifacio Executioner. Then the guy gets to add a leg every time he kills."

"Manhood," I said. "Who wants to walk around sporting a legless Executioner."

"You're more right than you know. Les Executeurs' motto is 'Corsica for Corsicans,' but since nobody really knows what a Corsican is, it gets confusing. Mostly, what they really mean is everybody on the mainland should die and everybody in Paris should die twice—which doesn't exactly make them unique. Half of Washington feels the same way. If Napoleon hadn't been born there, the French would have cut the place loose years ago. Basically, it's Chechnya with better weather."

"Putting Bruzzi aside, can you think of a reason any of these guys would be in Los Angeles?" I asked.

"I've been out of the loop. But whatever a Corsican's political jones is, he's still got to make a living and do some avenging whenever possible. And if he's not into waiting tables, that means working for the Sicilians. So it could be drugs, could be a three-hundred-year-old vendetta, could be a disagreement over a pack of Chiclets. To those murderous, superstitious fucks, it's all the same. If it moves, kill it. My guess is, though, that it's a onetime thing. Do the job, go home. They're not world travelers."

"You said superstitious? About what?"

"Neither of us has enough years left to get through the list. Let's just say they're like gypsies on acid. You say Tino likes knives?"

"And he's no rookie."

"Hey, Nance, you know that box in my study, on the shelf next to the *Culinaria* books? Can you get it for me, please."

"Sure, Jackie." Nancy got out of the spa, and she was a vision. "I'm going to get a beer while I'm in there. Either of you want one?"

We didn't, and she went in the house. A minute or so later, she was back with a bottle of Sierra Nevada and an eighteen-inch-long, polished wood box with a crest on it. She set it on the table and went back to the spa.

Jackie pointed to the crest, a gold shield bracketed by a pair of mother-of-pearl cherubs. And in the center was a left-facing, black enamel head wearing a white *tortil*. Sort of an edgy cameo. Jackie pointed. "*Testa di Moru*, the Moor's Head. You see it everywhere on the island, even on the flag."

I picked up the box. It was a little like looking at Tino, just darker.

Jackie went on. "There's considerable debate about why it's black. The usual answer is that it symbolizes rebellious slaves or medieval African soldiers, sometimes referred to as Moors. But since there's no consensus on exactly what a Moor was, and versions of the head are found on coats of arms throughout Europe, it's a mystery without a solution. The face is usually depicted with features atypical to Africans, so I think it's entirely possible an artist somewhere along the line intentionally made it dark to showcase the *tortil* . . . which is as good an answer as any."

Jackie opened the box and turned it toward me. Inside, in green velvet, lay a foot-long knife with a gently curved blade very similar to the one Tino had flashed at me on the freeway. The handle on this one was ivory, and there was no question that the blade was razor sharp.

"Beautiful workmanship," I said.

"Some people think they make the best knives in the world. And since the French won't let a Corsican anywhere near a gun, the kids there grow up handling them as naturally as an American teenager with a Nintendo."

As I picked up the knife, I remembered Walter Kempthorn. The balance was perfect. Even though Delta training includes knives, I wasn't a fan. If you're that close to an enemy, something has already gone wrong. And knives aren't efficient. Unless you make a perfect cut in one of a very few places, it takes a long time and a lot of wounds to just slow someone down, let alone kill them.

Most professionals I know feel the same way, but there are a few who walk a different road. They almost always do so in life as well. Loners. There's something about a guy who likes knives that subconsciously tells other people to keep their distance.

Jackie must have been reading my mind. "A Corsican doesn't stick his enemy. He slices at muscles, tendons, ears, anything that will terrorize. Sometimes they purposely leave victims dying, but alive . . . let them bleed out thinking about it. The rule is, if you come across a Corsican with a knife, shoot him. If you can't do that, get the hell away, fast."

Suddenly, Annie bolted out of her sleep and ran over to the edge of the patio, putting her head over the short wall, snarling and barking. Jackie and I leaned forward and looked down. Thirty feet below us, on another cul-de-sac, a golden retriever was prancing along beside his owner, oblivious.

Nancy called out, "Bet it's the retriever."

Jackie yelled back, "Yep." To me, he said, "For some reason, she can't stand retrievers. But then, she's German, so there doesn't have to be logic involved."

I stood up, and after saying good-bye to Nancy, Jackie walked me around the side of the house. Annie darted ahead of us. At the gate, I said, "Since you didn't say anything when I mentioned it, I gather City of War doesn't ring any bells."

Jackie shook his head. "I was thinking about it while we talked. Never heard that one before."

I told him I was going to invite him up to the yacht club for a sunset cruise one of these days.

"You're on," he said. "I'll see if we can dig up some clothes for Nance. And come back if you need anything else. Just call first," he winked. "At this age, I'm unpredictable."

When I got back to the boat, Archer and Brittany were playing Buddy Holly at eardrum-piercing level, laughing, dancing and trying on clothes. Boxes and shopping bags were strewn everywhere, and I saw that Archer had gotten her hair done so that it swept over her right eye again. She still wore my Ray-Bans though.

She saw me eyeing the mess and shouted. "That's the problem with working in the fashion industry, you're never shopped out. By the way, three guys came by with a cart and loaded a bunch of food in both refrigerators. You having a party?"

I turned down the music and said, "I thought we might take a run down the coast. Get you out of circulation for a while."

"How long?"

"Till we get bored."

"Just the two of us?"

"That a problem?"

"No, but how am I going to show off my new clothes?"

"When the mood strikes, we'll hit some restaurants."

"Terrific. This morning, I called a neighbor and asked him

to check on the house. Everything's fine. The doors were even locked. I'll call back and ask him to keep an eye on the place. He's home a lot because he's got a bum knee."

Gary, I thought. He'd already been around to see Archer. He'd be really happy to know I was involved again. "Just don't tell him where you are," I said.

As Brittany left, she turned to me, winked and gave a thumbs-up.

18

Doritos and Buffalos

As I was preparing to move the *Sanrevelle* out of her slip, I asked Archer, "You know anything about boats?"

She pointed to the bow. "That's the front."

I rolled my eyes exaggeratedly. "Okay, your job is to watch the stern—that's the other front—and sing out if you see anything coming."

"Cool."

"*Cool* is not a nautical term."

"It is now."

We left the harbor and rode out into a calm sea. Sunset was still an hour away, but the light was already playing tricks on the water, and a pair of pelicans was making runs at something just below the surface. It was a marvelous night to be alive.

Archer brought us a couple of beers, and we sat in the captain's chairs and enjoyed the ride. No conversation necessary. Half an hour later, I made a long, gentle turn to the south. The sun was now dead ahead, and it was so large and red that it didn't seem real.

"I can't believe how beautiful this is," said Archer. "I

haven't felt this good in more years than I care to count. Thanks, Rail. I really mean it, thanks."

"None necessary. It's always a better experience shared."

She reached over and put her hand in mine. "Do you mind? I just want to touch someone for a while."

I didn't, and we rode that way for a long time.

It had been dark for an hour when Archer went below. A few minutes later, she returned with two Serrano ham sandwiches on hard-crusted Spanish bread, dressed up with Mahon cheese, portobellos, arugula and fresh tomatoes. Archer had drizzled on the olive oil and balsamic vinegar that Emilio had packed separately. On the side was a large bag of Cool Ranch Doritos, which I'm a sucker for, and some of the best guacamole this side of Guadalajara. He'd also sent along a bottle of '98 Capçanes Cabrida to wash everything down.

"Forget eating out. This is unbelievable," she said with her mouth full and guac running down her chin.

"Emilio knows his hungry girls."

"And his Doritos. I think in some places they'd throw you in the slammer for mixing cultures like this."

Just after 10:30, I turned the *Sanrevelle* slightly westward and ran straight out to sea for a while. Then I eased her ever so gently north.

A few minutes later, I saw Archer looking at the compass. "I don't know much about boats, but where I come from, 'down the coast' means south."

"I thought it might be better if no one knew where we were. I've been watching for anyone following us, but with some pretty ordinary tech, they could be laying just over the horizon, and I wouldn't know it."

"Captain, whatever you do is okay with me. I never want to see land again."

We were off the West End light when I turned southeast on the backside of Catalina. This late, I didn't expect much traffic, and, in fact, there was none. I ran along the island's windward side for ten miles, counting only five campfires onshore and a dozen lights at anchor at Parson's Landing. Everything else was dark.

I brought the *Sanrevelle* around again and ran at five knots northwest, scanning the horizon for another vessel making the same maneuver. Other than a line of cargo ships in the distance, I saw nothing.

The cove I was looking for was nearly empty, the water perfectly calm. I couldn't have asked for a better welcome. The only other occupants were two small sailboats lying next to each other, both dark except for running lights.

I eased the *Sanrevelle* in, staying two hundred yards from the sails. When I read our depth at forty feet, I cut the engines and let her drift until I'd halved that, then went forward and winched the bower anchor down. It caught immediately, and we gently swung around ten degrees and held. I stood for a moment and watched for dragging, but there was none. We were in for the night.

It took me half an hour to tuck us completely in, and when I finished, Archer was lying on a sofa in the darkened salon watching television. I sat down next to her. She seemed completely at ease.

"Where are we?" she asked.

"Last Tycoon Cove. On the windward side of the island."

"Interesting name."

"F. Scott is supposed to have written some of his final novel sitting out here on Louis B. Mayer's yacht. But I don't believe it."

"Why's that?"

"You can only get so much booze on a boat, and there isn't a bar in sight."

She started to laugh, but it turned into a yawn.

"Why don't you turn in," I said.

"Because I'm so damned comfortable."

"Well, you wouldn't be the first one to spend the night right where you are."

"Was Kim . . . ?"

"I thought I explained. Kim was never on the boat."

"You did. I just keep trying to . . . you know . . ."

I did know. People who've been parted by sudden death—especially estranged ones—want to reconnect. They go to the same places, drive the other person's car, sometimes sleep in their beds. They want to see ordinary things through their loved one's—or not so loved one's—eyes. To try to imagine what they might have been thinking at a particular time. And every once in a while something special occurs. It's why I put more faith in the perceptions of lovers and family members than I do in psychics. If they let themselves, sometimes those who were closest feel things others can't.

I noticed that Archer's breathing had become deep and regular. I got a blanket, covered her and turned off the television.

I was tired too, but I had some calls to make.

When I awoke, the sun was well up, and Archer was swimming. Her eye was uncovered, and she seemed not to be self-conscious at all.

"Not a good idea unless you tell someone," I called out over the rail.

"If there's a shark around, I'll just wish him a good morning. How can you not love a day like this?"

"Mostly, it's about getting a cramp."

"Oh, please, other than from your parents, when was the last time you heard of anyone drowning from a cramp? Especially in weather like this."

I had to admit, it was California at its best. Warm sun, no clouds.

"Come on in," she shouted. "Work up an appetite for that sumptuous breakfast I'm going to unwrap."

I looked at her, but it wasn't Archer any longer.

Sanrevelle was waving, holding up a large piece of pink coral as she snorkeled off the stern. Damn it, I thought, how many times had I told her not to go out there alone. Especially not now. Hadn't she been listening when the doctor told her not to take unnecessary risks? That her mother had miscarried twice before giving birth to her?

But Sanrevelle never listened to anyone. She just smiled and tossed her head and did whatever she wanted. It was maddening sometimes, but it was also one of the things I loved most about her. Like the jaguars in her native Brazil, she couldn't be tamed, and I was now the second generation of Black men unable to resist a Carioca wild streak.

I turned, looking for one of the crew to relay a message to Captain Long that I was going in with her, but I didn't see anyone. I motioned for Sanrevelle to get closer to the boat. Though the beach of Clarissima lay only half a mile away, we had seen barracuda yesterday, and they have a habit of lying in ambush, then swooping in to tear off a piece of flesh.

At 235 feet, my father's ship, the Amarante, was still magnificent, but it was getting long in the tooth. Wildly expensive to operate, it had been an extravagance Lord Black could not bring himself to give up, using her to cross to England twice a year and holding board meetings aboard to defray some of the cost. With his death, I had kept her, more out of loyalty to the crew than for any practical reason.

I climbed two flights and went forward through the center passageway. My table in the owner's dining room was half set for lunch, but none of the four stewards was in sight. I had pared the permanent crew from thirty to seventeen, but even so, it was strange not to see someone, even a deckhand going about his business.

I crossed the dining room and looked into the galley. The chef lay on the floor, eyes open but seeing nothing, a bullet hole in his chest. I left and ran forward.

As I passed a guest stateroom, I heard a muffled cry. I tried the door. Locked. Using my master key, I entered and found a steward on his knees, moaning, his hands pressed against his scalp, blood running between his fingers. The other four stewards lay facedown beside him, dead, a single bullet hole in the back of each man's head.

"Holden," hissed the wounded steward, "and Quinn."

Tony Holden was the ship's engineer. He'd been with us less than a month, hired on an emergency basis by Captain Long after our longtime engineer had taken ill and returned home to Glasgow. Norris Quinn, Holden's cousin, had come aboard as a deckhand. We hadn't needed him, but we couldn't sail without an engineer, and it had been a package deal.

I got the steward a towel for his head and headed for the bridge, remembering what I could about Holden and Quinn. Long had hired them through our London crew broker, Oceania Personnel, but the men had said they had come directly from holiday in Greece and weren't carrying their engineer and seaman's certificates. Technically, this made it illegal to have them aboard as crew, but when faxed copies of the certificates arrived from Oceania, Long accepted them pending arrival of the originals from the men's homes in Liverpool.

But the promised courier never came, and Long had finally confronted the men and told them that if they did not produce the certificates by the end of the week, they would have to leave the ship. That had been yesterday.

Just outside the wheelhouse, I found the first mate. He had obviously struggled with his attackers, because there was blood splattered along a wide stretch of deck. But he had eventually succumbed to several shots in the upper body.

Since I had been in my quarters and heard nothing, the weapons were almost certainly fitted with suppressors. But what the hell was happening? And who were Holden and Quinn?

I feared what I was going to find when I opened the door to the wheelhouse, but it was worse. Three bodies. Captain Long was dead in his chair, shot once in the back of the head, and the second and third mates had been gunned down over the navigation table. I felt under the control con-

sole for the Glock Long kept there. I found it and checked the magazine. Full.

There was a loud scraping sound above. I ran outside, leaned over the port railing and craned my neck upward. Suddenly, a jet ski fell out of the sky, coming within inches of taking me out. It hit the water with a tremendous splash, and the scraping sound began again. Moments later, a second jet ski followed. Then two men came hurtling down after them.

Holden and Quinn in wet suits. I aimed and squeezed off two quick shots at each man. A hole opened in Quinn's wet suit, but both men managed to drag themselves aboard their jet skis, then pull handguns and open fire on me.

Splinters from the railing kicked up, and bullets ricocheted off the ship's superstructure. Miraculously, I wasn't hit. I heard the jet skis scream to life and watched as they accelerated quickly out of range. But instead of fleeing toward land, they headed out to sea.

I scanned the water and saw another boat two miles further out, turning and coming to meet them. It was an old trawler, painted gray and with no markings.

Sanrevelle!

I ran back through the ship at breakneck speed, leaping down to the afterdeck. She was swimming toward the ship. When I reached the transom, she was only three feet away. I extended my arm . . . felt her hand go into mine . . .

And the Amarante *exploded.*

"So are you coming in or not?" Archer shouted.
I had sweated through my shirt and cutoffs. Whitened knuckles gripped the brass railing, my palms as slippery as if they had been greased. Somehow, I managed to leverage myself up and over, knowing the water would soon rush up to meet me.

And like that morning so long ago, it seemed to take forever.

* * *

After a shower, I came into the salon, putting on a sport coat over my jeans.

"You going somewhere?" Archer asked.

"Not me. *We*. I've got a meeting up the coast, and afterward, we'll find a nice little clam house, knock back a couple of brews and gorge ourselves on chowder."

"Not a chance, buster. It's a 5-Star day, and I'm sitting on a yacht off what might as well be my own private island. And if I want a beer, all I have to do is walk ten steps to the refrig. I wouldn't leave here on a bet."

"I'm sorry, but it's too dangerous for you to be here by yourself."

"Come here," she said, and she went out on the forward deck and waved her arm in a circle. "Look around. You see anything ready to jump out and get me? Relax, Rail, you've done an incredible job. The only person who knows where we are is maybe God, and if He were a blabbermouth, He'd have slipped me the lottery numbers a long time ago. I sure as hell asked often enough."

I had to admit it was peaceful, and she was probably right. The chances anyone knew where we were, were remote. I relented, but not all the way.

An hour later, we heard the deep-throated rumble of a pair of racing engines running at high speed. "That'll be Eddie," I said.

Archer followed me out on deck. Eddie Buffalo and his petite Asian wife, Liz, were waving from the cockpit of *Zydeco*, Eddie's fifty-one-foot Outerlimits GTX. The orange flames on the black superstructure made the racing yacht seem fast even at considerably less than its 160-mph top end. Another man rode with them—tall, tapered and heavily muscled. Despite the setting and the weather, he was dressed in black jeans and a black leather jacket. He did not wave.

"Wow," said Archer, putting her hands over her ears, "that thing sounds like a rocket."

Just then Eddie cut the engines to idle and drifted *Zydeco* in. When he got astern of us, he threw two fenders over the side and eased close until the boats touched. Liz stepped up and onto the *Sanrevelle*'s transom with the grace of someone who'd spent her life around boats. As soon as she hit the deck, she dropped the overnight bag she was carrying, ran to me, threw her arms around my shoulders and kissed me with vigor. I felt a stab of pain as she jammed my ribs but managed not to wince too badly.

"God, Rail, we were so worried about you. And then Mallory told us not to come to the hospital. Are you okay?"

I held her away from me and said with a smile, "Getting there."

Liz turned to Archer. "You must be Archer. Well, you're just as pretty as Rail said you were."

I rolled my eyes, but I saw Archer flush. I was afraid she was going to cry, but she got a grip on herself. Smart-ass tough but fragile, I thought. Need to pay attention.

For the first time, Archer took note of the leather-jacketed man. He'd also come aboard, and now he unzipped the jacket and slipped it off, revealing a shoulder holster over a black T-shirt that barely contained his massive upper arms. Archer took a step back and looked at me.

"Morning, Mr. Black," he said in Cajun-accented English.

"Morning, Jimmy."

"Archer, this is Jimmy Buffalo. He'll be staying with you and Liz."

"Good morning, Miss . . ."

"You can call me Archer."

Jimmy smiled. "Fine. Morning, Miss Archer."

Archer opened her mouth to say something, then decided not to. To me she said, "Is this really necessary?"

"No," I said, "you can still go with me."

She turned on her heel and said to Liz, "I hope you brought your swimsuit, the water's fantastic."

I said, "We'll be back in time to take everyone to the trendiest restaurant on the island."

"That better be a promise," laughed Liz. "Usually, I can't get anything but burgers and beans out of Mr. Stay-at-Home."

I wasn't nearly as graceful getting into Eddie's boat as Liz had been getting out, but I managed to avoid going in the drink. I looked up at Jimmy standing over us and said, "Nobody comes aboard. No exceptions."

"Yes, sir, Mr. Black."

As Eddie revved the engines, I called out to the two women, "There's plenty of food and some DVDs in the cabinet next to the television."

Liz laughed. "Are you kidding? We're girls. We're gonna talk. Then we're gonna talk some more. I've gotta get her caught up on all your faults."

I shook my head, and Eddie lumbered the GTX out of the cove, then opened it up before I was ready. "Goddamn it, Eddie," I yelled as I banged into the seat.

Eddie laughed and gave it more gas.

Unlike my reluctance to buy a large boat, a big plane became a necessity. But this time, I didn't get a deal. Full retail and the price of four Ferraris to finish it out.

I had tried fractional ownership, but after getting a couple of planes where the previous users had left behind an odor best left undescribed and a Lear that the pilot told me he'd rather not take up because of skipped maintenance, I realized that just because somebody has money doesn't mean he's any more conscionable than a slum lord.

So I bought Jake Praxis's old Gulfstream when he upgraded. A first-rate plane with excellent technology, but I still got tired of ducking every time I stood up. Imagine walking with your head down for ten hours.

Eventually, I swallowed hard and bought a Boeing BBJ3, which is a 737-900ER configured for private use. There are fewer than a hundred in service, and I was lucky to get mine. Somebody on the waiting list died, and my check got to Boeing first.

After my first flight, I wondered why I'd ever flown anything else. With the main cabin outfitted like a plush living room and the stateroom expanded to accommodate a mammoth bed and an extra-large walk-in shower, it was as comfortable as a New York penthouse. And since most commercial airports have at least a passable level of security for hire, if I put down someplace primitive or dangerous, I use it as my office and hotel as well.

Eddie Buffalo didn't quite come with the plane, but I hired him the day I bought it and charged him with overseeing its fitting-out and shakedown. I'd known Eddie marginally, seen him fly at some air shows and knew he was considered one of the best pilots around. But also a handful. One of the guys he used to fly for told me he'd never felt safer with any other pilot, but he couldn't stand dealing with Eddie, the person. He said that he was such a control freak that he used to tell everyone onboard where to sit, and that once he refused to take off unless a fat guy got off. Said that in case of an emergency, he wasn't going to burn trying to pry the guy out of his seat.

Eddie's real name is Bufreaux, but that got corrupted to Buffalo early on, and he went with it. He's a New Orleans boy whose family runs a major portion of the waterfront. But Eddie didn't give two hoots about long tons and long-shoremen. His dream was to fly, and he was in a cockpit at nine and had his license by fifteen. Then he got himself a scholarship to Embry-Riddle and graduated at the top of his class.

His problems began after he completed his probationary period at United and refused to join the union. He told the rep that his Uncle Donald had been the business manager for three unions and stolen so much money his nickname was "Donny Dues." Eddie said he'd be goddamned if he was going to hand over part of his paycheck to some thief he didn't know just so he could keep his job. And that if the union didn't want to represent him, fine, don't. I think he might have thrown a "fuck you" or two in there as well.

They were going to bounce his ass then and there, but Eddie made a call, and somebody in his family who knew the secret handshake called another somebody way up in the pilots' union food chain, and Eddie stayed. But even if they had to let him work, they didn't have to like him, and most pilots wouldn't get in the cockpit with a guy they called a scab. That made fielding a two-man crew almost impossible, so mostly, Eddie got paid for playing golf. He kept his hours up by moonlighting for a Mexican freight company, then said fuck it and went private.

None of Eddie's idiosyncrasies bothered me. In the first place, I rarely fly with anyone else onboard, and I told Eddie that if he wanted to tell them where to sit during takeoff and landing, no problem. But after that, he was out of the loop. And if he ever tried to tell a guest to get off my plane—for any reason—I'd knock him on his ass, then fire him. And since I was paying him twice the going rate, I figured I had that right. He agreed, and we've never had a problem.

Jimmy's a different story. He's Eddie's brother, and he keeps bouncing between New Orleans and L.A. When he first showed up, Eddie wanted me to put a word in for him with some of my Hollywood friends, so I had Jake do a background check. When it came back, Jake had rolled his eyes but said that Jimmy wasn't wanted by the law. So as far as I was concerned, if he'd had some scrapes on the Big Easy docks, they weren't relevant.

Jimmy freelances around town doing security on movie productions and once in a while shows up on-screen as an extra. I use him for the occasional odd job and have never found him to be anything but loyal and competent. Plus Eddie knows it's his ass if his brother screws up.

So once again, no problems.

19

Bad Asses and a RIFALO

Pelican Bay State Prison's warden, John Z. Kelly, looked me up and down. He reminded me of Vince Lombardi without the warmth. His landmark isn't on any tourist board list of California's wonders. Tucked into the state's northwest corner, far from anything or anybody, it's a powder keg filled with the worst of the worst, and it explodes every now and then without the outside world ever hearing about it.

You want to hire somebody tough, forget the bullshit ads in *Soldier of Fortune*. Recruit a Pelican Bay guard. They're called corrections officers, but in a Supermax, there isn't any correcting going on. It's warehousing only, and it's a high-tension and deadly business.

The first thing I noticed was the smell. Jake Praxis calls it piss and punishment, and in my opinion, the punishment part's stronger. Warden Kelly made it clear he didn't like guys like me showing up to talk to guys like Reynaldo "Twenty-Two" Cruz, leader of Los Tigres. Even though I'd cleared the background checks, he was convinced Cruz was going to use me to ferry a message to his underlings on the outside. And there was nothing I could say that was going to change his mind, so I didn't try.

"You've got half an hour," he said. "And there'll be someone listening to every word. Step out of line, and they'll slap a pair of cuffs on you, and you can leave here in a squad car. Understand?"

I stood up and turned to leave.

"Where you going?" he growled.

I turned back to him. "That wasn't the arrangement. So I'll come back with my attorney and Cruz's."

He looked at me with cold contempt.

"Who the fuck do you think you are?"

"Just a citizen with a visitation agreement. I've got no agenda with you, Warden, but I do have to see Cruz. The half hour is fine, but in private. I'm not trying to change anything; you are."

He snorted and called out to his secretary. "Have the captain come up."

Sometimes stereotypes don't do an individual justice. In this case, they were dead-on. "Twenty-Two" Cruz wasn't big, maybe 5-7 and 160 pounds, but he exuded danger. He was dressed in a pair of orange prison pants and a white T-shirt, but I could see enough tattoos running down his arms and up his neck to picture what the rest of him looked like.

It was a noisy entrance. Cruz was being escorted by four guards dressed in riot gear, and they'd already been into it. I saw spit on the Plexiglas face masks of two of them. Reynaldo was in leg and arm restraints, and one of the guards walked behind him with a huge paw gripping his neck.

Cruz was motherfucking them all the way and hurling out a string of Spanish invective that at least one of the guards must have understood because he suddenly jabbed his baton into Cruz's ribs hard enough to get a gasp.

The visiting attorney's room wasn't like the movies. It was a fifteen-foot-square wooden box with one-way glass on all four sides sitting in the middle of a steel-barred cage. The roof-mounted air conditioner alternately hummed and groaned.

The metal table and four chairs were welded to struts

poured into the concrete floor. Jake said that they used to use bolts to hold things down, but some choirboy had managed to get a chair loose somehow and beat his attorney into critical condition before the guards got to them.

There was a two-inch steel eye formed into the tabletop and two more protruding from the floor on either side of his chair. The guards locked the gang leader's leg shackles into the eyes on the floor, during which Cruz made it as difficult as possible for them, and got a rap in the head for his trouble.

When they were finished, the leader of the guard team, breathing heavily, looked at me. It wasn't easy to see through his spit-covered and scratched face shield, but I got the feeling he wasn't excited about having to wrestle this guy around, and he wanted me to know it.

He pointed to the steel eye on the tabletop. "You gonna want him to look at any papers? If so, I'll put his hands up there. Otherwise, he stays in the shackles."

I shook my head, and the four guards left.

Cruz and I stared at each other. Now that the guards were gone, his expression was one of casual indifference. I sensed no anger or tension. He didn't have to show the flag with me.

In Mexican-accented Spanish, he made a couple of remarks about the incompetence of his lawyer, which I answered by telling him I'd never met the man. He smiled, and I realized he had been testing my linguistic ability. I also saw why he was a leader. He had that same combination of charisma and command you find in the best generals and the most effective presidents. And he knew it.

"So do we do this in English or Spanish?" I asked.

"What the fuck do you want?" he answered in English. "All that cocksucker lawyer of mine, who can't get me the fuck out of isolation, said was that it was in my fuckin' interest to see you. But I don't fuckin' see how."

There wasn't even a trace of an accent, so there was a lot more going on inside Mr. Cruz than he wanted the outside world to know.

"I'm here because I think I can do something for your son."

I saw his eyes change. "My son? Arcadio?"

I nodded. "Yes, Arcadio."

Suddenly, his voice dropped. "He is named for my grandfather. A simple farmer from Chiapas. One day, the government gave his land to another man. A very rich man who was a friend of the vice president. And when my grandfather complained, the police came and took him away. Nobody ever saw him again. Fuck the fuckin' police. All of them." Cruz paused. "Okay," he said. "For Arcadio, I will listen."

I laid out what I wanted. It didn't take long. When I finished, Cruz didn't say anything for a moment.

Then, "This kid . . . Kiki Videz . . . he was just an associate . . . and a pussy. He would never have made full member. And Los Tigres don't cut off arms. We fuck you up when you're alive, but once you're dead, that's it. Who the fuck do these cops think they are, makin' this shit up?"

I waited to see if he had any more in his system. He didn't.

His voice was calm now. Businesslike. "So let me get this straight. My lawyer says you're gonna do somethin' to Los Tigres, but you don't want me to do nothin' back."

"No, you have to actively not do something. There's a difference. Some of your people aren't going to understand and might want to try to impress you."

"So I've gotta make sure somebody stupid doesn't do somethin' stupid."

"Correct. And you're not going to be able to tell them why. They either won't understand, or they'll talk or both."

"What makes you think I can control people from this place? I don't even have a fuckin' window."

I just looked at him.

Finally, he said, "And for all this doin' nothing, what happens?"

I gestured at the walls. "Do you want this for Arcadio?"

He bristled. "I am a man of respect."

"True. That's why I'm here. But is this the life you dream

for a four-year-old whose favorite things are teddy bears and cherry Jell-O?"

Cruz looked away. My words had hit him harder than I'd expected. Now he was remembering. Maybe he was holding Arcadio. Maybe walking with his grandfather. You could cut the irony with a knife. This man who had deprived countless others of their sons and brothers and fathers was thinking about his own blood. I disliked even breathing the same air, but it wasn't about me.

Bearing down with a pair of cold, deadly eyes, he said, "And you will give me your word, that this plan of yours is just a fuckin' act? That as soon as you get what you want from the cops you'll stop?"

"I've got to find someone, and I need the police to do it. But I've got to have leverage. Other than that, I have zero interest in Los Tigres."

I watched as his face softened. Suddenly, he was no longer Twenty-Two Cruz, murderer. He was Reynaldo Cruz, father.

"What can you do for Arcadio?"

I told him about Sister Vonetta and the St. Regis School. When I was finished, he said, "And you will promise to put him there . . . to watch over him?"

"Yes, but that's not enough. For him to have a chance—a real chance—he and his mother have to move away from the influence of the neighborhood . . . and Los Tigres. And Arcadio has to hear his father tell him it's the right thing to do. I can handle the first part, but only you can make it happen where it counts—in his heart."

He looked into my eyes. "How soon?" he asked.

"As soon as you tell me."

He didn't even blink. "Now," he answered.

As Eddie and his first officer, Jody Miller, put the black-and-red plane down at LAX and began the long taxi to the General Aviation Terminal, I checked the cabin clock. It was going on 6:00.

When we stopped, Jody came back, opened the door and lowered the steps. "Eddie said to ask if you're going to be needing me any more this week, Mr. Black. I'd like to take a run up to Tahoe and spend a few days with my mom."

"How's she doing?"

"Well, if she doesn't stop winning at blackjack, the Cal Neva's gonna put her name in the book with the card counters."

I laughed. "Don't discourage her. Someday you might want to upgrade that old Stearman you're flying. Maybe get something with a roof."

"Never," said Jody.

I stepped onto the tarmac and told Eddie I'd meet him at the heliport in an hour. "Figure forty minutes back to Catalina and to pick up your boat, then a half-hour run to Last Tycoon. That should still give us time to grab a shower and make a nine thirty dinner."

"Where we eating?"

"Titanium."

Eddie rolled his eyes.

"I know, I know," I said, "but I promised Archer a first-class dinner, so get on the horn with that pain-in-the ass Bernard, and let him know we're coming. And when he goes into his song and dance about closing the kitchen at ten—which he will—tell him I'll pick up the chef's overtime, but I don't want to be rushed."

Eddie shook his head. "You'd figure a guy in a service business would want to accommodate his customers. But not that asshole. He spends more time telling people why they can't come to his joint than he does taking reservations. You know, he put me and Liz on the bar once for an hour, and the fuckin' place was empty? I almost punched him in his snotty little face."

"Yeah, but then you started thinking about his tuna tartar."

Eddie chuckled without mirth. "I just hate it that I love the shit he serves. But all kidding aside, telling him you'll pay extra to keep the kitchen open is like handing that cocksucker a license to pad the bill for a week's worth of over-head. And the chef won't see a fucking dime."

"You're right. Tell him anyway, and when we get there, I'll make my own deal with the kitchen."

"Much wiser, amigo."

The late afternoon glare across the bar at Encounter was particularly unpleasant. I dislike the place anyway. I could never understand why anyone would think that suspending a flying saucer under a giant pair of white arches was aestheti-cally pleasing or a worthy landmark for a world-class airport like LAX. The most nonsensical building in the city, it also wins hands down for preposterous interior décor. Liberace minus subtlety. And if it's possible to be even more unap-pealing, try the expensive, watery drinks or food an airline wouldn't serve.

The only good news is that the place is such a pain in the ass to get to that if somebody's following you, you'd have to be blind to miss him. So it's a favorite meeting spot for clan-destine operators. That's why Carl Noon said he'd chosen it, but since Carl was four years out of the business on a medical, I think it had more to do with his having once met a surfer there who'd gone home with him for a month.

Carl and his partner, Al Exie, were one of the CIA's "husband-wife" teams—at least they were until Carl had had a heart attack, and they took early retirement. Now they live at Lake Arrowhead and only come to the city to party.

Bill Colby was the DCI who finally figured out that being homosexual didn't obviate one's ability to conduct espio-nage. In fact, it might be the best way into some targets. But until then, if a clandestine officer was gay and wanted to play in the big leagues, he needed a very deep closet.

There's a story that the Soviets once filmed Carl in a Vienna hotel having a romantic liaison with a Bolshoi dancer, then invited Carl on a Danube cruise to screen his performance and try to "double" him. Carl, who'd been tipped, arrived in ballerina drag accompanied by a camera crew and a dozen male prostitutes. He managed to get some terrific footage of ten KGB guys pulling their coats over their faces and running like hell. One poor fool panicked and threw himself over the side, where he was run over by a water taxi. All these years later, no Langley Christmas party is complete until they pipe Carl's film through the in-house system. So much for the gravity of spook work.

I like Carl, but not Al. Al's the guy who screwed up the Lisbon operation where some friends of mine died. Part of his problem is that he's never been wrong. Just ask him. The other part is that he's got a photographic memory, so he thinks he's a genius. The joke about Al is that if he had lunch with a brain surgeon, he'd be ready to scrub up by 2:30.

He's also big on cloak-and-dagger crap, which makes my ass tired because I know he beat feet in Lisbon like a fuckin' schoolgirl, and probably some other places too. He's what we call a RIFALO—a guy who reads Ian Fleming with all the lights on.

Carl knows how I feel about Al, so I thought maybe he wouldn't bring him. But there he was. I walked to their table against the wall of windows.

Al stood and put out his hand. "Hey, how's my favorite member of the lucky sperm club?"

I stepped almost against him and grabbed his testicles in my right hand, squeezed medium-hard and held. I heard the wind go out of him and watched the color drain from his plastic-surgery-sculpted cheeks. He went almost limp.

"What the fuck . . . ," he gasped.

"I didn't come here to talk to you, Al, so just sit down and keep your mouth shut, or I might decide to even the score for those who can't be here to speak for themselves."

I released his crotch, and he sank into a chair, looking smaller than he had a minute earlier.

"Do I need to stand, or can we just shake hands?" deadpanned Carl.

I smiled. "Nice to see you, Carl."

"Same," he said.

Too much waitress packed into too little dress came by with a strange look on her face that said she'd seen what happened. I ordered a beer, and she almost ran to get it.

Carl looked at me. "Since we're obviously not here to socialize, what do you need, Rail?"

I looked out the window. A Singapore Airlines 747 was on final approach. I nodded toward it. "You worked the airlines, didn't you?"

Carl looked at the 747, then back at me. "Best gig we ever had. People forget how it was before 9/11. Hell, you could still smoke on most overseas carriers. And the food was terrific—at least in first class." He winked. "But don't mention that to the inspector general."

"And every airline had its own personality," I offered.

Carl looked wistful. "Swissair ran just like you'd expect. Compulsive precision. If you needed to be somewhere on time and with no bullshit, they were it. Remember the old line about why Hitler didn't take Switzerland? He didn't want to be *that* efficient."

The waitress brought my Heineken, and Carl waited until she was gone. "And then there was Alitalia. Best food in the air served on the dirtiest planes, creaking and groaning all the way to Rome. But, boy, was it a party. I remember one pilot who came out, poured himself a glass of Chianti and strolled the aisles singing opera.

"And El Al? Jesus, you couldn't smuggle a hatpin aboard, and the stews all had their smiles surgically removed."

I added, "That's because they were Mossad or army. 'Would you like dinner, sir, or should I just shove it up your ass?' "

After we laughed together for minute, I said, "So what about Egypt Air?"

"Then or now?"

"Let's start with now."

"Wouldn't go near them. The only thing the terrorists hate more than us is the guy in Ras el-Tin Palace."

"And before 9/11?"

"I was a regular. We all were. Good maintenance, professional pilots, and as long as you weren't carrying drugs, they didn't much care. One of the best bridge and drop airlines."

"Meaning?"

"No rough stuff. You needed to meet somebody you couldn't be seen with, you booked a seat, took a ride, did business and were home for dinner. A bridge.

"Drops, you left your baggage checks in the seatback and just got off. You never saw the other guy. Or vice versa. Sometimes, your pickup might be under the sink in the first-class john. Then you'd have one of those keys the service guys use, and just before landing, you went in and got it."

"What happened on Flight 990?"

I saw a slight flicker in his eyes, but it was gone just as quickly. "That's a bullshit question to ask an old friend. Especially after only one beer."

I gestured to the waitress for another round, and she nodded.

Carl looked at me. "I can't be much help. I wasn't around."

"Yeah, but there's always talk."

"The fuckin' pilot did it."

"No shit. But why?"

"Pick your poison. Some people think it was a dress rehearsal for what came later. I don't. You can't do that kind of operation more than once. Too easy to fuck up. And it's counterproductive for planning purposes. Shows too much of your hand.

"If the pilot wasn't completely nuts, then it was about the military guys onboard. Under ordinary circumstances, you might be able to get one or two at a time, but thirty-four on one flight is a planner's wet dream. And if that's what happened, then the guy who got on without paperwork would have been Target Numero Uno."

I didn't say anything for a moment while I thought about what he said.

The beers came, and Carl took a long swig. "You into this big?"

"Not the way you're thinking. I'm interested in a courier who was on the plane. Just a victim, I think. But can you find out if he was carrying something official?"

"Probably, but first tell me if the guy was an operator."

"I don't think so. He was a schmuck, but not one of you."

"I don't care how many medals the fucking queen pinned on you, Black, you're still an asshole. So what's this schmuck's name?"

"Truman York. Used to be an airplane driver."

"I'll ask around."

"And while you're at it, see if anyone's ever heard of something called the City of War."

"What the fuck's that?"

"That's what I want to know."

As I got up to leave, I said, "One more. Balkan Airlines."

"Ah, the Assassin Express. Everybody clanked when they walked, and nobody ever took off their coat. You know, except for the flight attendants, who all looked like Dick Butkus, I don't think I ever saw a broad aboard."

"At least not one without five o'clock shadow," I added.

"I'll call you," said Carl.

"Good-bye, Al," I said.

Al didn't respond.

I paid the check on my way out, and as I was waiting for the too-small elevator, Eddie burst through the emergency exit door, out of breath from the stairs.

"I've been trying to call Liz, and there's no answer. Same for Jimmy."

I took out my cell phone and dialed Archer. It was ringing when the elevator came, and it was still ringing when we got out.

20

Handcuffs and Deep Water

It was the first time I'd ever ridden in a boat with Eddie when I hoped he'd go faster. As it was, he incurred the wrath of every boat owner in Avalon Harbor after opening up the GTX as soon as we pulled away from the dock. Turning my head, I saw our wide, deep wake almost capsize two small outboards.

We made it to Last Tycoon Cove in fourteen minutes. The *Sanrevelle* was still riding at anchor the way she had been when we'd left. It was then that I noticed the dilapidated twenty-five-foot Chris-Craft cruiser sitting dark a hundred yards to the south. The two other boats that had been there overnight were gone. The cruiser was at least thirty years old, with peeling paint and one side of its windshield broken out. It might just have been somebody taking a nap or getting laid or hiking onshore, but it didn't feel right. And then I noticed there was a dive line over the transom. Not a good sign. Too late to be underwater.

The sun was getting low in the sky, but I didn't need light. No one had come out on the *Sanrevelle*'s deck despite the noise we made coming in. Eddie feathered the GTX up to the stern, and I threw out the fenders then jumped aboard with a line. He brought *Zydeco* alongside, and I tied it off on the *Sanrevelle*'s starboard side.

Eddie clambered aboard, and I motioned for him to go up top. I went inside.

The first pool of blood was on the teak floor just inside the door. I knelt and felt it. It had congealed considerably. Probably at least three hours old. I listened. Other than Eddie's quiet footsteps above me, nothing.

There was more blood in the salon, sprayed, like someone had stood in the middle of the room and squeezed it out of a ketchup bottle. Some of the furniture had been overturned, and the flatscreen Philips had a hole through it. There were also several bullet holes in the walls, like Jimmy had been trying to hit a moving target.

There was another possibility. He'd been badly wounded and was firing wildly. I pushed that thought out of my mind.

Suddenly, Eddie called out. "I got a dead guy up here. On the flybridge. Never saw him before. Everything else is clear."

"Stay there," I yelled back. "I'll be up in a minute."

I checked the galley. More things scattered, the microwave ripped out of the wall . . . blood. I could picture two men, locked in a deadly embrace.

I followed the trail down the center passageway and into my stateroom, where a shot had pierced the ceiling and another had found another of my Vettrianos over the bed. The blood was extremely heavy here, almost too much for even two people.

Jimmy's body was in the master bathroom, half in, half out of the shower stall. Not unusual. Mortally wounded people sometimes try to get to water. Maybe to try to wash it all away.

Unless the guy upstairs was big too, Jimmy must have been dead on his feet by the time he got to where he died. I knelt over him and checked his wounds. They were legion.

He'd been cut at least fifty times on his hands, arms, back, sides and chest. One eye was pulp and both ears were just barely hanging on. What had killed him, though, were a pair of incisions on each side of his neck, each about four inches long. One had taken out the jugular, probably the first major hit—then a coup de grace to the carotid.

He still had his Glock in his hand. The slide was locked in the open and empty position. A guy this big and who knew how to use a gun, had fired at least fifteen rounds and still died. Jesus, who the fuck was the other guy?

"Oh, God. Jimmy."

I looked over my shoulder and saw Eddie. He was going to see him sooner or later anyway, so I got up and left him alone with his brother.

I made my way up to the flybridge and found Jimmy's killer crumpled facedown under the control console. He was a slightly built guy, and when I dragged him out, he was caked in blood, head to foot. But except for some scratches on his bare back, I didn't see any open wounds.

I turned him over, and a knife clattered onto the deck. It wasn't like the one I'd seen at Jackie Benveniste's or that Tino had flashed on the freeway. This was a dive knife with a wide, tapered blade, honed to scalpel sharpness with teeth at its bottom edge. He was also wearing a handcuff on his left wrist, the other cuff open and dangling.

I pushed his long, still-wet hair off his face and got my second jolt of the last few minutes. It was the kid who'd shot me at Tacitus. Seventeen at the most, maybe younger. And just in case I thought I was imagining things, there was the one-legged spider on his left forearm. He was probably waiting until he got back to Corsica to add Kim's.

I looked into his face. He could have been Kiki Videz's brother, confirming my suspicion that Marta's youngest son's only connection to the Corsicans had been his resemblance to the real killer. He had an earring in his right ear with a tiny interlocking *D* and *N* dangling from it.

I jerked it through the lobe, pocketed it then checked the body for the decisive wound. It didn't take long. His wind-pipe had been crushed. Either under the hands of Jimmy Buffalo, or maybe the butt of his gun. Fifteen shots and not one had connected. The kid had died of asphyxiation.

Suddenly, I heard a boat engine. I stood up and looked toward the cove entrance. Harbor Patrol. Three officers. It had to be about the dozen or so laws we violated when we roared out of Avalon. I left the body and hurried downstairs. Eddie was just coming out of the main cabin. He looked pale and shaken, but his focus was on the patrol boat, same as mine. I shook my head almost imperceptibly, and he nodded.

"Is that your GTX, Buffalo?" The uniformed officer on the bridge was using a bullhorn, and his voice had an edge to it.

"Hey there, Henry," shouted Eddie. "You know it is. Hold on, I'll be right there." He moved quickly to the *Zydeco* and untied it.

"Stay where you are," the bullhorn commanded.

But Eddie was already in the boat and had it started. Fend-ers flapping, he drove straight at the patrol vessel, then at the last second veered off and cut his engines to idle. His mo-mentum caused him to drift past the cops so that they had to make a U-turn, which took their line of sight and, hopefully, their attention off the *Sanrevelle*.

I heard the bullhorn again, and the officer wasn't happy. "Goddamn it, Eddie, I said, stay put."

"Sorry, Henry," Eddie shouted back to him, "I know I was wrong, driving so fast in the harbor, and all. But I paid four hundred large for this sucker, and sometimes I just can't help myself. You know how it is."

"Eddie, shut the hell up!" Officer Henry shouted through his bullhorn. "And prepare to be boarded."

"Oh shit, Henry, give the badge a rest. How long have we known each other? I'm already late picking up Liz, so why don't you just follow me back to Avalon, and we'll straighten this out there. That way, if I end up in jail, Liz can take care of the boat."

And with that, he jammed the throttles forward, and the GTX rose up out of the water and roared away. It took the officer-in-charge ten seconds to make a decision. Then he took off after Eddie.

As the sound of the two boats died away, I turned back to the cabin. Just as I was about to go inside, I heard someone calling my name. I squinted into the gathering darkness and saw two figures onshore, jumping up and down and waving their arms.

Archer and Liz! And then they were in the water, swimming hard toward me.

I got the old Chris-Craft tied onto my boat using a line attached to a port cleat so it would ride out of my wake. The two women, now in dry clothes, had been alternately crying and talking ever since they got onboard, but I didn't have time for a recap. Neither of them was hurt, so I told them to find something to calm their nerves, and they chose wine.

I figured Eddie would be back. Unless you're stone drunk or there's an injury, residents of the island usually get a lecture and a summons for violating wake laws. But I wanted to get the *Sanrevelle* out of there in case Officer Henry sent somebody around to check us out.

If that happened, they'd come from Avalon then circle the island on their way back, so I put Archer and Liz in chairs on the afterdeck and gave them a fishing knife out of my tackle box with instructions to cut the cruiser loose if they saw any indication it was taking on water. Liz didn't want to touch the knife, but Archer didn't hesitate. Then I turned off my running lights and headed straight out to sea at a fairly robust ten knots.

Three miles out, the sun had set completely, but there was enough moonlight to see the silhouette of the patrol boat as it entered Last Tycoon Cove and used its spotlight to sweep the area. After several minutes, the light went off, and the cops accelerated away in the direction of West End. I waited half an hour, then slowly eased back in.

Eddie showed up just after midnight.

He and Liz spent a long time in each other's arms. I took Archer into the galley, where we restored some order and brewed a pot of coffee. Then all of us went into the salon with a glass of wine, picked up the overturned furniture and sat—Eddie on a sofa with Liz holding onto him, and Archer and me on the floor, where she curled as close to me as she could get. I put my arm around her, and she seemed to welcome it.

"It was about noon," Archer said. "The Chris-Craft came in and the guy threw out an anchor and a dive line. Then he stripped down to a bathing suit, put on a snorkel and went over the side. He had a big knife in a sheath on his belt."

"Where was Jimmy?" I asked.

Liz answered, "He was with us when the guy first appeared. But after watching him dive for a while, Jimmy went inside to get us lunch."

"The guy was just going up and down, bringing up things from the bottom and throwing them in the back of his boat."

"Probably nothing but rocks," Eddie said. "But getting you comfortable with his being there."

I agreed. "When did he come aboard?"

Archer looked at Liz. "I'd say about an hour later."

Liz nodded. "Jimmy was up front, and all of sudden, the guy was standing right there." She pointed to the doorway. "With a knife and something weird, a handcuff on his left wrist. The other cuff was open, just dangling there."

" 'Phones, give me your phones,' he said, and we handed them over. The guy had an accent, but his English was good. He threw the phones out the door past the deck. I heard them splash."

Archer was nodding. "I think Jimmy did too, because that's when I heard him coming."

Liz started to whimper, and Eddie pulled her close. "Oh, Eddie," she said, "Jimmy was so brave."

He patted her, and Archer went on. "Jimmy had his gun out, but the guy just stared at him and smiled. He wasn't afraid at all."

I remembered the night at Tacitus. And what Dr. Abernathy had said about the killer. Archer was right. This Corsican had stones.

Archer continued, "Before I knew what was happening, he grabbed me and clipped the other handcuff on my right wrist and pulled me in front of him. Then he told Jimmy to put the gun down. That he was taking me with him."

Liz said, "Jimmy motioned for me to come, then he pushed me past him and told me to get the hell off the boat. So I went out the front and over the side."

Archer said, "When I saw Liz go, I said to myself, 'Fuck this guy. Nobody's gonna cut me again without a fight.' So I grabbed a fistful of his hair and started jerking his head back and forth. He went crazy, and Jimmy charged."

Archer took a sip of wine, her hand trembling. "It was like being on one of those rides that whip you all over the place. You know, where you get off feeling like your insides came loose. I'm cuffed to the guy, and Jimmy's locked up with him, and the three of us are sweating and yelling and banging into everything in the place. Jimmy's gun went off so many times I figured we were all gonna die.

"Then we fell over that big chair over there and rolled into the galley in a tangle. While everybody was struggling to get up, I got my hand in the guy's pocket and got lucky. The key was there. I managed to get the cuff off, and the next thing I knew I was sprinting for the deck and diving over the side. I saw Liz swimming for shore, and I took off after her, figuring maybe we could find somebody with a phone."

She lowered her voice. "All the way in, I kept hearing shots."

When she got her breath, I told her how brave she'd been. I also kicked myself for leaving her alone—Jimmy or no Jimmy. Once the Corsicans had shown they wanted Archer—and me—it had been a stupid risk.

"Now," I said, "we've got a decision to make. To call the authorities or not." I let the words hang there.

Archer looked at me. "You know who the guy is, don't you? And don't bullshit me. I can tell."

I nodded. "He's the man who murdered your sister."

She didn't say anything for a moment. Then she whispered, "Jesus Christ." Then, "What do these people want with us?"

"At first, I thought they were tying up loose ends, but not any longer. He was going to take you. That means they think you know something—something Kim might have told you." I didn't have to mention they thought the same thing about me.

"I don't know shit, except that I'm scared to death."

"I believe you, but unfortunately, we can't send them a telegram."

"But you understand more than you're telling. . . ."

"A little, but there's a lot more I don't know. I'm trying to find out as fast as I can, but I'm not there yet. I do think, though, that I might be able to create a momentum shift in our favor, but if the cops get involved . . ." I looked at everyone. "If the consensus is we should report it, I'll go along."

Eddie looked at me. "With Jimmy's history, no cop's gonna shed any tears over him. And our mother doesn't need a camera crew chasing her down Bourbon Street. Besides, I can see it coming. Two dead guys who killed each other. One's served time, and the other's probably an illegal. Case fucking closed."

Archer nodded. "I've got a past too, and some of it I don't need to relive. Especially on the front page. I saw what they did to Kim."

"Liz?" I said.

She didn't hesitate. "Screw the cops."

                         * * *

At dawn, we were 125 miles northwest of Catalina, and 100 miles beyond the trans-Pacific shipping corridor. Here, the Patton Escarpment ends, and the ocean floor begins to taper downward sharply. When we had at least five thousand feet of blue water beneath us, Eddie shut down the *Sanrevelle*'s engines, and I did the same on the Chris-Craft. I'd have liked to have gone another hour, gotten closer to thirteen thousand feet, but the cruiser was running on fumes.

We'd left the GTX at Last Tycoon Cove. I had wanted to send Liz and Archer back to Avalon in it, but neither woman would go. Liz said it was the least she could do for Jimmy—be present at his burial—and Archer said she wasn't going anywhere without me. I told her I was flattered, considering I hadn't done anything to merit that much confidence. In fact, I'd almost gotten her killed.

She answered me with tears in her eyes. "Mister, since I left home, not one person has given two shits whether I live or die, and right now, I'm going to hang on for dear life to the only one who seems to—whether he likes it or not."

Before we'd left Last Tycoon Cove, Eddie and I had gotten the young Corsican's body back onto the Chris-Craft, along with as many blood-soaked pieces of the *Sanrevelle* as we could pry loose or rip out. In the mildewed cabin, I found a suitcase containing several lacy negligees and an assortment of women's silk underwear. Under this were the pantsuit and lime green accessories Kim had described from Ralphs.

It took a minute before it hit me. The argument between Tino and Dante that Kim had overheard. "Maybe you watch, you learn zee man way!"

I took the dead kid's earring out of my pocket and looked at it. If the *D* was Dante, then the kid had to be *N*. I looked at the filthy bunk and didn't know whether to be pleased at my detective work or revolted at the squalor. I settled for hoping to have a little heart-to-heart with Dante.

The only other things I found were the kid's shoes and shirt, which he'd probably taken off to dive, and a red *tortil,* which I saved, along with a photograph of the spider tattoo I took with my digital camera. There wasn't a single scrap of paper aboard to identify the kid or the boat, not even a hull number belowdecks. It had probably been a derelict, abandoned or sold for scrap and purposely kept anonymous.

Using a small axe I kept aboard the *Sanrevelle* to build campfires, it didn't take long to break a hole through her below the waterline. The wood was like wet cardboard. Maintenance hadn't been a priority.

I used the open handcuff to secure the Corsican to the bilge pump so he wouldn't float away and waited until I was sure the cruiser was going down. Then I slipped the axe handle into a belt loop on my cutoffs and eased into the water, clenching the Ziploc containing the kid's red headband and my camera between my teeth. I swam the few yards to the *Sanrevelle* without looking back, and by the time I climbed aboard, the Chris-Craft was almost gone. As the last of her top slipped below the surface, I knew I was almost certainly sinking the boat that would have taken Kim on her final ride. There was a certain justice to that, but I kept it to myself.

Getting Jimmy's body out of the head, through the boat and onto the afterdeck of the *Sanrevelle* was a grueling, gruesome job. No matter how strong or strong-stomached you are, handling a body is difficult. Handling one the size of Jimmy Buffalo was twice so, and I insisted that Archer and Liz stay in one of the forward staterooms while we did it.

After we had him on the afterdeck, Eddie and I removed the stainless steel door of my Sub-Zero refrigerator, rolled Jimmy onto it and wired both into a piece of blue canvas. This far out, the door was probably overkill, but the sea can be peculiar about disgorging secrets, so I wanted something really heavy. Jimmy's gun went into the water, along with some broken glass from the shower stall that we hadn't found earlier.

When the four of us assembled on deck around our makeshift body bag, Eddie and I were dripping with sweat, and the women looked like they'd been through the mill. We were all affected. No one with a conscience can be around violent death and not be, no matter how many times you've seen it before.

After some discussion, we determined we all knew the 23rd Psalm. So Eddie told a couple of stories about his brother—one of them so funny we all burst out laughing—and Archer and Liz thanked him for saving their lives, then we began, "The Lord is my Shepherd . . ."

A few minutes later, Eddie and I slid Jimmy Buffalo into the water, where he could sleep for eternity.

As I climbed to the flybridge, Eddie, Liz and Archer went into the cabin. "Call me if you need me," Eddie said. "But if I don't lie down for a while, I'm going to drop."

I was getting the *Sanrevelle* ready to go when I heard Archer coming up the stairs. She was carrying two cups of coffee. "I hope you drink it black . . . and strong."

I took the cup. "I can't think of anything I'd rather have."

Archer sat down on the chair next to mine. "Mind?" she asked. "I need to be close to someone."

Once again I was reminded of Kim. I said, "I'd enjoy the company. If you see me nodding off, just slap me. There's not much to run into, but it's not a good time to get careless."

When I looked at her a few moments later, she was sound asleep, curled up in the captain's chair like a cat. I took the coffee cup out of her limp hand and set it in the holder next to mine. A following wind was picking up. I eased back slightly on the throttles and let the breeze help push. There wasn't any hurry, and I wanted to think.

I'd been playing games against civilized people for so long that my instincts had dulled. It happens. Holding an edge is difficult. But the alternative is that people die. Well, if I'd needed to get reacquainted with what the world is really like, I just had. Time to wake up.

But there was something else. Something I kept locked

away in a dark place. And now, as it pushed its way to the surface, I felt the familiar coldness run through my soul, and I did not welcome it. This was not a man I liked very much, but he was here to stay until this was over.

I dialed Jake Praxis's office and got his voice mail. "This is Rail. Call your friend, the reporter," I said.

Then I adjusted the *Sanrevelle*'s course and headed home into the rising sun.

21

Maximus

The rain came down in sheets, reducing my footsteps on Liverpool's worn cobblestones to a faint sloshing sound. I hadn't expected to see many people out this late in this kind of weather, and I hadn't seen any, but I was grateful for the cover of the downpour anyway. The streetlights were also dim and placed far apart, so other than an occasional flash of lightning, I remained an anonymous shape in a world of black shadows.

I turned into a narrow alleyway lined with delivery doors and garages. Here, shopkeepers' carts and lorries rested alongside buildings, waiting for daybreak and the call of commerce. A drenched cat ran along the wall to my left, focused on something only it could see then disappeared under an iron gate.

A quarter mile ahead lay the river. I could smell it, and I could hear a solitary ferry horn, but the rain and darkness obscured any view of it. I slowed. In yellow letters on dark green steel, I read:

E.L. TYRCONNEL & SONS
PURVEYORS OF FINE SCOTTISH SPIRITS

I knocked once, and before I could bring my hand down a second time, the door opened, and I was facing a small, bald man in white shirtsleeves accented by a pair of tartan sleeve garters—Tyrconnel Clan. I closed the door behind me and shook off as much water as I could. The little man looked at me, taking in my height. "Aye," he said in a light Highlands brogue, "a Black, for sure. Now, give me your hat and coat."

I noticed that in spite of the circumstances of the evening, there was a twinkle in the man's eye. "I loved your father," he said. "When those fucking Canadians tried to run us out of business, he loaned us the money to stay afloat and arranged for Tyrconnel & Sons to become sole suppliers to the Crown. Then, his newspapers wrote about our good fortune." Tyrconnel chuckled. "They don't drink much Scotch down Buckingham Palace way, but suddenly, all of Europe wanted to do business with us. God bless Lord Black."

I knew the story well, and I smiled back as I handed over my things. "He always spoke warmly of you, Mr. Tyrconnel. Especially about how you permitted him to hide newsprint in your warehouses during the strike so that when everyone else's presses went dark, he was still turning out two editions a day."

He waved his hand dismissively. "Twas the least I could do. There's a drop or two of Tyrconnel blood running through the Black line, you know. And call me E.L., please. Come now," he said. "We have a little time."

I followed him down a long hallway until he stopped before a narrow door. He fished a large ring of keys out of his pocket and inserted one. When the door swung open, he turned a switch, and a light came on.

The stairway was steep and narrow, the ceiling extremely low. I had to bend my knees and duck as much as I could to keep from touching it, but there was nothing I could do about my shoulders, and they brushed both walls. Delta instructors teach you to count stairs on the way into a place in the event you need to make a fast exit. Forty-two. Assuming a rise of six inches, we were now at least twenty-one feet belowground.

The basement smelled of oak and leather, and when Tyrconnel turned on more lights, I was surprised at its size. At least one hundred feet long and half that in width. And in sharp contrast to the stairs, the ceiling was high—twelve feet, perhaps more.

Row upon row of tall wooden racks ran the room's length, giving it the appearance of a vast wine cellar. Only instead of wine, these racks held thousands of bottles of Scotch awaiting their final destination. In a break in the racks about halfway down the room sat a grouping of oxblood-colored leather armchairs, worn to a fine patina. It was here that E.L. led me.

"Please," he said, gesturing for me to sit.

As I did, I noticed a white nylon-covered fire hose running down the far row of racks, and out of sight beyond. The hose was tightly inflated, indicating liquid was flowing through it. I closed my eyes and listened. Deep in the bowels of the building, I heard a faint humming, clanking sound.

E.L. left for a moment and returned with two cut-crystal glasses and a decanter of deep amber liquid. He poured two fingers in each glass and handed one to me. I took a sip, and the warmth of fine Scotch washed over me. It was like nothing I'd ever tasted. Rich, extremely smoky, but somehow as smooth as velvet.

I smiled, and it was clear my appreciation pleased him. "If you don't mind my asking," I said.

"Bowmore 40," he replied. "Remarkably elegant. Something for momentous times."

I took another sip. "I'll be adding it to my cellar."

"Yes, you will," he smiled. "There's a case on its way to you."

"I'll instruct my office to send you a check."

He held up his hand. "I am pleased to have been asked to help. Consider it an expression of gratitude."

"Shouldn't it be the other way around?"

"No, it most definitively should not."

I let the moment stand.

A young man's voice called from upstairs. "E.L., we need to be getting along."

I rode in the backseat of the Jaguar sedan as we drove along the Mersey, its centuries-old stone and concrete banks reminding me of St. Petersburg and the Neva. There were three of us. Jeremy Tyrconnel, E.L.'s oldest son, was at the wheel, his brother, Ian, to his left.

"We would have gladly brought him to you," Ian said.

"I know, and I'm appreciative, but I need to do this myself."

"I understand. I'd feel exactly the same way. Your father was one helluva chap, Mr. Black. My brother and I were still in school, but we were devastated when he died. And E.L. says that Amarante was the most beautiful woman he ever saw. He attended their wedding, you know."

"I know," I said.

Ten minutes later, we slowed and turned into an ornate, eighteenth-century building sitting on the high north bank. The driveway angled downward, and on the lower level, we pulled up to a porticoed glass entryway. It was brightly lit, but no one was in sight.

"We'll do our part, then be right here," said Jeremy.

I got out and entered the building. The door was unlocked, and no one was at the security desk. I remembered the elevator. I hadn't been in it since I was a boy, but it still creaked and groaned and shivered between floors. It had always been small, but now it seemed tiny.

The empty secretaries' area on the third floor was also frozen in time. Mahogany desks, brass lamps and scattered green leather chairs for those who came to call. There was only one man to see now, and as I pushed open the heavy door to the conference room that led to his office, I heard *his voice, angrily speaking on the telephone. I made my way around the long, ebony table that had once belonged to Charles I and stopped in the dark a few steps from the open office door.*

"Captain Crowell, I don't give a good goddamn what the dockmaster says, you sail tomorrow, period. That beef has to be in Santos Friday, and there's a storm moving in. I'm already suspending you for this delay, and if you have to spread money around to get an exit stamp, that'll come out of your pocket too. So before you end up working all year for nothing, you'd better find a way to get out of Buenos Aires—and quick. Do I make myself clear?"

Apparently, he didn't need an answer, because he slammed the telephone down.

I stepped into the doorway.

Maximus Rhein sat where he always had, on the right side of the immense rosewood partner's desk up against the wall of arched windows. The desk was in exactly the same place, but its ivory inlays of armor-clad warriors slaying dragons were not nearly as terrifying now as they had been to a seven-year-old.

A fire in the oversized fireplace crackled with warmth.

"Good evening, Max," I said.

He looked up, noticed me, then returned to reading something on his desk.

His voice registered no surprise. "We've got nothing to say to each other, Black."

I walked across the thick carpet and sat in my father's old chair. I swiveled, looked down at the river. A long barge was going by, nudged on course by four tugs. "Two centuries ago, we could have looked out these same windows and seen four-masted slavers departing for Africa."

"And that's supposed to mean exactly what?" Rhein said.

I ignored him. "But long after such sorrow-laden ships no longer plied English waters, there were still those who traded in flesh. And the financial gain for ferrying today's slaves be-

tween nasty ports dwarfs even the grandest dreams of those who pioneered such commerce." I turned and looked across the desk at him. "And some of those men still sit in these windows—and bank their profits in British sterling."

Rhein picked up the telephone and pressed two digits. Moments later, a rough-looking, broad-shouldered man wearing a dark tweed coat and a black turtleneck came through the door.

"You called for me, Mr. Rhein?" the man said.

"Yes, Brooks. Escort Mr. Black the hell out of the building, then fire the security person who let him through. And if he should happen to fall down the stairs in the process, make sure he lands on his face."

Brooks looked squarely at me, then at Max. "I'm sorry, I can't do that," he said.

Rhein's voice became angry. "Are you deaf? I said throw this man out."

"I'm sorry, sir, but I don't know what you're talking about. There's no one here but you."

Rhein looked at me, then at Brooks. "What the . . ."

"I'll be going now, sir. Mrs. Brooks is nursing a touch of the flu. Good night, Mr. Rhein." And Brooks departed.

Rhein picked up the telephone and began to dial again.

"The phones are now off," I said.

Rhein listened into the receiver, then slammed it down. He picked up a cell phone.

I reached across the desk, took the cell out of his hand and threw it ten feet into the fireplace.

"What the hell do you want?" he snarled.

"Nothing."

"Nothing?"

"Well, as close to nothing as one can get. I came for you."

Max Rhein sat, his mouth open but no words coming out. I got to my feet, walked over to his side of the desk and hit him in the face with my fist. Not hard enough to hurt him badly, but hard enough so that it stung my hand. Here, in *this office, the decisions had been made, and I wanted to feel something. Anything.*

Rhein sat next to me in the back of the Jag, pressing a handkerchief against his nose, dabbing at blood that had already stopped.

"So this is the great Maximus Rhein," said Ian Tyrconnel, half turning in his seat. "Growing up in Liverpool, I heard his name, of course, but I don't believe I ever saw the man. Pardon me for saying so, but he doesn't look like much."

Jeremy looked over his shoulder. "They're comfortable with blood on their hands. But when it's on their suits . . . ah, that's a different story."

Rhein looked at me as if a light had suddenly gone on. "Holden," he said.

"I found him in Tunisia," I said. "Living in La Goulette, hiring out on sardine boats. Not a happy man. Said you reneged on the money you promised for the explosion that killed my fiancée. By the way, in case word didn't reach you, Quinn died from septicemia brought on by the bullet I put in him. Holden said he lay in that cheap Panamanian hotel for two weeks, screaming, waiting for the doctor you were sending. The one who never came."

Rhein slumped in his seat.

"You know how naïve I was, Max? Until Holden started talking, I had absolutely no idea you were behind my parents' deaths. I didn't even suspect my father hadn't died in an avalanche. That he'd been pushed into a crevasse. And that the men who shot my mother and Charlie Fear were a pair of Coral Gables teenagers just picking up some fast money. If someone had given me a thousand guesses and a thousand years, I wouldn't have come close to figuring out that the trail to all this death would lead here."

"Goddamn," breathed Jeremy Tyrconnel.

After a moment, Rhein tried to speak, but his voice broke.

I said, "For the record, Max, Tony Holden's dead. I know what a sensitive guy you are, so I'll spare you the details.

But I think, on the whole, he would have rather been in Philadelphia."

Rhein found his voice. His fury was palpable. "Your father stole my ships out from under me! I worked my whole life building that business, then, just like that, it was gone. Sucked into the Black empire without so much as a thank-you."

I looked at him. "All the money in the company was my father's, Max. Or did you forget? And it was his name on the door that brought people in, not yours. You came to him a failure, and with his capital and his contacts, he made you richer than you had a right to expect.

"And how did you repay him? By using his ships to transport kidnapped Pakistani children to India as carpet slaves. By shanghaiing Dominicans to Haiti to cut sugarcane. And by shipping Sudanese ten-year-olds to North Africa for . . .

"You disgusted him, and you disgust me. You were lucky all he did was terminate your partnership. He should have had you thrown in prison. And he didn't leave you destitute. He carried you until you were back on your feet. Even today, you work from a Black property. And for that, you sick old fuck, you tried to wipe his name off the face of the earth."

At first, Rhein didn't want to go down the Tyrconnels' basement stairs. It was important to me that he wasn't dragged, so I hit him just off the center of his throat with the edge of my hand. His eyes went wide, and he choked a couple of times, but he found his footing and decided to go under his own power.

E.L. met us at the bottom of the stairs, and the four of us followed him to the far reaches of a section of the basement that had remained darkened earlier. Now we were guided by work lights rigged along a rough passageway just wide enough to allow two men to walk side by side. The inflated fire hose ran along the floor to our right, and the humming noise I had heard earlier became louder.

At the end of the passageway, we came to a large manhole cut into the concrete floor. An iron grate covering it had been removed, and more work lights and the hose ran down into it. The top of a steel ladder extended a foot above the rim, and without hesitating, Jeremy and Ian disappeared down.

Max froze, but I prodded him hard in the back, and with shaking hands and legs, he managed to get onto the ladder. As I followed him down, I saw the broken remains of ancient, iron handholds protruding from the rock. However, as we passed a distinct, still-wet waterline on the walls, the handholds disappeared. Rusted away.

Thirty-five feet later, we dropped onto black bedrock, wet and slippery with algae. We were in a round chamber perhaps twenty feet in diameter. Along the walls behind the ladder lay coiled ropes and pressure hoses, acetylene and oxygen tanks, a pair of welding masks, heavy gloves and a torch.

To the right extended another lighted passageway, this one slightly narrower than the one above. Its entry was through a hinged, vertical iron grate as tall as I was. It reminded me of a bank vault.

Ian had to raise his voice to be heard over the humming noise now. "This is where they held African slaves bound for London. The U.S. gets most of the human trafficking vitriol, but beginning around 1700 and running for a hundred and seventy-five years, Britain had her own issues. The Trade Triangle they teach you in school—guns and trinkets to Africa; slaves to America; then tobacco, sugar and cotton back here—is only part of the picture. What they don't mention is that some English owners of American plantations couldn't say no to cheap labor and imported domestic help right from the outset. Cooks, housekeepers and liverymen mostly, but some were brought for sex—all kinds."

He looked at Maximus Rhein. "Welcome, Mr. Rhein. They say if you listen carefully, you can still hear the screams." To me, he said, "Everything you requested is about halfway in, Mr. Black. There's a wide spot cut into the rock, where mothers used to sit and nurse their babies."

"What's that noise?" Rhein demanded nervously.

Jeremy pointed to the hose. "A pump. We're about twenty-five feet below river level. Perhaps you noticed the waterline on the way down. Eighty years ago, the city fathers flooded the catacombs to keep history as non-visual as possible. It's a criminal offense to be down here." He winked at Rhein. "Don't tell, okay?"

Jeremy Tyrconnel stepped aside, and Ian entered the passageway. I pushed Max after him.

"What do you think this is going to solve?" Rhein shouted over his shoulder, trying to sound belligerent but not pulling it off.

"Solve? I'm not trying to solve anything."

"Then why bring me to this dreadful place? Okay, you win, I'm terrified. But you could have just shot me in my office. Dead is dead."

"Max, I'm surprised at you. This is England. I'm not carrying a gun."

Ahead, the tunnel began to widen, and shortly, we were standing in a much larger area, about the size of a hotel suite. Stacked against the far wall were a wet suit, mask, regulator and four individual scuba tanks.

"Get changed," I said to Max.

He looked at me with palpable terror. "I don't dive anymore," he stammered. "I'm too old."

I reached out and took his suit coat off him. "It's just like riding a bicycle."

As Max Rhein stripped, he began to weep. He didn't beg or cry out, he just sobbed to himself. And like in the office, I tried to feel something—anything—but nothing came.

Just then the pump stopped. The silence was momentarily startling, and the hose immediately deflated. Then Ian came into view, carrying the hose and coupling over his shoulder *like the head of a giant, dead anaconda. He disappeared in the direction of the entrance.*

Max was in the wet suit now, his business clothes folded neatly and sitting on his shoes so they didn't touch the damp floor. I noticed that the wet suit was a little large, making him appear smaller than he was.

He had stopped sobbing, but his throat still spasmed like a child's. "What happens now?"

"Without the pump, this chamber is going to start filling with water. About two inches an hour, I'm told."

I saw him look up at the ceiling and do a rough calculation. Eight feet. Forty-eight hours.

"That should give you plenty of time to scream yourself hoarse and run back and forth a few times before you get exhausted and settle down to do some serious thinking. Maybe even spend a minute or two on some of the children you sentenced to live in agony thousands of miles from their parents.

"Roughly two days from now, you'll need to strap on the first tank. That will buy you another hour. There's one for each of my parents, one for Sanrevelle, and one for our baby. My wife was pregnant, or didn't you know? By the time you reach the end of the fourth tank, maybe you'll be halfway to some of the anguish you've caused others. Of course, there's always the possibility you'll go mad and forget the tanks, and that will be okay too."

As the reality of what I was saying washed over him, I saw he was about to become hysterical. I stepped forward and slapped him—hard. It brought him back.

"Please, don't do this," he cried. "I'm begging you. Just kill me. Oh, dear God, please, just kill me now."

"Max, God has nothing to do with this." And with that, I turned and walked away.

As I exited the chamber, Ian closed the iron grate behind me and padlocked it, then he turned off the work lights, and the slave chamber went dark. Turning, he began to help

Jeremy, who was now wearing the welding gear and rolling a massive, steel plate over the grate.

Just before the plate hit home, I thought I caught a glimpse of Maximus Rhein running headlong toward us, his face becoming a skeleton. But I couldn't be sure.

And then Jeremy fired the acetylene.

22

Late-Night NFL and RICO

I left the *Sanrevelle* with Eddie with instructions to go through it with a fine-tooth comb and a bottle of bleach. Afterwards, he and Liz were to sail it down to F&G Yacht Design in San Diego for a refit.

F&G's owner, Preston Gage, is as discreet a man as exists, and if Eddie and I had missed something, he wouldn't. He's another Delta guy, but we didn't serve at the same time. Preston lost a leg in Sierra Leone, and somebody we both knew called me when the VA was putting him through a Catch-22 for a prosthesis. They wanted paperwork, which they couldn't get because the mission had been off the books, so as far as the bureaucrats were concerned, Preston might as well have lost his leg in a bar fight.

Bert Rixon got him fitted with one of his prostheses, then hired a therapist to teach him the intricacies of muscle and nerve manipulation. During the long hours of learning to walk again, Preston picked up a design magazine in the therapist's office and got hooked. Fabrics and colors aren't a traditional career path for former special ops guys, but as Preston is quick to point out, "There's a lot more money in Ralph

Lauren than checking car trunks at a nuke plant." Rhonda used to work for him before she struck out on her own.

I wanted to avoid the heliport, so I borrowed *Zydeco,* and Archer and I ran flat out to San Pedro. There, we grabbed a cab and headed for Dove Way.

It wasn't as bad as I expected. Tino and Dante evidently hadn't stuck around after Mallory had gotten away. I called Melvin Rose again and told him to get his Russian women out to the house as soon as possible. I also asked him to get someone to board up the window the two Corsicans had broken on the way in.

My preference for temporary quarters would normally be the Beverly Hills Hotel, but as nice as it is, there are too many ways in and out, and the bungalows are set off by themselves. I decided instead on the Beverly Wilshire, right in the middle of downtown BH. Also, a personal friend, Duke Pennington, a former SWAT commander for the Sheriff's Department, is head of security.

They offered me the Pretty Woman suite, but I opted for a penthouse in the much less conspicuous Beverly Wing next door. To belt and suspenders it, Duke assigned an extra security man to the desk next to the private elevator. He also called in a marker and had a couple of uniforms come by and run Archer home to pack some fresh clothes.

I gave Archer the bedroom facing west, and I took the one with the view of the Hollywood Hills. We were both exhausted, so I found an NFL game on television and we ordered Beverly Wilshire baby shrimp salads and a bottle of merlot from room service.

I don't know what time we went to bed, but the game wasn't over yet, and I was asleep before I hit the pillow. I awakened at 2:30 and lay there for a moment, looking at the lights in the hills as the second hand on the electric clock clicked softly on the nightstand.

I heard Archer come in. She wasn't wearing anything, and

she had her hair pulled back in a ponytail, leaving her scar and eye uncovered. She looked as sexy as any woman I had ever seen. She didn't say anything, just pulled back the sheet and got in next to me. I turned, and she kissed me deeply.

I started to put my arms around her, but she put both hands on my chest and pushed me back gently. She kissed my chest and lingered at my nipples, teasing them with her teeth. Then she slid the rest of the way down and took me in her mouth.

I started to stroke her hair, but she stopped me again. "Don't," she whispered. "I'm very good at this, and I want to do it for you. But I'm so keyed up, I'm about to explode. If you touch me, I won't be able to concentrate."

So I lay back and looked at the hills again. Shortly, they wouldn't stay in focus. She was right. She was very good.

I wanted to see Jake, so Duke assigned Doreen Cantwell, his second-in-command at the hotel and a former county jail supervisor, to go with Archer while she got her hair done at José Eber and picked up some makeup at Neiman Marcus. Doreen is black, pretty and built like a linebacker, and I could imagine how many wiseasses she'd straightened out during her time in uniform.

I was waiting for my car on El Camino Real, the private street that runs between the two wings of the hotel, when a voice came up behind me. "I see you're famous again this morning." It was Duke, a perfectly tailored, blue pin-striped suit draped over his six-foot-five frame and looking more like Julius Erving than usual. "Front page of the *Times,* and you didn't even have to get shot. Is that why you're hiding out in my crib?"

"Partly. If any reporters show up, I'd appreciate it if you could keep them out of my hair."

"You're already invisible on the hotel computer, but I'll keep my eyes open."

"Thanks."

"I figure you're not stupid enough to do something like this without a plan. So whatever it is, I hope it works, because from where I sit, you look like a dead man trying to find a place to lie down."

"Thanks for the vote of confidence."

I saw my Rolls crest the hill from the underground garage. There was somebody sitting in the front seat with the valet. The kid stopped the car and got out looking nervous. He didn't wait around for a tip.

Sergeant Manarca leaned across the seat. "Well, if it ain't the Duke himself," he said. "How's the house dick business?"

Duke looked down at the detective. "Morning, Dion. Hope you're not applying for a valet gig. How many department cars you wrecked this week, or do you still have that dimwit spic driving you around?"

Manarca smiled. "What's a big day for you now, Pennington? Busting a weenie-wagger at the pool?"

It was just a bullshit exchange between two cops, but you didn't need a decoder ring to know there was a history, and it still had bite.

"Get in, Mr. Black," Manarca said to me. "Let's take a ride."

He smiled, but it wasn't friendly, and I got behind the wheel. This hadn't taken as long as I thought it would.

As I pulled out and turned onto Rodeo Drive, Manarca said, "Never been in one of these fuckers before. About four hundred grand, right? Humidor in the glove compartment, safe in the trunk. Makes you wonder how Toyota stays in business, don't it?"

"Where would you like me to drop you?" I said, ignoring his question, which wasn't a question anyway.

"Oh, no place in particular. Just drive. My partner's behind us."

I looked in the mirror and saw Detective Pantiagua behind the wheel of a black sedan that might as well have had "cop" emblazoned on the windshield.

I turned onto Wilshire and headed east. Manarca had a

folded newspaper in his lap. He opened it so I could see the headline. It was the one Duke had been referring to.

BEVERLY HILLS SHOOTING VICTIM
SUES STREET GANG
Forbes 400 Billionaire to Los Tigres: "Lawyer Up"

"You know what two words you never want to hear your cellmate say?" Manarca asked.

"I have a feeling I'm about to find out."

"Nice dick."

"You make that up or steal it from your wife?"

Manarca seemed to like that. "You're a clever guy, Black. Quick too. You want to take a stab at why it fits into what we're talking about?"

"I wasn't aware we were talking about anything, but go ahead, enlighten me."

"I'm gonna give you twenty-four hours to drop your bullshit lawsuit, or I'm gonna find a way to bust you just long enough to get you into the general population at County. There's probably a hundred Los Tigres in there who'd love to give you their deposition—no lawyer necessary."

"Looks like I hit a nerve."

"Oh, you hit a nerve, all right. About ten thousand of them. The entire fuckin' department. It's not bad enough we gotta risk our lives protecting assholes like you. Now you want to haul us into court and get into our files. You don't give a rat's ass about Los Tigres. This is only about making cops look bad. Well, it ain't gonna fuckin' happen."

"And you drew the job of telling me."

"Think whatever you like."

"Well, you can tell your associates that's why I filed in federal court, not L.A. Superior, where you guys get treated like Vatican cardinals. And my lawyer told me this morning we drew Judge Cavalcante."

"Cavalcante? That cocksucker. He never met a cop case he couldn't fuck up."

"Ordinarily, I'd agree with you, but this time, I see it the other way. I'm anxious to watch you go through that jigsaw puzzle routine of yours with him. See if he sees Paris."

The simmer was turning into a burn. "I didn't figure I was gonna have to draw you a picture."

"And I didn't figure you for a room-temperature IQ."

Manarca didn't like being talked back to. He pulled out his service weapon and laid it in his lap. "Is that enough IQ for you, prick?" he said.

I pointed to a small dot on the dashboard. "While you were studying up on safes and humidors, you must have missed the page about in-dash cameras. Comes in handy in case of a carjacking. Or a cop making threats with a gun in his lap."

If a guy can turn redder than Manarca did, I've never seen it. And his voice had a tremor in it that made me glad he didn't have his finger on the trigger.

"Now," I said, "would you like to put Mr. Smith & Wesson away and start over, or should I use the handy Rolls-Royce voice-dial to get Jake Praxis on the line?"

Very deliberately, Manarca put the gun back in his shoulder holster, and we rode in silence for a few minutes. Finally, he spit out, "Okay, cocksucker, who you gonna serve your lawsuit on? Last time I looked, Los Tigres doesn't publish a list of officers or have an address."

"That's what I thought, but Jake found out that a couple of years ago the Feds slammed them with a RICO action."

"So what?"

"That makes them a criminal enterprise. Meaning as far as the law is concerned, Los Tigres is an entity with standing in the system, making them legally liable for all kinds of things. We served them the same way the IRS did. Through some scumbag attorney in a fancy office downtown."

"You're shittin' me."

"It also means that if I win a judgment, I can seize assets, which includes their relatives' homes if a member has slept there just once."

"I figured they'd kill you before the week was out, but I'm revising my estimate. You might not make it to the next stoplight."

"I doubt it. They've got bigger problems than me. And tomorrow they're going to get sued again. By Marta Videz."

"She related to the shooter?"

"His mother. But you and I know her son didn't shoot anybody."

Manarca chewed on that.

I said, "And sometime next week, there'll be a suit filed on behalf of Walter Kempthorn."

There was genuine puzzlement on Manarca's face. "Who the fuck is Walter Kempthorn?"

"The third victim. But then, you find it more comfortable not to know a lot, don't you, Sergeant?"

23

Power Plays and Security Oaths

It took the district attorney and the cops exactly thirty hours to get their act together. They sent three DDAs to the meeting at Jake's. Manarca was there too, along with his boss, Commander Roy Rogers, an unfortunate name, I thought, but after considering the size of the guy, I doubt anyone made fun of it. The other person was Captain Juliette Luna, head of the LAPD's gang detail. Pantiagua was nowhere in sight.

After everybody was seated in the conference room, and the deputy district attorneys had taken in the floor-to-ceiling views of the L.A. Country Club and begun wondering why they weren't in private practice, Jake said, "I appreciate your coming."

Captain Luna wasn't so polite. "So what exactly is it you fucking want, Praxis?"

Jake decided to handle the attitude first. Speaking to a bald DDA named Fontaine, he said, "The first thing we're going to do is drop the I'm-a-cop-and-you're-not bullshit. When I'm satisfied we're all here to cooperate, we'll start. Until then, I'll send somebody in to get your coffee order. If that doesn't suit you, the receptionist will validate your parking on the way out. Come on, Rail." And we got up to leave.

Fontaine looked at Luna, who glared at Jake, then at me. Just as we hit the door, Commander Rogers said, "Let's not waste any more time than we have to on this. We've all got other things to do."

We sat back down, and Jake started again. "First, Captain Luna is going to meet with Mrs. Videz and tell her that her son didn't murder anyone. That the police made a horrible mistake, and she's there to personally apologize. Then the department will issue a press release to the same effect. No tricky language, no ambiguity. The release will also say that you're reopening the investigation into the kid's death and Dr. York's. And I'm being charitable when I say 'reopening,' since there wasn't an investigation to begin with."

I thought Captain Luna's head was going to explode, but she held her tongue. I knew she was picturing herself being grilled by a herd of reporters smelling blood.

"Next, Sergeant Manarca will go out to LAX, hunt up Mitchell Adams and interview him about his nephew. Then he'll make a deal with the Manhattan Beach cops to get that case transferred to LAPD."

I saw Manarca look at me, surprised. He'd been expecting to be slapped. Instead, we were throwing him a bone. He nodded his appreciation, and I nodded back. It wasn't because I suddenly liked him, but he was probably a good detective who, for whatever reason, laziness or politics, didn't do his job. Now he was getting a second chance, and if he did it right, no one would remember the first go-round.

But Jake wasn't going to let him off scot-free, which probably had more to do with the Pantiagua incident at the hospital than it did with Manarca. "And then, Detective, if you haven't figured it out for yourself by now, you're going to interview Marta Videz. And while you're at it, I suggest you take along a police artist, because she actually saw one of the guys who murdered her son—something she could have told you if you'd bothered to ask."

Manarca got a little darkness in his eyes, but it evaporated quickly. He was already figuring out how he was going to get personal mileage out of this.

I slid over the photograph I'd taken of the killer's tattoo. "One of the other guys, Tino, will have this on his left arm—only it'll have more legs."

Manarca looked at the picture. "You couldn't get a face to go with this?"

"He moved when I clicked," I said.

"So it's the Tacitus shooter, and he's dead," Manarca snorted. "I hope you didn't do this. Where's the body?"

"You're the only one talking about bodies. Last time I saw the guy, he was in handcuffs."

"Handcuffs? Where?"

"If you two don't mind," said Jake, cutting in. "Finally, I want a copy of every scrap of paper and every piece of information you've got on the shootings at Tacitus. And, when they start coming in, on the deaths of Kiki Videz and Walter Kempthorn. All the interviews, all the forensics and all the computer runs—everything. And I want it to keep coming as long as the cases are open."

It was Rogers's turn to show the flag. "Not a fuckin' chance. We've got sources and techniques to protect."

Jake looked at Rogers like a schoolchild. "Commander, I expect you to redact informants' names. If I want one, I'll ask, and you can put it through channels. As for techniques, I haven't seen any yet. So let me know when I do, and I'll reconsider."

Without even looking at Rogers, Fontaine said to Jake, "You've got it."

This scene had probably been rehearsed beforehand to give the commander cover, but he was still furious and not hiding it. He snorted and crossed his big arms.

Fontaine looked at Jake. "Just tell me one thing. How did you manage to get this case in front of that ACLU shill, Cavalcante?"

Jake didn't bat an eye. "I'm surprised at you, Counselor.

You know nobody can influence judicial assignments—at least not at the federal level." He paused for effect. "But if I had to guess, I'd say that *60 Minutes* piece last year had something to do with it. How did that LAPD captain put it? You remember—the guy they filmed behind a curtain to protect his identity. 'Ask anybody, there's just some people, like that asshole Cavalcante, that if they call a cop, we're gonna sit back down and play another hand of poker. Maybe even order lunch.' "

Fontaine nodded. "That's what I told the chief—and that you'd probably subpoena him first, just to twist his tit. Was I right?"

"Faster than he can get to a photo op."

"So what can we expect in return?" asked Fontaine.

"I'll hold the other two lawsuits, and I'll ask Judge Cavalcante to extend the deadline for starting depositions on Mr. Black's action. Then I'll take the Los Tigres depos first. That should buy you a couple of months."

"Since you're getting everything you want from us, why can't you just drop the whole goddamn thing?"

"As Chuck Colson used to remind Nixon, 'When you've got 'em by the balls, their hearts and minds aren't far behind.' My best to the chief."

On the way back to the hotel, my cell phone rang. It was Carl Noon. He skipped the hello. "What the fuck are you into?"

"The name Truman York jog somebody's memory?"

"Classy fuckin' guy."

"How classy?"

"Let's do the professional shit first," Carl said. "Your boy's last posting was Incirlik."

"Turkey."

"Correctomundo. Found himself a nice sideline using his plane to hump heroin around the Med for some Mafioso named Gaetano Bruzzi. Then, like they all do, he decided to get into the business. Siphoned off half a million bucks of jet fuel and traded it for some Grade-A Afghan smack.

The *carabinieri* arrested him in Rome, in a suite at the Hassler, no less, sucking on some prostitute's toes with ten kilos under the bed."

"Wonder how they knew where to look," I said sarcastically. "That stuff was probably resold before he got fingerprinted."

Carl laughed. "Hey, the guy was a pilot. Ever met one who didn't think he was a fuckin' genius? But get this. There was no court-martial, not even a hearing. He even kept his oak leaves and full retirement. The air force just wanted him the fuck gone."

I thought about it. The military gets real attitude when you sell their stuff and don't invite them to the toe-sucking. But they get a major hard-on over drug trafficking. The theft was worth maybe eighteen months and a dishonorable. That much horse was twenty to life.

"Who'd he know?" I asked.

"That's what I thought too. It took a little digging to find out what really happened."

"And . . ."

"He was already in trouble for knocking up the daughter of some Turk mayor."

"And let me guess, she was underage."

"I think even in Sandland, you can't consent at twelve."

Somehow, I wasn't surprised. "The local code probably calls for a hot blade and an audience. So why didn't they just turn him over? Walk away."

"Because the mayor demanded the base general too. Said in his tribe a daughter's honor demanded the perp *and* his father, but he'd settle for the CO. The JAG had no choice but to get them both out of Dodge. There was no career move in prosecuting him and maybe having the media get hold of it, so they just cut him loose."

"That it, or is there more?"

"Oh, I'm just getting warmed up. This guy was a peach."

"Skip to the end, okay?"

"Well, no sooner did Major York rejoin the real world and

get his special courier certificate than he got hired by the G again. Only this time it was the army."

"They didn't know?"

"Hard to tell, but before Turkey, York had flown a refueler for the SR-71."

I rolled my eyes. "So he had clearances up the ying-yang, and, of course, the only thing the Pentagon cared about was that he'd never violated his security oath."

"You oughta go on *Jeopardy*."

"What did they entrust him with?"

"No one's talking, but that last flight, Egypt Air, wasn't a vacation. My guess is something very big went down with everything else."

"Anybody think it was related to the crash?"

"No, the cause was that crazy motherfucker upfront—high on God or politics or thinking he was Wile E. Coyote."

If there was anyone on the planet who'd deserved that last ride, it was Truman York. I'd have paid to see the look on his face. I shifted gears. "You ask about the City of War?"

"I did. And if Truman York got their attention, that lit them up like a pit bull at a petting zoo."

"So what the hell is it?"

"Don't know. But some people at the Pentagon want to talk to you. You're supposed to catch a plane."

"When?"

"Yesterday."

"Who do I see?"

"I wouldn't worry about that. The way they sounded, they'll be meeting everything that flies."

It's always nice to know you're important. "Carl, I'm going to need something else."

"Jesus H. Christ, now what?"

"I want to talk to someone who was close to Flight 990."

"That ought to be some trick, since they're all fuckin' dead."

"You know what I mean. And not an investigator. I want somebody who was there that night."

"Let me think about it. But if I come up with something, it's going to cost you."

"Name it."

"I've got a big birthday coming up. One that ends in a zero, and I want to throw a party on that goddamn yacht of yours. Nothing fancy. Ten, twelve good friends. A little three-day cruise to nowhere."

"Done."

"Not so fast. And I want that stiff limey who works for you to do the planning. What's his name again?"

"Mallory."

"Yeah, Mallory. Personality like a black fuckin' hole, but I'll never forget that housewarming he threw when you moved into San Simeon up there in the Hills of Beverly. Unbelievable."

"I'll guarantee the boat, but you'll have to talk to Mallory yourself. He's the most independent man on the planet."

"Deal. I'll get him laid. What's his preference?"

"Not my arena, but I'd pay plenty to hear the conversation."

Carl laughed, and we hung up.

24

Safe Houses and Spitters

Hollywood usually depicts safe houses as grubby apartments in a seedy part of town. Sometimes they are, but not very often. Slum residents know who belongs in their neighborhood and who doesn't. They also know a lot about each other's business, and they get suspicious when they can't determine where somebody fits in. Not a conducive environment for strangers coming and going at odd hours, or for someone who might have a houseful of strange equipment or be running people in and out.

In reality, safe houses are usually in respectable communities, where, as long as you pay your rent and don't make noise, people will generally leave you alone—if only out of politeness. And for serious operations, swanky is always best. There's nothing more anonymous than a Park Avenue co-op or a New Jersey horse farm. Most of the time, you can come and go without seeing anyone, and if you do happen to bump into a neighbor, when was the last time a rich stranger struck up a conversation with you? Money can get you attention, but it's particularly useful when you want to be invisible.

My real estate agent, Jhanya Devereux—exotic names are de rigueur in Beverly Hills real estate—called five of her high-end counterparts in Washington, D.C., and told them she had a client who was looking for a luxurious building where he could spend a month. Jhanya said her client was doing some consulting at the White House, and if he found the right place, he'd be open to purchasing a floor as his Washington residence.

"What he's really looking for," she breathed into the phone, "is a place to give parties and showcase his art collection." She added that there was no cap on the budget, and, of course, the agent stood to receive a handsome fee plus a bonus for being discreet.

Four of the five got back to her within an hour, and I chose the Watergate. It had several things going for it. First, its location in Foggy Bottom and a steady stream of cabs make it easy to get around. Second, its labyrinthine layout is difficult to surveil. And third, it was a place I knew. There have probably been more clandestine operations run out of the Watergate than any comparably sized plot of land on the planet.

I also know a lobbyist who lives just up the road in Georgetown. Freddie Rochelle's a horse's ass, but he's so greedy and unscrupulous that, for the right price, he'd roast his pet toucan for hors d'oeuvres. Hell, for a little extra, he'd chew it for you. As a rule, I try to avoid lobbyists because it takes a month to bathe them out of your pores, but I've come to appreciate that if you need something unconscionable done, guys like Freddie can be useful. Look in the phonebook under "Weasel-Fucks."

I called Eddie and told him to get the plane ready and file a flight plan to Reagan National for Monday—three days away. I also asked him to book rooms for us at the Hay-Adams—under our real names. Eddie started to ask questions but then backed off.

Duke Pennington responded to my page in fifteen minutes, and when he arrived, I asked if he knew anybody who would like to use the penthouse for a couple of days—all expenses paid.

"You want to tell me why?"

"I need it to look like I haven't left. You know, room service, dirty linen. But with the drapes closed in case someone's sitting out there with a pair of binoculars."

"Manarca?"

"Probably a little more heavy duty."

"Starting when?"

"About two hours from now."

He thought for a moment. "You particular about color?"

"I've got an aversion to chartreuse. It gives me vertigo."

He gave me one of those looks. "My daughter and son-in-law are trying to have another baby, but they can't get much together time with four-year-old twins. And I know my ex-wife would like to get her hands on those kids for a while without their parents hanging around to screw up her spoiling."

"Then tell your daughter I hear caviar helps fertility, but you've got to eat a lot of it and wash it down with Dom Perignon."

He laughed. "Shit, maybe I should do this job myself."

I shook my head. "Nobody'd stay cooped up with you for more than an hour."

Duke used his elevator key to take us down into the Beverly Wilshire basement, where we crossed under Rodeo Drive through one of the tunnels that connect much of downtown Beverly Hills. The passageways were built after the city became a mecca for celebrities so they could move around town without being bothered by ordinary folk. Since 9/11, though, just about anyone with any pull at all uses them.

We came up in Barney's and went out the back door, where the valet put us in a cab. As we pulled away, my phone went off.

It was Jake. "Manarca picked up your friend, Dante."

"Remarkable what people can do when they're motivated," I said. "Where was he?"

"The loading dock supervisor at Home Depot remembered him. Said he stopped in a couple of months ago and wanted to know if teenagers ever came around looking for work. When the supervisor said they showed up mostly on weekends when there wasn't school, the guy came back every Saturday and Sunday for a month."

"Shopping for a look-alike for his shooter. And one day, in walks Kiki Videz."

"That'd be my guess. Super thought the guy might be a perv, so he wrote down his license number. Turns out the van belongs to some French chef in Toluca Lake. And guess who was bedding down in the guy's garage."

That explained the gasoline smell on the pillowcase over Kim's head. "What about Tino?"

"Just Dante. And the van, which they've impounded."

"Where is he now?"

"Beverly Hills lockup. Manarca said he wanted to make it easy for you."

"And I'm sure that's exactly how he put it," I said.

Except for a couple of cramped rooms used by attorneys, BHPD isn't set up for prisoner visitation, so Manarca and a Beverly Hills detective named Kahane had Dante in an assistant chief's office on the third floor. They had both his wrists cuffed to a chair at a round table, with the two cops seated on either side of him.

I left Archer downstairs, where there was a coffee machine and a stack of law enforcement and gun magazines. She'd wanted to see the man who'd helped orchestrate her sister's murder and tried to kill her. Tell him what she thought of him. But I needed information, and a scene wouldn't help. To make her feel like she was doing her part, I told her to call Symphony Limousine and have a car sent over.

"Speak to D. J. Kaplan and tell him to have the driver bring an extra pair of socks. Something light that won't be too hard to carry."

"Socks, what the hell . . . ?"

"He'll understand. And when the car gets here, go out and wait in it."

The assistant chief's office faced east looking down Santa Monica Boulevard. The courthouse was a block over. But despite the nearness of the traffic and the comings and goings of the court, no noise seeped inside. Other than the breathing of the room's occupants, the only sound was the gentle clicking of a Harley Davidson wall clock with a large, white skull on it, which Dante was staring at.

When I entered, Dante made eye contact with me, then went back to looking at the clock. He was smaller and heavier than I expected, but then I'd only seen him once before, and he'd been sitting in a vehicle in the dark. His face was pocked with deep, ridged acne scars, and I could smell the strong odor of scared sweat that's always on the recently arrested, even the most hardened criminals.

Manarca introduced me to Kahane, then said, "Meet Dante Bruzzi. He came in on a French passport under the name Gerard Paul. But he's not frog. He's Italian."

"Sicilian, you fuckin' cocksucker," Dante snarled.

Manarca smiled. "We've bonded."

I looked at the prisoner. "Hello, Dante, remember me?"

He twisted his head toward Manarca. "I want a lawyer."

It was the same voice I'd heard that night on the 405. But here I could detect an accent. Its edges had been worn smooth, but it was there.

Manarca shot back, "What for? There's nothing official going on. In fact, you're not even here. You're downstairs taking a nap." To me, the detective said, "Normally, international crap takes forever, but this guy's prints popped a sheet so fast, he must be quite a star back home. Lives in some shit town called Apollonica. On Corsica. That's a frog island in the—"

"I know."

Manarca nodded. "Mr. Bruzzi spent seven years in Florida. Was supposed to be going to school in Tallahassee, but there's no record he ever attended a class. Call me a cynic, but I don't think he was cleaning pools either."

I looked at the prisoner. So now I knew where he fit. Dante

was the Hyena's English-speaker. Nobody ever shoots the translator. I guessed his age at thirty-five. His eyes were as coal black as his hair, and his skin was dark Med. He'd never been handsome, and the acne scars didn't help. Suddenly, the Sicilian took a deep breath and pursed his lips. Instantly, Manarca drove four fingers into his solar plexus, and Dante began coughing violently and gasping for air.

"He's a spitter," said Manarca. "I found out the hard way."

"You want to tell me why you killed Dr. York?" I asked.

Dante just looked at me. "Fuck you," he said.

Manarca said, "That's his version of the Fifth. Pretty much all he says. From the looks of the garage where we picked him up, at least two more people had been staying there, but they're gone. One of them was probably your friend, Tino."

Suddenly, Bruzzi said, "I didn't kill anybody."

"Not even Kiki Videz?" I countered.

"Never heard of him."

"Before she died, Kim told me about the City of War," I said.

I saw Manarca's eyebrows arch.

Dante stared at me and almost stopped breathing. Then he suddenly relaxed. "Fuckin' Americans. And your women are the worst—especially the educated ones. All this freedom shit . . . and lawyers. The rest of the world doesn't work that way, but you never get it. Not until it's too late. Did she really think we'd let her publish an article? And those fuckin' pictures? I'm glad she's dead. You're next."

The door had finally cracked open. I tried to give it another push. "It must have really pissed you off when she just ignored you."

He sneered, "Like I said, your women are the worst."

"So is that why you gave her the handjob in the back of the van? A little Mediterranean humiliation before she got dumped in the ocean?"

He exploded. "A Sicilian would never do that! And I stopped Tino as soon as—"

I interrupted him. "Now that you bring him up, where is Tino?"

"Fuck you."

I looked at him. "And the Hyena? Or do you just call him Uncle Gaetano?"

I didn't expect an answer, and I didn't get one. So I added, "Well, if you happen to be talking to him, tell him I'm looking forward to sticking a Glock up his fat ass."

He tried to come across the table at me, chair and all, but Detective Kahane put a pair of meaty hands on his shoulders and pulled him back down. Then Kahane got a good grip on a handful of Dante's hair and held on.

Bruzzi writhed and snorted and tried to bite the cop, so Manarca dug his fingers back into his gut, and the show stopped.

I stood. "Not much more to learn here," I said.

Manarca nodded. "I could have saved you the trip, but since we're just getting acquainted, I thought you'd want to see for yourself. Care to tell me who Uncle Gaetano is?"

He was right. I wouldn't have trusted him. But next time I might. "Gaetano 'The White Hyena' Bruzzi. Some kind of Sicilian godfather. That's all I know." I could tell Manarca wasn't buying in, but, to his credit, he let it slide. "What are you charging him with?" I asked.

"The guy whose garage he was living in has an expired visa, so we're gonna keep them both on ice until we get everybody's papers straightened out. The way the Feds move, that'll give me at least a month to come up with something of my own. And right now there's a Detective Davis in Manhattan Beach comparing Mr. Bruzzi's prints to the ones they found in that Kempthorn kid's house."

I looked at Dante, but if he was worried, he didn't show it. "Maybe you'll catch a break," I said to Manarca.

He winked. "I've got a hunch."

I stood and walked around the table. I could see Manarca and Kahane weren't sure what I was doing, so the Beverly

Hills detective took a firmer grip on the prisoner's hair. Dante was wearing a long-sleeved shirt. I undid the button on his left cuff and pulled it over his forearm. His skin was unmarked. I did the same with the right. No spider there either.

Dante locked eyes with me, and I could feel the hatred. "Like I thought," I said. "Not a warrior. *Il leccaculo.*"

Despite the cuffs and the grip Kahane had on him, Bruzzi nearly levitated out of his chair. Saliva flew, and he let go with a stream of obscenities that were impressive even from a criminal.

Manarca burst out laughing.

"What did you call him?" asked Kahane.

Manarca answered for me. "*Il leccaculo.* 'The ass-licker.' But it goes way beyond that. In the old country, one of them would have to die."

I turned to leave, then turned back. "I almost forgot," I said and slid the gold earring with the interlocking *N* and *D* across the table. It stopped in front of Dante. His stare was all the confirmation I needed. To Manarca, I said, "You might want to give County a heads-up. Mr. Bruzzi here likes them before they start to shave. Dresses them up like Barbie."

I saw Kahane dig his fingers a little tighter into Dante's scalp.

Manarca walked me out. When the door closed, he said, "We found the mate to that earring in the frog's garage. Where'd you get yours?"

I didn't answer.

He started to say something else then decided it would be a waste of time, so he switched gears. "City of War?"

I looked at him. "You now know exactly as much as I do."

25

Private Sanctuary and Silent Requiem

I'd expected D. J. Kaplan to send my preferred town car or SUV, but when I got downstairs, Archer was sitting in a super-stretch Caddie up to her elbows in a platter of Spago sandwiches he'd included. Add in the case of designer water and the Nate'n Al's chocolate chip cheesecake, and I smelled a favor request coming from D. J. before long. Archer offered me a ham and cheese. I declined.

I asked the driver, a burly guy named Buck who had Brooklyn written all over him, if he had the socks, and he handed me a brown paper bag. I opened it and found a Beretta 9mm. I'd have preferred something smaller, but at least D. J. hadn't sent a Magnum.

Archer looked at the gun but made no comment and went back to her sandwich. I gave Buck the Princeton Street address. Then I dialed Benny Joe. I was pissed at myself for not having done this before, especially after my conversation with Marta Videz, but better late than never.

The phone rang for easily three minutes before he picked up. He sounded half-asleep. "What the fuck time is it?"

"How you doing with those negatives?"

"Guy was a helluva shooter. Had a real fuckin' eye. I'll have something for you tomorrow."

"Forget it."

"What the fuck! You got any idea how many hours I put in!"

"You can have the Babe Ruth pictures for your trouble."

"You fuckin' shittin' me?"

"Nope, consider them yours."

"Tell that rat fuck Praxis, okay?"

"Okay. Now here's what I need, and you don't have to do anything but exercise that brain of yours. You awake?"

"Wait'll I open a beer."

I heard rummaging, then a can being opened and its contents being gulped. Finally, Benny Joe said, "Bedroom fridge. What a fuckin' country. Okay, shoot."

"Where would a woman hide photographs?"

"This is like some kind of fuckin' joke, right? Okay, I'll bite. Tell me."

"I'm serious. They would be important enough that they might get her killed."

"In her snatch. How the fuck should I know?"

"Stand up."

"What?"

"Get the fuck out of bed."

I heard groaning sounds and a loud burp. "Okay, asshole, I'm up."

"Now walk around the room. Get the blood flowing." I waited a few seconds. "You moving yet?"

"Yeah, yeah."

"Now listen to me. You're a genius with all things photographic. That means you think differently when it comes to cameras and film. If you were half as good at poker as you are at pictures, you'd know exactly what a civilian had when he bet out."

"Jesus, what I do ain't a fuckin' game."

"Oh, it's not? Then why does the government keep trying to get you to come back? And why are all those assassination photos hanging on your walls? Because guys like you would stop in the middle of getting laid if an idea came to you that would beat one of your competitors at some bullshit thing no one else would even notice. You're the ultimate competitor, Benny Joe. So kick Lee Harvey out of your fucking head for a few minutes, and put those cells to work on the problem."

There was silence.

"Okay, what were her hobbies?"

"Art, same as her business."

"This is about that fuckin' broad who got killed, isn't it?"

"Forget that. Focus."

"Left- or right-handed?"

I had to think for a moment. She smoked and ate mostly with her left hand. "Left," I guessed.

"Age? No, forget that. It only matters that she was a broad. Car?"

"Mustang. GT. Silver."

"House or apartment?"

"House."

"Favorite movie?"

Favorite movie? What the . . . ? "We watched *Papillon* once."

Benny Joe groaned. "Jesus Christ, Rail, just about everybody with a pulse has had to watch *Papillon* with you. You're gonna show McQueen to a broad, it's gotta be fuckin' *Thomas Crown*."

I rolled my eyes. "I'll try to remember that. I don't know what her favorite movie was."

"You're sure not making this any fuckin' easier. Next time you're going to get shot up with some chick, ask some fuckin' questions beforehand, asshole. Okay, give me something personal. Something she might not have told anyone else."

I thought about how she liked to have her nipples worked, but I didn't think that was what he had in mind. And I didn't need another lecture about how I was doing that wrong. Then it came to me. "She was probably molested by her father."

"Jesus Christ. Why the fuck didn't you say that before?"

"Explain."

"Pictures aren't like jewels. You don't put them in a safe-deposit box and trot them out for parties. They're fuckin' personal, man. You need to have them close—so you can look at them whenever you need a fix. And if they're important enough to fuckin' hide, then they've got to be someplace you think is safe—even if it's not. Like me and my fuckin' hole in the yard."

I understood. "So her bedroom is out."

"Right, it's where her father would have come to her. The whole house is fuckin' out if it's the one she lived in with him. It wouldn't matter if he was dead a thousand fuckin' years. He'd still be there."

Suddenly, it came to me. "Cactus," I said out loud.

"I thought you just said cactus," said Benny Joe.

"I did. And you *are* a genius. You've earned the right to go back to bed."

"Nah, I just opened a fuckin' beer, remember?"

As we drove toward Princeton Street, I asked Archer about the greenhouse in the backyard.

"It was my mother's," she said. "Everything she touched died, but that didn't stop her. Went through her tulip phase, then orchids, the works. I finally figured out that it didn't matter if anything grew or not. It filled time."

"What about Kim?"

She thought for a moment. "As soon as she and Truman moved in, Kim was out there puttering around. I don't remember what she grew, but Bess said everything green loved her."

"What about cactus?"

Archer looked at me. "I saw that stuff in the yard, but Kim must have put it in later. Growing up, it was all hedges and flowers."

Buck let us out in front, and I told him to get a cup of coffee and come back in an hour. I didn't want him sitting there in seven miles of black steel.

Archer stood behind me as I pushed open the greenhouse door. She looked at the wilderness of needles. "Jesus Christ, a cactus Amazon. What was she doing with all this shit? There used to be just a couple of boxes of dead daisies and a million fucking spiders. Willy City."

I knelt down where two massive organ-pipe cactus in identical pots pressed against each other. At least eight feet tall and with spines reaching out six inches, they looked lethal. But something was different about them. Everywhere else, smaller bunches of cactus had been shoved into the spaces between the larger ones, creating a solid curtain of green. Here, that hadn't been done.

I noticed that twelve inches of spines had been clipped off one of the stalks. Same with the adjacent one, leaving a clearance the width of my hand. On a hunch, I reached through. Nothing. Gingerly, I extended my arm and reached from side to side as far as I could, half-expecting to be impaled, but all I hit was more empty space.

Pulling back my arm, I rocked one of the organ-pipe pots back and forth until I had widened the gap a couple of feet. Squinting into the darkness beyond, I could see a narrow passageway. I turned to Archer. "In the kitchen cabinet next to the water glasses, there's a flashlight."

A few moments later, Archer was back with a small halogen Maglite. As she handed it to me, I noticed brown dirt in the grooves of the grip, and I had a feeling it wasn't the first time it had been out here.

With the Maglite between my teeth as a headlight, I wriggled on my hands and knees between the two large cactus. I was a lot bigger than Kim, and my sides and back brushed against the sentry plants, making the going painful.

About five feet in, I was no longer crawling on the bare plank floor but instead on carpet remnants, carefully cut and tacked down.

"Where the hell are you?" Archer called. "I can't see anything."

I thought back to that first night with Kim. *I think ev-*

eryone should have a completely unexpected place in their home, don't you?

"Ali Baba's cave," I answered.

"What?"

"Where Kim came to get away from her father."

The tunnel wound around and through the plants, but because each had had its spines clipped off high enough for passage, I was able to avoid most of the hazards as long as I stayed low. Finally, I saw an open area ahead, and I guessed I was near the far corner of the greenhouse, where the thorny creeper overhead made the place almost completely dark.

I don't think anyone could have prepared me for what I saw next. Reflecting back at me in the glow of the flashlight were the whites of hundreds of eyes. It took me a few seconds to realize they were dolls. In all shapes and sizes, some new, most old and well-worn, lined up row after row on makeshift brick and plank shelves that reached up at least five feet.

The space wasn't high enough for me to stand, but I could crouch without too much discomfort, and I found two thin, battery-operated lights shaped like candles. They'd probably been pilfered from Bess's Christmas decorations years ago. The first one was dead, but the second came on and lit the area well enough for me to turn off the flashlight.

I heard Archer. "Hey, I see light over there. I sure hope it's you, because if not, I'm outta here."

"You want to come in?" I called back.

"Not a chance. I'll live it on the replay."

I took in the rest of Kim's furnishings. A stack of children's Golden Books, some doll furniture, an air mattress, two pillows, a blanket, a small picnic cooler and a cigar box of costume jewelry. There was dust, but not a lot. It hadn't been that long since she'd been here.

Kim had created a safe place the only way she'd known how, and I wondered how many nights she'd crouched out here in the dark while Truman York prowled the house in a sexual rage. Spiders, mice and cactus had been a lot less threatening than her father. And like Benny Joe had said, even dead, he was still there. And I'd been rough on her because she hadn't told me the complete truth the first time I'd asked. Even though I hadn't known, I still felt small.

I looked at the rows of dolls and said quietly, "I'm sorry, Kim. I can't make it right, but maybe I can make it even."

Some of the dolls were almost in tatters. She'd rescued them and brought them here to be safe for the rest of their lives. Just like she'd wished someone had rescued her. It felt like a violation to even touch them, but I had no other choice.

I started down the rows, picking each one up, checking it, then putting it back. Moments later I found the camera behind one of the dolls. I opened it, but the memory card slot was empty. I put it back where I'd found it. Give or take one Olympus, the Getty would survive.

Then, something on one of the lower shelves caught my eye. Sandwiched in between the dolls was a single, planted cactus. I pulled it forward and saw, around its stem, a tiny brass tag that read, HUG ME—I'M LONELY, just like the one Abernathy had sent home from her office.

Using the blanket to keep from getting stuck, I pulled the plant gently out of its pot and set it aside. Then I probed the dirt with my fingers. At the bottom was a small Ziploc containing a smooth silver object slightly smaller than a Bic lighter.

A computer flash drive.

I put it in my pocket and replanted the cactus. Then I took one more look around, switched off the candle-shaped light and went back out the way I'd come.

I told Archer about the cactus womb Kim had created and about the rescued dolls. You didn't have to have a degree in psychology to put it together. I saw her lip begin to tremble, and she turned away. "That poor child."

I needed to go in the house to get Kim's computer. Archer

said she'd wait in the car. "I don't think I'm going to be able to go back in there for a while," she said.

As Buck drove us to Santa Monica Airport, I put the flash drive in the laptop. It contained two items, a slideshow and a text document.

I opened the document first.

26

The Flash Drive

CITY OF WAR
WAR, DUPLICITY AND STATECRAFT
IN THE ART WORLD
Investigated and Written by Dr. Kimberly York

SUMMER, 1941

As the two-million-strong German army raced un-checked across Russia, Soviet defenses were out-manned, outgunned, outcommanded and in chaos. To save what troops he had left from the slaughter, Joseph Stalin withdrew his regular army units east to Moscow and beyond, leaving the west to be de-fended by a poorly trained and ill-equipped militia.

On August 14, a young army captain named Niko-lai Tretiakov, who had been pulled back from Kiev, was summoned to the Kremlin by General Dimitri Zhuk, Chief of the General Staff. Only two years earlier, Captain Tretiakov, a graduate of Leningrad's prestigious Academy of Art, had been an associate curator at the Hermitage Museum. Called to military service, he had left the life of beauty to become a combat officer, and as evidenced by his advanced rank, a good one. .

Now, as he stood at rigid attention, his heart racing at the grandeur of his surroundings, the general outlined the gravity of the war situation. When Zhuk finished, he handed Tretiakov a notebook. In it were listed forty museums situated on a geographic line extending from Smolensk in the north to Odessa in the south. These museums housed thousands of irreplaceable, priceless works of art, and now they lay directly in the path of the onrushing Wehrmacht.

Zhuk explained that were the treasures to fall into Hitler's hands, the economic impact would pale in comparison to the propaganda disaster that would befall the nation. Stalin had decreed that such an embarrassment could not happen.

Captain Tretiakov, a man who had once dreamed of spending his life preserving art, now learned that he had been handpicked for a mission to do exactly the opposite: to penetrate German lines, locate the museums and destroy their contents. Failure, he was told, was not an option.

And so, in as bold an operation as was ever conceived, Tretiakov and a team of twelve handpicked men set out, not to safeguard Russia's culture but to erase it.

But what Zhuk and Tretiakov did not know was that, at that very moment, a unit of battle-hardened Waffen-SS troops were preparing to move on those same targets. Under the command of Colonel Heinz Schellenberg, this Nazi treasure-hunting team had its own list—one prepared by Hitler's architect, Albert Speer—of art and artifacts to be secured for transport to Berlin, where many would adorn the Hall of Victory in the newly constructed Reichstag.

In the early going, Tretiakov had remarkable success. The German battle plan did not call for occupying cities but to keep moving eastward. So, as the enemy camped in the countryside, Captain Tretiakov entered the deserted towns relatively unmolested.

But when he laid eyes on what he had been sent to destroy, the former art student could not bring himself to burn such treasures. Instead, he removed from the vaults the most valuable pieces, wrapped them as best he could, divided them into lots and secreted them throughout the area.

Some went into remote tentacles of the cities' sewer systems, some were buried beneath stalls, and others were slipped between the walls of abandoned libraries, stores and private homes. And as he worked, Captain Tretiakov drew detailed maps—twenty-two in all—in the notebook Zhuk had given him, carefully noting the locations of the hundreds of hidden works.

It was inevitable that Captain Tretiakov, moving south, and Colonel Schellenberg, advancing north, would eventually collide. It happened in the town of Kharkov in the eastern Ukraine, and in the bitter fighting that followed, ten of Tretiakov's men were killed, and the captain himself was severely wounded.

By the time Tretiakov and the two surviving members of his team made their way back to Moscow, it was December, and the city had been encircled by German troops. Stealthily, they picked their way through the enemy and once again gained entrance to the Kremlin.

General Zhuk had long since given Tretiakov up for dead, but now, as the young captain told his story and presented his twenty-two maps showing the locations of the secreted art, the general immediately grasped his very enviable position and moved quickly to secure it.

After medical attention and a night's sleep, Tretiakov was brought again before Zhuk. In a make-shift ceremony, the general presented the captain with the Order of the Red Banner, one of the Soviet Union's highest military awards. As Zhuk placed the medal around the soldier's neck, he kissed him on both cheeks.

It was the last thing Nikolai Tretiakov would ever feel. Immediately, one of the honor guard stepped forward and shot the young captain in the back of the head. Tretiakov's remaining men were already dead, their gasoline-soaked bodies set afire in the Kremlin dump.

General Zhuk now reached deep into the immense gulag of the Soviet Union. There, he culled from the population twenty-two of the most radical dissident artists. Brought one by one to a temporary studio in Lefortovo Prison, each was handed proper materials and told to paint anything he wished.

But the canvases they were given were not blank. Tretiakov's maps had been carefully reproduced on them by army draftsmen, and the artists would now cover them with oils.

Most of the artists sensed that this would be their last painting and brought to life images designed to evoke the hatred of Soviet rulers for a thousand years: pornographic depictions of Lenin, Stalin as a male prostitute, Molotov as a beggar. Yet others reached deep inside themselves and painted scenes of such breathtaking beauty and poignancy that their guards wept.

Eventually, all of the maps were covered, and each artist was in an unmarked grave in the prison cemetery, along with the draftsmen. General Zhuk was finally alone with his secret.

But the enemy was at the gates. And as they pressed into the western suburbs of Moscow, and

German occupation seemed only days away, the foreign embassies were being hurriedly relocated east to Kuybyshev.

General Zhuk approached the American military attaché, Lieutenant Colonel Christopher Crawford, and pressed him to take his paintings to safety, planning to retrieve them after the war. It is unknown if Crawford's boss, Ambassador Steinhardt, was apprised of the additional crates that were loaded onto the fourteen-truck American convoy that fled Moscow east to Kuybyshev on New Year's Eve, 1941. If he was, he made no record of it.

But unforeseen events can overtake even generals. A month later, Stalin began a new round of purges, and Zhuk's number came up. Dispatched to join Captain Tretiakov and the artists, Zhuk became one more casualty of what would eventually grow to be twenty million Soviet victims of that terrible war.

And the paintings disappeared. For fifty-six years.

In 1997, retired Air Force Major Truman York was working as special courier for the Pentagon. Special couriers hold various security clearances, and Major York's was one of the highest.

Summoned by a general whose name I will reveal later in this article, Major York was given the assignment of escorting twenty-two paintings to Russia—those that have come to be known as the Tretiakov Collection.

For security reasons, special couriers do not usually know what they are transporting. But Major York was told what his cargo was and that the job would require one trip a month for twenty-two consecutive months.

I will leave it to someone else to tell the story of the paintings' journey from the Soviet Union to the United States so many years ago. What follows is Major York's story.

It is one devoid of glamour. Rather it is filled with treachery and death. I dislike even knowing it, let alone telling it. But it is of vital importance to the art world I love so much . . . and to me personally.

Major York, you see, was my father.

Dr. Kimberly York
Santa Monica, CA

27

Babushkas and Black Granite

I opened Kim's laptop again as Jake Praxis's G5 began its takeoff roll. Her written introduction had been riveting, but I was still no closer to unraveling why she'd been killed. The subsequent slideshow contained twenty-eight items, beginning with the four photographs Marta had witnessed Kim's taking at the Biltmore.

In the first two, Gaetano Bruzzi was clearly recognizable, as was his nephew, Dante. The third showed the man he was there to meet, but he was no one I had seen before. However, the Asians in his security detail didn't look Japanese, Korean or ethnic Chinese. They were large-framed, with thick necks and light hair, characteristics I had seen more often in Siberia and Mongolia than farther east or south. Quite possibly, the unknown man was Russian.

The fourth photograph was the man in the jeans and leather jacket Marta had described getting off the elevator. She had been correct. He was an American. But his clothes and attitude were irrelevant. I knew him. Not well, but well enough. I said nothing, and Archer gave no indication of recognition. Marta, however, had missed something, or perhaps simply neglected to mention it. The American was carrying an attaché case.

I went back to the first three photographs and looked at them closely. In the background of the one showing Dante, I found what I was looking for—a pair of tan leather suitcases held by two of the Asian security men. It seemed a safe assumption it wasn't laundry. So at a minimum, the Biltmore meeting was an exchange. It didn't take much of a leap to guess what was in the suitcases, and since the contents of the attaché had contributed to four deaths that I knew of, it probably wasn't laundry either.

Continuing, the next two photographs were of a man in an artist's studio at work on a large canvas. He was painting with his left hand while he held his palette in his right, and what was visible of his work looked like a battle scene from the era of the Light Brigade. In the first, the man's back was to the camera, but in the second, he had turned in profile, as if someone had called to him.

His clothes were old and paint-spattered, and he had a prominent and quite crooked nose. But it was his smile that was out of place. It wasn't one of mirth. Rather it seemed fatuous, almost silly. I thought for a moment that he might be putting it on, but when I studied his eyes, I didn't think so.

Photographs 7-27 were of ornate buildings, and under each, Kim had typed what looked like a title followed by an artist's name. None were familiar, so it was likely that the buildings were museums or archives, and the typed information noted the Tretiakov painting residing inside. Since most repositories of fine art do not permit photographs to be taken of their collections, that would account for only showing the building.

Suddenly, Archer said, "Go back a few slides."

I did, and shortly she stopped me. "I've been there," she said, pointing. "That's the museum at Klenova in the Czech Republic. Just across the German border. I did a shoot for *French Vogue* at an old castle there. We took a train from Nuremberg, and it was like stepping into Hansel and Gretel.

Mountains, forests and gingerbread houses. And that title. *Scourge out of the East*. It's a painting. I saw it."

"Tell me about it."

She closed her eyes, remembering. "There was a skeleton riding a white stallion and waving a sword over his head, like this." She whirled her arm, like she was handling a lariat. "The rider had on a red cape that billowed out behind him, and the horse's nostrils flared into big, black holes."

"Dramatic."

"No, awful . . . and sad. The skeleton's mouth was open—screaming—and there was this ominous, deep purple and crimson sky hanging over a landscape littered with bodies torn to pieces. And in the foreground was a group of terrified men and women clutching each other, like they were waiting their turn."

"What about the artist? Petr Stech. Remember anything about him?"

She shook her head. "There was a plaque, but all it said was what's on the slide with the word 'Communism' at the top. I guess that's what it's supposed to represent. It was hanging by itself in a little room off the main gallery, and it had a three-sided brass railing around it so nobody could get too close." Suddenly, she laughed.

"What?" I asked.

"There was a guard. He didn't speak English, but he pointed to the painting and whispered, '*Dissidentski*.' I whispered back, 'No shitski,' but he didn't get it."

The twenty-eighth and final slide—what would have been the twenty-second painting—wasn't a photograph. It was just a blank screen labeled:

OFFERING OF THE BABUSHKAS
Illya Andreyevich Orlov, 1942

Archer made the observation on her own. "That would be the painting Truman was carrying when . . ." I nodded, and we rode in silence for a while.

Finally, she said, "I have a question. I don't know where those other buildings are, but I do know the Klenova one. Kim's article says General Zhuk got his artists from the Soviet Gulag, but Czechoslovakia wasn't part of the Soviet Union until after the war. So why would there be a Czech artist in the Tretiakov Collection?"

"I think I can give you an answer. After the 1917 revolution, Lenin threw open the doors to his new 'Workers Paradise.' It was an orgasmic moment for sympathizers around the world, and a lot of them packed up and headed east. Merchants, tradesmen, doctors, even thousands of Jews lured by the marquee of social equality. Not to mention artists of all stripes. Musicians, painters, writers. Remember John Reed?"

"My mother was completely cracked over Warren Beatty. She had every movie he ever made, and some weekends, she'd stock up on popcorn and beer and marathon it. Bess wouldn't have known a Trotskyite from Kryptonite, she just thought Warren had a great ass. But give me a fucking break with that self-indulgent piece of shit, *Reds*—and I'm a goddamn liberal."

"Yeah, but what do you think about Warren's ass?"

"*Splendor in the Grass*—hot. *Bugsy*—old and flat. Go on with your story. We were skipping toward Moscow with smiles on our faces."

"Well, like all big lies, one day, everybody woke up. But the exits had been nailed shut. If you were in, you were staying. And if you were complaining, you were staying too, just minus a pulse. For a lot of the true believers, it was one mother of a jolt, and by the time World War Two rolled around, some of their children were old enough to start becoming radicalized in the opposite direction."

Archer was quiet for a while. "What's going on, Rail? And who is that man painting in a studio? He's not one of the others."

"I don't know . . ." I let my voice drift off.

Archer finished it for me. "But Kim did, and it got her killed."

"Yes."

Just after midnight, the Gulfstream put down at Carl Spaatz Field in Reading, Pennsylvania. Reading, like a lot of the old coal and steel belt, is a down-on-its-luck town, and the airport reflects it. Nobody goes there who doesn't have to.

Somewhere over Nevada, I'd told Archer about my meeting with Dante Bruzzi. She'd taken everything in and asked only a couple of questions. Then both of us had gone to sleep for the rest of the trip.

We deplaned in a light fog with the engines still running. Rubbing the sleep out of her eyes, Archer looked around and said. "Jesus, *Clockwork Orange*." I gave a thumbs-up to the pilot, and he retracted the stairs and taxied back onto the runway. He was headed to New York to pick up one of Jake's music clients, who was escaping to Vegas to cool off after a throwdown with his former Playmate wife. Made perfect sense. Where else?

We found an ancient cabdriver at a run-down lunch counter in the terminal. He was drinking coffee with a couple of UPS guys. "How much to take us to D.C.?" I asked.

He never turned around. "Don't drive that far. Arthritis acts up."

I counted out five hundred dollars, slapped it on the counter and pushed it into his line of sight. "There's another five when we get there."

"Shit, Elroy," one of the UPS drivers whistled, "you don't do it, I'm gonna call in sick and run them down there in Big Brown."

Elroy thought about it a moment, then swiveled on his stool and looked up at me. After a head-to-toe appraisal, he said, "You're that basketball fella, ain't ya? The one gets hisself suspended all the time."

I didn't say anything.

"Thought so," he said. "The grand, plus two autographs for my nephews."

"Eleven hundred and no autographs," I countered.

"Twelve. Cause then I got to buy them off eBay."

"Done."

"And all of it up front."

The UPS guys shook their heads as I counted out the remaining seven one-hundred dollar bills. Elroy scooped up the cash and had it tucked away before I got my money clip back in my pocket.

The Watergate doesn't look like any other building in Washington. Designed by an experimental architect, it's an inconsistent mix of styles one critic called Guggenheim meets college dorm. But the place grows on you. And when you mention the name to people outside D.C., it always gets a response.

Elroy Webb, former boxer, former short-order cook, former aircraft carrier steward and currently full-time Reading, Pennsylvania cabbie, had kept up a running stream of chatter for the past hour and a half. And now, as I directed him onto New Hampshire Avenue and into the quiet Watergate complex, he didn't slow down the commentary.

"Don't look like they got the red carpet rolled out," he observed. "Figure they'd be a little more on the ball with a celebrity coming to town and all."

"Well, Elroy," I said, "it's after two in the morning."

"Shit, you'da come home with me, the whole neighborhood'd be up to say hello."

Archer, who seemed to be enjoying Mr. Webb's stream-of-consciousness rambling, said, "Well, maybe we should just turn around and go back."

I rolled my eyes, but Elroy wasn't having any of that either. "Not a chance. I ain't tellin' nobody—specially Mrs. Webb—about this money. Gonna take me a run up to Atlantic City one a these days. Maybe turn it into somethin' serious. Or maybe just get me a bottle of Mr. Beam and a Silver-Tongue Suzie and lay in for a weekend."

I had to give the guy credit. He was seventy-five if he was a day. Considering he only stopped talking to breathe, my guess was Mrs. Webb didn't keep the reins that tight.

The South Tower night deskman, wearing a blue blazer, maroon turban and a name tag that read Pradeep, buzzed us through the front door. I identified myself as the client of Jhanya Devereux of Beverly Hills, and he handed me a manila envelope containing two sets of keys and a piece of heavy stationery embossed with:

WANDETTE HOPE RADCLIFFE
SEA TO SHINING SEA PROPERTIES

In broad, feminine script and rich purple ink, Ms. Radcliffe had written

Dear Mr. X . . .

Welcome to the Watergate!!!

Jhanya said you're a VERRRRRRRY important person . . .

So if you need even the teensiest of anything,

just put your lips together and whistle!!!

Or call me!!! Anytime!!! Day or Night!!!

I took the liberty of putting a few things

in the fridge to get you started!!!

Hugs a bunch!!!

Wandie

PS. Jhanya said you're a really big guy,

so I got you a Mercedes SUV

It's in Space 11 in the garage!!!

Hope to meet you while you're here!!!!!!!!!!!

I handed the note to Archer, who read it and made a gagging sound. "Wandie Radcliffe and Hugs a Bunch. I guarantee you, she's a big fucking peroxide blonde with veneered teeth and a pair of gazongas out to here."

"In that case, would you mind if I dropped you at a Holiday Inn?"

I told Pradeep I'd find my own way, and we took the elevator to the top floor. Three units had been combined to create a several-thousand-square-foot open space with a 270° view of the Potomac and the lights of the suburbs beyond. The décor was burled wood and hunting trophies accented with modern paintings and several stylized busts.

I'd no sooner closed the electric drapes than Archer took the control box and opened them again. "If I'm going to live on the run, then when I've got a view, I'm goddamn well going to look at it," she said.

I started to say something about security, then dropped it. She wandered into the kitchen, and I heard her open the refrigerator. "Look at this, will ya. Ten ounces of Iranian beluga, a jeroboam of Pol Roger Winston Churchill and some kind of chocolate-covered turd. Oh, and two champagne flutes on ice with another note."

Dear Mr. X . . .
If you don't like drinking alone . . .
My number's on the letterhead!!!

W

"What a vacuous cunt. Where the fuck are the bacon and eggs in case we showed up in the middle of the goddamn night? I'll lay you 8 to 5 Wandie couldn't pour piss out of a boot."

You don't hear the C-word word a lot, especially from women. I took it as a sign anger was replacing fear. Wandie just happened to wander into the process. I moseyed into the kitchen and saw Archer had the caviar open and was digging at it with two fingers then ramming it into her mouth.

I said, "I think there's an all-night diner just over the Key Bridge. Since we don't have time to sleep, you want to rough it on finger food or take a ride?"

Pointing to a piece of taxidermy, she said with her mouth full, "I could eat the ass end out of that warthog, so lead on, Frank Buck. I need calories."

"Give me a minute." I left her in the kitchen and went through the apartment until I found what I expected—a gun safe. You want to find a firearm in any major city, look for the richest neighborhood and go to the master bedroom. Every time I'm invited to a party, I test my theory, and I'm rarely disappointed. Manhattan's Upper West Side, Beacon Hill in Boston, my town, Beverly Hills. It's not about politics. Regardless of which editorial page you believe in, when you know you're a target, you don't leave the lives of your loved ones to the tender mercies of a minimum-wage switchboard operator or high-school-dropout security guy.

This safe was locked, of course, and to my surprise, the combination wasn't taped to the bottom of a nightstand drawer. Nor was it slipped between the pages of one of the leather-bound volumes of French nudes on an adjacent shelf. I stopped and thought for a moment. Rich people are usually as lazy as everybody else, meaning they like to keep their passwords and combinations within arm's reach.

But after a couple more false starts, I was about to chalk this guy up as being one of those rare ones who commit things to memory. Then I noticed there was a lamp that wasn't on. When I'd entered, I'd hit the wall switch, and six lamps scattered throughout the place had lit up. But jammed between the seven-foot safe and an even taller armoire was a glass and brass floor lamp that remained dark. But even if it had been on, placed where it was, it wouldn't have illuminated much of anything. I stepped forward and looked through the top of the shade. The bulb was black.

I crossed the room and flicked off the wall switch. The

room went dark. Then I walked back to the floor lamp and turned it on. Instantly, a series of numbers glowed on the door of the safe.

From the doorway, Archer said, "What the . . . ?"

"Phosphorescent marker and a black light," I said. "The owner's recall isn't any better than anyone else's, but he gets bonus points for clever."

I spun the dial of the lock, and the door popped open. Inside was an impressive collection of both long guns and pistols, and in one of the two drawers, I found what I wanted—a Sig Sauer .45 threaded for a suppressor. The professionally manufactured silencer itself was in the second drawer. I slipped the Sig in one pocket of my jacket and the tube in the other. D. J.'s Beretta I put in the drawer.

As I was closing the safe, Archer said, "Bwana Watergate has some interesting stuff, but when it comes to shotguns, Purdy may have great resale, but you can't beat Bertuzzi in the field."

"The lady is full of surprises."

"The guy who owned my modeling agency had a hunting lodge in the Adirondacks. We lived together long enough for him to teach me to shoot just about everything. By the way, isn't getting caught with a suppressor a mandatory seven?"

"Federal, yes. D.C. local, who knows? Maybe the needle."

"Wouldn't it be smarter to take the Glock .40? Better stopping power and a bigger magazine."

"And pulling the trigger is like dialing 911. I hope I don't have to shoot anybody, but if I do, I want to be able to get some miles between us before anyone figures out what happened."

As we drove toward Arlington in Wandie's silver SUV with all of eleven miles on the odometer, Archer seemed lost in thought. It was confirmed when we passed the Lincoln Memorial and she didn't look. Not easy to do. Finally, she said softly, "You say this guy, Dante, was a shrimp."

"John Wayne, he wasn't. Why?"

"Well, you'd like to think a guy trying to kill you is fucking scary. At the very least, imposing. That little fuck on the boat still pisses me off. If he hadn't gotten those cuffs on me, I could have kicked his anorexic ass to fucking Seattle."

The C-word *and* attitude. She was going to be okay.

It was going on 3:30 a.m., and we were full. Archer had ordered everything on the menu and done her best to finish it. We'd just crossed back over the Key Bridge when a car passed us at breakneck speed, weaving wildly. I'd seen him coming and pulled to the curb, and even then, he'd almost gotten us.

"Probably a congressman late for a vote," I said.

Archer was fixated on something else. "Is that what I think?" she asked, pointing.

I looked and answered, "Yes."

"Take me there," she said.

I turned left at the next intersection and found a parking spot on the street. There are always people on the Mall. Thirty below in a sleet storm, and there'd still be strollers. This was only early fall, so even a couple of hours before dawn, there were a dozen or so insomniacs walking and talking.

As we approached the Vietnam Memorial, Archer grabbed my arm and held tight. "You haven't done this before?" I asked.

She shook her head. "Please don't let go of me."

The Vietnam Wall is a haunting place. Like the white crosses at Normandy, if you listen closely, the voices of the fallen whisper on the wind. I checked the directory for the location of Commander Cayne's name, then Archer and I walked slowly down the long, gentle path into the black granite canyon. As always, there were small, private offerings along the way. A picture of a young man throwing a football, a white rose, a tattered teddy bear, a purple heart, a folded note with "Gil" written on it.

When we came to the panel I had noted in the directory, I slowed, but Archer pulled on my arm, and we kept walking.

At the intersection where the east and west walls meet, we stopped. Here, the memorial rises to its highest point, and here, the acoustical nuance pushes together the quiet prayers of everyone along the paths.

We stood in silence until Archer finally said, "Okay, I'm ready now."

We retraced our steps back along the west wall until we reached the panel we had passed earlier. In the third row was the name Alexander Connor Cayne. Archer reached out with the hand that wasn't holding onto me, and I stepped forward so she could touch the letters.

She ran her fingers over the cut stone, and I felt her knees begin to buckle. I put my arm around her, and she swayed against me, then regained her footing. I asked if she would like to make a rubbing of her father's name. She shook her head no and buried it in my shoulder.

As we walked up and out of the basin, there was an older lady, backlit by the Lincoln Memorial, standing in the grass alongside the path. She was wearing a long, black cloth coat and a matching wide-brimmed hat, and she had her hands thrust deep into her pockets. Even in the dark, she was elegant.

When we reached her, she stepped forward and looked at Archer. "Pardon me, miss, but you are so beautiful I just wanted to look at you more closely. I'd like to think you are the kind of young lady Mark would have brought home."

Archer smiled and put her hand on the woman's shoulder. "Was Mark your son?"

The woman nodded. "First Lieutenant Mark Stephanie. My only baby. He was due home on Christmas Eve, and the whole family was there to surprise him. We didn't know his platoon had been ambushed two days earlier, and he'd died carrying a wounded man to safety."

"I'm so sorry," said Archer tenderly.

The woman's eyes were wet, but she seemed to need to tell the story. "Mark's body was never recovered, so after my husband died, I sold my home in Minneapolis and moved here to be close to the only thing I have left of him, his name. There are a lot of us—mostly mothers. We don't socialize, but we know each other. It helps a little."

The woman turned and looked up at me. "You were a soldier, weren't you?"

"Yes, ma'm, I was. United States Army."

"Just like Mark. Would you mind if I held you for a moment? It's been so long. And I'd like to feel the warmth of someone who wore a uniform."

I stepped forward and took her in my arms. Held her. Felt her shudder. After a few seconds, she let go and thanked me. Then she turned and walked away.

28

Manfred and Marlon

Archer hadn't said anything since we left the Wall, but now, as we drove east toward Annapolis, she looked at me. "You know, ever since I met you, I've been trying to figure you out."

"How's it coming?"

"It only took half an hour on the Internet to get the broad strokes, but that's just packaging. I've spent half my life around rich men, and you're not like any of them."

"They tell me I'm a better swimmer."

She ignored me. "As a breed, people with big money are arrogant, thin-skinned and lost in any conversation that isn't about how incredible they are. But for all the vibe you give off, you could be a plumber."

"Talk about rich."

"Knock it off, will you. This is important to me."

I concentrated on driving, and she continued. "Before that guy came aboard the *Sanrevelle*, Jimmy Buffalo told me you saved his life. By stopping him from killing somebody."

I hesitated, then said, "That's probably right."

"What happened?"

"It's not that interesting."

"Humor me."

I took a breath. "When Jimmy moved out to California, he needed transportation. But he was stone broke. He found an old pickup for a grand and borrowed the money from the owner of the gym where he worked out. Guy by the name of Manfred."

"Why didn't he just borrow it from his brother?"

I looked at her and saw the light come on. "Pride," she said. "What else? The curse of the pure heart."

I went on, "The deal was that Jimmy would pay Manfred back once he started knocking down some real money. In the meantime, he'd work weekend security at the gym—gratis. Jimmy didn't like owing money, so even though some weeks he went hungry, he managed to pay back almost seven hundred dollars."

Archer interrupted. "Then, of course, he hit a rough spot."

"He couldn't even cover his rent, so he was living in the truck under a viaduct and grabbing government cheese and ten pounds of potatoes on Welfare Wednesday. Then one day, on his way back from showering at the Y, he saw Manfred and two goons hooking his pickup to a tow truck."

Archer was incredulous. "For three hundred fucking dollars?"

"Not to mention the countless hours of free security. When Eddie called me, he said he had Jimmy at his house, but he wasn't sure how long he was going to be able to keep him there. Jimmy was just waiting for a friend to come by with a gun."

Archer said, "So you paid off Manfred."

I shook my head. "Eddie could have done that. But it didn't matter to Jimmy. He was going to kill him anyway."

Archer rolled her eyes. "Jesus, I just hate macho bullshit."

"It wasn't like that. In Cajun country, when a man's down, you don't screw with him. Period. Not his house, not his woman, and especially not his car."

"But it wasn't your fight."

"I've got this thing," I said, "about people who lend money. If you've got more than you need, and somebody needs some, then you give it to them . . . or you don't. But you don't lend it."

"Is that Ghandi or Marx?" she asked.

"Let me ask you a question. You're a carpenter, and a guy on your crew gets his tools stolen. The next day, he shows up for work and asks to borrow your extra hammer. Do you give it to him?"

"Of course."

"And when he buys new tools but keeps your hammer, what then?"

She thought for a moment. "I might ask him for it, but maybe not. What the fuck, it's just a hammer."

"Okay, so instead of a hammer, the guy asks you for twenty bucks to buy a new one."

"Same thing."

"Really? So when he gets paid and doesn't give you the twenty back . . ."

I saw the wheels turning. "I'm pissed."

"Why?"

"It's money."

"And that's logical how?"

"A hammer is a hammer. Money I could be using for a lot of other things. Besides, it's like being slapped in the face."

"So even if the guy's got four kids to feed, and he had to go into hock to get new tools, you want your twenty back first."

"How am I supposed to know about the kids?"

"You aren't. But the way I operate, once I give the guy the twenty, it's over. If he pays me back, fine. If not, I never think about it again."

"And you don't feel like you've been had?"

"Never. Because the pleasure's in helping, not having another twenty bucks. When it comes to money, there's a special kind of pain that some men who have it visit on those who don't. It's about power, and it doesn't matter how classy the guy is in the rest of his life or what a prince he is with his family. When he gets a chance to fuck with somebody who's down, he usually does."

Archer was nodding. "I think I know what you mean. He wants the good feeling *and* the cash. And he gets righteous and indignant. Maybe even tells a few mutual friends how you stiffed him so he can shove in another knife without your knowing it."

"No, he wants you to know. In fact, he makes sure of it. He's a victim now, remember."

"So how did you handle Manfred?"

"I bought the land and building where his gym was and gave it to Jimmy."

"You *what*?"

"Gave it to Jimmy. And when Manfred hit a rough spot and missed a few rent payments, Jimmy stopped by and showed him the deed."

"Fucking priceless."

"Eventually, he got behind far enough that Jimmy evicted him, then he sold the building to some burger chain. Made a nice deal too. Tried to pay me back with interest, but I told him to use what he didn't need to help somebody else."

Archer let a moment go by, then looked at me. "Did Kim know about this side of you?"

"She started out asking questions."

"So who helps you with yours?" she asked.

"My what?"

"Your demons."

"What makes you think I have any?"

I could feel her eyes on me. "Because what you do is about coping. There's something inside that hurts so bad that the only way you can handle it is by helping somebody else."

I didn't say anything.

"Someday, you're going to tell me what it is."

I smiled at her. "Don't make book on it, Sigmund."

* * *

At 5:45 a.m., we were sitting in a quiet residential neighborhood in St. Michaels, Maryland, watching the first rays of morning break over the Chesapeake. The houses were unpretentious, but that was deceptive. The St. Michaels waterfront is home to professionals and entrepreneurs who earn seven figures tapping into the trillion bucks the Feds ejaculate into the area economy each year.

Not many government types live in St. Michaels, but Army Chief of Staff Marlon Hood's wife, Suzanne, was a Connecticut Wentworth—the same Wentworths who helped invent the New York Stock Exchange—so his paycheck was getting a lot more traction than most.

Archer and I watched a pair of pelicans glide just above the surface of the bay as they window-shopped for breakfast. It was so still that when my cell phone rang, it sounded like a fire alarm. Mitchell Adams was on the other end.

"They matched up a palm print in Walter's house with that guy, Dante," he said.

"I figured they might."

"Unfortunately, he won't be around to stand trial."

"What happened?"

"They transferred him last night, and during processing he disappeared. A janitor found him in a stairwell . . . shanked in the neck."

I wasn't surprised. "Los Tigres," I said.

Mitchell didn't answer, then he said, "Rumor has it, it was a brother."

I thought about it. A guy like Mitchell Adams would have connections and be owed favors. In his position, I'd have done the same thing.

When he decided I was on the same page, he said, "Before he died, he chatted a bit. Tino's full name is Celestino Negroni. He's from Apollonica, Corsica. I checked the place out with a pilot over at Air France. It's rough country. Rougher people."

"So I've heard."

"There was a third guy. Tino's younger brother, Nico. But nobody knows what happened to him. Dante seemed to think he was dead."

Obviously, the guy who'd quizzed Bruzzi the Lesser in the stairwell had been more persuasive than the cops. It's always easier when you don't have to worry about civil rights. I was glad to have a name for the guy who'd killed Jimmy Buffalo. Nico Negroni. May the fuckin' fish eat him twice.

I said, "Thanks, Mitchell. I hope you find some peace."

"I appreciate the thought, but there's no satisfaction in knowing a piece of shit is dead."

"If it helps any, two pieces of shit," I said.

He didn't say anything for a moment. "Thanks for letting me know."

General Hood came out of his house at six sharp and got behind the wheel of a red Infinity M-Class parked in the driveway. They say the fourth star is the heaviest, but Marlon looked like he was wearing his well. He was as ramrod straight as I remembered him, and if he'd had any more gold on his uniform, he'd have needed a forklift.

Hood had always been a soldier's soldier, not just a guy who dropped by to get his ticket punched, so the show of fruit salad seemed out of character. Then I remembered that his boss, the Secretary of the Army, had recently had a heart attack, so he was probably spending a lot more time on Capitol Hill these days. And even politicians who don't like the military give battle ribbons a wide berth.

Archer leaned forward and stared at him. "Jesus Christ, it's the guy in Kim's picture! You know him?"

"Marlon Hood. When I was at Bragg, he was Special Ops CO. But I was a sergeant, and he was a bird colonel, so we weren't having dinner together."

"Looks like he's moved up in the world. I count four stars," she said.

"Army Chief of Staff. Not a surprise. Marlon was no-body's fool."

Just then, the door of the house burst open, and a tall woman vaguely reminiscent of Jackie Kennedy came flying out in a rage, a coffee mug in her hand. Barefoot and wearing nothing but a yellow bathrobe with the front flapping open, she was shouting obscenities and giving the departing general the finger. Lady Suzanne, I assumed.

As General Hood backed his car into the street, the woman ran down off the porch and rifled her coffee mug at him. It bounced across the hood of the Infinity and shattered on the blacktop. The general gunned the car and took off.

"Probably forgot to mow the lawn," Archer deadpanned. "You want a recount on the 'nobody's fool' remark?"

I said nothing and started the SUV.

Archer turned to me. "So not telling me about the general was another one of your tests, huh, asshole?"

"A little while ago, I was a damaged soul with demons."

"Hey, fuck you. How's that for your soul?"

"Okay, you're right. Sorry. Next."

"So make it up to me. What else?"

"He's the reason Bruzzi—and probably the other guy—had to come to the States. A general can't travel outside the country without approvals all the way up the chain of command. And in Hood's case, probably the president's okay too. So whatever it is those three are doing, the general is driving the train—or at least thinks he is."

I told her to turn on the laptop. When she had the right picture, I pointed out the suitcase and attaché. "They could have had emissaries do a simple exchange."

"So there was something that they had to discuss. Why L.A.?"

"Probably a city of convenience. Far enough from Washington that Hood wouldn't run into anyone he knew, and just one nonstop for the other guys."

"But Kim was onto it regardless. It could have been

Patagonia, and she'd have been there . . . with her camera."
Archer's voice told me she was over her anger and proud of
her sister.

As soon as he crossed the bay, Hood hooked a hard right
at the first exit. I wasn't ready for the move and almost blew
by him. I thought he might have picked up the tail, but he
pulled into a Starbucks, got out and never looked around. It
was still early, and the place was mostly empty, so I parked
and watched him buy a *Washington Post* from a machine
and go inside. I gave him five minutes, then followed, leaving Archer in the car.

Hood had his coffee and a bran muffin and was seated
at the very back of the L-shaped room. He was facing the
door but absorbed in his paper. I made my way to his table,
stopped and said, "You're mighty cavalier about security,
General. Don't they insist on drivers for guys like you?"

His eyes shot up. It took him a second, then he broke into
a broad smile. "Jesus Christ, if it ain't the Duke of Delta
Force. Excuse me, you must be a count by now."

I laughed. "If you're going to hobnob with the international set, you'd better brush up on your heraldry. No counts
in the UK, General. And the British equivalent, an earl, is
downwind from a duke. But I'm serious about the security.
Not procedure."

Hood smiled. "Sons of bitches hang around and listen to
all your business. Then they talk. Fuck that."

"In other words, there's a girlfriend someplace who doesn't
throw coffee cups."

His eyes narrowed, but he recovered quickly. "No comment," he said. "Besides, none of the guys in the driver pool
has any combat experience. If the shit hit the fan, they might
panic and shoot me. I handle my own security." He tipped
his chair back just far enough for me to see the chrome-
plated, ivory-handled semiautomatic on his lap.

"You take that off a pimp?" I asked.

"Gift from some sheikh," he grinned as he slipped the gun

in his pocket. Then he got to his feet, came around the table and hugged me. "Goddamn, Rail," he said, "it's good to see you. Get yourself a cup of coffee and sit down."

The hug didn't fit with our relationship, so he was checking me for a weapon. I hoped he'd felt the Sig.

I pulled out a chair. "The coffee can wait."

When we were both seated, he asked, "What are you doing way the fuck out here? And strapped?"

"You don't believe in coincidence?"

"You're driving a silver SUV, and you change lanes too much."

I smiled. "One of the hazards of morning surveillance. Nothing to hide behind. I was hoping you might shed some light on why I've been summoned to your place of business. I hate meetings where I'm the only one who's going to be surprised."

Marlon Hood looked uncomfortable, and I suddenly remembered that even though he'd acted startled when I'd approached him, he hadn't tensed up. And he hadn't put his hand on the gun in his lap. I don't care how cool you are, that green and gold General Staff badge on his right breast pocket put him near the top of Sandland's hit parade, and he'd be getting regular briefings on a shithouse full of bad guys who'd like to earn their six dozen virgins by taking him out.

"So you were expecting me," I said.

He looked at me. "You were as good a special operator as anyone I've ever known, so I put it down as a definite possibility. What do you think it's about?"

I put my hand in my pocket and keyed my cell phone. Thirty seconds later, Archer came in carrying Kim's laptop. I made the appropriate introductions, and we all sat. Archer opened the computer and switched it on. While it was warming up, I noticed that Hood was having trouble taking his eyes off the former model.

Archer did it for him. "Pay attention to the screen, General. My sister gave her life for this."

Hood bristled. Flag rank officers live in a world where people jump up, salute then hang on every word. But he recovered and turned to Kim's article on the laptop.

When he finished reading, Archer started the slideshow. I told her to run it manually. After the four Biltmore photos, I asked her to stop. To Hood, I said, "The white-haired gentleman is Gaetano Bruzzi, but maybe you can enlighten me about the guy with the steroid entourage."

I watched the general. He seemed to be weighing something. "How long have you had these?" he asked.

"Since yesterday."

Hood shook his head, then looked at Archer. "Whether you believe me or not, miss, I would never have sanctioned what they did to your sister. I don't think Serbin would have either. That was all Bruzzi."

Hearing the admission, I thought Archer might become emotional, but she held her iron and shot back, "I'm sure that was a great comfort to her as the bullet entered her brain. The last thing she probably thought was, 'Boy, is General Hood gonna be pissed.' "

I let the moment sit. Marlon had my blood on his hands as well. Let him think about it.

Finally, he seemed to deflate. "What do you want to know?" he asked.

"Let's start with Serbin," I said.

"Konstantin Serbin. It used to be Colonel Serbin, but after the Soviet collapse, he discovered he could make more money selling tanks than commanding them. He also produces most of the steel in Eastern Europe."

"A real go-getter," I said, "but evidently, not everyone's a fan. Presidents travel with less security."

Hood nodded. "Serbin's an egotist. He likes to make a show. But some of the extra guns are warranted. Time was, if you were a friend of the Kremlin, no one would breathe in your direction. Moscow has limited reach these days—and less respect. So certain people can't be too careful."

I nodded to Archer to advance the slideshow.

Hood said, "You haven't asked me what we were doing together."

"I don't want the rehearsed answer, so I'll come back to that," I replied.

The two photographs of the unknown artist were next, and as they came up, I focused on Hood's eyes, the way a magician does during a card trick. Right on cue, the general's pupils dilated, meaning the picture triggered his brain's recognition receptors. But he shook his head no, and I said nothing.

We went through the next photographs without comment. And then the blank screen with the Babushka caption came up. As soon as he saw it, Hood took a sharp breath.

"Familiar?" I asked.

He didn't blink. "The buildings are the museums where the paintings from the Tretiakov Collection now reside. That was Serbin's goal. The artists' bodies weren't recoverable, but by placing each man's final work in the city of his birth, he was, in effect, taking him home—offering a kind of immortality. That blank screen refers to the painting by Illya Orlov. By far the most valuable of all of them. It went down on Egypt Air with . . ." He stopped and looked at me. "But you already know that, don't you?"

No answer was necessary.

Hood took a sip of coffee. "You still own all those newspapers?"

"There are a lot of dead people, General. And I've got some attitude about being shot myself. This isn't about a newspaper story."

I saw him turn something over in his mind then look at his watch. He stood. "I've got two hours before I have to be on Capitol Hill. I drive fast, so try to keep up."

29

Russians and Cities

Hood hadn't lied. Gone was the commuter pace. I had to fight to stay up with him as he wove in and out of traffic at speeds topping ninety miles an hour. I dialed Eddie Buffalo and woke him up. When he heard it was me, he said groggily, "Let me guess, this isn't an invite to Denny's for a Grand Slam."

"How soon can you get in the air?"

"At this time of the morning? Depends how quick I can find a copilot sober enough to read off the runway markers. Couple of hours maybe."

"Make it less."

"Where am I going?"

"I'm not sure yet. I'll be in touch."

"I'll need to file some kind of flight plan."

If anyone was watching, and they almost certainly were, they already knew I wasn't in L.A., so they weren't going to believe any flight plan Eddie filed anyway. But maybe we could make them work for their money. "Do paperwork for Chicago by way of St. Louis. Then change it midflight to Denver by way of Detroit," I answered. "I want you laying up there at forty thousand feet about halfway across the country. Stay refueled, drive slow and make a couple of un-expected stops."

"I've always wanted to see Memphis," Eddie said. "Hear they got great ribs. This got something to do with the guy who killed Jimmy?"

"Yes."

"Promise me you'll let me tear those sons of bitches. . . ."

"Get in the air," I said.

I didn't like cutting him off, but I didn't want—or have time for—stupid talk. The kind that comes from rage with no outlet.

Also, since Marlon was doing his best to cause a twenty-car pileup, I really needed both hands on the wheel. I flipped the phone into Archer's lap, told her to put it on speaker and called out Bert Rixon's number.

He answered on the first ring. "Doesn't sound like you were asleep," I said.

I could almost hear the smile in his voice. "Brittany and I were just—"

"Bert!" I heard Brittany yelp. "Don't you dare."

"Hey, Rail is the one who told us to do it as often as we could."

Bert's voice sounded thicker than when we'd last spoken. I hoped it was just the early hour and not the disease acceler-ating. Archer smiled. "Bert, a lady doesn't take out an ad."

"I'm no lady, and if you could have heard her a few min-utes ago, you wouldn't confuse her for one either. Hell, I'd wear a sign if she'd let me."

I had to swing across two lanes to avoid being sideswiped by a bread truck the general had cut off. "Bert, I need a favor. You up for a little work?"

"Name it. Brittany can only go for the gusto about three times a day, and I need something to do while she's rest-ing."

Archer and I laughed. "Bert," I said, "when you were in the prosthetics business, the Pentagon was a customer, right?"

"My biggest. But I never made a dime off them. Sold only at cost, and if some soldier didn't meet the military's criteria for an arm or a leg, we gave it to them."

"Then I need you to track down one of those bureaucrat friends of yours and remind him of your generosity. Got a pen?"

"Nothing wrong with my memory."

"Major Truman York. U.S. Air Force. Tanker pilot. Deceased. I need to know everything there is to know about his time in the service. His DD-214 will be a starting place, but it's going to be deficient."

"Shouldn't be a problem. If this guy York ever had so much as a hangnail, he'll be in the medical database, and somebody will know how to get the rest. What else?"

"I want the same thing on an army four-star. Marlon Hood."

"That name sounds familiar," said Bert. "Should I know him?"

"He's the Army Chief of Staff," I answered.

"Current?"

"Current."

"This should be interesting."

"His bio will be on their website," I said. "But if I'm right, it'll be selective too."

"That's a switch. Usually, generals can't blow their horn enough. By the time the PR guys get finished, a weather delay passing through Tokyo ends up sounding like a Far East Command."

Bert was right. Creative writing was probably invented by some lowly centurion who got handed a clay tablet with orders to write his general's resumé. I said, "Then I want you to overlay York's tours with Hood's. See if you can find any intersections, mission or geography."

"I'm on it," Bert said. "Anything else?"

"Yes, but this one will just take some Internet time. The guy's name is Konstantin Serbin. Used to be a colonel in the Red Army."

Bert interrupted me. "And now he owns one of the world's foremost collections of Russian art."

"You never fail to surprise me."

"Christ, Rail, some of us enjoy things besides cars and Steve McQueen. If you'll think back a few months, I invited you to a reception at the Norton Simon. Serbin had lent them part of his collection and was in town for the opening."

"I hope my excuse was original."

"Mallory was making venison stew."

"What did I tell you? One of his best dishes. But you went?"

"We did, and it was magnificent. I've still got the catalogue around here somewhere."

"Dig it out and get a messenger to take it to my hangar at the airport."

"Now? It's still dark out."

"I'll bet that for a hundred bucks and a chance to drive that Aston Martin of yours, one of the kids in the club kitchen can be persuaded. And call Eddie and tell him not to take off without it. He's on his way there now."

"When I get this other stuff, you on your regular number?"

"Yes, but the phone's going to be off intermittently, and I don't want it on a voice mail. Leave a message, and I'll get back to you."

"Will do."

After Bert hung up, Archer said, "Isn't that a reach? Hood and my stepfather weren't even in the same service."

"That's why we're looking. If there's a connection, chances are it'll be by design, not coincidence."

I followed Hood off the Beltway, through Georgetown and into a city garage near Constitution Avenue. The first open space was on the fourth floor, and the general waited until we pulled in. I didn't like getting into someone else's car, but he'd made it clear that where we were going, if we didn't arrive with him, it was a no-go.

"Standard procedure," Hood said. "One car they can verify."

I didn't say what I was thinking, which was, *Bullshit, that doesn't protect anyone from anything*, but I suspected he'd called ahead and set it up that way. Strictly a power issue. Before getting out, I took the Sig and the suppressor out of my jacket and slipped them between the seat and the console. I had to assume the car would be searched while we were gone. The suppressor would give them something to think about.

The building was a standard glass and steel office highrise in a busy part of downtown. The red Infinity hadn't yet stopped rolling into the no parking zone in front before two soldiers in black berets and green camo gear, their pants bloused into highly polished combat boots, came running down the two dozen steps to open our doors.

Normally, a pair of sergeants confronting a Chief of Staff would throw themselves to arch-back attention, snap into crisp salutes and shout, "Good morning, Chief!" But that didn't happen. They all but ignored the general and focused on hurriedly conveying Archer and me up the steps and into the building. Once inside, a second pair of sergeants with M-16s slung across their backs handed our escorts their own rifles. Hood saw me taking note and said, "Guns outside make tourists jumpy."

Straight ahead, across the black marble lobby, between two banks of chromed elevators, a man sat behind a half-moon reception desk. The logo on the front—a silver star bracketed by a pair of silver parentheses—was one I didn't recognize, and the receptionist also had it on the breast of his black blazer.

Hood nodded to the man, and he immediately picked up a telephone. While we waited, I wandered over to the building directory and ran my eyes over the columns of occupants. It was the usual mix of law firms, trade organizations and consultants. Nothing that screamed government.

Just then, a pair of doors on the right bank of elevators opened, and two men in business suits got out. They were engaged in conversation, but even though they had to walk past four combat-ready Rangers carrying M-16s, they never looked up. No one does that. We were standing in a domino.

Like the mask it's named for, a domino is a thin veneer of disguise placed on something important to make it look ordinary. In this case, the directory would be a phony. And the logo. Even the address, 1116, wouldn't be in any city directory. And the receptionist would have a MAC-10 clipped someplace handy and probably a supply of flash-bangs and tear gas. This was the government operating on all cylinders.

The receptionist put the phone down and nodded to Hood.

"Ready, Sergeant?" the general asked, and I realized he was looking at me. "I know you're not foolish enough to have brought that pistol along, but if you or Miss Cayne are carrying any cameras or recording devices, please leave them with reception. In a few minutes, you'll be checked."

A twenty-second drop in a high-speed elevator isn't unusual—unless you're doing it starting at ground level. D.C. is mostly reclaimed swamp, meaning that if you dig down more than a few dozen feet, you hit water—lots of it. However, there is a geological aberration of a narrow spine of bedrock several miles thick that runs through the District, and interestingly, the buildings of certain agencies and departments that might be able to make use of a considerable amount of unseen space are built along it. This clearly included the building we were in, because at an average commercial floor height of twenty feet and a rate of descent of one floor per second, when the elevator doors opened, we were deeper than some coal mines.

Our small group was met by a one-star whose name patch read Damon, and two more camo-clad Rangers with M-16s. The soldiers who had accompanied us down stayed aboard the elevator and disappeared back upstairs.

We were standing in a green, steel-walled alcove that reminded me of San Quentin's gas chamber. There was barely enough room for all of us, and the close air harbored a sharp odor of sweat. An imposing steel door across from the elevator contained a thick pane of one-way glass, and since there was no handle on our side, I assumed that once we had satisfied whomever was watching, it would open.

"How about a recount?" Archer said. "I'm claustrophobic as shit."

"Sorry, ma'am," General Damon said, in an unlikely Texas twang. "The scan takes a couple of minutes."

"What kind of scan?" she asked, but Damon didn't answer.

Shortly, the door banged full open, and a Ranger captain, also in camo and brandishing a .45 with the safety off, shouted, "Chief coming through!"

Not wanting to risk getting one between the eyes, I stepped aside so Hood could lead, then took Archer by the arm and followed. The passageway was long and the same green steel as the holding area. The floor was metal too, and our footsteps reverberated in the tight space. I noticed a slight give under my feet and suspected the tunnel was riding on some kind of shock absorber, which probably allowed the entire apparatus to be collapsed and removed.

We passed through two more locked doors following the same procedure. "Chief coming through!"

Archer looked at me. "Like this place is so fucking high-traffic, they might confuse him with the pizza guy."

I heard General Damon laugh behind me and decided we weren't being led to the lions. And then the passageway suddenly ended. I'm not easily surprised, but nothing could have prepared me for what lay before us. I heard Archer suck in her breath.

We were standing on a wide balcony looking through a four-story wall of glass into a space too big to be called a room—almost too big to be called a cavern. It was as if someone had strung together several dozen aircraft hangars, front to back and side to side, until they had become one giant open structure. The girdered ceiling, some seventy-five feet above, was supported by evenly spaced rows of vertical I beams, X-ed at regular intervals for strength, and the light pouring in from somewhere was natural enough that I had to remind myself that we were hundreds of feet below the earth.

Below us, on the other side of the glass, dozens of workers—men and women—in white coveralls, white surgical hats and white plastic covers over their shoes drove forklifts and golf carts along wide, shiny cement thoroughfares that extended to vanishing points. Essentially, what we were looking at was a massive clean room far beyond anything NASA or private industry had ever conceived.

The focus of all this excess and activity were thousands of stainless steel storage vaults, each the size of a doublewide, stacked on braced shelves, reaching to the ceiling. Each vault contained a safe-type door with an electronic locking device and its own environmental system, indicating that the contents required individual regulation. They were being tended by mammoth blue cranes that rolled along the aisles on ten-foot balloon tires.

One crane was attempting to inch a long, coffin-shaped box into a vault on the third level, and the two men on the platform were having difficulty lining it up. When the crane rammed the box into one of the supports, the reverberation almost knocked the men off their perch.

"I'd be willing to bet not a single politician has ever seen this," I said to Damon.

The general looked at me with mild amusement. "Why do you say that?"

"Anything this big would need to be carved up and moved to their districts."

He laughed. "I think you're right."

I turned back to the glass and said to Hood, "The City of War, I presume."

"Officially, Combat Impact Trust Installation 3. Short-hand. CITI-3."

"CITI-3. The City of War. What are 1 and 2?"

Hood was slightly irritated. "I'm letting you peek up my skirt, Sergeant, not spread my legs." Then he quickly turned to Archer. "I apologize for my crudeness, Ms. Cayne."

"I'm sure I'll survive," Archer replied.

Hood looked at General Damon and said, "Tell Dr. Cesarotti we're coming in."

"Yes, Chief," Damon said and departed.

30

Assholes and Apelles

They had some trouble fitting me, but half an hour later, dressed like a team of biotech scientists, Hood, Archer and I made our way through three gas disinfecting airlocks and into CITI-3. A very pretty, dark-haired, dark-eyed lady around forty was waiting for us. She extended her hand to me. "Dr. Bibiana Cesarotti," she said, with a pleasant Tuscan accent. "And please call me Bibiana."

Then she turned to Archer. "You're Archer Cayne, aren't you?"

Archer looked surprised. "Have we met?"

"The Michelangelo Caravaggio Competition," Bibiana answered. "I'm the one who stopped it."

Suddenly, Archer threw back her head and laughed. When she finished, she saw my blank look and said, "You ever see any Italian television?"

"Naked weather girls can pretty much erase a bad day."

"I'm sure. Well, when I was living overseas, one of the networks decided to run a contest to find the next Caravaggio. Grand prize: a hundred million lire."

"What was that back then? About a hundred grand?" I asked.

"Less," said Bibiana, "but it didn't matter. In America, everybody wants to be a singer. In Italy, every good family has at least one successful priest and one failed artist."

I liked this lady.

She continued. "At that time, Signorina Cayne was the most beautiful woman in Europe. People would go wild just seeing her step out of a taxi." She turned back to Archer. "How many magazine covers?"

Archer was enjoying the trip down memory lane. "I did thirty-seven . . . not counting the North African knockoffs."

Bibiana looked back at me. "The network's plan was to put the Caravaggio contestants through a series of competitions. And at the end, the two finalists would paint your friend."

"In the nude, I trust," I said.

"Absolutely," said Archer. "And on national television."

I had to admit it beat the hell out of some plus-sized dame choking out a Celine Dion tune on *American Idol*. "So how did this show not sweep the planet?"

Bibiana turned very serious. "*I* am what happened. There are scholars who devote their entire professional careers to Caravaggio. And ordinary people who spend their life savings to just walk past one of his paintings. He's an Italian national treasure, not a subject for a voyeuristic gangbang. And as Deputy Minister of Culture, I had the prime minister's ear."

General Hood smiled. "In addition to being beautiful, the lady has integrity."

I saw Dr. Cesarotti blush, and she wasn't the blushing type. You didn't need a program to know this is where Mrs. Hood's coffee cup had been aimed. "So what do you do in this place besides *not* produce reality shows?" I asked.

Bibiana looked at Hood, who nodded.

"Let's proceed while we talk," she said. "It's more productive." And she commandeered a small electric bus, which we climbed aboard.

While the driver threaded his way through the skyscraping caverns of vaults and past more blue cranes, General

Hood took over as tour guide. "When the current army was organized in 1791 to deal with Indian conflicts, it quickly began to accumulate artifacts and treasure. In a time when long-distance communication with battlefield commanders was spotty at best, and not wanting a mercenary fighting force that might choose objectives to enrich themselves, Congress drew up rules governing anything of value that might fall into the military's hands. These were loosely called the Museum Regulations, but they had nothing to do with museums as we think of them. They simply designated the army to hold in trust all items of real or intrinsic value until a final disposition could be determined. And to free fighting units from additional burden, the army created special collection teams to secure the spoils.

"There the matter sat for almost a century. By then, we had hundreds of warehouses full of all kinds of things, and there still wasn't enough space. So even though the regulations had initially precluded lending, we began contracting with public institutions for long-term storage, often just to get stuff out of the rain. For the accommodation, we expressly didn't limit what these institutions could do with the items, thereby opening the door to study—and display. Today, many of the collections in our most prestigious institutions—especially Native American artifacts—are still technically army property. We don't want them back, but the paper trail is there."

"And classified, I'm sure," Archer said.

The general became thoughtful. "I'm not at liberty to comment on that, but for the past several decades, we've been working to return identifiable objects to their original tribes, presuming they are still in existence. The difficulty is that record keeping at the time of collection was highly unreliable. And there are many competing claims."

We had arrived at an open square where tables and chairs were arranged for workers to take breaks. On one side of the square was an elaborate clean room within the clean room that was lined with thick windows through which I could see people painstakingly restoring paintings and sculpture. On another side was a glass-walled laboratory containing rows of bench-mounted microscopes that generated images on high-resolution monitors. These were manned by technicians, some of whom were matching colors to a spectrum while others compared metals and stone to photographs. The third and fourth sides of the square were taken up by an L-shaped, windowless, two-story building.

As we dismounted from the bus, Hood held us for a moment. "By the turn of the twentieth century, what had begun as a temporary custodial program to safeguard important and valuable items had mushroomed into a conservator and arbitrator responsibility. And no one was happy about it—especially at budget time."

"Such are the responsibilities of victory," I said.

Hood nodded. "They are."

"And thus, CITI-3."

Archer looked up at the stacks as if for the first time. "My God, so many wars. I can't even imagine what's here."

"Neither could we. That's why I lured Dr. Cesarotti to America. It was time to find out." Hood smiled and put his hand on Bibiana's shoulder. "She's the absolute best there is."

Bibiana looked admiringly at Hood. "The general says if I work fast, I might finish in twenty-five hundred years."

The cutie-pie act was a bit much, so before I had to put on my hip-waders, I said, "With all due respect, Doctor, with your background, you're not here for the tom-toms and tee-pees."

There was an uncomfortable silence and an exchange of glances with Hood before she answered. The lovey-dovey had disappeared. "No, Mr. Black, my expertise is European art. Why don't you follow me."

I saw Archer look at me; she mimed touching a hot stove and pulling her hand back sharply. You can get two things from hitting a nerve—silence or justification. Shortly, we'd find out which I'd prompted.

When we entered the L-shaped building, it was dark. Then the lights came up, and I still wasn't sure what I was seeing. We were in a long center aisle, and on either side were rows of tall, thin, vertical walls like you'd find displaying bedspreads or Oriental rugs. Only these were thirty feet high and twice that in length and draped in heavy-gauge, clear plastic. I wandered between the two nearest walls and realized that they were made of stainless steel and perforated like pegboards. Affixed to them were hundreds of battlefield drawings and paintings, some framed, most not.

General Hood came up beside me. "The essence of battle. Drawn by eyewitnesses." There was a catch in his throat, and I believed it was genuine. Though many of the works were of uneven quality, they projected the kind of drama that a dispassionate observer could never achieve. Hood pointed to a small painting of a World War I doughboy straining under the weight of a wheeled cannon. The work was entirely in shades of brown. "Done in the artist's own blood," he said.

It was indeed powerful, and I said so.

"We used to rotate these in and out of army installations," he said. "Then we discovered that many weren't coming back. So now, Bibiana has hired artists to reproduce them, and those are the only ones that go on the circuit."

"There must be thousands," said Archer.

"Eleven thousand six hundred and four, to be precise," answered Hood. "But it's only about a fifth of the collection. In 1775, newspapers began sending artists into the field with the Continental Army to document the Revolution. It was one of the only ways to get the story, and often, accounts of battles were written not from a correspondent's observations but from an artist's drawings and description. In the 1800s, soldier-artists began to emerge alongside the civilian ones, and the army finally went exclusively to military personnel during the First World War."

"What happened when there weren't any wars going on?"

"The artists would travel to various installations and memorialize commanders, camps, equipment and sometimes more frivolous endeavors."

"So embedded reporting wasn't invented in the desert," said Archer.

"You'd be surprised at the names on some of the early work," answered Hood.

"Let's go into the other wing," said Bibiana.

She and Hood led, and Archer and I followed.

Unlike the first room, this one needed no explanation. The stainless pegboards here ran along the center aisle, and on them were hung life-sized portraits of some of the world's most bloodthirsty despots and mass murderers.

"I call this the Walk of Assholes." Bibiana smiled. "Unofficially, of course."

The description was apt. The first dozen paintings, each at least eight feet tall, were of Himmler, Goebbels, Heydrich, Goring, and the rest. Most of the canvases had sustained water or bullet damage or both. "From our Reichstag collection. Danced under by kings, prime ministers and presidents. Also Charles Lindbergh and Henry Ford," said Bibiana. "Curiosity pieces of no particular monetary value but historically worth preserving."

As we passed another of a white-uniformed Joseph Stalin being handed tulips from adoring schoolchildren, Hood said, "This was hanging in the Grenada post office. Evidently, they hadn't gotten the memo he'd been dead for thirty years."

It was a unique rogues gallery. Kim Il Sung (seized by MacArthur from a spy in Inchon), Juan and Eva Perón dancing the tango (a gift to a U.S. military attaché), a young Che Guevara (courtesy of the Bolivian army), Pablo Escobar (from an informant in his Medellín villa) and, of course, Saddam Hussein. I said to Hood, "I've always found it fascinating that murderers and despots can't have their portraits painted often enough . . . or large enough."

"Immortality," he said. "Hard to come by. I have mixed emotions even having this crap around, but the EPA vetoed my request for a bonfire."

"You'll have to forgive me," I said, "but so far I haven't seen anything that couldn't be protected with a padlock and a rent-a-cop."

"You're correct," he said, and just then, we turned a blind corner. Thirty feet ahead was a massive bank vault with a seven-foot, circular door. The word *overkill* came immediately to mind. In this vast hole in the ground, surrounded by hot and cold running Rangers, why on earth did they need a holiest of holies?

The vault door was open. We entered, and Michelangelo proved me wrong. So did Auguste Renoir and Camille Pissarro. Uccello and Da Vinci and Raphael. Antonio Stradivari and Fabergé. Guttenberg and Shakespeare. And at the center of this pageant of the inconceivable, a King John version of the Magna Carta.

The collection, set in a space the size of a large ballroom, seemed endless. Hundreds of works, from paintings to porcelain to sculpture to musical instruments to tapestries to manuscripts scholars would sell their mothers to get their hands on. Each sealed in its own custom glass case.

At the very rear of the room sat three long, mahogany tables set with rows of green glass and brass lamps that reminded me of the New York Public Library. And surrounding the tables along three walls were scores of black, lateral file cabinets running from the floor to at least ten feet in height, each drawer fitted with a combination lock.

"Recognize this?" Hood was pointing to an easel behind glass. Inside was a canvas that looked like it might suddenly turn to dust. On it were three very fine horizontal lines—one red, one blue and one black—painted so closely together that from a few feet away, they appeared to touch. However, when I bent to examine them, they clearly did not. The piece was unsigned.

Neither Archer nor I had even a guess.

"We're not certain, but it may be the famous three lines of Protogenes and Apelles, Alexander's portraitist. From the fourth century BC. If so, it once hung in Julius Caesar's villa and was supposedly destroyed in a fire."

"Is there a word for beyond priceless?" Archer asked, only half in jest.

Bibiana smiled. "If it is indeed that work, it belongs in Greece, perhaps on Rhodes, where it would have been painted."

"How in the world did the army get it?" Archer asked.

Bibiana shook her head. "We have absolutely no idea. There isn't a shred of paper about it anywhere."

"That's why Dr. Cesarotti is so valuable," said Hood. "No one here would have even recognized it, let alone understood its value. It was just sitting in a container with a hundred others, some equally old, that we haven't begun to identify."

Bibiana waved her arm around the room. "This represents two years' work, and we've only opened twenty containers."

"How many more are there?" asked Archer.

"Seventy thousand that we know for certain contain things that need to be examined. Another fifteen thousand with no inventory at all, like the one with the Apelles," she replied.

Archer took a moment, then replied. "I think twenty-five hundred years is optimistic."

"So what happens to this and whatever else you find?" I asked.

"It's not entirely clear," said Hood. "We're plowing new ground. By statute, the army is forbidden to sell anything, so our hope is to repatriate as much as possible. However, that's easier said than done."

"I would think it would be simple," said Archer. "Just put it on a website."

Hood looked at her with some amusement. "That would

be like a theatre manager posting a picture of a wallet he'd found containing a hundred bucks and no ID."

"Couldn't you be vague?"

"Much of this is so rare that any description at all could be deciphered by someone with a little expertise. And though it may sound crass, the army isn't prepared, nor can it afford, to hire several thousand attorneys to sort through claims, let alone go to trial."

"I can see what you mean," she said. "So why not just declare the stuff ours and give it to the Smithsonian?"

"Personally, I'd love to, but unfortunately, finders-keepers doesn't get much traction in a court of law—and even less in the court of diplomacy. Right now, all we can do is wait for governments or individuals to bring us an impeccable description of what they're looking for along with ironclad documentation of their right to it."

"Like the Tretiakov Collection," I said.

"That was well before my time here," Bibiana answered quickly—too quickly. I looked at her, but she didn't meet my eyes.

"Technically, before mine, as well," said Hood. "The Chief of Staff has direct oversight of all CITIs. However, I was also the previous chief's aide, so I was peripherally involved. The Tretiakov Collection was our first large-scale, national heritage repatriation since 1945. It became something of a test case. Everyone watched very closely—State, Justice, even the CIA—to see if we raised the temperature of any interesting groups. Fortunately, we didn't. There were a few glitches, but it went smoother than anyone could have hoped for. Largely because the Russians were able to provide us with indisputable provenance, along with descriptions of all twenty-two works."

"From Konstantin Serbin," I said.

"Through him, yes."

"Correct me if I'm wrong, General, but I've always thought of national heritage as pieces of foundational culture. The things citizens collectively revere . . . get misty-eyed about. Like the Declaration of Independence and the Pyramids. According to Ms. York, only a tiny number of people had any knowledge of Captain Tretiakov's mission, and only General Zhuk knew about the paintings. Then Zhuk was executed, and they disappeared.

"I'll accept that they might be valuable, but national heritage, no. So who would even know to ask about them? Even more intriguing, how did somebody convince Yeltsin's people, who were as culturally deaf as the Taliban and didn't even seal the state museums until three years after they took power, that a little-known World War Two junior officer and some phantom artwork deserved any kind of priority? Now you've got Putin, or whoever is fronting for him this week. I'm not a Russia expert, but it would seem to me that as soon as he learned about Tretiakov, he'd be sweating our ambassador for a lot more than some unknown dissidents' meanderings. They're still looking for the Amber Room, aren't they?"

Hood stared at me like he was trying to make a decision. He turned to Archer. "I'm sorry to be rude, but there's a security issue here. Because of his background, I can make an exception for Mr. Black." Hood then looked at Bibiana. "Perhaps you could show Ms. Cayne our restoration facilities."

"How about a ladies' room and a cup of coffee instead," said Archer.

"Sounds pretty good to me too," said Bibiana, and they left.

With no further conversation, Hood led me to one of the tables at the back and asked me to take a seat. As I did, he went to a file drawer and worked the lock. Shortly, he brought back a large, red box about twenty-four inches square and sealed with two wide bands of yellow plastic tape that had to be scissored off.

With the open box in front of me, Hood said, "Half an

hour should be enough. I've got some calls to make." He started to leave, then turned back. "I don't think you'd violate my confidence, but just so there aren't any embarrassments, each item is impregnated with a microscopic security strip that would be picked up on your exit scan."

"If Sandy Berger shows up, I'll let him know."

Hood didn't say anything.

31

Nehemiah and the Tooth Fairy

The key document was on top. Unfortunately, it was maddeningly incomplete, either by incompetence or design.

The Tretiakov Collection had been discovered at 21:03 on December 22, 1996 in Vault C3-44777 by a Corporal Nehemiah Jacobs, a research assistant in the Army Documents Division. Corporal Jacobs had been attempting to locate a copy of a 1901 treaty between Germany and the Ottoman Turks, but what had led him to that particular vault wasn't noted. Nor was it noted how he'd learned the name Tretiakov, or even how the paintings had been packed or labeled. He also didn't mention other contents of the vault, assuming there had been any, or the name of the officer who had given him the assignment. Not surprisingly, he also didn't say whether or not he had found the treaty.

Jacobs's two-page report had been copied to three army departments and the assistant secretary of defense, but it was not even marked Confidential. In other words, his find had raised no alarms, sent no one into immediate motion. File and forget.

So what had happened to elevate it? And how had it been determined even what the Tretiakov Collection was? I checked the staple holding the two pages together but saw no evidence of an attachment that might have been removed.

Under Jacobs's report was a folder containing a set of extraordinarily high-resolution photographs of the paintings. I knew from things I'd seen at Benny Joe's that they were satellite imagery size, eighteen by twenty inches, and the detail was so precise that if I'd had an enlarged version, I would have been able to count individual brush strokes. Obviously, somebody had thought it necessary to bring in pros to do the documenting.

I stood and laid the photos side by side, then went down the line absorbing the details of each. The styles varied widely, but each was the work of a very talented person. Petr Stech's *Scourge out of the East* was one of the most intriguing, and I was immediately impressed with Archer's power of recollection. The only detail she'd omitted was a shield carried in the skeleton's rein's hand.

The last photograph, however, literally took my breath away. It was Orlov's *Offering of the Babushkas*. No one, not even Vermeer, had ever drawn a finer line. Even in a photograph, Orlov's hand reached out and touched you.

The scene was Moscow's Red Square under a full moon. St. Basil's Cathedral loomed to the left, and the Kremlin to the right, their haunting shadows giving the wide concourse the look of a brick-paved cavern. The windows in the Kremlin were dark, many were broken. At St. Basil's, flames poured from the oblong apertures beneath the spires, and one dome had collapsed. On the street below, in the left foreground, prowled a pair of fierce-looking, yellow-eyed dogs, perhaps gone mad in the search for food.

The detail was so precise that the roughness of the buildings' mortar seemed tactile and the broken glass sharp. But the real business of the painting was a throng of women, milling about the square. Each wore a different patterned babushka and carried in her arms the limp, dead body of a young man dressed in a Soviet prison uniform. Their burdens clutched tightly to their breasts, the women actually seemed to stagger under their weight. Further adding to the drama was that, like the women's, each young man's face was so flawlessly drawn that it was actually an exquisite tiny portrait.

I knew how many there were going to be, but I counted the women anyway. Twenty-two. Then something caught my eye, and I leaned closer. Tucked into the shirt pocket of all but one man was an artist's brush. The one who did not have a brush was at the very front, and his bearer, unlike the other women, who were of obvious peasant stock, was tall and slender, her dress fashionable. Likewise, her scarf was a brightly patterned blue and not threadbare, and instead of boots, she wore high heels of the era. A crucifix dangled from her neck, catching a tiny ray of moonlight.

Her young prisoner wore dark-rimmed eyeglasses, his face very much her own. And his paintbrush was held between his fingers as he would have done in life. Almost certainly, this was Illya Orlov. And the others were the mothers and artists of the remaining twenty-one paintings.

Orlov had left a record . . . the only way he could. I felt a little sick inside and was surprised that a painting could have such an effect.

There was nothing else of major importance in the box. Certainly nothing to merit the drama Hood had evoked before he'd left the room. The formal repatriation request on Office of the President stationery and signed by Yeltsin was almost generic. No impassioned, dramatic language like one would expect for something so dear—or wordy in the extreme like everything else Russian. The only passage relating directly to the paintings stated that they no longer had any value as road maps, because Tretiakov's notebook had been discovered among Zhuk's effects, and the surviving items had been located and moved back to museums in 1946. And the attached descriptions of the paintings were sketchy at best. They didn't even identify the artists.

The only thing that nagged at me was that Serbin had written a separate letter to the secretary of state, claiming that

Russian researchers had been unable to locate any record of how and when the paintings had gotten out of Russia after they had been given to the American attaché. Why even say this? If it was even true, all these years later, who cared? More to the point, nothing could be less Russian than admitting ignorance.

I put everything but the file of photographs back into the box and busied myself looking at some of the other glass-protected exhibits until General Hood returned. When he saw me, he looked uneasy. "You're a fast study," he said.

"General, with all due respect, there isn't anything there you couldn't give to the *New York Times*. There aren't even manifests for Major York's trips. The Orlov was on the last flight, but what about the others? Was he carrying just one painting per trip or something else too? For that matter, did he ever carry a Tretiakov? You can't tell from what you showed me. And the only provenance is that the Russians say they're theirs and sort of wave at describing them. To paraphrase A. A. Abernathy, if somebody tried that on me, I'd call the FBI."

"Who is A. A. Abernathy?"

"Not important. But I don't believe you're that sloppy around here, so it looks like this is some kind of exercise to cut off my banging around where you don't want any banging."

Hood's face turned red, but he held his tongue, confirming my suspicion. While he was uncomfortable, I pressed. "Let me try it another way, General. Who verified the Russians?"

He hesitated. "I'm not sure what you mean."

"The repatriation request. Take out the word *painting* and insert *baling wire,* it reads the same. There had to be a ministry or department or museum involved. But that letter is so nonspecific, it could have been created at Kinko's. So who vetted it?"

I had to give the general his due. He went from salty to

conspiratorial in a nanosecond. I was obviously now on ground he'd rehearsed for.

"Actually, it wasn't an official-official, government request. It was sanctioned, of course. Yeltsin signed off, as you saw. But it was only a half dozen years after the Soviet collapse, and the country was still operating like a start-up. Feeling their way. Navigating icebergs in the dark. We were anxious to have them succeed at nation-building, so we did everything we could to help. When the paintings were returned, each was sent to a different museum. There were unveilings. Parties. Press. It might not sound like much now, but at that moment, the symbolism really mattered."

"I'd like to speak with Nehemiah Jacobs. I'm sure he's long gone from the army, so maybe your office can dig up his whereabouts."

Hood didn't even blink. "I'm sorry, but Corporal Jacobs was killed in a motorcycle accident."

"When?"

"As I recall, a couple of months after he found the paintings. Hit by a truck on his way down to Norfolk."

"Make that five bodies."

Hood ignored me and picked up the file of photographs from the table. "You neglected to put this back."

"That's because I'm going to take it with me."

"Why would I permit that?"

"For the same reason you're going to send me copies of the repatriation request and Serbin's letter to the secretary of state. Because Dr. York has earned the right to have her research completed and her paper published."

"And if I refuse?"

"Then when you stop at Starbucks tomorrow for the *Post,* you're going to see your smiling face under a headline that reads, 'United States Army Chief of Staff Under Investigation for Conspiracy to Commit Murder.' And somewhere in the story, the reporter is going to have a quote from the Russian ambassador about the current state of 'national heritage repatriation.' What do you want to bet that'll get you a couple of calls from the White House?"

"That's preposterous."

"Try me. Better yet, call Sergeant Dion Manarca of the LAPD. Mention there's a picture of you standing next to a guy named Dante Bruzzi."

"Dante Bruzzi?"

"Gaetano's nephew. And real piece of shit with a record from here to the Med." I neglected to mention he was dead.

"Why would that matter to me?" He was perspiring now, and making no move to hide it.

"Because Sergeant Manarca's career is on the line, and ten minutes after he hears your name, he's going to start screaming for a subpoena. People are dead, General. Probably more than I know about. And your fingerprints are on all the Monopoly pieces."

An army staff car dropped us in the parking garage and sped away almost before we were out. Unlike the door-to-door service earlier, this time we had to take the elevator to our car. I was paying the attendant when Archer looked at me and burst out laughing. "Well, they did it with dignity, but they sure as hell threw us out of there in a hurry. What in God's name happened?"

"I think he was pissed you disrespected Caravaggio." I handed the file of photographs to her.

She took it and spent the trip back to the Watergate looking at them. When I parked, she said, "I don't think I can describe how I feel, especially after looking at the Babushka painting."

"That's exactly what happened to me."

I had the reception desk call the Watergate Hotel next door and arrange for us to use their indoor pool. The outdoor facility in the residential complex was too exposed.

After a swim, Archer opted for a massage and a facial, so I headed back to catch a nap. On the way, my phone rang. It was Eddie.

"Where are you?"

"Right now I'm over Omaha. Stopped in Boise for lunch and a blow job, but only came away with a bellyful of ribs."

"My condolences. Who's riding shotgun?"

"Jody Miller."

I could hear a voice in the background. "Hi, Mr. Black."

"I thought he was visiting Mom in Nevada," I said.

"Hit the wall talking bunions. I found a deadheading Southwest pilot to sit right seat up to Reno. Now, you've got the regular crew."

"Where's your next stop?"

"Jody says he knows a couple of chicks down Texarkana way who live in a mansion one of them clipped from an ex-husband. If we're gonna have a layover, I'd rather not do it in a Motel Six with a pizza."

"I won't ask about Mrs. Buffalo."

"Hey, I've never been unfaithful while we were in the same town."

"I think that's in the Bible. Look, I should know tomorrow what I want you to do, but it could be sooner. So keep the line open. No matter what."

"Right, boss. Hey, Jody, get on the horn and call that Arkansas cooze of yours. Tell 'em to pack in some Red Bull, we're gonna go all night."

I shook my head and hung up.

Before I lay down for the nap I'd promised myself, I called Jackie Benveniste. The answering machine came on, and remembering my visit, I waited through the message, then asked him to pick up. A few second later, he did.

"Sorry to bother you," I said.

"No bother at all. Nance and I were just trying to cook something we saw on *Iron Chef,* but mostly we've been drinking beer and throwing the ingredients at each other."

"I'll make this short. What can you tell me about Konstantin Serbin?"

He didn't answer for a moment. "I presume you want more than the broad strokes."

"I know he was an army officer who's now a business-man and art collector. I'm interested in how he might have gotten hooked up with our friend the Hyena. On the surface, it doesn't seem like they would run in the same circles."

"Really? Why's that?" said Jackie, seemingly amused.

"Well, for starters," I said, "Bruzzi is a violent, profes-sional criminal, and—"

Jackie interrupted. "And Serbin's what? The Russian Billy Graham?"

"Sounds like you're going to stick a needle in my logic."

"No offense, but the colonel didn't go from tanks to lim-ousines because he had a nice smile and knew how to over-price steel. Every one of the so-called oligarchs got rich the same way—by putting a gun in somebody's ear. To his credit, Serbin actually held his himself. Criminals at that level never stop being criminals. They're just a lot more media savvy than most people give them credit for."

"I'm listening."

"You have a dog?" Jackie asked.

Strange question, I thought. "I grew up with six Gordon setters."

"Pretty big, aren't they?"

"Seventy-five pounds, give or take," I answered.

"Okay, suppose you tried to put out a bowl of food. What would happen?"

"One bowl for six dogs?"

"One bowl," he said.

"If I lived, I'd probably have to be hospitalized."

Jackie chuckled. "Okay, let's figure you survived, and they've eaten. Now you refill the bowl and try again."

"Same thing."

"And a third time?"

"They'd keep it up until I either ran out of food, or they died of old age. Get full, throw up and start over. Genetics."

"That's twenty-first-century journalism too. Editors used to say, 'Get it first, but first get it right.' Now, it's, 'We don't give a rat's fuck if you make it up. Just write it loud. And if you can squeeze in a celebrity, here's a bonus.' So the bowl moves around, and they all chase it.

"You'd be amazed how many timetables get advanced when the press gets busy with some white-hot piece of crap. I think there were two coups while they were burying Princess Di. And the really slick operators have learned to set out a bowl of perfumed cat shit and wait for the morons to get the scent. Then they get down to doing business in the dark. It's like a fucking joke everybody's in on but them.

"In Rome, it was my job to monitor criminal networks and relationships. Pay attention to how Thug A is affecting the orbit of Gang B. And you know who I ran into? Not just obvious assholes like Bruzzi. But Arab terrorists. Japanese tech thieves. Brazilian drug smugglers. Tanzanian gunrunners. Even an occasional Washington spy humping secrets. But there were also what we called 'borderlines.' Shady oil barons. Shipping tycoons. Private bankers. Nuke scientists."

"And Russian steel magnates," I added.

"And everybody doing business with everybody else. No lone wolves. No filter on who would deal with who. Need something? Pull up a chair, order a Campari and sit back. It'll find you. The world's shrunk for everybody, including the bad guys. But the Med isn't unique. Carve out a landing strip in fucking Antarctica and leave it unattended. In six weeks, the exact same people will be doing business in snowshoes." He stopped. "Sorry," he said. "You hit a nerve. You got time for this?"

I not only had time, it was exactly what I wanted. "I do," I said.

"Just a minute," he said, and I heard him call out, "hey, Nance, screw the Food Network, we'll order in and put on some Nat King Cole. And bring me another Sam Adams, would you, sweetie?" Then he was back. "Okay, where was I?"

"Getting rich selling snowshoes."

He laughed, and I heard him take a swallow of beer.

"Every now and then, I'd invite a reporter in to shoot the shit. A lot of the stuff I dealt with was classified, but some of it, all you had to do was go out to the airport and watch who got on and off. Shining a light on rats gets them moving around, and you learn things. So I was always trolling for press guys who were bright but lazy. Guys who would run what I gave them. Shadows, mostly, but if you looked close, there might be a picture."

I thought of Manarca.

"There was this go-getter running the Rome desk for one of the New York papers. A Mississippi grad too, so I might have been grading on the curve. Donny McGuirk. Seemed to be busting his ass. Filed twice as many stories as his colleagues. So since I was about to retire anyway, I decided to open up the safe. Give Mr. McGuirk something that would put the world on notice that things weren't as neat and tidy as they'd been led to believe. And for Donny, minimum guarantee, a fucking Pulitzer."

There's nothing I like better than a good story told by a good storyteller. And Jackie Benveniste was good.

He continued. "Got to go back to the beginning. August 2, 1990. My thirty-seventh birthday. Iraq invades Kuwait, and the Republican Guard unleashes an orgy of violence not seen since Himmler dropped by Warsaw. By week's end, relatives of Saddam were carpooling over for a few days of rape and concentrated looting. But while the lower phyla pilfered BMWs and gold brocade furniture, Mr. Hussein's personal goons were systematically dismantling the country's infrastructure and sending it back to Baghdad. Mainframes, oil rigs, fire engines . . . they even went into hospitals and tore babies out of incubators.

"One of the items they came across was a Boeing 757/767 simulator. Since Iraq Air didn't fly either plane, there was no immediate relevance, but hey, when a madman sends you to loot, you loot, and the simulator got packed up too. You with me?"

"Not completely, but keep talking."

Jackie went on. "Well, a simulator isn't a refrigerator. You don't just plug it in. So Saddam sent word to start burning out Kuwaiti eyes until somebody gave up the technicians."

"How long did it take?"

"Less than forty-eight hours. Two Boeing-schooled engineers and their boss, the senior training pilot for Kuwait Airways. Welcome to Mesopotamia. Hope you brought a change of clothes."

"And you told this to McGuirk?"

"Oh, I did better than that. I showed him where the simulator went when it left Iraq. In March 2002. Twelve years after it was stolen and a full year before 'Shock and Awe.'"

"Syria?" I guessed.

"Nope, and not Iran either. Al Jawf, Libya. A place nobody goes. Not just because Qaddafi would have you gang fucked by camels, but because it's the end of the goddamn earth. And fifty weeks a year, you can bake a pie in the shade."

Jackie stopped talking for a moment, and I tried to get a rope around my thoughts.

"Anything come to you?" he finally asked.

"Yes," I said. "Rewind to 9/11. Two 767s, two 757s."

"Bingo. What else?"

"The Kuwaiti techs would be dead, but the computer memory would be able to tell you what runs had been practiced. I'd also want to look for fingerprints. And DNA. A match with any 9/11 hijacker ends the war debate. Forever. So why haven't we already gone in and gotten it? A Delta team could do that in their sleep."

"Because Uncle Muammar lets us use his airspace for all kinds of shit that nobody wants public. Complicated world."

I had to agree. "So what about McGuirk?"

"This is the best part," said Jackie. "After I finish laying out the intelligence reports, radio intercepts and surveillance photographs of the simulator coming off a Libyan freighter in Benghazi—any one of which could get me life in Leavenworth—McGuirk looks at everything, then leans toward me and says, 'You maybe got something in Barcelona? They're having a real bad winter in New York, and my boss wants to catch some sun and get laid.' "

"You're kidding, right?"

"Who could fucking make that up?" he said. "And here's the PS. A year later, McGuirk writes a book. Ready? *Saddam, 9-11 and the Tooth Fairy*."

I shook my head. "First thing I've got to do is check with my London managers and make sure Mr. McGuirk doesn't work for us."

Jackie said, "Don't worry, he doesn't. Somebody put two rounds in the back of his head in a Tunis alley. Goddamn if I didn't lift a toast. Probably another pissed-off source. But back to your original question. Konstantin Serbin. When the Soviet Union collapsed, no one was watching anything, especially not the museums. The rumor was that Serbin, then chief of internal security, just bellied up to the bar. Bruzzi was the middleman for the stuff that left the country."

"And I don't suppose any of it went where it might stand a chance of being repatriated," I said.

"Museums don't have a pot to piss in," Jackie scoffed. "Plus they've got boards that sit around wringing their hands over provenance. Private collectors are where the action is. And a larger percentage of them than you'd expect don't give a flying fuck where something came from. They've got no intention of selling, and they're certainly not exhibiting. It's about bragging rights."

"Sooner or later, sellers become buyers. Any guesses what the colonel might be into?"

"The Afghan and Iraqi stuff was hot for a while, but it's mostly gone. Serbin's known mostly for paintings anyway. He has a standing offer of five hundred million for the *Mona Lisa*."

"You're kidding."

"When it comes to thieves, you never know. Good advertising too. It guarantees he's the first call for every major score."

"And if you're really ambitious, he'll go a billion for Apelles' *The Calumny*."

Apelles again. But not the one Hood had. "I don't know what that is."

"No reason you should. It was done about 300 BC and probably didn't survive. It shows a man being whispered to by two beautiful women—one in each ear. Ignorance and Suspicion."

"No comment."

"Me neither. Anything else?"

"Yeah, why did you retire? Seems like you're exactly the kind of guy who should still be on the job."

"Allen Dulles said that in case of war, the best thing we can hope for is that the State Department remains neutral. We left neutral behind a long time ago."

32

Balconies and Jengo

Archer and I tore into an armada of Premium oysters at Blacksalt and chased them with a couple of troughs of Bangkok seafood stew and a bottle of Pinot Grigio. The place was jammed with the usual assortment of expense account guys sprinkled with a few senators. I still missed Jean-Louis—the restaurant and the man. Lung cancer at fifty-five, but while he was alive, he went at life with both hands. Someplace, a joint full of angels is sitting down to a helluva dinner.

We walked back to the Watergate, enjoying a mild night and crowded sidewalks. I watched our fellow strollers, but nothing seemed out of the ordinary. Pradeep at the front desk had another note from Wandie, who'd dropped off a box of French pastries. Archer tossed the note before I could read it and was into something flaky and gooey on the way to the elevator.

Despite our previous encounters, we were still new to each other's intimacies, so later, in bed, it was awkward for a few moments. But I always study hard and pass my exams, and pretty soon, we were exploring each other with reckless shamelessness.

She was a magnificent lover, and I had no trouble twice. The second time, she ran to the kitchen and came back, with Wandie's caviar, which she used to lubricate us both before guiding me into her anally. Then, while she bucked her hot wetness against me, she seemed to go into a trance. I may have joined her.

Afterward, we showered together, which led to a wetter, soapier interlude, then fell into a deep sleep in each other's arms. Just before she drifted off, I think she said something nice about Wandie, but I could have been dreaming.

The change in air pressure in the room awakened me. Someone had opened a door, and Archer was still sleeping soundly a few inches away. I looked at the clock. It read 3:15, so it probably wasn't the housekeeper. The skyline of Virginia blazed away in the distance like a night-light, making the bedroom a lousy place to be caught by someone with bad intentions.

I rolled silently out of bed, eased the bedroom door closed and turned the dead bolt. I pulled on a pair of cargo shorts and screwed the suppressor into the Sig. Then I knelt and put my hand over Archer's mouth. She came instantly awake, and I took my hand away and touched my finger to my lips. She nodded. I led her by the hand onto the balcony through the sliding glass door. The night had gotten cooler, and she shivered. I went back inside, took the blanket off the bed and wrapped it around her shoulders.

The balconies of the Watergate curve with the building and are continuous, except for small dividing walls between rooms and units. We were on the opposite side of our living room, so I motioned for her to climb over the next three walls and hide on that balcony. I didn't know the layout next door, but that would hopefully put at least one full condo and a hundred feet or so between us and provide as much safety as I could manage on short notice. Without batting an eye, she took off the blanket and held it under her arm so it wouldn't interfere with the obstacle course she was about to run. Even though I had things to do, I couldn't help but admire her body in the moonlight. I hoped it would have the same effect on anybody who might awaken and see her.

I went over the wall in the other direction, which put me on the balcony outside our living room. I silently thanked Archer for insisting that the draperies remain open. The six feet or so of gathered material gave me cover and minimized my silhouette inside.

I lay down on the AstroTurf and inched my head around the drapes. There was a man with a gun standing just inside the foyer. Then I heard the whump of a door being kicked open and something hit the glass in the bedroom. Then twice more. Not loud. About like somebody throwing marbles. I leaned back and saw that my landlord had security concerns of his own—either that, or he was worried about wayward pigeons, because the glass in the condo was shatterproof. I'd heard no firearm reports, so whoever was inside was suppressed too, but there was no mistaking the three deformed slugs lodged in the centers of three glass webs.

Voices came through the open door, and it was only a matter of time before someone checked the balcony. I got to my feet, bolted past the living room window and vaulted onto the balcony on the other side. The sliding door in the adjacent condo was open, and I eased inside and stood in the dark, trying to keep the sound of my breathing to a minimum.

The king-sized bed across the room was occupied by a heavyset man on his back, snoring. His wife, however, was sitting straight up, staring at me. She saw the gun, and I thought she might scream, so I put my hands up to show her I wasn't there to harm them, and she lay back and watched.

I could hear men talking softly on the balcony next door. I couldn't make out what they were saying, but I had to assume the lookout had seen me run past the window, and now they were deciding what to do next. When I heard them go back in, I stepped outside.

There were three of them, and they were standing in my living room, arguing. From a crouch I had a clear shot at the left knee of the biggest guy, and as soon as the Sig spit, the man cried out and went down. I leaned back out of sight, and at least a dozen bullets smacked into the wall of glass and stuck there. A few came through the now-open door and kicked up chunks of cement.

I gave myself a 10-count, then reached out and fired through the door again. Two shots, without looking. I heard something crash, then the front door open. I moved to where I could see, and one man was helping his limping partner out the front door. The third intruder lay in the foyer, not moving.

In the bedroom, I grabbed a shirt, jacket and my wallet and slipped into my Top-Siders. The bed was riddled with holes, confirming there wouldn't have been a Q&A. I dropped an extra clip of ammunition into my pocket.

As I ran through the foyer, I saw some blood and pieces of bone on the slate floor. The dead man's knees were intact, so somebody out there was in a lot of pain.

I opened the door. The hallway was clear. I skipped the elevator and took the stairs.

The reception desk was empty, so Pradeep was either lying behind it waiting for the coroner, or he'd gotten out. Either way, I probably didn't have a lot of time before the place would be crawling with cops. The smart move would have been to go back upstairs, collect Archer and run. But I was roaring fucking mad, and I wanted those other two cocksuckers.

I held the gun under my jacket and stepped outside. If somebody was waiting to shoot me, the bright lights on the Watergate portico would have made it easy, but nothing happened. I looked in both directions but saw only empty street. Then, a block away, I heard a car start and tires squeal.

A black Yukon Denali with two men in front headed up New Hampshire and into the city at breakneck speed. As they passed me, the driver reached out and put a red flashing light on his roof.

A lone taxi hunkered in the dark just beyond the portico.

It was a lime green Crown Victoria, and the driver, a burly black man, was sitting in his backseat, asleep with the door open.

I slammed his door shut and jumped behind the wheel. The guy came awake in a heartbeat, but I had the Ford started and was after the Yukon before he could react. I looked at the license clipped to the dash. Jengo Mutumbo.

"Jengo, I'm sorry as hell, but I can't lose that car. I promise, I'll make it worth your while."

His accent was African. Nigerian, I thought. "Christ, mon, I the best damn driver in D.C. No shit."

"No argument here. So once I see where these guys go, you can take over."

That seemed to satisfy him, and he sat back. By the time we blew past the White House, I was on the Yukon's ass and could see that it had no plates. I couldn't believe we hadn't already attracted a cop.

Then from the backseat. "That embassy car you chasin', mon."

"How do you know?"

"Red light. All security guys got dem. Not sposed to, but the cops don' mind. Make it easy. No stop."

I'd caught a break. The police would just think we were a procession. Then a bullet hit the windshield, shattered it, and all vision disappeared. I jumped on the brakes and was all over the street, trying to steer while looking out the window. With my free hand, I brought up the Sig and shot the windshield from the inside. It exploded out, and we could see again.

"Shit, mon. You fuckin' crazy."

"I think you're fuckin' right."

When we hit Wisconsin Avenue, all I had to do was hang back a couple of blocks and watch which embassy my quarry turned into. Unfortunately, the driver of the Yukon had a different plan. Banging along at sixty miles per hour, he suddenly threw the big SUV into a reverse 180, using the wall-to-wall parked cars like bumpers.

When I saw him accelerating back toward me, I knew it wasn't a scare tactic. These guys had been sent to kill me, and they must have decided that if they had to die in the process, it was better than reporting home as failures.

There was no place to go, so I did the only thing I could. I threw the taxi into its own skid so that we took the crash from the rear. It was a helluva jolt, but nothing like what it would have been head-on. And I was already pulling away before the whiplash ended.

The Yukon didn't fall back, however. Denied the semi-honorable end of a kamikaze, the driver stayed against my bumper, literally pushing me faster than I was accelerating. I jammed both feet on the pedal, but the Crown Vic's brakes weren't up to the task. They burned out after a block, and the Yukon kept pushing, while we sent up smoke and sparks and a squeal that woke dogs in Philadelphia. Then they started shooting.

Jengo was lying on the backseat, but he seemed remarkably cool. "Jus like downtown Kinshasa."

So he was Congolese.

We were saved by a garbage truck. It was stopped in the middle of the street while a couple of sanitation guys were rolling a Dumpster out to it. It wasn't going to move, and we couldn't stop, so the inevitable happened. Fortunately, the Dumpster the scow was airlifting on its front forks absorbed most of the shock, and the Crown Vic's air bags hadn't been ripped off by a crackhead. Jengo ended up on the floor in the back, but undamaged.

Almost before the air bag deflated, I had changed clips in the Sig and was out of the cab, firing. The Yukon's driver jammed it in reverse and backed away, but not before I got several rounds into his windshield. I saw blood splatter on the passenger side just as the SUV got turned around.

The driver looked out his open window, and we locked eyes. Then he spit, "Yebat!" If I hadn't already guessed, I no longer needed to know which embassy.

As the Yukon squealed away, I turned and saw the three

sanitation workers running in the opposite direction. Jengo was just standing there looking at his wrecked meal ticket.

"I need another favor," I said to him.

He started to take out his wallet, and I laughed. "No, not that. I want you to give me your cell phone and one of your business cards. Then I want you to handle this mess. A man named Jake Praxis will call you. Tomorrow."

"He gonna make dis all right?" he asked.

"Trust me," I answered, "more than all right."

I had put a block between myself and the crash when I heard the first siren. I dialed my new phone and heard the familiar, "411 Connect. What city, please?"

The Russian embassy answered on the first ring. It was a male voice, and he didn't sound like a receptionist.

"I know this is being recorded, so I'm only going to say it once. No questions." I waited for a response.

"Go on."

"One of your associates had an accident in my living room. Doesn't seem to be able to get up. I'll be gone in an hour, but I'm going to pin a note on him who to contact, so I suggest you deal with the problem before my housekeeper shows up in the morning. She's probably a screamer. I'd leave a key, but you evidently already have one."

"Is that all?" asked the voice.

"No, tell the two guys who survived the cluster fuck that I'll see them again." The voice on the other end started to say something, but I hung up.

My next call was to the apartment. Archer answered. "My God, where are you?"

"On the way back. We're leaving."

"Before I get to meet the president?"

"Next time, I promise."

"Rail, there's a man in the living room. He's . . ."

"I know."

I tossed Jengo's phone in a sewer and began looking for a cab.

* * *

When I walked into the Watergate, Pradeep was at his post, eating. He gave me a nonchalant wave with a drumstick the color of a fire truck. Maybe the first time a craving for tandoori had saved somebody's life.

"Can you get me a limo?" I asked.

"How soon?"

"Forty-five minutes. But I'll meet him at the hotel."

Pradeep didn't seem to care one way or the other, which could have been that he was used to odd requests or bored or both.

Fortunately, the guy in my foyer wasn't a bleeder. In fact, if it hadn't been for the kneecapping, there would have been very little at all. I went through the corpse's pockets and found what I expected—nothing. There wasn't even a label in his suit, and his gun, a German Korth, had the serial number filed off. Not surprisingly, the suppressor was professional grade. I left the weapon on his chest and stuck a note between his teeth.

PROPERTY OF KONSTANTIN SERBIN
RETURN POSTAGE GUARANTEED

Archer had already packed her few things, and I did the same. I had two messages on my phone. The first was from Bert to call him.

The second was from Carl Noon. "The name you want is Bastet Nazarak. She was the ramp agent that night. Family runs a commercial nursery outside Alexandria. She was there as of yesterday. Steer clear of chanting pilots, buddy. Cheers."

I called Eddie and told him to meet me at the Northeast Philadelphia Airport the day after tomorrow. And to be well rested with the fuel tanks topped off.

"Where we goin', boss?"

"Chart us to Reykjavík, and we'll take it from there."

"Ice bunnies, nice."

Though it probably wasn't necessary, I wiped my landlord's gun and suppressor clean of prints and put them back in the safe, taking back my Beretta in the process. The guy was probably going to notice that his gun had been fired and wonder what happened. It would just have to be one of those unsolved mysteries of life.

I pried seventeen slugs out of the windows and six out of the mattress and flushed them down the toilet. I probably missed a couple, but I wasn't going to take the time to look. Then I fished Wandette Hope Radcliffe's welcome card out of the kitchen wastebasket. She answered like she was poised over the phone.

"Wandie. Your tenant at the Watergate, Rail Black."

"Oh, my God!" she shrieked. "*The* Rail Black. You know I used every trick in the book to drag your name out of Jhanya, but she wouldn't even give me a hint. Lord, you're not only rich, you're like the most handsome man on the planet."

Who was going to argue with that?

"Look, Wandie . . . may I call you Wandie?"

"I'd rather you nudged me for breakfast, but absolutely."

She had a great laugh, but somehow I didn't think Archer would be impressed. "Wandie, I'm leaving this evening for a couple of weeks, and I'm embarrassed. I had a few drinks too many last night and got carried away."

"Don't you worry about a thing," she purred. "The man who owns that place runs a game reserve in Zimbabwe and almost never comes to Washington. So whatever it is, we'll handle it, and he'll never know. Let me guess, you tried to throw that god-awful warthog from the balcony to the pool."

"I wish I'd thought of that. No, I got out a couple of my guns and kinda shot up the place."

There was silence on the other end of the phone. But only for a second. And then the question wasn't what I expected. "Do I need to come bail you out of jail?"

I laughed. "No, nobody heard anything. At least if they did, they didn't report it. But you're going to need a good glass guy and a new mattress."

"Shit, I can do that with my eyes closed."

"Great. Say, when I get back, how would you feel about dinner?"

"Hell, I'll pay. Then when I wrestle you in the door later, I'll feel I'm owed." She laughed.

I did too. "Good, I'll be in touch. In the meantime, tell Jhanya to have Jake Praxis call you about getting paid. And don't cut any corners. I don't want the Great White Hunter looking to put me next to the warthog."

When I hung up, I realized what a lame explanation I'd come up with. But she seemed to have bought it. Besides, everybody knows rich people are loons. I left a voice mail for Jake to be ready for Wandie. And to call Jengo Mutumbo. I also made it clear I wanted him to handle the guy like he'd saved my life.

33

Greedy Lobbyists and Dreamy Eyes

The limo took us to Dulles Airport, where we got out, took the escalator downstairs and caught a cab back to Georgetown. It might have been an unnecessary exercise, but there was no way to know, so it's what you do.

As was to be expected, Archer had a lot of questions, most of which I didn't know the answers to. All I could offer was a ticket home, where it probably wasn't any safer. It didn't matter, she said. She wasn't going anyway.

Freddie Rochelle's place was just off M Street in a tree-lined neighborhood where every house was a slice of history. Freddie's was one of the most lovingly restored, which contrasted nicely with the schmuck who owned it. But like I said before: You need a friend you can buy, find a lobbyist.

I hadn't called, because there was always somebody there, and they'd know how to reach him. I heard the dogs when I rang the bell. They're a pissy pair of miniature dachshunds named AK and 47 with no charm. Freddie opened the door himself wearing a pair of white silk pajamas and matching robe, his bald head pink as a flamingo's ass. He was carrying a large martini glass with something yellow and frothy in it.

The dogs made a snarling beeline for me, saw my stare and thought better of it.

"Oh, Jesus Christ, shoot me on sight. If it isn't the mad Brit himself. My God, Rail, it's been for fucking ever." He hugged me, then noticed Archer. "Oh, I'm sooo sorry, miss. My God, Rail, are my eyes playing tricks, or did you bring me Archer Cayne? She's even more gorgeous than her pictures. Come in, you two maaaaaarvelous people . . . come right in."

How the hell he knew who Archer was I couldn't guess, but then he made his living knowing things. Archer stepped forward and took his hand, and he led her into the house. I followed and heard him call out. "Leon, Leon. Look who's here. Whip up another batch of Banana Banshees, doll, and don't skimp on the banshee." He and Archer both thought that was funny as hell. I was already wishing the Russians had been better shots.

You only have to see Freddie at home to know he's gay, but in his business life, he plays it straight as a Presbyterian preacher. Office full of cowboy art, antique guns and his real passion, Thoroughbreds. He owns pieces of some of the best bloodlines in the world and is rumored to have made millions advising Saudi royals on racehorses. Knowing Freddie, the information he gets in return retails for more than the nags.

Leon, his longtime companion, is roughly Freddie's age and a really nice guy. He's an architect with a platinum client list, and he has the same beef with his housemate that I do. Everybody in town knows Freddie's gay, and nobody cares. They afford him his charade like they should. But like everything with Freddie, he's not happy unless he's manipulating, and he overdoes the sales job. Cuban-heeled boots with his Savile Row suits. Mirrored aviator sunglasses. Death's head signet ring. And a flashy Rolex on the same wrist as a thick gold bracelet he calls his Bay of Pigs Memory Band. Nobody gave out bling for fucking up the Bay of Pigs, and even if they had, Freddie was still riding a tricycle when the operation went down.

But he doesn't stop there. There are constant suggestions about dark ops in deep jungles when the closest he's ever been to physical danger is getting his jaw broken by a Boston prostitute after refusing to pay the guy. My personal favorite, though, is watching him tongue kiss every woman he meets. Nobody knows why he does it, it's just part of his MO. The less charitable like to say Freddie's been slapped more times than Bill Clinton but wouldn't know what to do with a pair of tits. I wanted to be there if he tried to slip his Gene Simmons between Archer's lips.

Leon met us in the tastefully decorated living room with a pitcher of something too thick to tempt me, but Archer was game. The dogs took over a sofa, and Freddie didn't waste any time getting down to business. He suggested I join him in his office.

There are dozens of examples of Freddie's greed and moral vacancy. One that comes immediately to mind is the married European diplomat who discovered his Chevy Chase girlfriend was seeing somebody else. So naturally, he tied her to a tree and burned down her house. Freddie arranged to get the guy out of the country before the cops could find him. His fee: $2 million. His defense: "Heavens, I haven't watched TV or read a newspaper for days."

Freddie skated. The girlfriend wasn't so lucky. She committed suicide.

I disliked him, but I needed him. We took seats in a small sitting area opposite a rolltop desk Freddie brags belonged to Jesse James. I doubt it. Jesse wasn't much of a desk-sitter. He grinned at me like a skinner eyeing a plump hide. If there are any disadvantages to being wealthy, this is one. "Whatever can I do for you, Rail?"

"I need visas into Egypt for Archer, myself and my two pilots. We'll be arriving day after tomorrow."

"Oh, you're staying over. Delightful. We just redid the

guest room. And why don't you ask for something hard? Egypt? Sounds intriguing. Do tell me."

"Not a chance. And it's not that easy. My pilots aren't in town yet, and Archer and I can't leave the house. You'll have to do it on charm."

His grin got wider. "You know the old saying: you can get more with a kind word and a gun than just a kind word. I've got some juice with an embassy guy who likes to . . ."

I held up my hand. "Not something I need or want to hear."

Freddie laughed. "Anything else?"

"I want to be able to land my plane without the whole world knowing. Maybe a small airfield up north."

"Alexandria."

"Yes, but not Borg Al-Arab International. I've got a history with that place."

"Now there's a story I'll bet I could make some hay with. How long will you be in-country?"

"Just a few hours. One meeting and out."

"So you'll probably need to get around some. I've got a friend up that way who leases cars. What say we get you into a new Maybach. Maybe a driver too. Egypt's not an easy place to find your way. Dangerous too."

What he meant was, how about letting me add a spy. "No driver, just the car."

"That it?"

"Archer and I could use somebody to do some shopping for us. We're both a little low on clothes."

Freddie clapped his hands with genuine joy. "Terrific. I've got just the guy. Vittorio. He's got the best taste."

"I'm not interested in his taste, only his ability to follow instructions."

Freddie shook his head. "Still a goddamn fashion dud. I'll bet your lady friend will be more receptive to a little adventure."

"If she wants to trust you, that's up to her. But I should

warn you, the lady can shoot. Okay, Freddie, time for your favorite question. How much? And don't use Chevy Chase arsonists as a benchmark." I couldn't resist the jab, but Freddie was impervious.

He looked off into space like he was calculating. If he was, it was how big a number he could throw out without having me grab him by the neck. "What say I do it out of friendship?"

I was ready for him. "Then be on the hook for something down the road? Not a chance. I was on the receiving end of that once before, remember? It cost me about five times what the original favor was worth, not to mention the respect of a really good man."

Freddie frowned. "That guy was a fucking asshole. You're better off."

"How much, Freddie?"

"Let's say a quarter."

"A quarter of what?"

"Don't be coy."

"For four visas and a landing permit? That yellow crap you're drinking must be LSD."

"You ever hear the one about Mike the Butcher?"

"If you think it's worth two hundred and fifty grand, knock yourself out."

Freddie leaned toward me. "Lady comes in and asks Mike, how much are pork chops? Five ninety-nine a pound, he tells her. Jesus Christ, she says, Lenny down the street sells them for three ninety-nine. Then buy them from Lenny. The broad gets upset and says, I can't, he's sold out. So Mike leans across the counter and says, I should be sold out, you can have them for three ninety-nine."

"A hundred grand, not a penny more."

"Go see Lenny," Freddie said. "Price of pork chops here is a quarter million."

The prick had me, and we both knew it. I sighed. "For that I get your car too."

"My Bentley? Not a fucking chance. It's worth that much all by itself."

"I don't want to buy it, Freddie. Just use it. When I'm on my way, I'll call, and you can send somebody to pick it up."

"Why not just let me drive you to whatever airport you're using?" he asked. "What damage could I do?"

"It's the other way around, Freddie. Being seen with me right now has nothing but downside."

The coward in him told him not to press. "Okay, but only if you promise to park it indoors."

"Done."

My cell phone rang. I looked at the screen. Bert.

"Jesus Christ, Rail, why didn't you call me back?"

"I've been a little busy."

"What the fuck is going on?" he said.

I had no idea what he was talking about.

"Haven't you seen the news?" he asked, his voice rising.

"No."

"Well, get to a television. Fast. Then call me back."

I started to point to the television across the room, but my professional eavesdropper already had a picture coming up. The reporter on CNN was standing in front of the Pentagon.

"In an eerie parallel to Admiral Boorda's 1996 suicide, Army Chief of Staff General Marlon R. Hood evidently shot himself in his office early this morning. He was found by his secretary, and last rites were administered before he was transported to Walter Reed Medical Center, where he was pronounced dead.

"The president has been notified and will make a statement at four o'clock this afternoon. The general's widow has gone into seclusion, and some members of Congress are saying that he should not be permitted to be buried at Arlington until there is a full investigation.

"Several colleagues of General Hood said they saw no indication of any problems, but there is an unverified report

*that a coworker had recently noticed a pistol on Hood's
desk, and when he asked about it, the general said it was
a gift, and he was just waiting for a display case he'd ordered.*

"General Hood began his career . . ."

I motioned to Freddie to mute the sound and thought about
the chromed gun I'd seen at Starbucks.

"You know Hood?" Freddie asked.

"We were at Bragg together," I answered. "Way back."

He started grinning again. "That call wasn't about way
back."

The look I gave him got my point across, and he shrugged.
"Okay, but if you're interested, his wife had recently filed
for divorce—for the umpteenth time. And word was she was
finally going through with it."

"How long had they been married?"

"Thirty-two years. You know who she is, don't you?"

I nodded. "A Wentworth."

"Correct, so there went the meal ticket. Four-stars do
okay, but they live in subdivisions, not the Maryland shore
and Park Avenue."

"Cause?"

"What else? Too much pussy, not enough time. The good
general fucked just about everybody in town. Hell, he mighta
fucked me and Leon too, if we'da stood still. His latest piece
of strange was some Italian beav."

"Bibiana Cesarotti."

"My compliments. You ever get tired of clipping cou-
pons, you can come work for me." His laugh made my skin
crawl.

When I called Bert back, he was still animated. I let him
talk, then asked if he'd come up with a connection between
Hood and Truman York.

"Yeah, but it wasn't easy."

Bert wasn't a guy who needed a pat on the head, but some

people have to get it out their own way. It was also the most excitement he'd had for a while, so I think he wanted to make it last.

"Once I got their complete service records, I plotted their stations. They were within a few hundred miles of each other a couple of times, but, according to a talkative lieutenant in the air force pension office, there was no official connection unless it was a temporary duty situation, which wouldn't have been logged. I figured that was too much of a long shot, so I went looking for something else."

"Your medical guy."

"Yes. Kim told you there had been two Mrs. Yorks before Bess."

"Right."

"Actually, there were three. The first was while Truman was still in flight school in Colorado. Pamela Mason. Local girl. Young. Seventeen. She was killed a year later."

"How?"

"Skiing accident is how it was reported. Novice mistake. Took a wrong turn and went over a cliff. Broke her neck, but apparently not York's heart. After picking up a hundred grand in insurance, he was off to Lackland in San Antonio. Six months later, he married Charlette Nunley, daughter of a wealthy rancher."

"A hundred grand in insurance. On a seventeen-year-old. What foresight," I said.

"Wasn't it?"

"How'd Wife Number Two work out?"

"Lasted less time than it took the ink to dry, but at least she got out alive. I managed to track her down. All these years later, and she's still spitting fire. Damn near broke my eardrum shouting, 'Yippee,' when I told her Truman had bought the farm. Said he beat the shit out of her so bad, her daddy had to step in. Annulment, and a transfer—compliments of a well-placed phone call to the Pentagon from a powerful congressman. And there was something else. . . ."

"What?"

"Charlette said that after Truman was gone, there was talk that he'd been molesting a couple of young girls. Junior high age. It made her so sick, she went out of her way to avoid finding out more."

"How long did it take the next Mrs. York to arrive on scene?"

"Quite a while, actually. Truman was a captain and stationed in Germany. He was on leave in Paris when he met a young art student named Abigail, who was studying at the Sorbonne. Kim's future mother. Incidentally, Abigail was an artist. Don't you find that interesting?"

Bert and I had had this conversation before. We both believe that genetic predisposition is one of the reasons some families mint doctors and some, criminals. "What about the father?"

"Banker from New York. One of the wealthiest families in America. Wentworth. And Abigail's body was never found."

I thought my age put me beyond that kind of surprise. It didn't. I felt my face flush. In some ways, it was good to know that part of me was still in there somewhere.

"How did she die?"

"Rental boat capsized off Ibiza. Truman survived."

Something wasn't working for me. "Why would a family as powerful as the Wentworths not move heaven and earth to get that child?"

Bert hesitated. "I'm sitting here holding two Spanish death certificates. One in the name of Abigail Montrose Wentworth, age twenty-three. And the other for Cassandra Paulette Wentworth-York, age one year, seven months."

It took a minute for the full impact of it to hit me. And then Kim's words. *I don't know why, but I have this almost sickening fear of drowning. And I'm terrified of boats—especially small ones.*

Truman York hadn't cared about the Wentworth money.

He only wanted the daughter. His own daughter. Somebody too young to remember her mother. And somebody who could never file a complaint. I felt the nausea welling up and fought it back, only marginally successfully.

"Rail, you okay?" Bert asked.

"No, but I don't expect you are either."

"The implication is almost too depraved to contemplate."

"How did you come up with this?"

"My Pentagon medical guy. He had a hard-on for Hood—something about cutting benefits for World War Two veterans—so he put two people on it. I've got a full dossier on both men. Where do you want them sent?"

"Hang onto them. I'm going to be traveling. And frankly, I'm not sure I care to know any more."

Freddie, like he always did, delivered, and Archer and I met Eddie and Jody at the executive terminal of Northeast Philadelphia just after 6:00 p.m. the following day. I parked Freddie's precious Bentley in the VIP area, which, unfortunately, wasn't indoors. So along with the keys, I left a five-hundred-dollar check in the glove box and a note to get his ride detailed on me.

Eddie hugged Archer, and she got teary, which isn't unusual the first time you see someone after a tragedy.

Northeast, where many Europe-bound private aircraft embark, was, as usual, standing room only. "Fuckin'-A," said Eddie. "I had to grease the maintenance chief a grand just to move up five slots."

"You, a grand?" I asked.

"Well, I promised you'd come by and take care of him."

I found the guy—Bruno—and after some blue-collar, South Philly negotiating, we got our food and fuel loaded, passed inspection, and were told to roll into takeoff position.

Half an hour later, we were passing through ten thousand feet, and Jody—a master navigator—had put us on a heading east of Halifax, over Nuuk and into Reykjavík. Assuming continued good weather, we'd be having pickled herring and scrambled eggs for breakfast. I dialed Freddie and told him where he could find his car.

"Northeast is one airport I've never been to," he said. "They have inside parking, right?"

"Of course." There was no reason to stress him out on the drive up.

"Bon voyage, my friend. I've already called Jake about the money."

"You'd have disappointed me if you hadn't."

When we reached our cruising altitude, Archer suddenly reached over and took my hand. "I can't even begin to guess how much you've spent."

"Neither can I."

"I wouldn't blame you for calling it quits. Nothing's going to bring Kim back, and I'm finding comfort in her finally being at peace."

I smiled. "I appreciate it, but not a chance. Those fuckers shot me too."

A little while later, she turned to me with dreamy eyes. "Rail, morning will be here soon, and I won't have the courage anymore. I need to say this. I love you."

I patted her hand.

"No," she said, "it's not just talk. I really love you."

By the time it sunk in, she was sound asleep. I picked her up and carried her to the bedroom. Eddie—or more likely, one of the ground crew—had the covers turned down and smooth jazz purring. I undressed her and slipped her between the sheets.

Before I left, I smoothed back her hair. The scar through her bad eyelid was almost invisible in the soft light. I bent down and kissed her. I didn't know how I felt, but it had been a long time since my touch had been so light.

I went back to the main cabin and started through the catalogue for Konstantin Serbin's Norton Simon exhibition. Bert had highlighted some things, the most interesting of which was that Colonel Serbin didn't live in Russia anymore. He had moved to London. Belgravia, to be precise. The catalogue said his new residence had once been the Yugoslavian Embassy. I knew the place. My grandfather had built it.

I dimmed the cabin lights and watched the blackness of the North Atlantic for a while, thinking about Kim. No wonder she had been so terrified of drowning.

I did the math. Kim had died at thirty-one, so Hood and Suzanne had married before York and Abigail had. Which meant they'd known about the baby.

In leverage terms, the general had owned York. There was nothing, however, that indicated Kim ever knew who her mother was or what happened to her. I couldn't decide whether that was good or bad, but probably good. I'm a big believer in the truth, but sometimes too much of it is worse than none at all. Not something you'll hear in church—or from a cop. Sooner or later I was going to have to tell all of this to Archer, but not now. I wasn't finished processing it myself.

When I awakened, the sun was breaking over the horizon, and we were in our descent into Iceland.

Jetway Drivers and Dark Places

It was foggy and raining in Alexandria, and visibility was nonexistent. That only happens a dozen times a year, and it paralyzed the tiny airport at Al Qasr. Despite Eddie's cajoling, ground officials insisted on diverting us to Borg Al-Arab. As I told Freddie, that was not a place I wanted to go, not to mention there was an Egyptian military installation on the grounds, and they'd make it a point to inspect a private jet from the States, especially one this size.

I was standing in the cockpit door. "Eddie, is this bucket of bolts as sophisticated as the brochures say?"

"I could put it down on Fifth Avenue in a blackout," he said.

"Then land," I told him.

Eddie grinned. "I love shit like this." He keyed his radio and spoke into the headset. "Clear the runway, we've got an emergency." Then he hit the intercom so we could all hear. The controller's voice, screaming in Arabic, filled the plane.

"Sorry, no habla," Eddie replied. He lit a cigarette and exhaled toward the radio. "Coming in. Smoke in the cockpit."

The tower hadn't been lying. We didn't see ground until

we touched it, but Eddie and Boeing brought it in on a wire and Velcroed the wheels to the tarmac. By the time we got parked, the rain had stopped.

There were angry words with two guys who looked like they'd bought their suits from the KGB, but after everybody got done venting, Eddie and Jody headed off to lunch with them. Eddie had wanted to go with me, but there are horses for courses, and this wasn't one for a fire-breather. The lone customs official assigned to Al Qasr was on holiday in Cyprus, so we were free to go.

Freddie's car guy, Osiris Vagotis, was a slender young Greek in a business suit who looked like he should have been in the movies rather than peddling cars. He was waiting for us just outside the one-story terminal, and as we approached, I saw him discreetly admire Archer. When he introduced himself in perfect English, I decided to take a chance, Freddie notwithstanding. "You busy this afternoon, Osiris?"

"No, sir."

"What would you want to drive us for a few hours?"

He smiled. "I know all the sights. The restaurants too. You can pay me what you think I'm worth at the end."

Good answer. We got in the car, a silver Maybach. Archer said she might want to nap, so I got in front with Osiris. As we pulled out, I turned to our driver, "One more thing."

"Sir?"

"The gentleman who arranged for this car . . ."

"Yes, Mr. Rochelle."

"Your relationship with him is what?"

"My father used to be deputy trade minister. He engaged Mr. Rochelle to make inquiries about a Texas gentleman who might be offering bribes for Egyptian oil leases."

I almost laughed out loud. The Texan had probably been one of Freddie's clients. And if he hadn't been, when Freddie got finished, he certainly was. "How did it turn out?" I asked.

"Not particularly well. My father said Mr. Rochelle spent

a lot of money traveling and entertaining but never seemed to come up with anything. And no matter how many times he promised, he wouldn't submit a detailed list of expenses. He'd just send in a number on a piece of stationery."

How many times had that tune been sung. The only people more skillful than lobbyists at ripping off a foreign rube are Washington's legion of security consultants. Guys like them and Freddie you had to flat rate. No matter how expensive it seemed, it was nothing compared to what they could do on an open ticket.

I said to Osiris, "So whatever you might see or hear today would stay among us."

"My father would shoot me if I betrayed the confidence of a customer. No matter how he came to us."

I nodded. "We're going south."

"There's not much to see out there, sir."

"Maybe we'll find something."

The sun was out again and turning puddles into vapor, which had the effect of making Egypt's heat visible, even through the darkly tinted glass of the Maybach.

Young Mr. Vagotis had started out wanting to be a soccer player. But unknown to him, his father had paid a coach from Manchester United to attend a few of his games and assess his skills. The report came back that he was good but would never be more than a bench player at the professional level.

"I was very angry at first," he said. "I thought it was none of my father's business."

"And now?"

"He was right. And deep down, I knew it too. I just wouldn't admit it." His voice took on a new quality—pride. "You know, when I joined the company, we leased Mercedes exclusively. Now, we have over one hundred Ferrari and Aston Martins on the road. And next year, we're going to be the first leasing company to open in Tripoli."

"And how many of your wealthy clients' fathers have tried to make a match with their daughters?" I asked.

He smiled. "One of the hazards of the business. But

the first time I went down that road and didn't marry the girl, word would go out. And in Egypt, that would end my business—and my love life."

"Handsome, ambitious and smart," Archer said. "What are you doing Saturday night?"

We all laughed.

We drove for an hour and a half across an unchanging moonscape. Occasionally, there would be a cart on the side of the road or some low, brown houses in the distance, but other than the thinning traffic, scenery was all but nonexistent.

And then out of all this brown arose an ocean of green. It was like we'd blinked and been transported to an endless Dutch countryside, broken occasionally by long rows of palms. We drove for miles surrounded by this lushness before coming to a turnoff marked by a sign in English and Arabic.

NAZARAK NURSERIES

I was impressed that the private road was as well-paved as the main highway, and as we followed it, I asked Osiris if he had seen this before.

"When I was in school, sometimes we would bring our dates out here. We'd pull off the road and have a picnic in one of the fields. It smelled so wonderful. Like nothing in the city. It was almost a guarantee your girlfriend would want to make love. You had to watch for the sprinklers though." He laughed.

We rounded a curve and a city of covered work areas came into view. Scores of men were potting plants and placing them onto skids that others then wrapped in plastic. A little further on, the road branched, and Osiris took the right fork. "I'm not sure this is correct," he said. "I'm guessing."

He was on the money. Very soon, we were passing a ten-foot stucco wall on our left that ran as far as the eye could see. A little while later, we came to a gate and turned in to face a pair of wide steel doors etched with stylized cartouches. There seemed to be no way to summon anyone, so Osiris got out and pushed on the gates. They opened, and we drove through.

I'm not sure anyone could have prepared me for what lay ahead. Mr. Nazarak had replicated Luxor's Avenue of the Sphinxes, and for a hundred yards, dozens of massive sandstone sentries stood guard over a tree-lined lane. At its terminus sat a columned palace draped in the most beautiful hanging gardens since Babylon.

Archer came awake and looked out at the magnificence. "My God, where are we? Newark?"

Suddenly, there were men running at us from all directions. They wore white turbans and khaki uniforms and were pointing Kalashnikovs—locked and loaded.

From the backseat, Archer said, "Yep, Newark."

Amen Nazarak spoke English, but he was much more comfortable in Arabic, so bringing Osiris had been fortuitous. However, in any language, he was adamant that no one was permitted to see his daughter.

As we sat drinking honeyed tea in a vast room of low sofas, Oriental rugs and randomly strewn cushions, we looked out over a man-made lake, where snow white swans and blue herons seemed to have been designed into the view. Amen was cordial, if not warm, but Bastet, he explained, was still traumatized by Flight 990. All these years later, she still required medication to sleep and had lost some cognitive ability. She frequently became lost in unfamiliar surroundings, and she had difficulty remembering friends' names.

Trauma is an indiscriminate debilitator, and I do not ever minimize its power, but this seemed excessive for someone who had only been a ramp agent for a doomed flight. When Osiris put my comment to Amen, he flashed angry, then he put his head in his hands. "It was not the tragedy, it was the torture afterward."

Gradually, haltingly, he revealed that in the wake of the

crash, Egypt Air became obsessed with convincing the world that their pilots did not commit suicide. Regardless of the cockpit voice tape and the telemetry from the flight data recorder and ground radar, Egyptian aviation officials—under intractable and threatening orders from the government—worked backward from a conclusion of engine or structural failure. That most people with any IQ laughed at them didn't matter. It was their story and they were sticking to it.

Partly, it was to establish a defensive position for the litigation certain to follow; partly, it was a very real concern that thousands of future horrified travelers might just up and cancel their Egypt Air reservations; and partly, it was cultural. All of it was stupid, because in the end, even though the investigative team noted the airline's and government's objections, the official NTSB report is unflinchingly brutal. For whatever reason, rational or psychotic, Relief First Officer Gameel Al-Batouti deliberately dove his 767 into the ocean at close to the speed of sound, taking with him 216 innocents.

But what did any of this have to do with Bastet Nazarak, surely the lowest person on the totem pole that night? Not even her father could answer that. Bastet had never confided any of the specifics to him, and afraid he might further compromise her already delicate mental state, he hadn't asked. It looked like we were at a stalemate when all of a sudden, a quite tall, extremely pretty, dark-haired young lady walked into the room. She was wearing faded jeans and a dark blue blouse and had her hair pulled back in a ponytail. She would have been over thirty, but she looked much younger.

"I heard my name," she said, looking at me. "Are you here about the crash?"

We all stood, and Amen started to say something, but our driver stepped in. "Miss Nazarak, my name is Osiris Vagotis. These people are friends of my father's. He is a respected businessman in Alexandria, but we used to live in Cairo. We left after he was imprisoned for having a Jewish partner. Of course, that was not the reason given on the arrest warrant.

That said he was accused of tax improprieties, but during the beatings, all they asked was why he was friends with a Jew."

Bastet came all the way into the room and sat down across from Osiris. She looked at him with wide, expressive eyes. "Please call me Bastet. What is your father's name?"

"Mathias. Mathias Vagotis."

"Is he . . . still alive?"

Osiris nodded. "Very much alive, and he never misses an opportunity to tell people what happened. He believes evil can only survive in the dark."

I saw her lower lip tremble. After a moment, she said, "They beat me too."

Osiris leaned forward and took her two hands in his. Her fingers were long and slender, and she wore a thin silver bracelet on her right wrist. "Your father has told us. He's deeply concerned about you. But if Mathias were here, he would urge you to do what he has done. Shine a light on bad things."

Bastet looked at Archer and me for the first time. "What are your names?"

Archer answered. "This is Rail Black, and I'm Archer Cayne."

"I've seen your picture in magazines," she said to Archer, then turned to me. "Are you an American too?" she asked.

"Yes," I answered.

I could see Amen Nazarak in my peripheral vision. He was sitting back in his chair, the tension on his face gone. This was probably the first time his daughter had said anything about Egypt Air in his presence.

"And you're not with the government or the NTSB?" she asked.

"No, Bastet, I'm not."

"Then what is it you would like to know, Mr. Black?"

"Truthfully, I'm not sure. Maybe if you could just walk me through that night."

She collected her thoughts. "It was raining, and the agent who parked the jetway when the plane arrived hadn't done a very good job. There was a gap at the top letting water in. So during boarding, I put on my coat and held an umbrella over the space to keep the passengers from getting wet." She paused. "There were children, you know."

I did know, and it was heartbreaking, but I didn't want her to get bogged down in the sadness. "Which door were you using?"

She came back to the present. "Number one; 767s board through first class. Most of the passengers were already onboard because the flight had originated in Los Angeles. It didn't take long to get our few on, along with the relief pilots."

"Did you know anybody in the crew?"

"EA's not a big operation in the States. Everybody knows everybody, but flight crews socialize more with each other because they're on the road together. The rest of us go home at night."

I understood and nodded.

"After everybody was aboard but still getting settled, I folded my umbrella and stepped into the plane. I saw the pilot talking to some military men in business class. The conversation was animated, and since normally the pilot would be in the cockpit, I asked a flight attendant what was going on. She said one of the military officers had gotten on in L.A. without his paperwork."

Bastet must have seen the question on my face. "Military personnel have to carry several documents. The most important are their orders. It determines how the airline logs the seat, and who will reimburse them. Pilots have to fill out a lot of extra forms and can be fined if they don't get a copy. It doesn't happen often, but I've seen pilots insist that a military passenger without paperwork get off. Most of the time, though, they just give the guy a lecture and make arrangements to get it later."

"The captain was El-Habashy."

"Yes, and pretty soon, he came forward, shaking his head, and went into the cockpit. I looked down the first aisle and saw that most passengers were already seated, so I went back onto the jetway and waited for the order to close the door."

I started to say something, but Bastet put up her hand. "Let me tell this my own way." Her tone had a new urgency to it, and it struck me that this was going to be the first time she had told what was coming to anyone.

"While I was waiting, the man sitting in Seat 1-B, a special courier who'd gotten on in New York, was talking to a woman standing in the aisle. The woman seemed upset about something. Then a flight attendant told her she'd have to return to her seat in coach because they were getting ready to close the door. The woman started back, but she looked terrified."

I remembered Archer's telling me how fearful Bess was of flying. She'd just suffered through five and a half hours in the air, and now she was about to have to endure ten more. She *was* terrified.

"A few seconds later, the courier stood up and unbuckled his case from Seat 1-A. Special couriers have two seats—"

"I know," I said. "One for them, another for their case. Then what did he do?"

"He got off the plane."

Bastet continued talking, but they were just words coming from far away. My mind was racing. I was pulled back to reality by Archer's shouting, "THAT MONSTER IS ALIVE! OH MY GOD, THAT FUCKING MONSTER IS ALIVE!"

Amen had a look of shock on his face at the outburst, and Osiris seemed a little taken aback too. The only person who wasn't rattled was Bastet, who just stopped talking and calmly waited for things to settle down.

I got my arm around Archer. "We'll explain later," I said to Bastet and asked her to continue.

"As soon as the courier went past me, the woman he'd been talking to came running up the aisle in a panic. She was yelling, 'Truman, Truman, where are you going?' I knew the man's name was Truman York, because as the ramp agent, it was my job to put special couriers on the plane before general boarding began and to inform the rest of the crew who they were. Mr. York had also been on that same flight several times before, and I remembered him."

Bastet paused, like she wanted to make sure she got the sequence of events right. "The senior flight attendant stepped in front of the woman and told her that she had to return to her seat, but she just kept yelling, 'Truman! Truman!'

"Then a strange thing happened. Mr. York came back down the jetway and stopped right behind me. He called out to the woman, 'I've got to do something, Bess. I'll meet you in Marseilles. Mascotte Vieux Hotel, remember?' And then he was gone. The woman wanted to get off too, but the flight attendant said she couldn't. By that time, some of the passengers were upset, and one of them told her to sit down. I saw her start back to her seat, but I'll never forget the look on her face. I can't lie down without seeing it. It haunts me every night."

"Why did they let the man off the plane and not the woman?" It was Amen asking.

"We're not even allowed to talk to a special courier unless he talks to us. If you tried to impede one, you'd be fired on the spot."

"Bastet. Can you describe the case?" I asked.

"Aluminum, about like this." She held her hands roughly three feet apart. "Maybe twelve inches deep, and the same width as a first-class seat. With wheels and a handle that pulled out so you could tilt it when you walked. It was the same one Mr. York always carried."

"And it was on a cable attached to him."

She nodded. "Yes, down his left sleeve, which I was told meant he was right-handed. I never saw him with a gun, but special couriers are permitted to carry one, so it could have been under his suit coat. He only had to show it to the captain."

"But the captain was occupied," Archer said.

"Like I said, Mr. York went on before anyone else. I don't remember where the captain was then. But the first officer could have been called out to see it as well."

I could feel Archer shuddering. I wanted to get out of there before she lost it, but I wasn't finished. Interestingly, Bastet seemed fine. Almost like a weight had been lifted.

"Had Truman York ever gotten off the plane before?"

"Not on any of the flights I worked."

"You didn't tell anyone about Mr. York when they interrogated you, did you?"

She shook her head. "Four months in that slimy cell, but I knew it would be a lot longer if I got into that. Nobody else who survived saw it, and it didn't have any bearing on the crash, so it was a matter of self-preservation."

"How do you know it didn't have anything to do with the crash?" Amen blurted. "It could have been very important."

Bastet looked at Amen with great tenderness. "Father, the relief first officer put that plane in the water. Everybody knows it, and it's wrong to pretend otherwise. Egyptians do commit suicide. They get depression like people everywhere . . . or they just do crazy things with no explanation. Like Osiris's father said, bad things live in the dark. We have to talk about them, not make believe we're different."

35

Missing Pieces and Body Art

I sat with Archer in the backseat. She was still huddled against me. "Thanks for your help," I said to Osiris. "Your father can be proud."

"Thank you, sir."

"I hope you'll also pass along my admiration for his bravery."

"May I respond the way he would?" he said.

"Of course."

"Do you know how many people there are in Cairo?" he asked.

"Sixteen million, give or take," I said.

"And how many operating synagogues?"

"I have no idea."

"None," Osiris answered. "So what does that mean? That there are no Jews, or that there are consequences for raising your hand?"

I thought back to Jackie Benveniste and Corsica.

Osiris went on. "My father says he's not brave, he just hates ignorance."

"I'm pretty sure I'd like him."

"That would last only until you had to negotiate with him."

We both laughed, and then he said, "If you don't mind, Mr. Black, I might drive out and see Bastet again."

"I think she'd like that. I think her father would too. How do you feel about farming?"

"Not a chance. I'm addicted to fast cars and bright lights . . . but she's lived in New York, hasn't she?" He grinned at me through the rearview mirror.

We rode in silence for a while, and I thought about Truman York. A lot of things made sense now. Truman had likely had an escort to JFK, so he'd had to go through the charade of boarding Flight 990, then simply gotten up and walked off. He didn't know Al-Batouti was going to auger in the 767, but since he was going to kill Bess anyway, when he heard, he probably high-fived himself.

I didn't know yet if he'd had a well-thought-out plan to steal the last Tretiakov painting or if it was a spur of the moment decision, but I suspected a plan. Based on their previous relationship in Turkey, York would have been the one who introduced Bruzzi to Hood, and it had been a lucrative arrangement. But he'd almost certainly grown weary of being run by his former brother-in-law, and this was a way out—with a retirement bonus.

For his part, Hood wouldn't have liked someone as reckless as Truman—and with as much personal baggage— having his fate in his hands. He'd gone to incredible lengths to monetize the City of War for his own benefit, and what had probably begun as a nest egg for the day his wife finally cut him off from the Wentworth fortune had turned into a multimillion dollar enterprise spanning three continents. He might have made a decision to eliminate the most obvious threat. A decision Truman had gotten wind of. Nehemiah Jacobs had died for a lot less.

As I saw it, Truman's biggest problem was that there was no obvious market for the Orlov painting. To realize its value, he would either have had to publicize its history, which would lead to unwanted attention, or have a buyer waiting in the wings. Since the latter made the most sense, Bruzzi or Serbin had to have had prior knowledge.

I didn't see an advantage for Serbin. All but one of the paintings had already been repatriated, so there was no reason to steal something you were about to get anyway. His people were presumably waiting in Cairo to take possession—or they were already aboard Flight 990. My bet was Cairo. If they had been on the plane, there would have been a hell of a commotion when Truman got off.

That left Bruzzi. The question was why. Perhaps it had just been a thieves' day out, but I didn't think so. Too many people had died to hide a simple grab.

A couple of other things nagged at me as well. That the deliveries had gone through Egypt rather than directly to Moscow, especially since the paintings' return was being hailed as a national heritage repatriation. I learned a long time ago, that when it comes to Russians, there is rarely a straight line from A to B, but I couldn't get past the fact that there had been twenty-two separate trips on a commercial airline instead of one military flight to a secure base. Perhaps there was some political issue that wasn't obvious, or maybe it had taken time to get the museums in place, but those explanations seemed flimsy.

Archer suddenly sat up. "Rail, I'm really sorry I fell apart back there. I didn't realize how much I hated him."

I took her hand. "Archer, there is a secret place down deep in all of us that holds emotions beyond the scope of our imagination. You, of all people, have nothing to be ashamed of."

"I've been sitting here reeling. Kim knew he was alive, didn't she?"

"Yes, she was getting money to him. Whatever he'd received for stealing the painting had probably long since run out."

I then told her about Brandi Sue Parsons, the Pasadena beauty queen, and the Kubicek watercolors. About Kim's commenting on the value of things in my home like the Alençon lace and the Vettriano painting. And about her finding an inconspicuous room by comparing the outdoor dimensions of the house to the indoor ones.

Archer said, "Ordinarily, when I stay with someone, I just try not to get caught raiding the cake stash. So she was shopping."

"I think so, but to give her the benefit of the doubt, let me make a call. Osiris, my phone isn't set up for Egypt, may I borrow yours?"

"Certainly."

After a moment, I remembered A. A. Abernathy's cell number from his card and dialed. It only rang a couple of times before I heard the familiar voice and told him who it was. "Sorry to wake you, Doctor."

"No problem. Need to be up anyway. I've got an early breakfast in Westwood, and I was just lying here planning my omelet."

"Tell me, did anybody ever notice anything missing at the Getty?"

"From the collections? You must be kidding." He sounded like I'd just called his mother a crack whore. I didn't have time to brush sand from a fossil one grain at a time, so I had to take a different tack. One of the things they teach you at Interrogation School is that softening your voice and using a person's first name immediately lowers the interviewee's heart rate and brings down his blood sugar level. With someone looking for the chance to be compliant, it can be like hitting him with 20 mgs of Tranxene.

"Yes, A.A., from the collections. I know that's something people in your line of work don't like to think about, but we all know the frailties of human nature, especially when weak people find themselves near extraordinarily beautiful or exceptionally valuable things."

He danced. "We're a museum, Mr. Black. We have millions of objects in our care and people in and out all the time. Sometimes items get misplaced."

Misplaced. We were getting there. "A.A., I'm thinking about anything Kim might have had access to."

He hesitated too long. I was losing him. So I told him about Kiki Videz. When I finished, he said, "It's a sad story, but I'm not sure why you're telling it to me."

"Think about it, Doctor. Kim's killers didn't need a fall guy or a gun for her. She was going in the ocean where she'd never be found. But they'd been following her. She lived alone and didn't have any friends. There was only one other person she had regular contact with. Probably had lunch with from time to time. Somebody who may have even taken her out once or twice despite what he told me."

I waited while my words sunk in.

Finally, he said, "There could have been a few items missing that I was concerned about. Not major pieces, but worthwhile."

"Things that could be easily sold?"

"Perhaps."

I took a breath. "A.A., is that the real reason you were letting Kim go?"

The silence went on so long that I thought we'd lost the connection. Finally, he said, "Much as I might like to, I really can't comment on personnel matters."

I didn't need any more. "How good are those security people of yours?"

"Damn good, I would imagine," he said.

"Then I suggest you send them over to Kim's. There's no one home and no alarm. Behind the living room bookshelves is a portfolio you might be interested in."

"Care to tell me what's going on?"

"Over dinner at Tacitus."

"I'll hold you to it," he said. "By the way, I came up empty on City of War. Any luck on your end?"

"Tacitus," I said and hung up.

Archer looked at me in disbelief. "She was stealing from the museum too? For that filthy son of a bitch? After what he did to her? It's unfathomable."

It wasn't, and I told her the rest of the sordid story. When I finished, she sat in stunned silence, then turned and silently watched the brown desert pass. After a while, she whispered softly, "Like I'm one to talk. Two years with a guy who eventually cut out my fucking eye."

Batterers and battered, abusers and abused. Researchers aren't even close to understanding their codependency. In my opinion, after a while, there's a chemical change in their brains, different from love, but just as powerful. But last time I checked, nobody was standing by waiting for me to weigh in.

Finally, Archer turned back to me. "But why the photographs? The article?"

"Two reasons. The first was self-protection. My guess is Hood, Serbin and Bruzzi all got copies. The second was money. Once she started running out of options, she tried to blackmail them."

"So they had to kill her . . . but they needed the flash drive to close the loop."

"Correct. And Bruzzi drew the contract. It's what he does for a living anyway. Remember how Hood tried to distance himself from Kim's murder? I also think Bruzzi and Truman had some kind of a side deal, and your stepfather, desperate and a fool, completely miscalculated. Bruzzi didn't just want Kim dead, he wanted her to suffer.

"The Hyena was most likely the man in the private plane Tino and Dante showed her to that night, and Kim knew exactly who it was. She also knew that once they had her out to sea, Tino was going to go to work on her with his knife for the location of the flash drive before he fed her to the fish. If the 405 hadn't stopped, she would have jumped out of that van even if it had meant dying."

Archer shuddered. "So what do we do now?"

"We're going to get you someplace safe, then I'm going visiting. There are some questions I want answers to. The photos at the Biltmore show Hood still in business with

Bruzzi and Serbin years after Egypt Air went down. So what else have they been taking out? And was Dr. Cesarotti part of it, or just the girlfriend?"

Archer said, "But most of all, you want to know where Truman York is."

"Not most of all, but yes, that's part of it."

She flashed, "I want to be there when—"

I held up my hand, and she stopped. A minute or so later, she turned back to me. "I didn't ask you this before, but you slept with her, didn't you?"

"I would have thought that by now, you would have realized I don't answer questions like that."

"Not even when it could help someone? Like me?"

"Never. And it wouldn't help anything."

"Then let me ask it this way. How could someone who had that happen to her over so many years still function . . . normally?"

"You mean, why didn't Kim become psychotic or a drug addict or end her life?"

"Yes, in spite of everything, she stayed connected to him. Almost like she was able to accept what happened. I think if Truman York had laid his hands on me one more time, I would have gone down to the beach and just kept swimming out to sea."

I looked at Osiris, who was driving smoothly, keeping his eyes on the road. "Osiris, you've heard this conversation. How do you think somebody could be brutalized her whole life yet appear to outsiders as if there were nothing wrong?"

"I think, sir, people find ways to adjust to even the most horrible things. I played a soccer game in Poland once, and the coach took us to Auschwitz. I couldn't understand how anyone could live through that and ever laugh again. But at the end of *Schindler's List,* there were all of these people who had not only gone on but lived productive lives. The only place it could have come from was inside. For some, it was being strong for a loved one. Others became living testaments. And I'm sure more than one made it on sheer hatred."

A wise young man, indeed. "The world is filled with walking wounded," I said. "It's what civilized people do: carry on, regardless."

Before I gave Osiris back his phone, I had one more call to make. Mallory answered on the first ring. I could hear seagulls in the background. "Let me guess, fishing," I said.

"Please, I'd rather have my teeth pulled. We're eating in some dreadful place built to look like a lighthouse. I think I was just poisoned."

I heard Jannicke laugh, "For somebody who doesn't like the food, you haven't stopped shoveling it in since we sat down."

I said, "I take it you're tired of Palm Beach."

"Palm Beach is fine. It's my sister's new boyfriend. He's some kind of professional wrestler . . . about half her age. Calls himself The Bazooka. My God, the body piercings . . . and the level of conversation. *Professional wrestling?* Is that even grammatically correct?"

I laughed, "How about if I sweep you and Jannicke away."

"Anything, please. I'd worship you."

"I'll hold you to it. I need a safe place on the Continent to put a friend. Something besides a hotel."

"Anyone I know?"

"No, but you'll understand when you meet her."

"How soon?"

"Starting tonight."

"I have just the place. Princess Veronique's villa in Cannes. She's just turned ninety, and you know how much she loves company."

"Why don't you make the arrangements, then get yourself and Jannicke to an airport."

"Waiter, check please."

Mallory wasn't usually this funny. He must really have hit the breaking point.

"Oh, Mallory," I said, "if you decide to go for a nose stud, make it tasteful—nothing larger than a carat."

"I think I'm going to be sick."

36

Tears and Beethoven

Princess Veronique didn't look a day older than I remembered her, and that was almost two decades ago. She was still one of the most interesting women I knew, full of eccentricities, like her 1930s wardrobe.

Her terraced villa, Le Trésor, is set into the hillside above Cannes with a commanding view of the Mediterranean coast. Outside, it looks like the Parthenon, and inside, it's filled with French chandeliers, Persian rugs and neo-Roman furniture.

There's also the matter of the world's most ill-tempered parrot, Bartholomew. Iron gates and tall hedges keep the curious away, but any fool breaking in would rather be arrested than have to deal with that bird. Bartholomew and I have a deal; he doesn't peck out my eyes, and I don't show him how the lawn mower works. To the best of my knowledge, he doesn't have that agreement with anyone else, because he's had some close calls.

When her husband, Roger, was alive, Veronique gave legendary parties attended by royalty, Hollywood stars and whomever she happened to run into on the street. Now, she lives with a scaled-down staff and relishes the occasional visitor, mostly writers whom she invites to stay as long as they like.

The current artist-in-residence was a guy named Pappy Meecham from New Orleans, who was writing about his blues singer father. Veronique said he hadn't gotten much work done because the days seemed to slip away while they played old records and drank absinthe. Part of me was jealous.

Archer immediately fell in love with Veronique and vice versa. They began chattering away like college roommates. Then Pappy poured her a glass of green liquid, and everyone forgot about me.

I made my way to the kitchen and left a note for Mallory with Veronique's cook, Brigitte. I asked him to spend as much time as possible with Archer and maybe get Jannicke on the case too. And I apologized for adding to his burden since the shooting and then almost getting him killed. Lastly, I thanked him for his friendship. Something I don't do as often as I should.

As I walked back to the taxi where Eddie and Jody were waiting, Archer came running up behind me. I turned, and she came into my arms. We strolled hand in hand across the lush grounds of Le Trésor and stopped next to a statue of David standing watch over a swimming pool where Cary and Audrey had frolicked. Her voice quivered as she looked up at me. "Rail, darling, I need you to come back."

I took her face in my hands and kissed her. "That's my plan too."

"No, you have to listen to me. I don't think I could bear losing you." She buried her head in my chest, and I felt her melt against me.

I stroked her hair while she cried. Women had clung to me before, but this time something stirred that I hadn't felt in a long, long time. I'd had only one deep romantic relationship in my life, and when Sanrevelle died, I assumed my turn at bat was over. And frankly, I was okay with that. It gave me distance from untidy emotions. What I was feeling now wasn't supposed to happen. But it also wasn't the time to try to sort it out.

I took Archer's hand and led her gently back to the house. Veronique, wise to unspoken cues, met us at the door. She looked at me with her legendary smile. "Don't worry one minute, Rail, I'll take perfect care of her."

Some film festival was in town, but I tipped a greasy guy in a stained suit a year's salary and managed to get Jody installed in a small hotel just off the Croisette. By the time he hit the room, he was already planning which parties to crash. Eddie and I found an Internet café and printed the photographs of the artist on Kim's flash drive. Then I mailed the drive to myself in London, and we caught a taxi to Montpellier Airport.

Coming in, we'd had to land at Nice to clear customs. It wasn't an ideal situation for people trying to be invisible, but Eddie told the hangar manager we were on our way to Monte Carlo to break the bank. Someone looking for us might not buy it, but considering the number of visitors to Monaco and the Principality's penchant for secrecy, it would take them a while to make sure.

Eddie was exhausted and concerned about flying any more hours, so we rented a silver Cirrus SR22, which I'm qualified to fly. It also has enough seat adjust to handle me, as well as a parachute in case I mistook the fuel dump switch for the landing gear. I'm the first to admit I'm not much of a pilot, so I could only imagine how tired Eddie was if he was willing to risk death to get some sleep.

I got us up. It was shaky, but my passenger snored through the whole thing—even when I momentarily lost sight of the Air France commuter ahead of me and had to listen to a ration of shit in gutter French from a controller.

The night was clear, and the first order of business for any bad pilot is to program the autopilot then don't fuck with it—no matter what. I put us on a course for Bastia, which is about as far as you can get from Bonifacio and still be on Corsica. Word might eventually reach Bruzzi that we were there, but maybe it wouldn't get to him before we did.

So while Eddie slept, I flew. And thought about what I'd felt holding Archer.

Even though Amarante talked about it all the time, in my first eighteen years of life, I had never seen Brazil. So when I took my mother home to bury her, I didn't know what to expect. Nobody could have prepared me for the two hundred "cousins" who showed up with their extended families and stood ten deep outside the church.

I was astonished at so much wailing and fainting until my Uncle Santos, Amarante's youngest brother, explained that most of the crowd had never met her. "They just know she had lots of money, so they're practicing the mantra of the favellas that maybe if you cry loud enough, some of it will fall on you."

Lord Black was in Sydney mired in some merger or union negotiation or deep-sea fishing or squiring a new girlfriend to the opera, so he couldn't make it. It was the only time I ever had an angry thought about him. But when I cooled off, I came to my senses. She wasn't his wife anymore, and she'd left him.

The priest asked me if I wanted to say something at the service. I told him no. What I didn't tell him was that Amarante and I had already covered everything on the trip down. Me in first class, her on dry ice. It was the first time since she started drinking that we'd had a conversation where she stayed put until it was over. She was a terrific lady in a lot of ways and extremely talented, but she wasn't someone who was interested in other people's problems. Mostly, if you weren't talking about her, you were doing it to an empty room.

As we left the cemetery, Santos steered me to his car. He was a highly respected businessman and a Brazilian senator, but he'd run afoul of the generals in charge, so he was spending most of his time at his villa on the coast. He suggested I come with him. I wasn't really interested, but then he pointed out the rough-looking intelligence officers in bad suits conspicuously taking pictures of the crowd, and he explained that sooner or later, they'd get around to "interviewing" me.

Like the Sistine Chapel, Ubatuba is one of those places photographs can't capture. It's both a mood and a place. Miles of pristine beach with hundreds of inlets, each more stunning than the next. White sand, black sand, rough water, serene lagoons—whatever you could imagine. And because the rich had bought up the land for miles, there wasn't anybody, anywhere, except an occasional fisherman in an ancient dory.

The deeply palmed red hills ran straight up from the sand, and it was on these that the owners built their oceanfront getaways. Santos's place was two stories of Phillip Johnson glass and steel with 360° views and a long, twisting sandstone driveway that must have taken hundreds of campesinos months to lay.

Santos landed his Cessna on a tiny dirt airstrip carved out of the rain forest, and immediately two dozen locals surrounded the plane, shouting instructions to one another in a patois I didn't understand while they unloaded the supplies we'd brought into a caravan of ancient Volkswagen Beetles. My uncle and I squeezed into the last car, and the convoy wheezed and coughed its way along a rutted trail barely wide enough for a bicycle, then labored up the steep drive at a pace half the speed I could have walked it.

The next morning, Santos went back to São Paulo to attend a board meeting, so before breakfast, I dressed in swim trunks, slung a towel over my shoulders and hiked down to the beach. I swam up and down the coast until I was exhausted, then bodysurfed in. I felt good for the first time since my mother's death. Alive . . . and hungry.

As I started back to the house, I saw two figures on the empty beach walking in my direction. When they got closer, I could see they were young women in their early twen-

ties, wearing nothing but high-hipped thongs. They walked easily, engaged in conversation, unashamedly topless.

I'd been all over the world and was recently no longer a virgin, but I still wasn't used to women with their breasts right out there for everybody to stare at. It wasn't like I hadn't seen it before. In France, you had to be careful because of all the grandmothers—but Spain and Italy, unbelievable.

Brazilian women tend toward the exquisite anyway, and some simply can't be described. These two were beyond anything I had ever seen—anywhere. When they got closer, I noticed that, in addition to her thong, the taller of the two was wearing a small, white seashell around her neck on a piece of rawhide, something that had the dual effect of accentuating her tan and drawing your eyes right to where you were trying to keep them from focusing.

She smiled at me with the whitest teeth I had ever seen and said, "Americano."

I grinned back and asked in Portuguese, "Como?"

With a long, perfectly formed finger, she pointed to her eye. "Olhos. Azul." Then in heavily accented English, "Eyes. Blue. And big, big tall. My English pretty damn fucking good, no?" Then she threw back her head and laughed. Her sun-bleached hair hung down her back, almost to her waist, accentuating her own height, which had to be close to six feet.

"Pretty damn good," I repeated, hoping she didn't notice the catch in my throat or the growing tent in my swimsuit. She gestured for me to drop my towel, then took my hand and led me, running, into the water. We laughed and splashed and dunked each other for a while, and then she came into my arms. Sometimes everything just fits. No uncertainty, no false starts. She kissed me, and I knew. And I knew she knew too.

When we came out of the water, her cousin was well down the beach. I gestured that I was hungry, and she led me to the tree line where an oyster fisherman had set up shop on top of an old barrel in the shade of some giant palms. While he shucked, we squeezed freshly quartered tangerines over the prize and wolfed them down. He also poured us martelinho glasses of milky liquid from an unlabeled bottle. My first cachaça . . . actually, my first several.

Sanrevelle Adriana Marcelino Carvalho—which she went to great lengths to make sure I pronounced correctly. And after Santos called and said he was flying down to Puerto Alegre for a couple of weeks to attend to a business emergency, I told the servants I'd be having a guest, and she came to stay with me.

Sanrevelle was twenty-three, and the week before, her fiancé, Carlos, had announced he was breaking their engagement to marry her cousin. So she and her sister, Sophia, had headed to Ubatuba to lie in the sun and bake the hurt and anger out of her system.

She was a classical pianist with little-girl dreams of touring the world. But after sixteen years of study with the best teachers in South America and two years in France with a virtuoso who was less interested in her adagio than getting in her pants, she'd taken a long, hard look at her talent and come to the conclusion that she was never going to be great. And so she packed her bags, ground out a cigarette on the Frenchman's Bösendorfer and caught a plane home.

And now the replacement dream was gone too.

Ordinarily, five years is a big gap, especially when the woman is twenty-three and the guy is just out of high school. But this was Brazil, not Beverly Hills, and despite what we both felt, we told ourselves we just wanted a fling, not a future.

At least once, everyone should have two weeks of nothing but good food, good weather, no clothes and shameless sex. You're a long time growing old, and this is a memory you deserve.

It's even better if you have a big house with lots of odd-shaped furniture.

A day after Sanrevelle came to stay, we gave up all pretense of getting dressed—except for the seashell around her neck—and Miss Sheltered Upbringing was showing me things I couldn't have dreamed of—and I'd been reading Penthouse Letters *since I was twelve.*

My personal favorite was where one of us played the piano while the other knelt in front of the bench. When the music stops, so does everything else. It didn't take long to figure out that your only chance of not getting lost in the moment was to play really fast, so we named this sweet torture Beethoven on Fire. I can now play a mean "Chopsticks" bathed in sweat.

During one break, I taught her "Christmas Always Breaks My Heart," which, when she sang it, took my breath away. Almost as much as the pianist.

Eddie stirred, then came awake. He looked at the autopilot and then at the GPS. "Not bad," he said. "The frogs don't know shit about maintaining electronics, but this thing's new enough they didn't have time to fuck it up. Want me to drive for a while?"

"Thought you'd never ask."

37

Cognac and Legionnaires

Everything looks better from the air, and Corsica looks better than most. Then you have to land. The scenery is breathtaking, the towns picturesque, but a couple of thousand years of conquerors, despots, corrupt politicians, violent criminals—and the French—have poisoned the populace into a dark, brooding people with the personality of a collection agency. It also doesn't help that terrorism can be just around any corner. But you've got to give the Corsicans props for equality. They don't like each other any more than they do anybody else.

It was a fight to get the plane hangared, a fight to rent a car and a fight to get directions that turned out to be wrong anyway. Our car, a wheezing Citroën with a seat adjustment range that would have cramped Napoleon, finally got us into Bastia. But I wanted privacy as well as a good night's sleep, and French hotel registries are too easily accessed. So tired as we were, we pushed on until we found the Maison de Casatorra, a bed-and-breakfast south of Borgo with sweeping views of the Tyrrhenian Sea.

The innkeeper was actually almost friendly, but not until he gave us a lecture on American foreign policy and what a fool Reagan was. The guy seemed to have memorized the Democratic talking points from the 1984 election, so I didn't have the heart to tell him the Gipper was dead.

But if the civics lesson was the price of admission for the comfortable sea view rooms and the extraordinary food, it was worth it. The Maison's dining room was twenty-six-year-old Paolo Adianio's first kitchen, and since we were the only guests in the hotel—and Americans—he laid it on.

Paolo was from Civitavecchia, a ferry ride across to the Italian coast, and he was experimenting with putting Roman accents on traditional Corsican dishes. He called it Etruscan-Corse, and after the first bite of the first appetizer—sardines stuffed with brocciu and grilled in olive oil—I knew I had to get him to Beverly Hills as soon as possible. His food was as exceptional as that at Tacitus, and I needed someplace to go where I hadn't bled on the tile.

Jackie had been right about the wine, though. And Paolo said he didn't have the budget to improve the Maison's cellar. Fortunately, there was plenty of Pietra, a local chestnut beer, which we followed with Corsican espresso and icy shots of Cedratine.

I had Paolo bring me a bottle of one of Bruzzi's reds so I could see the label. Much to my disappointment, no hyena.

When I hit the bed, if it creaked, I didn't hear it.

By the time Eddie found his feet and wandered down to the beach the next morning, I'd already pounded out a mile and a half in the chilly water, and whatever residue clinging to me from the night before was gone. I'm always amazed by the Med. Though it's bordered by some of the most ecologically irresponsible nations on earth, sometimes it's as pristine as Santa Barbara. Better yet, no sharks. Oh, they're there, but they're not particularly aggressive. The one time I did have to deal with one, I punched him in the nose, and he shot away like I was the town bully.

We had breakfast on the Maison's terrace. Double-yolk eggs, Corsican ham and baguettes with fresh butter. Evidently the money we'd spent on dinner and the tip we'd left the service staff had gotten everyone's attention, because when we checked out, the owner didn't mention politics once as he walked us to our car.

The night before, I'd shown Paolo the picture of the unknown artist, and he'd drawn a blank. Now as we put our overnight bags in the trunk of the Citroën, I handed it to the Maison's owner. He shook his head no and thrust the picture back at me so fast that I almost asked him to take another look. Then I saw the man's face. He wanted no part of whoever it was. I was also sure he wasn't going to tell anyone about it. He was terrified.

Of a painter? What the fuck was this?

Corsica is the most mountainous island in the Med, and 70 percent is national park, so the best roads are along the coast. But like most of Europe, they haven't grasped signage. Essentially, it's we know where we're going, so fuck you. Eddie drove while I pondered a map that only occasionally matched reality, and we regularly shouted at each other like we were married.

We entered the dramatic, cliff-clinging city of Bonifacio about an hour before sundown, and its electrifying splendor awed even the hard-bitten Eddie. "How in the hell can these people not see what they've got here?"

"Old World hardheads," I said. "Americans get excoriated for ignoring tradition, but at least we don't get bogged down with bullshit. Over here, if your great-grandfather had a hard-on for somebody, you have to piss in his salad. And if you try to break tradition, the enemy won't talk to you anyway, plus you go on the shit list with the rest of your family."

Eddie shook his head. "We could change all that with a couple of California developers. The only thing that slows them down is a grave. By the time the locals got back from lunch, they'd have these old buildings converted to condos and be running tract houses right up that fuckin' mountain. Bingo, brand-new culture."

Again I wanted to avoid a commercial hotel, and a bed-and-breakfast was out of the question, because someone as powerful as Bruzzi would be advised of every stranger who hit town. Having been to Corsica twice before, I knew there were homes for rent, mostly villas favored by wealthy French and Italians. The trick was finding someone who could show us one without turning on an air raid siren.

Because I'm so conspicuous, I sent Eddie into a bar next to a closed real estate office where we'd seen luxury rental property photographs in the window. Half an hour later, he came out with a well-dressed guy about thirty-five, who'd obviously had a couple of drinks and couldn't have been more affable.

"Meet Julien Borreau," Eddie said, smiling. "Property manager extraordinaire, and hell on a bottle of cognac."

Julien shook my hand through the car window. "Mr. Buffalo said you want to do some fishing and you're interested in a place that is very nice and very private." He appraised the battered Citroën. "Are you sure you can afford it?"

He had pronounced Eddie's name "BOOF-a-loo," and even though his speech was slightly slurred from drinking, his accent was mainland. A transplant.

I laughed. "It was either this or a Fiat with no hood. How'd you end up on Corsica, Julien?"

He grinned. "Every time I open my mouth, it gives me away, doesn't it? Started out as a thief. In Paris. Got pinched and did a turn in the Legion. Mustered out here. Everybody's so fuckin' busy being suspicious, you keep your nose clean you can make a good living dealing with the foreigners the locals won't talk to. Bother you?"

Not only didn't it bother me, I had to give Eddie an A. In a country of socialist xenophobes, he'd managed to find a friendly, if slightly tipsy, former criminal—maybe retired, maybe not—who was only interested in money. And being

Parisian, he probably wasn't wired to Bruzzi. "Julien," I said, "we're in your capable hands."

He turned and went into his darkened office. A few moments later, he was back with a set of keys and got in next to me. Eddie sat behind him. He directed us along the coast road, and with the sun now all but set, Bonifacio's skyline was dark except for a few random lights. As we passed a burned-out building on the beach, I asked, *"Qu'est-ce que ça?"*

Julien seemed to have to decide how to answer. Finally, he shook his head. "L'Hotel Eden. Forty-six lives. What is it you Americans say? Poof?"

"Poof?"

"Yes. A bomb. Three bombs, actually. The wedding of Lazzaro Santagatta. The most popular Nationalist leader. The police say it was terrorists, but everybody knows it was the man who owned the hotel. The one who invited Santagatta to have his party there. Gaetano Bruzzi."

I played dumb. "Why would anybody blow up his own property?"

"Cafoni," Julien half-whispered, half-spit. "Mafia. What the fuck do they care about anything except keeping things the way they are? Divided. Vendettas everywhere. An independent Corsica would bring Corsican prosecutors . . . Corsican judges. And so they support everyone . . . and then they kill the ones who become too powerful." He paused, then lowered his voice. "And they kill the people who get in the way."

I knew that tone. Whatever the sadness was in this man, it was deep and raw. I changed the subject. "I thought Les Executeurs were who everybody was afraid of."

Julien became immediately suspicious. "How do you know Les Executeurs?"

"My lawyer told me to be careful of them. That they are dangerous. And they like to cut people."

The Frenchman relaxed. "Your lawyer is stupid. They are *fantoche* . . . puppets. Here, there is only Bruzzi."

"Sounds like you don't much care for him."

He waved his hand. "I neither care nor don't care. I just earn a living."

I glanced in the rearview mirror and saw Eddie looking back at me. He slowly raised his forefinger and drew it across his throat.

Two miles out of town, Julien directed me off the main highway onto a narrow lane. As soon as we turned, overhead lights came on, and we twisted through thick woods until we were stopped by an eight-foot, wrought-iron gate supported on a pair of gray stone columns topped with copper eagles. Julien jumped out and dialed a code into the keypad affixed to the left column. The barriers parted, and instantly, more lights came on, showing a winding cobblestone drive leading upward at a steep angle.

Like its in-town brethren, the three-story stone house was cut into the mountain, only this one sat alone surrounded by trees. Unless someone down below was standing on his roof with a pair of binoculars and had just the right angle, it would be impossible to know anyone was here. I parked in the circular drive, and Julien went inside and started turning on lights.

The interior was also stone. Fifteen-foot ceilings, walk-in fireplaces and tall French doors off every room leading onto a wide veranda overlooking the coast. There was even an indoor-outdoor swimming pool and a full exercise room.

"Not too fuckin' bad," said Eddie as he headed toward the ebony bar. "Cognac, Julien?"

"Absolutely," Julien answered, "then I want to show you something."

Snifters of Paradis Extra in hand, we followed Julien across the courtyard to a stone stairway leading down the cliff. A motion sensor turned on lights built into the steps, and we descended.

A hundred feet later, we walked out onto a lighted, private beach recessed so deeply into the hillside that privacy was total. Riding at anchor a few feet offshore were two Aquascan Q20 inflatables with twin Mercury 250s on each. Eddie acted like he'd just seen a bare-breasted mermaid. He didn't even bother to take off his shoes before wading out to the nearest one and climbing in, cognac splashing.

"Goddamn, Rail, we've gotta go out right now. Come on, Julien," and he kicked a 20-footer to life.

Julien was grinning, obviously pleased with himself. The Q20 is a two-seater, so I told him, "I'll pass, but I should warn you, Eddie doesn't understand careful."

Julien laughed. "Couldn't be any worse than the guys in the Legion." He headed into the water and expertly climbed aboard. Unlike Eddie, he never spilled a drop.

I watched as they disappeared into the night in a deafening roar, then turned and headed back to the house.

An hour later, I heard Eddie come into the cove, engines at full throttle. A few minutes after that, he and Julien came through the patio doors, laughing and desperate for a drink. We sat on the large sectional sofa facing the Med, and I handed Julien a check for twice what he'd asked for a one-month rental.

When he looked at me questioningly, I said, "Like I said, we're going to do a little fishing. But I don't want to sign a lease. The extra's for you, and if we leave early, you can keep the difference too."

Julien had the check in his shirt pocket and was raising a toast before I put my pen away. After we sipped, I took out the photocopy of the picture of the artist in his studio and handed it to him. "Ever see this man before?" I asked.

I can't describe the look that crossed the young Frenchman's face. It was like something out of Stephen King. Without a word, he dropped the picture on the coffee table, stood and started toward the door. Then, remembering he had my check, he turned and thrust it back at me, his voice terse. "You may stay the night, but you must leave tomorrow. Now, please drive me back to town."

"Suddenly you don't like us?" I asked.

"Bonifacio is not a modern city. The people who come here to fish bring their own equipment. They also do not rent places like this. But your business is your business." He pointed at the picture on the table. "Except when it concerns that."

"Sit down, Julien," I said. "And hold onto the check."

He hesitated, then sat, took out a cigarette and lit it. Eddie went to the bar, brought back the bottle of Paradis Extra and poured him three fingers. Julien ignored it.

"You're the second person who has reacted to this picture. Who is it?"

"Are you with the American government?" he asked.

"No," I answered.

"Not the CIA?"

"Of course not."

He took a deep breath. "There have been people who have come here before . . . for information about Gaetano Bruzzi. They disappeared . . . into the mountains."

"This is personal, Julien."

"Then you are the kind of foolish no one can cure." He took a breath and pointed to the picture. "That is Gaetano's brother, Tiziano Bruzzi. They call him *Il Pazzo*."

"The Crazy One."

"People say he is the greatest artist in all of Corsica, maybe even in all of Europe, but he is not right in the head. He cannot speak, and he must wear diapers."

The artist's smile had been bothering me since I'd first seen it, and somewhere my subconscious had been wrestling with why. Now the tumblers started falling into place. "What does he paint?" I asked.

"Mostly, he copies famous works. Degas, El Greco, Cézanne, anyone really. Perhaps if you held Tiziano's side by side with the originals, the differences would be obvious, but I don't think so. They are very, very exact."

"I'm still working on the diapers," said Eddie. "Was he in an accident?"

"He would have been born that way," I said. "He's an autistic savant. Socially non-functioning, but artistically brilliant."

"A what?" said Eddie.

"Remember *Rain Man*?"

"Sure, great flick. I love Dusty."

"His character was based on a real guy named Kim Peek. Kim's genius was numbers and quantities. He also memorized ten thousand books."

"I remember every piece of ass I've ever had," said Eddie. "What's that make me?"

"If you remember their names, it makes you God," said Julien.

We all laughed, and I said to him, "Nice to have you back among us."

"I am interested in hearing more about *Il Pazzo*," he said.

I thought back to the extraordinary imagery Hood had arranged for the Tretiakov paintings. If you were just making a record, you could do it with any reasonably good camera. But Hood needed more. He had to be able to see the brush strokes, the color nuances . . . and the flaws.

I went on. "There are different kinds of savants, functioning at different levels, in different disciplines. Music, mathematics, languages, even design. One of the most remarkable is a Brit named Stephen Wiltshire who can take a helicopter ride around a city, then later draw it in panorama in perfect detail."

"Cool, but I'm not making the connection," said Eddie.

"Think about it. He sees Rome once then draws it from memory. So his brain is operating as three separate cameras—wide-angle, zoom and portrait. Simultaneously. Except that he doesn't have to change lenses or focus. At exactly the same time, each camera's view is recorded with such accuracy that later, another area of his brain can guide his eye to reproduce them."

I could see it beginning to dawn on him. "Fuck, that's why it took York so many trips. The Hyena had all the photographs, but his brother could only paint one picture at a time."

"Bingo," I said. "And if Tiziano is like most savants, the process wears him out. So he had to rest between sessions. But that was okay because the copies had to be artificially aged anyway."

"And if they ran into a glitch, the general controlled the timetable, so who gave a shit," said Eddie.

I nodded. "But Bruzzi stayed on schedule, and once a month Truman picked up a painting, flew to Washington, collected the original and headed to Cairo. There, the fake went to Russia and the original to Serbin's private collection."

"But wouldn't somebody eventually notice?"

"Based on what Julien says, probably not. But even if somebody did become suspicious, who was he going to complain to? Serbin? The police?"

"I don't know these things you're speaking of," said Julien, "but part of it sounds like Elmyr de Hory."

"I don't think Elmyr was a savant, but the concept is the same, yes?"

"Elmer who?" asked Eddie.

"El-MEER," corrected Julien, "the greatest art forger in history. His pieces are still bought and sold by respected collectors. Many hang in museums. But no one works very hard at uncovering them. Too much embarrassment . . . too much money at stake."

"And the scam went on even after York took a powder," said Eddie.

"Why not, it was like printing money. Dr. Cesarotti chose the paintings, and Serbin's people tracked down canvasses and paint formulas of the right era for Bruzzi. Then, with fake in hand, the general advised the appropriate country's government that he'd found one of their masterpieces, and the repatriation process began. Excitement would be at fever pitch, and everyone would want to believe the work was authentic, so the De Hory Effect took over.

"And for a few million in payoffs, Konstantin Serbin accumulated a billion dollars in art—not counting the passion premium. In those cases, we have to go back to Archer's question, Is there a word for beyond priceless?"

"How can I help you?" asked Julien.

"I thought you wanted to get as far from us as possible," I said.

He stared at me, and I could see him framing his answer. "When you said it was personal, it meant you intend to kill Gaetano Bruzzi."

It was the observation of a man who had been trained to hunt other men. I didn't need to answer, and I didn't.

"Then," he continued, "I already know too much. And I have my own reasons for wanting you to succeed."

I waited, but he didn't continue right away. He looked out the window toward the sea. "Do you know what they used to say about de Gaulle? That his fondest wish was to die in his own arms. This is not only true of peacocks. It is also true of men who murder for power. And it is time to give M. Bruzzi the opportunity."

I was suddenly very tired. "Julien, take the Citroën. Go home and get some sleep. Tomorrow we'll take a drive into the mountains. Since we seem to have forgotten our fly rods, perhaps we'll look for some land to buy. Maybe even see a winery or two."

38

Mountain Roads and Dead Pets

A sunny morning on the Med is pretty much as good as it gets. Julien had arranged for a local grocer to make a food run up the hill, and the guy had brought a truckload. I hoped we weren't going to be there long enough to need it, but in the meantime, the three of us sat outside and ate with abandon.

A little after nine, with Julien at the wheel of his car, a four-door BMW, we drove back to the coast road and turned north. Our guide had brought along notebooks, a camera and a pair of binoculars. Tools of the trade for land speculators, he told us. The camera was a top-of-the-line Minolta, and the binoculars military, well-worn and without markings. My guess was that the Legion was missing a pair just like them.

We stopped several times, got out and went through the charade of Julien's pointing things out while we nodded, made notes and occasionally used the binoculars or snapped a picture. I didn't think anyone was following us, but with so little traffic on the island, we were going to be noticed, and looking like foreigners being shown around by a local real estate agent was as good a cover as we were going to get.

As the coastline dropped farther below, it became a post-card. As dazzling as Amalfi, but without the crowds. It was a shame that so few outsiders ever get to see it.

A couple of hours later, we turned inland and met the rugged interior of Corsica. Here, the mountainous spine merged with a steep forest broken by bare rock outcroppings and an occasional towering waterfall thundering into an abyss. When the land would flatten, pristine streams would emerge stalked by hawks and tiger heron. But if there were human inhabitants, there was no indication.

We reached a stretch where a fast-moving river had slashed a deep gorge through the granite mountain, leaving passage possible only along a winding, narrow road cut into the rock. At its widest points, possibly two small cars could squeeze by each other, but otherwise, you had to wait for one of the engineered turnouts that appeared every mile or so. It was so treacherous that even the normally steel-nerved Eddie gripped the back of my seat.

"Not many people up here," said Julien, attempting to break the tension. "And the ones who are stay out of sight."

The place had a feeling of total isolation, and I couldn't imagine trying to haul somebody out who didn't want to go.

"It's also something of a Corsican tradition to romanticize our outlaws."

No sooner had Julien finished the sentence than two bright red trucks with aerial ladders mounted on their roofs appeared behind us. I'd seen them before—coming toward us on the coast road when we'd turned inland.

"Probably lost and trying to make up time," Eddie said.

"Well, they're stuck with our pace for the moment," said Julien.

"Jesus Christ!" roared Eddie.

I turned and looked out the rear window. It was filled with a grille I was intimately familiar with. Pinzgauer II, a six-wheel-drive British-made vehicle rarely seen outside a military installation. We'd used them in Delta because their narrow track and superb traction could take us places nothing else on wheels was capable of. In the right hands, they can climb almost anything, and the way these guys were driving, the hands were right. Regardless, it was way too much iron, way too close.

"Can you see who's inside?"

Eddie craned his neck upward. "Near as I can tell, a couple of lobotomy patients." He leaned out the window and shouted at them to back off. Their response was to accelerate and tap our bumper.

Eddie pulled his head back inside. "What's Corsican for 'motherfucker'?"

"Either of them wearing a headband?" I asked.

He shook his head. "Nope."

Julien gave the BMW a hit of gas, then had to back off when we came to a bend. That's when the Pinz hit us again—this time hard enough that we all flew forward.

We were swearing in multiple languages, and Eddie was giving the finger out his window. The next turnout was ahead on the left, and the BMW slowed as Julien braked and put on his blinker. But instead of easing off, the truck banged us again, and our left rear wheel hit the edge and hung out in space for a couple of seconds until our forward momentum pulled it back.

We skidded to a stop against the low stone wall of the turnout and were out of the car almost before dust billowed up. But the trucks were already past and accelerating away, their roof-top ladder assemblies banging as they whipped into the next bend. It was the white lettering on their tailgates that made the event even more surreal.

DANGER! EXPLOSIF!

Eddie wanted to go after them, but that was like a dog chasing a bus. So you catch them, then what? The BMW had only minor damage, and I told Julien I'd take care of it. So after we silently contemplated the several-hundred-foot free fall we'd narrowly avoided, we climbed back in the car. Like the tailgating record producer in the red Lamborghini, the world is full of assholes with driver's licenses. Sometimes the right ones died.

Half an hour later, we rounded a final bend and the Fortress of Apollonica rose into the cloudless sky like Kane's Xanadu. Turreted walls ran along a perimeter steep enough to stop an antelope, enclosing a spired, seven-story edifice that was almost a mirror image of the Abbey at Mont St-Michel. It was something out of a time when audacious engineering on high ground served notice to lesser folk not to fuck with the occupant.

"Power abhors understatement," I said.

"It was built during the French papacy. As a refuge for the Holy Father," said Julien.

"In case the natives got restless."

"The natives they could handle. It was the guys with armies that kept them awake. But as far as anyone can tell, no pope ever spent a night here."

Eddie had his own axe to grind. "That shit's why I left the church. Fuckin' high-and-mighty assholes spending other people's money."

"I'll put that down as Reason Number 133."

We laughed, but you couldn't help but wonder how many peasants had died hauling all that stone up there. But as Benny Joe—and maybe a pope or two—might have said, that's why we have peasants.

"When did Bruzzi buy it?" I asked.

"About twenty years ago. But what everyone thought was going to be an economic blessing didn't happen. Some of the nicknames he's acquired don't translate, but my favorite is a Corsican play on words that means 'Sicilian Who Sits in Eagle Shit.' "

It was hard not to like that.

The village of Apollonica fit neatly into a shallow gash in

the sheep-dotted mountainside directly under Gaetano's citadel. Julien turned left and crossed the gorge on an ancient limestone bridge probably built by the Romans. *Apollonica* sounded more Greek than anything else, and since this part of the world had been cross-pollinated for millennia, there was a good chance it was. Maybe the legion commander had been from Athens.

Halfway across, I looked down, and there, ten stories below us on a narrow access road along the water's edge, were the red Pinzgauers. They had their aerial ladders extended, and two men were up thirty feet or so, working on something along the rockface. Their partners stood watching.

"Stop the fuckin' car!" yelled Eddie. "I want to piss on those cocksuckers."

"It'd just blow back in your face," I said.

"They almost killed us."

"How many times has another boater thrown you the finger because you couldn't go by him slow?"

Eddie didn't answer.

"Let it go," I said.

Julien looked down. "I should have realized earlier. They're the fireworks crew for The Festival of the Return."

"Whose return?" asked Eddie.

"Napoleon's."

The town occupied only a small footprint of land, but its multistoried structures rose imposingly out of the hills. Everything, even the miniature streets, were straight up and straight down. Centuries of constructing dwellings one on top of the other and cantilevering others over them had created a skyline that from a distance looked like Tolkien but up close was a tall Hanoi.

"Not much wealth on the island," said Julien, "and the farther you get from the coast, the poorer it is."

"Kind of a shithole," observed Eddie, and he was right. The lower parts of the buildings were stone, but each successive generation of additions was framed in wood with walls that looked as thin as paper. The only paint in evidence was a pinkish-brown wash. Up close, Apollonica wasn't a travel poster.

The cobblestone square tilted with the mountain, but in contrast to the otherwise monochromatic backdrop, the facades of the buildings facing it were festooned with dozens of black-and-white Corsican flags and red, white and blue banners proclaiming "*Vivé Le Empereur.*" In the center of the square, amid this unexpected splash of color, was a small grass island containing a thick Ionic pedestal carved out of stone. Fresh violets were strewn around its base, and a large, intricate wreath of violets and olive leaves lay on top.

"Every village has its own Napoleon tribute," Julien explained. "They say it's to attract tourists, but the real reason is that he's still the only uniting force on the island."

"I still don't get it," Eddie said.

"They're honoring the return of his corpse from St. Helena. In 1840. The craftsman who carved his coffin, Octave LeDucq, came from Apollonica, and as far as the locals are concerned, the general's internment in Paris is only temporary."

What was it Jackie had said? *"My, but we are a stubborn people."* He was right, but without the Jewish exclusivity.

Julien continued. "At sundown Saturday, a funeral barge will come upriver carrying a replica of Napoleon's bier. It'll be brought here and placed on the pedestal."

"Then the party will begin," I said.

"Just until everybody gets drunk. Then the grudges will come out."

Julien parked next to an ornate, bone-dry fountain, and we got out. I stood and looked around the square at the flags, each depicting a black Moor's head adorned with a white *tortil*. I saw Eddie doing the same.

"Fuckers," he said.

"Eddie, get a grip," I said.

He shrugged. "Okay, but I'm adding fireworks guys to my list."

What few pedestrians there were looked us over quickly then moved on. I saw only one other powered vehicle, a Vespa, sitting on the sidewalk outside a bocce court. Two men were engaged in a cutthroat game while several others sat on benches smoking and offering advice.

Julien told us to wait, and he crossed the square and entered a building. A few minutes later, he came out with a uniformed policeman. "What's going on?" asked Eddie quietly.

When Julien and the cop crossed back to us, he explained. "I'm required to check in with the local authorities when I show property outside Bonifacio. Usually, it's just a formality, but when Lieutenant Santini heard you were from California, he wanted to meet you. He has a sister in San Francisco. Oh, by the way, he says this year's festival is going to be spectacular, and he wants to invite us to attend as his guests."

Unlike everyone else we'd seen, this guy couldn't stop grinning and bowing. He also spoke a local combination of French and Italian I'd never heard before. I understood most of it, but I let Julien translate. "His sister's name is Yvette Santini, and he wants to know if you've met her."

"Jesus," said Eddie, "doesn't he know there's like a million people in San Fran?"

"Look around," I said. "What do you think?" I turned to Julien. "Tell him we'll have to take a rain check on the festival, and that we haven't had the pleasure of meeting Yvette. But if he'd like to give us a message for her, we'll do our best to see she gets it."

Julien translated, and I thought the guy was going to kiss us.

Julien shook his head. "You don't know what you've gotten yourself into. He's going to have somebody put together a basket of her favorite breads and cheeses."

"That'll be great." I smiled and shook the lieutenant's hand, which sent him into another frenzy of bowing. I looked at Julien. "Now ask him where we can find our artist."

Julien looked like I'd slapped him. "I think it's wiser to be discreet. Wander around. Let me show you some apartments. That's supposed to be what we're here for."

"We don't have time to go house to house, and if we leave empty-handed, we won't get back. The man at the top of the hill will make sure of that. Now ask him."

Julien was perspiring. He started talking, then stopped, cleared his throat and began again. I listened to him rattle off a paragraph, and it didn't have anything to do with Tiziano Bruzzi. Rather than argue, I took out the copy of the photograph and opened it.

Julien wasn't happy, but instead of the usual reaction, Lieutenant Santini burst out laughing. Then he shot out a stream of sentences, punctuated by more laughter, and pointed in the general direction of the church. When he'd finished, even though I'd gotten it, I waited for Julien's translation.

"There was an incident. Tiziano took off all his clothes, including his diaper, and climbed the bell tower. He'd done crazy things before, so no one got particularly upset until . . . how do you say it . . . he pissed on the mayor."

We laughed, and that was the lieutenant's cue to go into another gale.

I looked at Eddie. "High places and urination. Must be the mountain air."

He ignored me and said to Julien, "What happened then?"

"They called his brother, and while he was trying to talk him down, he pissed on him too."

Now *that* was funny.

"Some men who work for Gaetano finally took him away. No one has seen him since."

"How long ago was this?" I asked.

"A month."

Tiziano was the meal ticket, so he wouldn't be in outside care. Hood might be dead, but the art hustle still worked. All you needed were connections, and Bruzzi had plenty. Not to mention leverage over important people. No, Tiziano was nearby, probably at the top of the hill.

"Ask the lieutenant if we can see his studio."

Santini was more than happy to accommodate.

"I can't believe he laughs so openly about Bruzzi," Julien said as we followed Santini across the square.

"I can. You live next door to evil, you're happy when it has a bad day."

I'm in pretty good shape, but I was gasping by the time we climbed the mile and a half up the steep dirt footpath. Tiziano's studio was literally the last house in town, a tiny cottage perched on a rough slab only a quarter mile below the citadel. It was old but well-kept, with wide windows and a rusty bicycle chained to the wooden fence out front.

Lieutenant Santini worked the padlock on the door and pushed it open. I was prepared for a mess, but the place was neat and smelled of nothing more than paint and linseed oil.

"The lieutenant says that Gaetano paid a woman to look after his brother and keep the place clean. She takes care of other troubled people too—the ones without families—and now she doesn't know what she's going to do, because this was the only income she had."

I reached in my pocket and came out with cash. I peeled off ten C-notes and handed them to the cop. He took them like they were on fire.

"Tell him to give it to the woman."

Julien shook his head. "It's too much."

"She had a good year. Tell him."

It took a little while, but Julien finally got through to him. I guessed there wasn't much charity going on in Apollonica. The lieutenant started thanking me, but I held up my hand and gave him another hundred. "This is for you," I said. "For your trouble."

Julien didn't have to translate that.

I walked to the back windows and pushed them open. The footpath continued up toward the winery, with the incline steepening even further so that the pope's former hideout seemed to be suspended over the town. "Where are the grapes?" I asked in French.

Santini answered in kind. "When you came over the bridge, there was a turnoff. It leads along the water and around the mountain. Beyond, the land is different." He made a gesture that indicated flatter.

There were a few unfinished paintings scattered about, but none I recognized. Tiziano was good, though. Very good. His colors were rich, and his images exploded off the canvas. Supposedly, there is some creativity in all of us, but in most cases, including mine, it's locked up pretty tight.

I found the spot where Kim had taken Tiziano's picture. I also saw where she had taken the photographs of the paintings. I looked at the cop and used my French. "There was a young woman. Kim York. Tall. Long hair. She would have come here to see Tiziano."

The lieutenant nodded vigorously. "Many times. Always with other men."

"Any Americans?"

"Yes, one."

Truman.

The scream was so loud, so shrill and so full of terror that I was halfway out the door before the second one came. Thirty feet down the hill, a full-grown hyena had its jaws clamped around the neck of a crying child and was trying to break into a lope as it dragged the struggling bundle up the path. Behind them, a young woman was giving chase, screaming from some deep, primal place.

When she got alongside the big beast, she began beating on it with her fists. The hyena turned, dropped the toddler and snarled at her. When she tried to grab the child, the animal leaped and hit her with its head, and she stumbled backward and fell. Its immediate problem solved, the hyena picked up the child and started back up.

I reached it before it oriented itself, and I kicked it in the ribs as hard as I could. I saw the surprise in its yellow eyes, but even though I had jolted it, it didn't let go of the baby. Instinctively, the animal moved far enough away to keep me from making another run. But not far enough that I couldn't smell the fear excretions from its anal glands.

Eddie, Julien and Lieutenant Santini had now reached us and were fanned out between the animal and the winery beyond. The hyena stood stock-still and, one-by-one, eyed those standing between it and escape. The child had gone limp. I hoped only from shock.

Santini had his gun out, a MAB 9mm, which is just slightly less accurate than throwing rocks. Even a direct hit probably wasn't going to kill the animal, but it might shock it into dropping its prize. I waited for him to fire, but he didn't.

"Jesus Christ, shoot!" Eddie yelled.

Santini didn't need to be able to speak English to know what to do, but nothing happened. Sensing the danger, the hyena began to move laterally away from us.

I looked at the lieutenant, saw the perspiration on his forehead and immediately understood. It was okay to get a laugh at the bully's expense every once in a while, but killing one of Bruzzi's prized hyenas was another matter. I had a feeling this wasn't the first time one had come to town, and I wondered how many children the citizens of Apollonica surrendered each year.

I moved quickly toward Santini and took the gun out of his hand. He didn't put up a fight. I aimed at the hyena's rear hip where the bullet would shock it but not jeopardize the child and squeezed the trigger. The MAB hardly moved in my hand, and the sound wasn't any louder than a clap.

The shot went low, kicking up dust as it skidded under the animal. Nice fucking gun. I elevated quickly and fired again. This time I heard a whump, and the hyena let out a bloodcurdling scream and left the ground with all four feet, dropping the kid.

Eddie ran forward, scooped up the child and kept going

like he'd just recovered a fumble. The hyena started for him, and I fired again. There are shots you brag about because you made every calculation. And then there is out of your ass.

I was just hoping to distract it. Instead, the bullet went in its right eye, rattled around its brain and exited through its throat. The hyena ran three strides dead, then dropped like a bag of wet sand.

For the first time, I was aware that other people, probably hearing the commotion, had come out of their homes and were gathering around us. Two of them were young men wearing red *tortils*. The older of the two had a spider with four legs tattooed on his left forearm. Both stared at the dead hyena, then at me.

The younger, shorter man seemed more unsure of himself, so I concentrated on him. Very slowly, he took a knife out of his hip pocket, held it at his side and flicked it open.

I'd been here before, so I raised the lieutenant's gun and pointed it straight at his face. He didn't blink, but his hand tightened on the knife. I told Santini that it was up to Dumb and Dumber, but I wasn't going to be cut.

Santini shouted something, and after taking enough time so we all knew they were the coolest of the cool, the men began walking away.

"Give my regards to Tino," I said.

The man with the tattoo turned, stopped and stared. Then, with great deliberation, he continued on.

Behind me, Santini muttered something that sounded like "fucking Americans," but I could have been just hearing things.

Julien and I both had some medical training, but his was a lot more recent. As he examined the boy, the kid suddenly let out a scream almost as loud as the hyena's and began twisting and turning and reaching for his mother. In Beverly Hills, you'd call your lawyer, then a backup lawyer, then the ambulance. In Apollonica, the last I saw of mother and son, they were walking back down the hill. The woman had opened her shirt, and the kid was having lunch.

When we left Lieutenant Santini, he was trying to organize a burial party and not having much luck. Apparently, the descendants of Napoleon wanted no part of Bruzzi's dead pet. Yvette's basket didn't make an appearance either.

39

Pradas and Poof

The road around the mountain started out rough, then turned into a smoothly paved ribbon of blacktop. It followed the gorge for a couple of miles, then forked at a 45° angle. The left fork was gravel and descended toward the river. We stayed right with the pavement and half a mile later appeared to be heading into an impenetrable wall of rock. However, as we got closer, an eye-of-the-needle pass appeared, so narrow and so deep that the sun didn't hit its floor.

Inside the pass, a shallow lake of standing water had turned the hard clay shoulder into a thick brown soup that had migrated onto the road. Julien had to slow down enough to keep from hydroplaning but still maintain enough speed to avoid becoming stuck. It was a choppy ride, and the BMW's wipers had to work overtime as waves of muck swept over the windshield.

When we reached the other side, the road was dry again, and the terrain became less severe. I was also immediately aware that the climate had changed. The cool, arid air of Apollonica had been replaced by a moist breeze that was easily fifteen degrees warmer than where we'd been. Then I saw why.

We had entered a lush valley completely encircled by towering peaks, which had the effect of creating its own ecosystem. Except for the pass, I could see no other way in or out, so the basin was protected from most extreme weather. Looking up and to my right, I could see the back of Bruzzi's fortress, but instead of the steep drop of the front, here the land sloped gently downward, providing his hundreds of acres of vineyard with natural drainage.

"I know this part of the country pretty well," Julien said, "but somebody had to show me this."

"It explains how he can be in the wine business in such an inhospitable place."

"Like another planet," said Eddie, then he leaned across the seat and pointed. "Ever see anything like that except at a nuke plant or San Quentin?"

Bordering the vineyard, a twelve-foot chain-link fence topped with coiled razor wire ran off to a horizon line, dotted at regular intervals by security cameras affixed to the top of twenty-five-foot poles. I motioned for Julien to pull over. I got out and walked up to the wire. Ten yards inside the first fence, there was another, identical one, creating a kind of no-man's-land between the road and Bruzzi's grapes. The warmth and conviviality one usually associates with wine-growing had been replaced by a malevolent starkness.

"All this scene needs is a guy running from a crop duster," said Eddie.

About thirty feet further down the line, something on the inside of the fence caught my eye. It was about eight feet up, and as I walked toward it, I presumed the swarm of black flies hovering over it was scavenging the viscera of a bird that had lost its bearings and flown into the chain link.

And then I saw the skeletal hand, severed at the elbow and clutching the wire with its dead fingers. An expensive gold watch was still strapped to its wrist, but the small mound of remains on the ground beneath it was unidentifiable except for a single black crocodile loafer containing an ankle bone.

I examined the hand from my vantage point below it, and though the maggots had been busy, there was still some sunblackened flesh between bone and wire. I estimated it was about a week old.

"Jesus Christ," said Eddie from behind me. "He lets those fuckin' hyenas run loose in that chute, doesn't he?"

"Well, whatever this poor schmuck's deal was, he didn't come dressed for fence-climbing wearing a Cartier and two-thousand-dollar Pradas."

Eddie looked up at the distant winery. "Gotta hand it to him, though. That's like a half a mile . . . in fuckin' loafers."

We got back in the car and drove until the road swung into a wide right-hand turn. Here, the fence gave way to a thick stone wall, its top even with the fence but minus the razor wire. The cameras continued, now accompanied by halogen floodlights. A mile later, the road ended at a modern interpretation of a medieval castle gate complete with impaling hooks, only this one had been fashioned out of two-inch tempered steel bars and was electrically operated. We pulled up facing it and got out. I recognized the emblem emblazoned on the gate as the Bruzzi winery label, and I could see through the bars that the hyena run ended here too.

I had wondered how long it was going to take before someone acknowledged our presence. As it turned out, not long. I heard the motorcycles before I saw them. They were hidden by the thick vines of the vineyard until they broke into the open twenty-five yards from the gate. Four men in red *tortils* riding Triumph Rockets.

The Rocket is a big bike, but the leader of this quartet wouldn't have looked out of place on a bigger one. In his early forties with black hair, unusually smooth skin and ice blue eyes, he was built like an outside linebacker—maybe six-six, 240. He also had the unmistakable look of command reinforced by the deadly-looking *lupara* strung on his back. Two of his companions were the guys from the village we'd seen at the hyena shoot. The fourth was Tino.

They sat across the steel bars from us with their bikes idling. Seeing Tino this close again moved my needle, and though it was thoroughly unprofessional, I wanted to get under the piece of shit's skin. And I didn't think telling him Dante was dead was enough.

"I ran into Nico out near Catalina," I said in French. "But based on his wardrobe, it might have been your sister."

Tino looked like I'd pressed his face against a hot stove, but he didn't say anything. The two men from the town could barely contain their laughter, so evidently, I wasn't breaking new ground.

I reached into my pocket and took out the red headband I'd been carrying since we'd sunk the cruiser. I stepped to the gate and held it through. "Thought you might like to have this. Dante got the earring."

Unsure, Tino looked at the big man, but the guy said nothing. Finally Tino dismounted and walked to the gate. As he touched the *tortil*, I grabbed his wrist and pulled him against the bars—hard. His arm came completely through, and his face slammed into the steel. I was pleased when I saw the blood coming out of his nose.

Over his head, I saw the two men from town start to get off their bikes, but the leader shook his head, and they stayed put. He was apparently curious about what was going to happen. I felt Tino move and saw him reaching his free hand into the hip pocket of his jeans. I didn't need a diagram to know what was in there, so I snatched his forearm with my other hand and pulled it through the gate too. I now had him pinned with his back against the bars. I twisted his wrists in opposite directions and pulled hard enough so he let out a gasp of pain. Then I leaned forward and said into his ear, "Interested in your brother's last words?"

His breathing was labored, but he didn't answer.

"Please don't cut off my arms."

He went completely rigid.

"I told him to take it up with Kiki when he saw him."

With that I put my foot against Tino's narrow back and propelled him forward so hard that he stumbled into his bike, and both it and he went down. The fall kicked the Rocket into gear, and it spun a couple of times before the engine cut off. Tino got up, spit spraying out of his mouth. "I should have cut your fuckin' head off that night on the freeway."

"You're welcome to try now."

He reached out to the big man with the *lupara* on his back. "Remi, give me the gun."

But the man called Remi ignored him and kept his gaze on me. "You are the man called Black," he said in French. It wasn't a question. "I would like to apologize for Tino's foolishness. We have no quarrel with you. You should never have been shot. However, it appears you have evened the score."

Tino had spoken English to him, so I did the same. "Since I'm the one with the bullet holes, I'll decide when we're even. You have a name besides Remi?"

He regarded me for a moment, and when he spoke, his English was accented but clear. "Terranova. My mother was French, my father Sicilian." He paused, then went on. "What is it you want?"

"Your little pal there . . . and the guy you both work for—*Il Iena Bianco.*"

His tone was light, almost amused. "Then you have come to look at our security. What do you think?"

"Visually impressive, but sloppy. Like the hand hanging on the fence."

Remi looked hard at Tino. It must have been his turn to pick up after the hyenas. Turning back to me he said, "Ah, yes, Andre. If he were here, he'd tell you he had it coming. Unfortunately, since he's not able to speak for himself, you'll have to take my word for it."

Tino had moved to Remi's side, and he made a grab at the *lupara.* The larger man caught his hand in a massive fist and squeezed. Tino went to his knees in pain, but Remi didn't release him. Only when Tino began to whimper and tears ran down his cheeks did Remi push him roughly away. He lay in the dirt, holding his hand, moaning softly.

"Tino's not having much of a day," I said, "but I'd prefer it if you shot him."

Remi looked down at Tino, then back at me. "M. Bruzzi is an indulgent man with those who have been useful. Sometimes too indulgent." He shifted his attention to Julien. "You are the real estate man from Bonifacio, no? M. Borreau? Why are you with these men?"

Julien crossed his arms and looked squarely at Remi, not answering.

One of the other two motorcyclists leaned close to Remi and said something. The big man nodded and turned back to Julien. "Ah, yes, L'Hotel Eden. My deepest sympathies, Monsieur. But your anger is misguided. We all hope for the day the terrorist scum is wiped from the island."

Julien's eyes never left Remi's. "Terrorist scum I'll leave to the authorities. My problem is with the Eagle Shit Sitters."

Remi looked hard at Julien. "My friend, I would suggest you go back to your business . . . and stop giving interviews."

Sometimes, when you're looking at the obvious, you don't make the connection. Then something causes the synapses to fire in the correct sequence, and you wonder how you missed the locomotive bearing down on you. The trigger was something Kim had said that first morning. I looked at Remi. "Who's shaving you these days?"

Remi's head jerked almost imperceptibly. He recovered quickly, but his eyes had lost some of their certainty. He stared at me while he collected his thoughts.

When a man hears something that only a woman with whom he's been intimate knows, he immediately believes that every breath of their relationship is in play. There aren't any statistics about the number of homicides that follow, but my money's on plenty. And right now, as far as Remi was concerned, if he liked to paint a lipstick smiley on his pecker, I knew about it.

"Kim always was a talker, especially after a good fucking. Did she also tell you her father taught her how? And that she used to do us both? The shaving too."

It wasn't a big leap, and suddenly, the air seemed unclean. But the other pieces now fell into place. Kim's ride to the airport in the van hadn't been about identification. Bruzzi wasn't waiting for her. Remi was. A very careful man making sure his boss's orders were carried out. And perhaps gaining some kind of perverse satisfaction.

"Truman was with you the night Kim was kidnapped, wasn't he?"

He smiled. "He was flying the plane. It wasn't easy for him, but he knew she had to go. He'd lost control of her . . . we all had."

I'd been wrong about Truman too. He hadn't had a master plan to steal the "Babushka" painting. Like the stupidity of getting caught in Rome with a hotel room full of heroin he'd had no way to sell, he'd simply walked away from Egypt Air 990 on an impulse then realized he was stuck. What had saved his life was that Bruzzi decided a good pilot can come in handy when you don't want your movements tracked. Especially one who knows that if he fucks up again, the next stop is hyena chow.

Kim was probably initially regarded by Bruzzi as kismet. Here he was in the art business, and another avenue into the system had just dropped into his lap. One that didn't include Hood and Serbin. She not only worked at the Getty, she was already stealing. And since he had the only piece of the process that couldn't be duplicated—Tiziano—he was poised to go into business for himself.

But somewhere along the way, Kim decided she'd had enough . . . of everything. And she began to document what they were doing. Maybe for law enforcement, maybe just to cleanse herself. And where once Bruzzi had seen more scores, he now pictured cops from around the world dropping by Apollonica for something other than the wine. She had to have known what his reaction would be, but she did it anyway. What a brave girl. . . incredibly brave.

The question that would never be answered was what had been the tipping point? I thought about the unaccounted for Kubicek watercolor and the missing beauty queen, Brandi Sue Parsons. Were those Truman's work? And had that been the seed that would sprout Kim's attempt at redemption? Or was it something else that none of us knew? Whatever it was now lay in a cemetery in Los Angeles, and that's where it would remain.

Tino was on his feet now, and he started to say something, but Remi ordered him to shut up and get back on his bike. He walked over to the gate and picked up Nico's headband, shook off the dust and put it in his pocket. The conversation was almost over, but before we air-kissed and made plans to do lunch, I decided to put a small burr of my own under a Sicilian saddle.

I said to Remi, "Did Boy Wonder there happen to mention he had a good time with Kim before they got to the airport? She didn't think it was so much fun, but what the hell, she was going to die anyway."

There's another phenomenon of pillow talk. Black Bart never likes one of his gang messing with his girl—even one he's finished with. Remi's mask of control disappeared, and he looked at Tino with such naked anger that I thought I smelled Tino's pants fill. Maybe they did.

Remi revved his Triumph, then roared away. The others hurried to catch up, but not before Tino and I looked at each other. There wasn't much swagger left in those eyes.

Eddie, Julien and I watched until they reappeared near the top of the hill.

As we drove back to Bonifacio, I talked, and Eddie listened. By now, Julien understood much of what had led us to his island, and I could see him processing. It was almost dark when I finished.

"Then I'm not sure what we accomplished except to let them know we're here," Eddie said.

"They already knew," I said. "A cop who's too timid to shoot a wild animal mauling a baby wasn't going to open Tiziano Bruzzi's studio to three strangers because we had nice smiles. And he certainly wasn't going to give us directions to a place only a few people are supposed to see."

"I don't get it."

"They knew who we were as soon as we hit town—maybe before—and they searched our car while we were on the mountain saving lives. That's why the security detail arrived essentially unarmed. All they wanted to do was lay eyes on us. Take our temperature."

"Wouldn't it have been a lot easier just to shoot us?"

"Bruzzi is so careful he never leaves the Med. Yet he flew halfway around the world to collect his cut of a deal—something Remi could have done for him. The Hyena went because he wanted to show the flag. Look everybody in the eye and remind them who their partner was—a guy who kills if you fuck with him. Kills ugly."

"So my question stands. Why not us?"

"Because right after security, Bruzzi's priority is money, and his reaction to our showing up means that they're not mopping up at the end of an operation. Hood's death wasn't fatal to the enterprise. It just entered a new phase, confirming what I've suspected since I met her; Bruzzi owns Bibiana Cesarotti. She's from his part of the world and traveled in heavy circles. And because larceny on this kind of scale is never somebody's first infidelity, she has a past. He just had to get her together with Hood, which wouldn't have been difficult for a guy with an eternal hard-on. But Hood and Serbin's plans go way beyond Russian artists nobody ever heard of."

"Any idea what?"

"No, but it's not important. It's only important not to underestimate him. Jackie Benveniste tried to explain it, but it didn't register. The world's shrunk for everybody, including the bad guys. Bruzzi and Serbin aren't just a couple of moves ahead, they're playing a different game."

"But you've got Kim's computer, and the pictures."

"And a dead woman to corroborate it. Or maybe a general who fucked his way through Washington then put a gun in his mouth. I couldn't get that through one of my own editors. No, as far as M. Bruzzi is concerned, we're just loose ends he can live with. That, and the last time one of his hired hands tried to kill me, paparazzi on five continents had an orgasm. And the last thing he's looking for are flashbulbs.

"But we did accomplish something today. Guys as smart as Bruzzi—and with as many enemies—don't run empires with the kind of lowlifes we've met up to now. There had to be somebody like Remi Terranova, and now we know he's every bit as competent—and as deadly—as one would expect."

I turned to Julien, who was driving with one hand and smoking a cigarette with the other. "It's none of my business, but what's your connection to the Hotel Eden?"

He flicked ashes out the window. "The night of the explosion, an agent in our office, Nicole Rolatte, had some contracts for Lazzaro Santagatta to sign. He was buying an apartment in Bonifacio . . . for his mistress. Nicole got busy, so she sent her daughter to the hotel with the paperwork . . . Christelle was fifteen."

He paused and lit another cigarette from the butt of the one he was smoking. "A week later, Nicole hanged herself, and the media couldn't get enough of the story. I gave an interview to French television that our friends on the mountain evidently didn't like."

I took one of Julien's cigarettes, a British Carlton, lit it and rolled down my window. The cool air rushed in. It felt good. We had just turned onto the coast road, and the lights of the boats dotted the harbor below. I thought of Julien's description of the hotel's explosion. Poof. Not much of a word for what it could do to people's lives.

* * *

The following morning, I sent Eddie back to Bastia for the plane. Julien knew a guy named Hugo who ran a skydiving club, and the members had cut an outlaw landing strip out of the scrub northeast of Bonifacio. Hugo said we could park the Cirrus there as long as we let his brother-in-law refuel it. After he explained the brother-in-law worked for Air France, it didn't take long to understand why or to calculate the profit margin.

Then Julien and I took one of the Aquascans and headed to Marseilles to do some shopping. It also gave us time to work out a plan.

Absinthe and Funeral Barges

I don't like 9mm's. I use them when I have to because they're the crabgrass of handguns, and you can find ammo in any cabbie's ashtray. But like in Washington, going up against professionals is like walking your pet in a bad part of town. You want a pit bull, not a chipmunk. The name of the game is stopping power, and my pit bull of choice is a .45. Nines are also contraindicated for hyenas.

So while Julien took a taxi to the Legion town of Aubagne, I walked to a formerly seedy neighborhood near the Old Port of Marseilles where fond memories were few and far between. The restaurants were nicer than I remembered, and some of the bars were on the verge of becoming trendy. I stopped at a place with newly installed white tile and polished brass and paid the bartender twice what a bottle of absinthe should have cost. Just so I wouldn't forget I was in France, he took my money and tip without eye contact or a thank-you.

Rue de la Trinidad was right where I'd left it, a tiny alley that still reeked of garbage and excrement and where the buildings hadn't changed in two centuries of neglect. Number 4 was the same shade of worn institutional green, and I climbed the stairs to the third floor, stepping over broken glass and things I didn't care to examine.

Apartment B was in the rear, the worn *mezuzah* on the doorjamb where it had always been. I knocked twice sharply, then twice again followed by three more. Nothing happened, and I repeated it, only this time changing the code by adding one knock. I heard someone moving inside, and I stepped to the side away from the hinges. If Mayer Luzzé still lived here, I didn't expect him to come out shooting, but he was as paranoid in his own way as Benny Joe, and not always as predictable.

"Qui?" a rough voice asked from behind the door, the Israeli accent discernable even from the single syllable.

"I have a bottle of Roquette 1797 that I can't drink by myself," I said in English.

I heard a chain disengage, the dead bolt turn, and the door opened a crack. I waited, and when nothing else happened, I pushed on the heavy wood, and it swung all the way in.

The apartment was as cluttered as I remembered it, but Mayer's tools were laid out on his workbench in perfect order. He was working on some kind of exotic pistol with an overly long barrel, but I knew better than to ask. Gunmakers are like diamond cutters—compulsive, secretive and with limited social graces. Now in his late seventies and still not needing glasses, he returned to his work without speaking.

I found a pair of small snifters in the kitchen and poured each of us two fingers of green liquid, then returned to the living room and handed Mayer his. "I expected you to be digging clams in Jaffa by now."

"Too many old Jews," he said, holding up his glass. "And I can't get this." He took a long swallow and closed his eyes, letting the sharp heat of the absinthe wash over him. I left him and walked through each of the four rooms, opening closets as I went. We were alone, as expected.

"Still careful at all the wrong times."

I waved a cat off the only other chair in the living room and sat. "Every now and then I get one right."

"That's too bad. Most people think you're a pain in the ass. What do you want?"

"Three .45s . . . Colts preferably . . . with suppressors . . . and some information."

"Two thousand each, and if you try to negotiate, three. But no suppressors. Market's gone. People just use a plastic bottle and throw it away. World's gone to shit."

"Euros or dollars?"

"Fuck euros. Propped-up tourist money. See how far out of town you get with a suitcase full of that shit if Hitler comes back."

"You know something no one else does?"

"You looked around lately? How long do you think before somebody says, 'Enough with these fuckin' Arab, and while we're at it, let's finish the job on their fuckin' cousins.' "

He gestured with his empty glass, and I got up to get the bottle. He took another draw, then looked at me. "What kind of information?"

"Remi Terranova."

"He works for that cocksucker Gaetano Bruzzi. Why aren't you asking about him?"

"What's to know? He's rich, so he's lazy. Terranova will be the problem."

Mayer thought it over. "He uses that army of kids to terrorize anybody who crosses him. You don't kill them first, they'll cut you and just keep cutting."

"Somebody else told me the same thing."

"Then listen. You've got a soft streak in you. Like you read the Bible and remembered the wrong parts."

"And Remi?"

"Doesn't lose his composure. You'll be a good match . . . if you get to him."

We drank in silence for a while, and I saw the cat eyeing me from under the workbench, probably wondering when he was going to get his chair back.

Mayer finally spoke. "The police'll want to give you a key to the city."

"I'll make sure you get the credit."

"Fuck keys. I only take cash."

"American."

"Better than gold. Never a question." He pointed to his glass.

Julien had done his job. Three sets of black commando gear, an Alpine package, and night-vision goggles, compliments of a GIGN counterterrorist unit commander looking to retire. "I can get him a job handling security for our high-end properties, like the one you're staying in," Julien explained. "And I gave him a thousand dollars to take his team out to dinner. These guys have people's lives in their hands, and they get paid less than street sweepers. I hope you don't mind."

It isn't limited to France. I'd have probably given him more.

Our last stop was the Musée d'Histoire du Marseille. I wanted to see if I could find something about the Fortress of Apollonica that might show a floor plan. We got lucky. A few years earlier, the museum had commissioned a photographic team to document Corsican places of worship. Technically, the fortress didn't qualify, but the team's leader had managed to wrangle his way inside anyway, and Bruzzi himself had shown them around.

The results were more than I could have hoped for. Hundreds of high-quality black-and-white photographs taken from every conceivable angle. Since the museum had a no-copy policy, we commandeered a table and began constructing a photographic schematic, and after a couple of hours of working with the images, we felt we had a good enough mental picture to get around. The only thing they had not gotten—either by Bruzzi mandate or photographer omission—was a shot of the monitoring station for the security system.

And so, just before dawn on Saturday, with everything stowed in waterproof seabags, we boarded the Aquascans and ran southeast through the Strait of Bonifacio. An hour later, Julien, who was alone in the lead boat, indicated that we were inside Italian waters, and we cruised another half hour until there were no other vessels visible. Using empty wine bottles we'd brought from the villa, it took us only a short time to sight in and get used to the feel of the .45s. Then we headed for Sardinia.

The Maddalena Archipelago on the northeast coast is accessible only by boat, but unlike their sour, wary Corsican neighbors, Sardinians are as warm as a Brooklyn wedding party. We put in at a pink sand beach, and a pair of smiling young men in their twenties waded out and took our boats. I was concerned about leaving our things aboard, especially the guns, but Julien said that theft wasn't a problem in the marina and the tip he promised the men would turn them into better security guards than the police.

We ate a huge breakfast of eggs, sliced lamb, fresh fruit and yogurt at a small sidewalk restaurant run by a beyond-friendly family named Cavalli, who kept bringing out more platters no matter how much we protested. Finally, we just had to get up from the table, exchange forty handshakes and kisses and leave.

Julien knew of a neatly kept tourist hotel on the beach, and after paying cash for three rooms, I changed and took a hard swim in the warm, calm water. Afterward, we sat in comfortable chairs under a cork tree and went over the plan one more time. Then we turned in and slept until late afternoon.

An hour before sundown, Napoleon's funeral barge rounded the protruding isthmus on Corsica's east coast sixty miles north of Bonifacio. Turning west into the mouth of the gorge, it fought its way past the foam of river meeting sea, the life-sized replica of the general's coffin riding high abovedecks and draped with his personal flag. A six-man, period-uniformed honor guard rode with the bier, one man standing at each corner, the others at the bow and stern.

Behind the barge came a flotilla of private vessels keeping a respectful distance but filled with partiers on their way to the festival. Some of the larger boats were strung with lights, while attractive young ladies caught the last rays of the Mediterranean sun. The decks of others were so dangerously full that they looked like entire neighborhoods were aboard. Regardless of the size of the party, however, alcohol was in plentiful supply, and a cacophony of music drifted across the water.

We were laying about a mile to the north in the Aquascans, watching through binoculars, and when the last of the parade disappeared upriver, we started our engines and followed. When we entered the gorge, the darkening 150-foot rock walls loomed over us, bouncing back the rumble of the big Mercs. I calculated that in a little less than two hours, the moon would be directly overhead. If we were lucky, we wouldn't be around to see it.

It was eleven miles from the mouth of the river to Apollonica, and we lagged well behind the other boats. Julien, riding only a few feet off our port side, called over, "A pair of police cruisers will be patrolling to make sure no one gets too close to the fireworks, but they'll be drinking too, and their boats are old and slow."

Forty minutes later, we rounded a bend, and suddenly the Roman bridge came into view. It was even more impressive from the water, only now, lining it and the cliffs on both sides of the river, stood hundreds of men, women and children, quietly watching the mythical drama of Napoleon's homecoming unfold. Along with the other boats, we cut our engines and drifted. The only sounds now were the low thump of the barge's inboard and the gentle rush of water against hulls.

With the sun low, it was difficult to see the faces of the onlookers, only their silhouettes. I thought of the terra-cotta soldiers at Xian. Though these Corsican sentinels were playing out a living drama, both were serving rulers whose only contribution now was to remind them of what they no longer had. It was hard not to appreciate both the irony of the moment and its theatricality.

Eddie didn't share the wonder. "Gives me the fuckin' creeps," he whispered. "All this make-believe bullshit."

"This from a guy whose people tell fortunes from chicken guts," I said.

Julien didn't quite grasp what I meant, but he thought it was funny.

The barge swung toward shore, and we now saw a priest and two dozen men, also dressed in period, standing along the river. One of the deckhands threw out a line, and the men eased the barge in. It took some time to get the coffin offloaded, but as soon as it was hoisted onto strong shoulders, the slow trek up the steep path to Apollonica began.

We had drifted backward with the current, separating us from Julien. Now he throttled back to us. "Once they get to the square, there'll be a speech by the mayor followed by a mass written specifically for Napoleon. At its close, the priest will lead the descendants of Octave LeDucq to the coffin to place violets on it. That'll be the signal to crack open the wine, sing 'Regina Salvo' a couple of times and head back to the river."

"And that will take ninety minutes," I said, confirming.

"Maybe a little less. If the crowd gets restless, the priest will cut it short. He knows everybody's there for the party, not to listen to him."

"Then he'd be the first," said Eddie. "My money's on the ninety."

We brought our boats to speed and drove past the funeral barge. I saw no one onboard. The captain and crew must have gone up too. Across the river, another long, low shape sat at anchor. The fireworks barge. According to Julien, it would be attended by at least two technicians, but if they were there, they weren't out where I could see them.

Two miles further upriver, we came to the road we'd passed a few days earlier. Unpaved, it descended steeply from the top of the ridge and looked too narrow for anything wider than a golf cart. However, the two red Pinzgauers were parked along the water, so unless they'd flown in, they fit.

The Pinzes had their lights off, but I could make out two men sitting on the bumper of one, smoking. As we turned toward them, they got up and started waving their arms and shouting. *"Non! Non!"*

We ignored them and beached the Aquascans on a small apron of sand. The men came charging toward us like they were heading into a bar fight. Without a word, Eddie stepped into the lead guy and slammed him in the face with his Colt. It sounded like a hammer going through a ripe peach—the gelatinous mashing of nose followed by the hard crunch of teeth.

The guy grabbed his face with both hands, blood running between his fingers. He went to his knees, then fell forward in the dirt, motionless. Just for good measure, Eddie kicked him a couple of times in the ribs. The kicks were over the top, and I probably should have stopped him, but I didn't.

The other trucker's attitude changed immediately. He stopped and shut up. Julien approached him and asked in French how many more there were. "Just two," the man replied. "With the barge." Then Julien hit him so hard and so fast I didn't see it coming. The man went down, but not out. Julien looked down and said calmly, "Learn to drive, motherfucker."

We taped them together inside one of the trucks, locked it and threw the keys in the river. Then we unloaded the boats and dressed quickly in our ops gear. I checked to make sure Eddie remembered how to operate the night-vision goggles and reminded him not to have them on when the fireworks began.

"How about giving me a little credit, boss," he said irritatedly. "I don't think I'm going to need them anyway. Where I'm from, you can't see at night, a gator eats your ass before you're five."

A couple of minutes later, he tied our Aquascan to his

and headed upstream to find a place where he could see the ridgeline. Julien and I got in the remaining Pinz, and I jammed it into gear and headed up the steep incline, our left side all but scraping rock and the other barely hanging on the edge. If all went well, we'd signal Eddie from the top, and he'd be waiting for us by the time we got down to the river. If that didn't happen, as soon as he saw the fireworks begin downstream, he'd head back to the bridge and wait for us there. Not a Good Housekeeping-approved egress, but all we had.

The mud in the pass wasn't an impediment to the Pinz. We blew through it at 35mph, and I turned off the headlights as soon as I saw the crescent moon peeking through the exit slit at the other end. Sometimes, the fate of missions hangs on the smallest of decisions—and luck. This was one of those times. Had I left the headlights on, their natural low angle would have kept me from seeing Julien's BMW sitting in the middle of the road. But backlit by the moon, its silhouette registered a half second before I would have slammed into it.

I jerked the Pinz right and felt that side start to come up. I wrestled the wheel into the roll and jammed the accelerator to the floor. We spun once in the wet slop, then slid back across the pavement to the other shoulder, where I finally brought us to a stop forty yards later, facing the wrong direction.

More angry at myself than anyone else, I dropped the Pinz into gear and headed back. We'd almost died before we'd even gotten to the dance, and it was my fault for allowing my brain to model the road as empty as it had been the only other time I'd driven it. Then I'd compounded my mistake by expecting the BMW to be waiting on the other side of the pass, not stopped in the middle of the fucking road in the fucking dark.

As I pulled alongside the car, I could see three shapes sitting inside. Julien got out of the Pinz and hurried to the driver's side window. He kept his voice low, but I could tell he was reaming somebody out. When he got back in, he said, "Alain apologizes."

We exited the pass, and I looked up at the fortress. Lights burned along the length of the wall, and several windows in the tower were illuminated. From this distance, I couldn't see anyone, but that didn't mean anything.

Julien and I put on our night-vision goggles and, instead of following the paved road, turned right and started overland, the twin chain-link fences on our left. Eddie had overflown the property on his way back from Bastia and reported that about a quarter of a mile in, the barrier turned uphill. It was rough going, and as the ground steepened, the left side of the Pinz rode higher and higher. Finally, the fences took the awaited 90° turn, and we went with them.

"It doesn't seem to make sense," said Julien. "Why go to all the trouble to build this then leave one side of the place exposed?" asked Julien.

"Technology and cost," I said. "Once people cover the obvious with cameras and sensors, they assume the show is enough. In the army, we used to train by penetrating secure facilities, and we always got in. Always."

It was steep but, with all six wheels of the Pinz engaged, climbable with only a minimum of backsliding. More difficult was the heavy underbrush and the occasional tree that would loom up. The brush disappeared as the trees became thicker, but a couple of times, we had to scrape our way between a pair of pines.

Finally, we reached the fifty-foot fortress wall, and I pulled the nose of the Pinz against it while Julien got out and chocked the wheels with rocks. I'd estimated our climbing angle at 30°, but here the ground was slightly flatter. The wall looked like it had seen better days, but it was hard not to be impressed with the size of the stone blocks that the anonymous builders had carried up the mountain centuries earlier.

I climbed onto the roof of the Pinz and engaged the aerial

ladder. It slid slowly up until all its sections were extended and I could bring it gently down against the stone. There was still a good twenty-foot gap between the last rung and the top of the wall, but that was acceptable. I nodded down to Julien, and he dialed his cell phone.

"Immédiatement," he whispered.

Julien and I walked along the wall to a spot where we could see past the trees and through the fence, and we took off our goggles to save battery life. Far below, the bright headlights of the BMW came barreling out of the pass and fishtailed along the fence, rap music booming from the radio. We saw it make the right turn where the wall intersected and disappear, but we could track its progress by watching the floodlights come on sequentially.

"Fast enough?" Julien asked.

I nodded. "We want Remi's adrenaline pumping. Who's in the car?"

"Alain, who works with me, and his friend, Guy. Playing you is Hassan, a Moroccan basketball player who keeps a place on the island. What if Remi doesn't react?"

"He might not believe it, but he can't ignore it. And everybody who doesn't go with him to the gate will be huddled in front of the monitors, watching. I just hope your friends stay cool."

"That's not a problem, but just in case somebody from Bruzzi's camp doesn't, Alain's father is a judge—a famous one."

Suddenly, a dark, four-legged shape ran by on the other side of the fence. Then another and another. Six in all. A seventh, a heavily pregnant female, stopped and looked through the chain link. We locked eyes, and she seemed to want to challenge me, as if sensing I was responsible for her missing mate. She took a step forward, bared her sharklike teeth and cackled, the mottled black and brown hair of her neck expanding and contracting. Then pack instinct took over, and she turned and ran after the others.

"I hope the judge is famous enough," Julien said softly.

We heard, then saw, the motorcycles racing down through the vineyard, only this time they were accompanied by two military-style Hummers.

I looked at Julien. "How do you say 'Showtime' in French?"

"Showtime."

I went up the ladder first, uncoiled the grappling hook, swung it a couple of times for momentum and heaved it over the parapet. I pulled hard on the Beal rope, and it held, so I dropped it to Julien, who tied it off at the ladder base. I redonned my goggles, attached two ascenders to the line and went up—fast. It was only twenty feet, but I remember climbing as being easier. A few seconds later, Julien followed.

Knights Quarters and Zeus

We had landed on a guardwalk on top of a perimeter building. The main residence was about thirty yards across a large courtyard. With the moon, we had exceptional visibility and saw no one. We moved quickly to find a way down.

What you gain with night-vision equipment, you lose in peripheral and depth perception. The first indication that we weren't alone wasn't from something I saw but something I heard. Running feet on stone—bare feet.

We were making our way along a wall under a portico bordering the courtyard. Julien was out front. I reached out and grabbed his arm, and he froze in place. I stripped off my goggles and swept the area in the direction of the sound. There was a stairway directly across from us on the corresponding portico leading to a level below. Someone was coming up, fast. I motioned Julien down, and we flattened ourselves on the stone. The moon was behind us, so our side remained dark while the other caught the light.

A woman appeared on the stairs. Naked. And frantic.

Just as she reached the top, a man wearing a red *tortil* came up the steps behind her and hit her with his fist in the back of the head. She sprawled across the stone. He bent down and said something I couldn't make out, then grabbed her arm, jerked her upright and pulled her back down the stairs. She was resisting a little, but most of the fight had gone out of her.

I motioned to Julien, and we rose and crossed the courtyard. From the top of the stairwell, we couldn't see anything. It was at least fifty steps down, and whoever was there was out of sight. We descended slowly, keeping our backs against the wall, and when we reached the halfway point, the backs of two Les Executeurs came into view, their pants around their ankles as they prepared to rape an attractive ash blonde, who was on her hands and knees, sobbing. The woman looked up and stared directly at me, and I knew that if we didn't move immediately, her eyes would give us away.

I took the guy on the right, and Julien hit the second rapist on the top of the head with the butt of his .45. He staggered, then fell. I grabbed the other man's head in the crook of my elbow and jerked him up and onto my hip while I wrenched his neck well beyond its intended arc. There was an audible snap, and he instantly became dead weight. I let him drop.

The surviving man was stunned but had gotten to a sitting position and was fumbling at his bunched-up jeans, almost certainly looking for his knife. Julien found it for him, flicked it open, stuck it in his throat and pulled hard right. Blood erupted, and the man's eyes went wide as he clutched at the wound with both hands. There was a loud gurgling sound, and his lips began to foam red. A few seconds later, he slumped over and died.

We were standing in a wide, pale stone room interspersed with graceful arched columns supporting a Gothic ceiling. Four corridors intersected at right angles, forming the shape of a cross and running off into darkness. The girl's clothes were in a pile near an upturned tray. Broken dishes and remnants of food were scattered about.

Julien helped the girl to her feet. She went to her clothes and began dressing. "Who are you?" she asked, her voice trembling.

Julien ignored her. "This is the Knights Quarters, right?" he asked in French.

She nodded. "But no knights, only prisoners."

"Prisoners? How many?"

"Two now. Sometimes there more. I bring their food. The guards too. But tonight . . ." She stopped. Now dressed, she knelt and began picking up the broken dishes.

"Where are these prisoners?" I asked.

She pointed at the corridor behind me.

"Guards?"

She looked at the two bodies. The blood pool was still expanding. "Only Marto and Louis."

"What do you want to do with her?" Julien asked me in English.

"My guess is she won't be anxious to tell this story." It was a dangerous move. One I would never have made in Delta, but I didn't want to traumatize her any further. We left her and walked into the dark corridor, Maglites out, guns drawn.

If indeed knights had once lived here, they hadn't been flashy ones. Each of the rooms was no bigger than a prison cell and furnished with only a crude wooden bed, a simple table and chair and bucket. Knighthood had probably gotten more romantic in the retelling.

We passed four rooms on each side, all empty, before seeing a light coming from under a door on the left. There was no lock, just a thick dead bolt that could only be engaged from the outside. A piece of hinged copper covered a slit no thicker than a paperback. I lowered it and looked in at an angle so as not to give anyone inside a target.

Tiziano Bruzzi's unblinking eyes stared straight into mine.

Only the thickness of the door separated us, and his rancid breath filled the air. I could see beyond his narrow face that the light was coming from a screen-covered socket high on the wall. His bed had been overturned, the sheets torn to pieces. I closed the peephole and moved to the next cell.

As I reached it, a deep male voice called out in American-accented French, "If that's you, Marto, you motherfucker, I need another blanket."

I pulled down the copper plate, and again looked in from a safe angle. The cell was pitch dark, and suddenly, something wet came splashing through the slit, missing me but hitting the opposite wall and running down the door. Its smell left no doubt what it was, but since the occupant probably wasn't going to have more urine for a while, I aimed the Maglite through the opening and swept the cell.

I knew it was going to be Truman York, but I was surprised by how fit he looked. Military straight, his six-foot frame was without paunch, his iron-gray hair neatly combed. Even his face was that of a man much younger than his sixty-five-plus years, the lines more character than age.

"Hello, Truman," I said.

"Who the fuck are you?"

"A friend of Kim's."

He hesitated a moment. "Thank God. Open the fuckin' door. I'm goin' nuts in here."

I wanted to ask him how Kim was, just to hear what he'd say. Down deep, I still didn't want to believe that a father could be so twisted. But I replaced the copper plate without saying anything.

"Jesus Christ, you're not gonna hold a fuckin' grudge over a little piss, are ya? Look, I'll let you smack me in the mouth. Couple of times if you want to. Just open the god-damn door."

I saw Julien looking at me, but I avoided his eyes. I returned to Tiziano's cell and unbolted the door. The gaunt, bent figure came out like a ghost, ignoring both Julien and me. But instead of heading up the corridor toward the exit, he went the other direction.

Julien and I followed, Truman's curses receding behind us.

Tiziano was dressed the same as in Kim's photograph. Baggy white long-sleeved shirt over baggy white pants, bare feet. His gray-streaked hair hung to his shoulders, and he walked in fits and starts, stopping for a few seconds then almost leaping forward as he seemed to remember his destination.

The wall that had once ended the corridor had been inelegantly removed, and the stone floor now turned into a steel walkway. I could tell from the change in sound that we were in a larger area than we had been, and when I trained my Maglite upward, I saw the ceiling was at least forty feet above us. The stone block walls, more roughly hewn here than in the corridor, framed a cavernlike space roughly eighty feet across.

Tiziano had gotten some distance ahead, but he suddenly stopped and looked back, his wild eyes glowing white in the beam of the flashlight. He leaned over the railing and pointed down, and Julien and I turned our lights into the black void.

We were standing on a footbridge built two stories off the ground using steel cross-braces, like a railroad trestle. The floor below was dirt and dotted with man-sized chunks of discarded building stone, interspersed with mounds of straw. A pair of low water troughs fed by a hose and the random piles of scat confirmed what I suspected. This was the hyena den, and the open, electrically operated steel door along the far wall would lead to the fenced-in run. Above the door, a long row of windows had been set into the wall, and through them I could see down over the vineyard to the floodlit gate. There was still activity there, but it was too far away to define.

I turned back and saw that Tiziano had swung open a hinged section of railing and was standing on a steel lift similar to the ones you see rising out of a New York sidewalk. I pictured Bruzzi and his entourage watching the man named Andre being lowered into the lair. Maybe he was one of those rare guys who had the cool to spit in his tormentor's face, but probably not. The door to the run would have been open then too, and when the lift stopped, Andre would have had no choice but to start running.

Perhaps the hyenas weren't interested at first, or maybe they were already outside, which is why he got as far as he did. But Bruzzi didn't seem like the sporting type. More likely, he would have starved his predators for a few days, then made sure they were waiting. Andre may have even survived the first attack, gotten up and continued running until he finally ran out of time where we'd found him. And Bruzzi had watched it all through the windows, maybe with a pair of binoculars that he passed around. However it had unfolded, Andre had left some of his terror in the room. I could smell it.

When I turned back to the footbridge, Tiziano had disappeared.

We came up through a dungeon door into the kitchen of the main residence. It was a large, industrial-strength place, where eight women, ranging in age from their early twenties to their late sixties, were at work preparing the evening meal. The young blonde woman from the Knights Quarters was among them. I motioned to Julien that we needed to get them out. He nodded and stepped into the room, holding his .45 at his side.

A white-haired, thickly built woman who seemed to be in charge saw him first. Julien put up his hand in a non-threatening gesture and walked toward her. As they spoke I stepped into sight. Seconds later, all of the appliances had been turned off, and the white-haired woman was ushering her staff through a doorway on the far side of the room.

"I told the cook they wouldn't be coming back," Julien said when I joined him. "She said she hoped we burned the place to the ground."

The Bruzzi magic.

"The security room is through that door and down the hall," he said, pointing.

There were three Headband Boys huddled around a bank of Sony monitors. We went in fast and put them on the ground with only minor resistance. One, a kid in his teens, began to sob, and an older guy with a full complement of legs on his spider lashed out with his foot and kicked him. Julien was removing knives from pockets, and he grabbed the kicker by the hair and banged his face into the floor until he was spitting blood.

I secured wrists to opposing ankles with 100-mile-an-hour tape, then we turned our attention to the monitors. Alain, Guy and Hassan were getting back into the BMW, watched carefully by guards with shouldered Kalashnikovs. I didn't see Remi, but with the confrontation over, we were about to get more company. I pulled the main cable, darkening the monitors, and we started out.

Julien was a step behind me, and when the shot rang out, the close confines made it sound much louder than the caliber that fired it. I wheeled, knelt and leveled my weapon at the three men. The young kid, tears still streaming down his cheeks, was holding a cheap .22 caliber that had been hidden in the pantleg of the bleeding man next to him. Mouse gun is what professionals call pissy little pieces of shit like that, and we'd both missed it. The problem is, history has a habit of turning on pissy little pieces of shit, and Julien was on his knees, grimacing and holding his left side.

I wanted to shoot the kid, but that would have accomplished nothing. I jerked the .22 out of his hand, bending his fingers the wrong way in the process, and threw it hard against one of the monitors. The glass spiderwebbed, and the cheap pistol broke into pieces that clattered to the four corners. The knives we had removed from the three were lying on a desk. I flipped one open, found the kid's spider tattoo—legless, of course—and sliced a deep X through it.

Junior had maybe fifty to sixty years left to live. He could look at that scar every day and remember.

I got my arm around Julien, helped him to his feet and closed the door behind us.

Keeping to the wall, we entered the refectory, a seventy-five-foot hall lined with white columns. Originally, it would have been set with long tables and served as a dining hall for monks and clergy. Now it had been turned into a forest of statuary. Huge marble emperors, philosophers, gods and goddesses—some on makeshift bases, some lying on their sides—were jammed recklessly amid scores of unopened crates and a pair of Fiat forklifts. One Iwo Jima Memorial-sized piece depicting a naked gladiator in combat with a bear and a lion seemed too large to have been moved at all, let alone to the top of a mountain. It had taken a bold thief and a bolder wallet to steal so many tons of stone, but a profit margin exceeding that of bad wine would be a good motivator.

We had gone halfway across the room when Julien began to stumble. I eased him down between a statue of Zeus and a seraphim-and-cherubim fountain, where I examined his wound. It was a through-and-through and bleeding profusely. Almost certainly, his intestine had been punctured.

"How you doing, partner?" I asked.

"Feels like ground glass in there. I'm not going to be doing any running. Go get Bruzzi. I'll occupy any assholes who show up."

"You're starting to swear like an American."

"It's that fuckin' Eddie."

Tough as he was, he wasn't going to get back over the wall to the Pinz either. I laid my .45 and extra clips down next to him.

He looked at them. "Don't be foolish."

I ignored him and checked my watch. "Think you can ride a motorcycle?"

"Who knows, but I'd rather die trying than lie here. They're using the crypt as the garage, right?"

"That's what the photographers' notes said. How's twenty minutes sound?"

"I'll be there . . . but if I'm not, don't wait."

I clapped him on the shoulder and was gone.

42

Everlast and Fireworks

Evidently, only God sleeps higher than a French pope, because his private quarters had been erected atop the main residence, shadowed only by the fortress's seven spires. Reached by a steep staircase off the refectory, it was not unlike a New York penthouse, a separate rooftop world of gardens, footpaths and fountains surrounding a two-story, layered limestone building that had been modernized for its current owner.

The main level was sixty-five feet long and set in from the roofline to make it invisible from the ground, which also prevented its 360° panorama from being contaminated by views of the Apollonican unwashed. What one might call Trump *Il Papa*. The upstairs was a third smaller, and presumably housed the bedroom, however, the Musée d'Histoire's photographers had not been permitted inside, so I was guessing.

Crouching at the top of the stairs, I could see two guards outlined against the night sky. One was average sized, the other squat and round. They both wore *tortils* and held Kalashnikovs. They were engaged in intense conversation.

"It was a gunshot," said the shorter man angrily in rapid French. "I know you heard it too."

"I didn't hear anything, but even if I did, Remi said not to leave under any circumstances, so I'm not moving."

"But what if—"

"You want to investigate, you're on your own."

"Shouldn't we at least tell Tino?"

"And tell him what? That you heard something I'm going to swear I didn't hear? Fuck off."

The short man hesitated, then said, "I'm going to the bottom of the stairs . . . take a look." He started toward the stairway, and I retreated back down and melted into the shadows.

I chopped him in the back of the neck just as he hit the last step and caught him and his rifle before they fell. When I dragged him under the staircase, he wasn't breathing. I left the Kalashnikov but took his knife. I don't like them, but sometimes stealth trumps firepower.

The other guard saw me coming through the darkness. I could tell he was unsure about my size. "Remi?" he called out.

I had the knife open at my side. I closed the gap between us and thrust it up under his sternum, jerking the handle back and forth to sever as many blood vessels as possible. I felt some resistance, then it gave way, and I knew I had gotten his heart. He died against me with only a slight rattle.

I dropped him over the side and moved quickly to the exterior of the building, positioning myself between two wide picture windows of four-inch-thick thermoplastic capable of flattening a high-powered rifle slug. The windows were permanently sealed, which was excellent against intruders, not so excellent if you had to get out in a hurry. Leaning around, I could see a study furnished with the masculine accoutrement of a man possessing money and power. Papers were strewn on the desk, and there was a fire burning in the large fireplace, but no people.

As I stood with my back against the thick stone, I suddenly felt a vibration, a thumping. Irregular, but ongoing. Bullet-resistant thermoplastic is specifically designed to absorb shock waves, so I leaned my ear against the window. Whatever it was seemed to be coming from the second floor.

The iron-strapped front door opened silently to my touch, and a heavily carpeted stairway was immediately to the right. Staying against the left wall, I went up.

The stairs opened into a large room whose centerpiece was an immense, silk-canopied bed of such intricate goldwork that only a pope could have afforded such artisans. Bookshelves lined the walls, dotted liberally with eighteen-inch reproductions of famous sculpture. No one was in sight, but the thumping was louder now, punctuated by grunts and an occasional snort of breath.

I crossed to a pair of French doors set into the wall on the right. One was open, and a mirror was positioned so that I could see into the next room. Gaetano Bruzzi, larger and broader than his pictures, was stripped to the waist, his hands taped, as he pounded on a heavy Everlast bag, the floor shaking with the blasts. Across from him, Tino was doing his best to hold the 150-pound piece of equipment steady, but the big man's fists hit so hard that he jolted the slightly built Corsican off-balance with each punch.

The Hyena's protruding jaw and mule-sized teeth were accentuated by his thick, white, wavy hair pulled back in a clump of a ponytail. The strands that had worked loose hung in damp strings along his cheeks, and his torso glistened with sweat that collected in half-moons along the waistband of his expensive, shark gray slacks.

I noticed a white dress shirt and matching gray suit coat draped over the back of a chair, which accounted for the thin, black Italian loafers instead of athletic shoes. Marta Videz had been right. He didn't lumber, he moved with the grace of a dancer, like Jackie Gleason, only much bigger.

He must have felt my presence, because he suddenly looked in the mirror, and we locked eyes. He then did a curious thing: he smiled and kept punching. Mind games. So I stepped forward and pushed open the second French door.

Tino, sporting a newly swollen left eye, probably courtesy of Remi, lost his concentration, and the next slam of Bruzzi's fist knocked him into an armoire. He recovered quickly and had his knife out in the same motion. There were no words this time. He simply crouched and moved in on me. I still had the dead man's knife, but I was not nearly skilled enough to face somebody like Tino with a blade, so I left it in my pocket.

I anticipated his first move, but the second was like lightning, and less than two seconds into the confrontation, I had blood running down the inside of my left arm. *A Corsican doesn't stick his enemy. He slices at muscles, tendons, ears, anything that will terrorize.*

I glanced over at Bruzzi and saw him closing in, fists cocked. But it was stupid to have taken my eyes off the guy with the knife, and I paid for it. This time, he got under my upraised arm and jabbed his blade just below my left nipple. I felt it hit bone, then it was gone again, and Tino was circling, trying to bring me into Bruzzi's range. This had all the earmarks of a samba they'd done before. It wasn't exactly a Black and Black, but I knew what was coming. Bruzzi would fake, I'd react and Tino would slice, probably my face this time.

Out of the corner of my left eye, I saw the fist coming, and I fought my instincts. Instead of jerking away, I tilted my head forward, and as the blow glanced off the back of my head, the steel blade went by my face where my eye would have been.

Bruzzi laughed, not even slightly out of breath. "Bravo, Mr. Black."

Tino wasn't as cool. He lunged at me. Now he'd made a mistake. I grabbed his wrist, and like the pro he was, he let his arm go limp and went with the pull. But as soon as I felt him coming, I jammed my foot into the carpet and changed direction. Bruzzi had moved in, and we banged against him, which could have been fatal if he'd been ready, but I was already falling and rolling, and I felt Tino's arm dislocate at the shoulder.

If I was expecting him to scream, it didn't happen. He sucked in his breath, reached across with his free left hand and took the knife out of his dead right one, backslashing a ten-inch gash across my chest on the return. The heavy nylon fabric saved my skin, but not the next jab, which went into my right thigh and cut something loose I didn't think I wanted cut. The little fucker was not only good, he was fearless. He was also going to get my throat. I let go of his arm and grabbed my windpipe with both hands, then rolled over him. The razor edge of Corsican steel tore open the backs of both my hands, but then I was gone.

I kept rolling until I was back in the bedroom, then got to my feet and determined that despite the blood and a searing pain in my thigh, I was okay. But if I survived, I was going to have a long talk with the guy who decided not to bring a gun.

Tino came through the French doors first, low and wary. His right arm drooped lifelessly, but his left held the knife with enough competence that I wasn't going to get careless. He might not have been as eager as he had been, but he was still dangerous.

When Bruzzi appeared, I feinted at Tino, and when he took a half-step back, he bumped into his boss. I lunged forward and caught the Hyena with a straight right to the jaw. It wasn't enough to put him down—not even enough to stun him—but bullies don't like getting hit, and he threw Tino out of the way.

I backed up and took a couple of punches off my forearms before I saw an opening and jammed him in the forehead. His eyebrow split, and blood began seeping down into his left eye. As he wiped it away with the back of his fist, I hit him on that side again, this time in the temple, and he suddenly didn't seem so anxious to get at me.

Bruzzi moved out of reach, dropped his arms and shook

them. He'd been hitting the heavy bag for a while, and now he was working on adrenaline, still a bull, but a tired bull. I closed in so he'd have to continue to work, and he caught me with a right to the liver that sucked the breath out of my future grandchildren. But I managed to get him in the lips, and the upper one split against his teeth.

He spit a gob of blood on the Oriental rug and hissed something in Sicilian that sounded like "Fuck your village," which didn't have the effect on me it might have had in Palermo. Then he grabbed Tino and literally threw him at me. I hit the slightly built Corsican with a forearm shiver that elevated him into a side table and sent wineglasses and a decanter of port flying.

I expected him to get up and come at me again, but he just lay there on his back. Then I saw why. The decanter was one with a wide, flat bottom and a long, delicate neck, and in the collision, a vertical section of the stem had sheared off, turning it into a lead crystal spike, which had impaled Tino at the base of his skull. He was very much alive but afraid to roll in either direction, and with a nonfunctioning arm, unable to push himself straight up.

Bruzzi had moved to the center of the room and was busy rubbing blood off his face. I calmly walked over to Tino and looked down. His eyes reflected panic, the kind he was more familiar handing out than experiencing, but he didn't say anything. It wouldn't have mattered. I placed my foot on the bridge of his nose and pushed down. Just before the jagged glass severed his spine and exited his mouth, I said, "This one's for Walter Kempthorn."

Meanwhile, Bruzzi had armed himself with a replica of Rodin's *Iris*. It was the size of an anvil and probably weighed as much, but the Hyena handled it like balsa. Normally, the only requirement for taking a blunt object away from an attacker is the willingness to accept a blow in a nonessential part of the body; then grab the weapon and break the guy's arm. However, when it's being wielded by somebody maybe six-seven and three hundred pounds, there's no such thing as a nonessential body part. So you go to Plan B, which means stay clear and hope the guy wears himself out.

Bruzzi's first swung was murderous, but wild, and I managed to get one of the bedposts between us. Rodin went through it like an axe, as it did a second. The next sixty seconds became step—step—duck—crash, until the only things left standing were the Hyena and me. He was gasping and wheezing and mumbling unintelligible curses. I was exhausted too but better at hiding it.

I waited for him to drop his head just a little, and when he did, I rushed him. Bad idea. He turned slightly and took the charge on his shoulder. Then, quick as a cat, he got me in a bear hug from behind. My ribs weren't completely healed, and the pain turned the world red.

For the next few seconds, I used every move I had to try to dislodge his grip, but he'd read the same book. Tired of being whipped around like a rag doll, I got my feet under me, and, with all my strength bent forward until I had him draped across my back. Then, with a burst, I started running backward. I had to guess where the stairway began, and I was a little early when I launched, but our momentum carried us past the top step.

I sledded Bruzzi down the fifteen steps to the first floor in roughly two seconds, and even though I was on top, it was a bumpy ride. Bruzzi's head took the full force of the stop on the marble foyer, and he groaned once, then was out.

I disentangled myself and checked his pulse. Fast, but strong. I taped his wrists together, then ran the roll around his neck a few times to pull his hands up to his chest. It was a bitch getting his sweat-slick body off the stairs and turned over. When I finished, I made a stop at the fireplace, then found a bathroom and cleaned up my wounds as best I could.

A pitcher of ice water brought the Hyena around, and when he regained his bearings, I told him to get up. I got the response I expected, so I went back to the fireplace, where I had the business end of a straight poker baking in the embers. When I returned, I saw his right eye following me, but if he was waiting for a threat, he was disappointed.

The hot tip went through his expensive slacks like they weren't there, and I smelled flesh burning about the same time I got six inches of searing steel up his ass. He bellowed and bucked and tried to roll, but I held him in place with a handful of ponytail in my free hand while I recited the names of the people whose lives he'd destroyed, giving the poker a rough twist for each. He vomited until he hit dry heaves, and when I thought he could stand without collapsing, I used his hair to pull him to his knees, then up the rest of the way.

"Now we're going to take a walk," I said and thrust the poker up a couple more inches to get him moving. Outside, I heard gunfire below. Kalashnikov bursts mostly, but interspersed with the solid thump of a .45. Julien was still on the job.

I knew there had to be a service stairway between the penthouse and the kitchen. The Marseilles photographers wouldn't have thought it important enough to document, but logic said that the way I'd come up was too far to travel when a pope—or a Hyena—wanted a hot meal. I found it in a corner of the roof, and it led to a small landing just off the pantry.

Though the gunfire was close, the kitchen was still empty. We had almost reached the door that led back to the Knights Quarters when a flash of white exploded out of nowhere, and Tiziano buried a cook's cleaver in his brother's shoulder. He jerked it free and was going for Gaetano's head when I managed to get hold of his shirt and throw him across a counter, taking out cookware and china in a colossal crash.

Blood poured down Bruzzi's back and chest. Already in shock, it wasn't going to be long before he passed out. Tiziano scrambled to his feet, found his weapon and started at us again. I stepped in front of him. He stopped, a look of confusion on his face, like he was trying to figure out who I was. I didn't want to hurt him, and if anybody had a right to kill this son of a bitch, it was his brother. Maybe that was the best thing to do. Just walk away.

Tiziano and I locked eyes, and we stood for a minute, neither moving. Then his face softened. As the wildness disappeared, I saw what he might have been a long time ago—a delicate, vulnerable man. Tears started to run down his cheeks. And then he turned and ran.

I found the light switch in the cavern this time. Bare bulbs brought it up to semidarkness, but it was enough to make our way back to the steel lift. With only a flat piece of metal to stand on and no handholds, it was a treacherous place for the unsteady, and Bruzzi resisted getting on. I hit him in the back of the neck, and he went down face forward, which allowed me to kick his legs far enough past the railing to clear the walkway. He lay sprawled, part of him dangling over the edge, a study in indignity.

I heard them coming before they appeared. The hyenas had returned from their run down to the gate, and they could sense something unusual was happening. They gathered under the lift, looking up, saliva dripping from their muzzles. Bruzzi was panicking now, but I ignored him.

I considered removing the poker but decided to leave it up to the last guy who'd made this trip. "What do you think, Gaetano? Did Andre have a sense of humor?"

Bruzzi began sobbing. "Good," I said, "then let's give him his money's worth." But for a second opinion, I asked the hyenas. One of them began a high-pitched laugh that obviously meant, "Don't go to any trouble on our account."

And so I hit the green button on the control panel, and the lift began its last descent. I was impressed by how smoothly it ran. Proper maintenance is important.

Truman York knew a shortcut to the crypt. The guy was scum, but he'd been in combat, so he didn't rattle. And he didn't ask unnecessary questions—even when he heard the gunfire. I was seven minutes past the deadline, and I expected to find Julien either gone or dead. He was neither.

He'd managed to barricade the door leading down from the residence, which had forced his pursuers outside, where they'd had to slide down a steep, grassy bank to get to the foot-thick, hinged vehicle doors. But Julien had stopped them there too by pulling one of Bruzzi's wine trucks against them. Now Remi and crew were trying to shoot their way in.

After wading through a foot of water in a medieval tunnel that smelled of rot and rat shit, Truman and I came up through a grate in the crypt floor. But now we were just as trapped as the bad guys. We were going to have to go back up the stone steps and through the house, and running wasn't going to work.

Truman had never ridden a motorcycle before, so that meant Julien was going to have to find the strength for one more push. He looked about as pale as a human being can look, but he forced a smile and got one of the Triumphs started. With my .45 back, I went up the steps to the iron interior door. I leaned against it, but with the gunfire downstairs, I couldn't tell what was on the other side. My bet, however, was that Remi would have it covered.

I slowly raised the thick security bar. Its hinge squeaked as it disengaged, and immediately two gunshots hit the metal from the other side. I counted to three and jerked the door open, double tapping right to left until my clip was empty. There were two grunts, and a pair of bodies hit the floor.

I waited but heard no reinforcements, so I retreated back down the steps and mounted the other Triumph with Truman sitting behind me. We blasted up the stairs, past the two dead sentries, then up two more long flights that were so narrow the bikes' handlebars barely cleared the walls.

I'd given the .45 to Truman along with an extra clip, and as we rounded the corner into the vast living room, he took out two more headband-clad shooters. Another riddled the walls and ceiling with Kalashnikov fire as we crashed through a wall of floor-to-ceiling leaded windows onto a wide porch, then down more stairs and finally onto level ground.

We were on the town side of the property. The driveway led right, but I had no intention of taking the long way home. Julien was even with me, the side of his blood-soaked jumpsuit visible in the moonlight. I pointed to the high wall in front of us, and he nodded.

I glanced over my shoulder and saw the headlight of Remi's Triumph emerge from the garage, a member of his crew holding onto his waist with one hand, a *lupara* in the other.

"We can't get out that way," Truman yelled in my ear.

I ignored him and opened the throttle onto a narrow footpath. It ran straight at the wall, then turned sharply left into an arbor of overgrown roses. In the dark, at speed, it was impossible to avoid the thorned tentacles reaching across the divide. Fortunately, most were below eye level, so I wasn't going to be blinded, and my ops gear kept them from slashing anything vital. My passenger, wearing light cotton clothing, wasn't as lucky. He leaned into my back as far as he could, but he still got raked, and I felt more than a little pleasure each time he grunted.

At the end of the path, there was a man-made stream that had probably been conceived as a place of meditation. Neglect had long since ended that function, and only a trickle of brown water now ran among the thick rocks in its bed. I steered into it.

The bike bumped and jerked and almost went over a couple of times, but I managed to hold it, and Truman didn't try to help me lean. A hundred yards later, with the wall still high on our right, we came to a place where the streambed had crumbled away completely. Over the years, water runoff from the mountain had eaten away the bottom of the wall, and at some point, a rockslide had come along and taken out a wide section, leaving behind boulders and rubble as high as the wall had been.

I gunned the Rocket and hit the scree head-on, pulling up and leaning back as far as I could at the moment of impact. The jolt jammed my teeth together and blurred my vision, but our momentum took us up the shale and airborne until we dropped tail first into the trough, then rollercoastered again twice more.

Once we cleared the debris, we barreled into a thick stand of trees above and east of Apollonica, and with the moon now hidden by the leaves, I fought to thread the trunks with only my headlight for visibility. I didn't need to look back for Julien, because I could hear him shouting, *"Merde!"* as he banged through the brush below and behind me.

Suddenly, there was a loud crack, and pellet splatter from the *lupara* cut away tree bark. Some of it flew past my ear so close that I heard it snap the air. Truman and I looked simultaneously and saw that Remi was not only still with us but gaining. His passenger was leaning out with the gun, and he fired again, kicking up dirt and loose stone. He wouldn't continue to miss, and if he got Truman in the head, he'd get me too.

I downshifted, put my foot down and swung the Triumph left, gunned it into a controlled slide, just missing a tree as thick as a bridge piling, then slammed the throttle wide open, heading back uphill. Before Remi could react, I was passing him in the opposite direction, and by the time he got turned, I was already a quarter mile away and directly above the town. I bore left and headed down. My headlight picked up something white, and as I sped by, I saw Tiziano, apparently heading home. I silently wished him luck.

The dirt street that ran past the artist's house appeared out of the grass, and instead of easing back on the throttle and allowing the steep downhill to take over, I kicked it even harder, and the bike began picking up the kind of speed that usually ends with someone sweeping what's left into a dustpan. I felt Truman involuntarily tighten his grip on my waist.

We were about a third of the way down when I saw the speedometer needle pass 117. At this speed, I couldn't chance looking back, but even if Remi was there, he wasn't going to let anybody fire a gun next to him. Suddenly, from a side street on the left, Julien burst back onto the scene and turned downhill—and because he wasn't carrying an extra 200+ lbs. of asshole, he began pulling away.

With everyone at the river, the town was deserted, and we hit the empty square and passed Napoleon's bier just as the first fireworks burst in the sky. For some reason, I noticed they were red, white and blue. Julien had slowed enough to let me catch him, and I kept the Triumph wide open and blew by. Then I felt something on my right. Remi had somehow come even with my rear wheel, and he looked over and smiled. The shooter was right-handed, so he had to arc the *lupara* over Remi's head to fire to the other side, which he was trying to do without impeding his driver.

Up ahead, another rocket went off, illuminating the crush of people lining the cliffs. No one turned toward us. The engines thundering down on them were lost in the explosions.

I had hoped to be able to slow and part the crowd enough to use the access road to get down to the water. And if that failed, to just drop the bike and run. But now, any hesitation would be fatal . . . maybe to a lot more people than me.

Remi had gained another few inches, and his passenger now had a clear sight line. I saw the barrel of the shotgun gaping at me and expected to see fire spit from it at any moment. At least I'd be dead before I crashed. As the shooter tried to adjust to the bounce of the cobblestone surface, I surveyed the crowd, looking for a spot where I'd kill the fewest citizens. Then I saw a narrow opening on my right. A pie-shaped wedge of cliff face had fallen away, leaving a deep V that spectators had avoided standing too close to. I leaned into the bike as much as I dared and aimed for it.

I don't know how fast we were going, but our momentum carried us well out over the river. I saw Remi to my right and heard the screams of onlookers just as a volley of fireworks rockets launched, their fiery tales shrieking by us.

But one did not get all the way by. It hit Remi's bike, shattering the gas tank and turning Mr. Terranova and Mr.

Lupara into Roman candles. Remi wouldn't be needing any more shaves.

I felt Truman disengage, and I pushed the bike right and tried to fall as far to the other side as possible. As the water rushed up to meet me, I hoped that if I didn't make it, Truman wouldn't either. And then I hit the river, and everything went black for a moment. Then strong hands were pulling me aboard an Aquascan.

43

Blue Jungles and Crimson Tents

What was it Julien had said about the patrol boats? Old and slow? Who the fuck had he been kidding? True, we had left a pair of Corsican police vessels far behind, but as we'd hit the open water of the Med, a French Navy coastal launch had jumped on our tail, its prow riding high and a couple of manhole-cover-sized searchlights turning the inky night into high noon.

Eddie and Julien were running a hundred yards to our starboard side and angling away. The French skipper had to make a decision, and he stuck with Truman and me. I did all the jukes I could and still remain upright, but the cruiser was still there with his siren dialed up to ear-split. We were roughly even with the coastline where I'd intended to put in, but that was out of the question with this asshole on me.

"He has a .50 cal," Truman yelled in my ear, "and there's a guy racking it."

There's such a thing as too much information. I was running flat out, and the wind was kicking up five-foot swells, which meant we were only one off-center smack from capsizing, so hearing that a stream of roll-of-nickel-sized slugs might be on the way wasn't data I could use. Suddenly, we hit an oversized wave head-on, and the little Aquascan nose-dived into the trough, bringing us almost to a full stop. The machine gun opened up at exactly the same instant, and I saw the tracers pass overhead. If we'd still been running at the speed we had been a moment earlier, we'd have been hamburger. I guess French for warning shots is "Eat this, motherfucker."

We had about ten seconds before even a blind gunner found the range. I jerked the rudder hard left for a two-count then jammed the throttles all the way forward and wedged the equipment seabag against them. The searchlights momentarily lost us, and the oncoming swells began to beat our bow, lifting it skyward then smashing it down at unnatural angles. One or two more times, and we'd be upside down and dead.

Over the siren, the engines, the wind and the pounding waves, I heard Truman yell, "Are you fucking crazy!!!"

I slipped the second seabag containing my personal effects over my shoulder, turned, took a step and wrapped my passenger in a tackle that took us both over the side. I tried to hit on my back, and almost got there. I saw the wake of the Aquascan go by and felt my legs hit its edge, flipping them over my head.

I was underwater when the cruiser went directly over us, and after being mix-mastered by the twin screws, I surfaced. Truman was ten yards away, choking out seawater but seemingly none the worse for wear. I heard the cruiser's engines change, and I saw it half a mile beyond come into a hard turn. I grabbed Truman and pointed him toward shore, wondering how much I had left.

We missed the outlaw airstrip on the first pass, then doubled back and saw the Cirrus's tail sticking over some low brush. Truman and I were both a little chewed up from the scrub, but our clothes had dried considerably. When he saw the plane, Truman started grinning. "Goddamn, whoever you are, you thought of everything."

I ignored him and paced off the minimum distance I needed to get airborne. Then I took a flare out of my seabag, lit it and dropped it in the grass. There wasn't much leeway before we'd slam into a copse of pines, and I made a mental note not to try to cheat an extra ten yards.

When I got back to the plane, Truman was standing beside the pilot's door. "I assume you've got a set of keys for this mother," he said.

"I do, but you're not driving."

Not getting it, he looked at me with that special kind of disdain pilots and surgeons reserve for mortals. "Apparently, you don't know I'm as good a pilot as there is—anywhere."

I looked at him and smiled. "Oh, I know who you are, Truman. But on this run, you're just freight."

While he puzzled that out, I hit him. It wasn't the best punch I've ever thrown, but it was the best since my father and I cleared out the Dragoon Bar in Belfast. I caught him on the button, and he went down, back of the head first. He wasn't completely out, so I bent over him and said, "From Kim." I saw his eyes start to focus and my words begin to penetrate. Then I hit him again and felt his teeth give. "From Archer." He missed the second dedication, but it didn't matter.

Lying behind me in the Cirrus, Truman York looked like a terrorist on his way to Guantánamo. I'd put a pillowcase over his head and run a loose line of tape around his neck, giving him some ventilation. A considerable amount of blood had seeped through the makeshift hood, but that came under the heading of it couldn't be enough.

I had also taped his wrists to his thighs and his ankles to each other. Buckled into the backseat on his right side, he was undoubtedly uncomfortable, but so far, quiet. That his daughter had once lain in an almost identical position was an irony not lost on me, but I couldn't bring myself to talk to this dirtbag again for any reason.

From time to time, I checked to make sure the hood was

expanding and contracting, and so far, he didn't seem to be fighting for breath. But frankly, if he had been, tough shit. I think he sensed that was my attitude, so he reached back into his pilot's training and avoided hyperventilating.

I held steady at 4,800 feet, high enough to be on everybody's radar and not be perceived as a threat, but low enough to have plenty of oxygen. We'd refueled once, and before putting down, I'd thrown a blanket over my passenger. He'd flopped around a bit, but if the grimy guy handling the pump noticed, he didn't say anything. He'd looked at my bandaged hands, then at the hundred-dollar bill I handed him, and evidently decided it was none of his business.

We'd been in and out of rain and wind the whole way, but the autopilot had kept us dead on course. Now as we entered the last leg, I suddenly noticed how stiff and tired I was, and I had to fight off the urge to fall asleep.

Fifteen minutes later, a voice came up in my headset. It was American with a little Alabama thrown in. "FRANCES, BAKER, BAKER, TANGO, ZEBRA . . . Come in, please."

"This is F-BBTZ. Go ahead."

"You are flying into restricted airspace. Authorization to enter is denied. Repeat, authorization denied. Do you copy?"

"Affirmative. Please ask your intelligence officer to come to the tower."

The voice got more aggressive. "If you are experiencing an emergency, please declare its nature. Otherwise, you must turn around. Repeat, turn around, now. Intercept has commenced."

"Listen, son, before we ratchet this up any further, let's agree your balls are bigger than mine and so are your guns. Now, call your intelligence officer and tell him Blue Jungle requests a runway assignment. Got that? Blue Jungle requests an assignment."

Military pilots and crew, clandestine officers and special operators are issued authenticator codes for emergencies. If you're on the run in hostile territory, it's how a search-and-rescue team knows you are who you say you are and not the enemy sucking them into a trap. And if you're captured, you try to find ways to get your code out so people know you're alive.

Some of the Vietnam MIAs actually cut their authenticators into hillsides and rice paddies, and our satellites photographed them. But McCain and Kerry and the rest of their goddamn investigating committee decided that the Defense Department's analysts were full of shit and left our bravest to the tender mercies of Hanoi's gulag. Some of them are probably still there. I often wonder what they must be thinking. I hope one day they get a chance to tell the John Boys—personally.

Originally, authenticators were nonsensical combinations of letters and numbers. Then somebody figured out that most people can't remember their old zip code a month after they move, and they switched to words. Since Delta operators are always subject to recall, our codes are supposed to be "hot" until we go to the big shooting house in the sky. They're also supposed to act as an unquestioned introduction anywhere in the world. I was about to find out.

I looked over the seat. "If we hit the drink, Tru, try not to float facedown."

A pair of F-16s showed up a few minutes later and streaked by like a couple of kids on skateboards buzzing a senior citizen. I switched off the autopilot and rode the turbulence by hand. It wasn't necessary, but when they pulled alongside, I wanted to look like I was doing something.

Shortly, they bracketed the Cirrus and were close enough to read the pilot's names under their canopies. Captain Brubaker was on my left; Lieutenant Montgomery to the right. I waved, and got a wing waggle from Montgomery. Brubaker apparently didn't like me. Then my headset got busy again.

"Blue Jungle, this is Bulldog One. We're going to ride with you while they sort this out downstairs. Copy?"

"Copy."

"So here's the drill. On my mark, we're going to climb to seven thousand and make a one-hundred degree turn to the west."

"Negative."

"I don't think you understand."

"Look, Captain, I've had a rough couple of days, and I'm dead fucking tired. You want to put one between my eyes, be my guest. Otherwise—"

I was interrupted by the tower. "Blue Jungle, this is Major Borden. G-2."

"Afternoon, Major, sorry to be such a pain in the ass."

"No problem, Sergeant. What can we do for you?"

Well, at least he knew who I was. "First thing would be to ask the Bulldogs here to back off a thousand yards. I'm sure they're used to flying this close, but I'm not."

The major gave the command, and the F-16s dropped out of my line of sight.

"Thanks, how's the weather down there?"

"A little overcast, but nothing significant. Five miles visibility."

"Good, I'm pretty lousy on instruments too. You got a runway I can drop onto so we can chat?"

"It'd be nice to have a mission name or an authorizing officer."

"How about Marlon Hood?"

Silence, then, "Use One-Four Right. See you in a few minutes."

"Major?"

"Yes?"

"I'm going to need a full set of shackles and a car. Nothing military."

"And just this morning I was saying nothing ever happens around here."

The road northeast out of Incirlik had turned hot, flat and empty. The red Chrysler with the super-tinted windows was

Major Borden's personal car. He'd bought it over the Internet from a dealer in Dallas and had it shipped out in a C-5. He said the air force had dinged him two grand for handling, but now he had the best air-conditioning in the country, and it was worth every penny. Looking at the temperature gauge and seeing 121, I agreed.

Truman had made some commotion during the switchover from tape to shackles, but when you're wearing a hood, it's hard to get a bead on your opponent, and I clocked him again. Now he rode alongside me, alternately grunting and calling me a motherfucker. The pillowcase was dripping blood now, so the last punch had either smashed his nose, or he'd bitten his tongue. I didn't bother to check which.

I hadn't told him where he was, but he knew. After you've lived abroad for a while, you realize that every place has its own unique smell. Southern Turkey's verdant green, salt wind, even the sun, all carried their portion of the region's olfactory identity. The rest was borne by the people themselves: baking bread, livestock, spices, decaying fish, blue exhaust and rivers of sweat. All giving dimension to a thriving democracy.

But Truman York wasn't interested in travel brochures, and neither was I.

Ilker Koca was no longer mayor of Tasar, but a kid named Farouk in white cotton shorts, a Cowboys T-shirt and a tattered fisherman's cap offered to lead me to him for twenty bucks. I followed the Vespa east for an hour and eventually into a dusty, sprawling town where camels and donkeys stood alongside big Mercedes. Here, Farouk had said, Ilker ruled over the extended Koca family.

A hodgepodge of two-story, vaguely European-style homes was set amid hundreds of tents, some small and worn, others large and ornate, and I struggled to keep sight of the Vespa as Farouk zigged and zagged through the impossibly narrow lanes, scattering dogs, goats and chickens. Once or twice I brushed against something I'm sure I wasn't supposed to, and I worried some curious citizen would wander out and I wouldn't see him until it was too late.

We finally stopped at the entrance to a majestic, bright crimson tent accented by woven gold. In the shade of the entrance's portico, several veiled women knelt on rugs working at something. I left the car running and got out. As I approached, I saw the women were sorting silver beads of all manner of design. None of them looked up, and my guide frantically motioned for me to go back to the car.

I leaned on the hot door while Farouk took off his fisherman's cap and entered the tent. I glanced at Truman, who was straining against his seat belt, as if by getting his head closer to the windshield he might be able to see through the cotton cloth.

Suddenly, there was loud shouting inside the tent, and the women scattered. A few moments later, a bearded man in his thirties wearing traditional tribal dress came out. He had Farouk by the neck with one hand and was brandishing a dagger in the other. The kid started struggling even harder, but the man tightened his grip.

He looked at me. "You, why do you come to this place?" he called out.

"I have business with Ilker Koca," I answered.

"I am Mehmet Koca, his son," he said. "Any business you have with my father, you have with me. But first, you will watch while this young fool has an eye taken for bringing a stranger to our village."

I looked at Farouk. The terror on his face told me it wasn't an empty threat.

"I forced him to do it," I said.

This seemed to take Mehmet off-guard. "How could you force him?" he said angrily. "He could have ridden away at any time."

"I told him that my business with Ilker Koca was of such importance that if he did not take me, someone would slit his throat for his negligence."

Mehmet looked at me for a moment, then laughed loud

and long. "I do not believe you, but you are clever and quick." He pushed Farouk away, and the boy stumbled to his Vespa and was gone in a heartbeat. "Come inside out of the heat," Mehmet said. Then, for the first time, he looked at the idling car. "Is there someone else?"

"Yes, but he'll be fine," I said. He's very good at waiting."

Given the blast furnace outside, the comfort of the tent was surprising and welcome. I removed my shoes and followed Mehmet onto the raised platform that constituted the main living area. Ringed by a ground-level walkway, it was roughly thirty by fifty feet and carpeted with a checkerboard of Middle Eastern rugs overlaid with animal skins.

A dozen squat dining tables with three-foot-round hammered metal tops dotted the room, and each of the elaborately carved support posts running down the center of the tent had a shallow oil bowl hanging from it to provide light. Along three sides of the far end of the platform was a long wicker sofa covered with crimson, green and gold cushions, and there, a group of bearded older men sat, talking among themselves.

Mehmet turned to me. All pretense of menace was gone, replaced by an amused look. "So, what is this important and deadly business, my friend?"

"I don't wish to offend you, but it is business for your father only. If he wishes to include you, I have no objection, but that must be his choice."

He started to say something, but I stopped him. "It is about the past, and it concerns your sister."

I watched his face change. After a moment, he turned and walked toward the old men. They spoke quietly, then Mehmet gestured for me to join them.

Ilker Koca had probably never been a large man, but now he was shrunken almost into his skin. His naturally dark complexion was a deep gray, and the whites of his eyes were yellow. Liver cancer, I guessed. Perhaps kidney failure setting in.

When he spoke, it was in a rasp, and he didn't waste words. "You have brought me something?"

"Truman York."

If he was surprised, he didn't show it.

"And the second man? The base commander?"

"He will not be coming."

Ilker Koca looked deeply into my eyes. "In good time," he said. "Is there something I can do for you?"

"You are doing it. My sympathies for what happened to your daughter."

When I got back to the Chrysler, they had already taken Truman away. I fingered the key to the shackles and decided they didn't need it.

I wheeled the big machine around and headed toward Incirlik. A mile out of the village, I stopped and got out. I threw the key as far as I could. When I got back in the car, I felt a lot lighter. I hoped Major Borden had a bed I could fall into.

44

Grandfathers and Ashes

It was a perfect autumn day in London. The wind whipped red and gold leaves across the Stansted Airport runway like welcoming confetti and pushed banks of clouds about the sky so the sun could alternately tease the landscape with the last remnants of the season gone, then plunge it into a preview of the coming months of gray.

Mallory had been staring out the window. "My grandfather spent his entire life soldiering for the Empire, yet every letter he wrote home opened with his memories of this lovely, gentle land. And each time I see it after an absence, I realize it is a stamp upon my soul I shall never lose, nor wish to."

Archer was seated on the opposite side of the cabin, and she had been quiet since we'd crossed into British airspace. "I've always flown into Heathrow or Gatwick. This is . . . how can I say it . . . more Englandy."

"I think you have a future in travel posters," I said. But she was right. The first great city after the Fall of Rome is making great strides at devolving into another neon-encrusted theme jungle engorged with chain hotels, logoed boutiques and Disney musicals. In my formerly marvelously quirky homeland, where unique was as ingrained in the national character as understatement, one can now order the exact same overdressed dish while sitting in exactly the same bilious décor as in a dozen other "world-class cities." Meaning that if you happen to drain an extra martini or two, it is entirely possible to forget which language to use when you stumble outside to hail a cab. One can only marvel at the advancement.

Some hard-core traditionalists chart the beginning of the end of British civilization to the day Harrods opened a pizzeria. I'm inclined to go with the razing of my favorite drinking establishment, The Four Swords—in the business of quenching thirsts since 1744—to make room for a day spa called U! U! U! The Philistines have clearly won, so "more Englandy," anywhere, is to be applauded.

The livery service had sent a pair of Range Rovers, but I released one after Eddie and Jody said they were going to fly Jannicke back to California the following morning. "It's not that I haven't had a marvelous time," she said as she embraced me. "How many opportunities does one get to escape assassins then hide out with a professional wrestler *and* a princess? But Neiman Marcus is jamming my voice mail, and if I don't start paying attention to business, I'll have to move into your screening room."

"I can think of worse things," I replied. "But I'm not sure I'd wish Old Grumpy full-time on anybody."

Mallory didn't disappoint. He grunted and led her away for a private good-bye.

"And I promised Julien I'd follow up on the new Aquascan," Eddie said. "And I really miss my boat." Then, after a look from Ms. Cayne, he hastily added, "Liz too, of course."

Of course. "Steer clear of Texarkana," I said.

"If you need me, I can turn around and come right back."

I shook my head. "You've done enough, Eddie. When I get home we'll have that dinner at Titanium."

"Good, that gives me an excuse to stop and slap that fuckin' Bernard around a little so he's with the program when we get there."

Archer, Mallory and I waited until they booked rooms at a bed-and-breakfast in Bishops Stortford and a car was sent. I thought for a moment that Archer might decide to join them, but then I felt her warmth against me, and I put my arm around her.

As our driver headed north, Mallory dozed in the front seat, and Archer nodded off beside me. We left the main highway at Nottingham, didn't see Robin Hood, and meandered through the autumn countryside until we turned onto the narrow, tree-lined lane that led to Strathmoor Hall. With no other cars on the road or houses in sight, the world seemed as if it belonged only to us and the large contingent of squirrels making hay while the sun still shone. I told the driver to stop, and as he did, Archer came fully awake.

"I'm going to get out and walk," I told her.

"Then I am too," she said.

"I should warn you, it's a couple of miles, mostly uphill." I looked at her shoes. "And those Ferragamos are going to feel like . . . like Ferragamos."

"Lead on, my liege. Need be, your humble servant will go barefoot."

We got out, and the Range Rover accelerated on. The lane ran along a narrow stream, crossed at intervals by stone bridges constructed when the property was just a farm. A few were only wide enough for foot traffic and connected paths once used as shortcuts to the grazing lands beyond.

Archer led me across a particularly narrow one, and as we

walked along the opposite bank, her heels sank deep into the soft ground. As promised, she took off her shoes and carried one in each hand. "Did you used to play here?"

"If there're any frogs left, it's a tribute to their ancestors' cunning."

She laughed with the first genuine joy I'd heard for some time. "How could you not want to live in a place as incredible as this?"

"Come back in a month."

"Don't be glib. That's not what I meant."

"It's a good question. Maybe I just don't want to be alone." I wasn't proud of myself for saying that. It wasn't true, but I thought it was what she wanted to hear.

"That kind of horseshit get you laid a lot?"

"Excuse me?"

I saw her face flush, and her voice rose. " 'Excuse me' doesn't begin to cover it. I'm not your fucking prom date, Rail. We weren't looking for one another, but the last few weeks have been . . . oh, fuck it, anyway."

I'm the first to admit I'm terrible at these kinds of conversations. When you're blundering through a scene with a woman you've slept with and you don't have a copy of the script, it's like waking up with a rattlesnake in your sleeping bag. You know that as grateful as it might have been for the warmth, now it's going to bite you. Sometimes the best thing to do is get it over with.

"I'm not very good at reading minds, so why don't you mime it." As soon as it was out, I knew it was the wrong thing to say. I tried to grab it and missed.

"You're an asshole."

She had me there. She turned and faced me, her cheeks red. It wasn't that cold. "I'm going to say two words, and I want an honest answer. Do I have your promise?"

"Maybe."

"That doesn't make it. Yes or no?"

Now *I* was irritated. "You want to know something, ask. If

I have the answer, I'll probably give it. But if it's something I prefer not to share, I won't."

I thought she was going to blow, but she didn't. "Okay. Konstantin Serbin."

I don't know what I was expecting, but that wasn't it. "And . . . ?"

"You're a smart guy, let your imagination run."

"We're in London because I have a board meeting. Period."

"But you intend to see him, don't you." It wasn't a question.

I took a breath. "Is he unfinished business? Yes. Do I have an agenda? No. One of the things a soldier learns is when to let things go. Otherwise, wars would never end. Every person who was responsible for the death of someone you cared about would have to be hunted down and killed . . . as would the person who gave the order . . . and so on . . . until there was no one left."

"Does that apply to atrocities too?"

"Especially to atrocities. Despite the revisionists, do you honestly believe there was anyone with a pulse in Nazi Germany who didn't know what was going on?"

"Of course not."

"So every ordinary citizen who kept his mouth shut contributed to the Holocaust."

"In their own way, absolutely."

"Well, all thirteen trials at Nuremberg netted the execution of only a couple dozen people. That's two hundred and fifty thousand to one in Holocaust victims alone. Add in military and civilian deaths, and it's ten times more."

"So you're saying nothing ever comes out even."

"It's not 'even' that matters. We're defined by the point we decide it's over."

She looked at me for a moment, then turned her head. But before she did, I saw a tear on her cheek. "Goddamn you," she said, but there wasn't any conviction in it.

* * *

Strathmoor Hall looked warm and welcoming, not at all like a place that hadn't been visited by its owner in over two years. Keeping four stories of eighteenth-century galleries, state rooms, paintings, grand staircases and bedrooms in good repair requires almost as many man-hours as it does pounds sterling. And, like many of its elderly brethren in the neighborhood, the undertaking is compounded by stables, lakes, a classical garden with an impossible maze and an auditorium-sized conservatory that, in its day, was the largest ever built.

Every grand home has a feature of architectural genius. Strathmoor Hall's is a man-made horseshoe waterfall one hundred feet across that plunges nearly silently into a pool adorned with naked statues of Grecian gods. My father, who thought the falls were a "goddamn eyesore," tried twice to have them torn out, but the blue-haired ladies of the National Trust, who aren't supposed to have any say over private property, somehow convinced a court otherwise. I never told my father, but I was glad.

As Archer and I stood looking at it, she said, "I tried to be nonchalant when we came up that boulevard you call a driveway, but this . . . I'm completely at a loss."

"My father was convinced the original owner put it in because he was impotent. He called it Compensation Falls."

She laughed. "It makes me want to pee."

When we walked through the back door, Mallory had our cook, Guinevere—an ample woman with breasts that could nurse a small country—waving two knives and screaming at him to get out of her kitchen, or she was going to cut off something to cook with bangers. On his way past us, he mumbled a retort, but not loudly.

"I see nothing's changed," I said as I kissed Guin's neck, and she turned and hugged me close.

"The nicest thing anybody's ever done for me was take that little fart to California," she said in her lilting Scottish brogue.

Archer burst out laughing and bolted for the bathroom.

* * *

Black Group, Ltd. operates out of a nineteenth-century, columned, granite-faced edifice in Knightsbridge. The boardroom, like most, is a monument to the company's successes:
framed front pages of history-making headlines, detailed
models of its great ships and photographs of its famous real
estate. It would take two rooms of equal size to exhibit its
failures, but as my father would say, "I never made a mistake
I couldn't erase in the retelling."

The primary item on the agenda was the acquisition of a
Rome media company we'd been pursuing for years only to
be rebuffed each time in that quaint way the Italians have of
six people waving their arms and shouting all at once. Now
they'd come knocking on our door.

"There's some upheaval in the family D'Antonio," explained BG's managing director, Sir Gregory Bone, to the
eleven men and three women seated around the table. "The
oldest son has a heroin problem, and the youngest a habit of
marrying prostitutes. The late Mr. D'Antonio's will made
it absolutely clear they were to have nothing to do with the
business, and their sister, Graciella, has been running it—
quite ably, I should add. Now the brothers have filed suit to
either be put in operating positions or have their percentages
paid out in cash. They'll lose, of course, but Graciella would
like to avoid the dirty laundry that would come out at trial."

Another director—Burton Evennette, the board's resident
curmudgeon—shook his head. "Italian courts. Only the
Americans have made more of a mess of a justice system.
By the time those corrupt bastards finish, the D'Antonios
will be bankrupt. We should stand down and pick up the
pieces."

Sir Gregory looked down the table at me. "Would you like
to speak to this, Mr. Black?"

"I see from the notes you provided that the asking price is
two billion euros. What does our due diligence say?"

"It's below market, and I believe that, under the circumstances, we might be able to wring out another ten percent."

I turned to Julia Rillington, head of BG's media group. "This would fall under your wing, Julia. What do you think?"

"I've met Ms. D'Antonio. She's smart and tough. If I could, I'd like to have her on my team."

"Sir Gregory," I said, "let me offer a suggestion. Negotiate the best deal you can, then I'll make up the difference to two billion. That way BG will be honoring its corporate responsibility, and I'll get a piece of an undervalued asset."

Julia Rillington never broke eye contact with me. "And Ms. D'Antonio will not feel as though she's had her father's company stolen from her. Thank you, Mr. Black."

I don't think Burton Evennette was as impressed, but then he rarely is.

At that moment, the boardroom door opened, and Mr. Wicks, BG's chief of security, came in. "Excuse me, Mr. Black, but there's a gentleman in the lobby who insists on seeing you. I told him you were not available, but he refuses to leave. Before I sent for the police, I thought I should ask. He said he works for someone named Serbin."

The man seated in the anteroom off reception was large and Asian. I recognized him immediately from Kim's photographs as one of the colonel's security detail. He stood quickly and handed me a rich-looking envelope with a red wax seal and my name inscribed in elegant calligraphy. As I took it, I thanked him in Mongolian, *"Bayarlla."*

That caught him by surprise, and he smiled slightly. Then he regained his stony countenance, nodded curtly, turned and left. As I rode the elevator back to the boardroom, I broke the seal and read the KS-embossed card inside.

Mr. Black,

Since our paths continue to be intertwined, I think it's time we met, don't you? I'm holding a small, black tie affair this Saturday to unveil some additions to my collection.

I'd be delighted to have you attend. Say, around 8:00? And by all means, please bring Ms. Cayne.

Konstantin Serbin

Paintings and Pageants

Archer came down the staircase with the same walk I had seen that first day back on Princeton Street. I'd been with her almost constantly since, but even though she always moved with an easy grace, this was different. Catlike. She was a woman who was used to being noticed to the exclusion of anyone else in a room, and down deep, she not only knew how to maximize it but she craved it as well.

She'd borrowed a dress from the London shop of Rudolfo Sanci, the designer who had launched her career in Europe, and there was no other word for it but imperial. Shoulderless black silk with aquamarine accents complemented by matching aquamarine Jimmy Choos. She'd also discovered a collection of jewelry in the house that I didn't know existed and selected a flat platinum neck chain with a single strawberry-sized aquamarine on a slide at her throat. On her wrists, she wore a pair of three-inch-wide mock French cuffs in solid platinum, each set with a single, large aquamarine where the cuff link would be.

Even Mallory was taken by her entrance. "My goodness, Ms. Cayne, you are likely to be spirited off to Saint Petersburg to live at Catherine Palace."

She smiled. "Only if I can order executions." She eyed my tux and said, "You clean up pretty well yourself."

I had elected to drive rather than call for a car. I hung my jacket on the hook in the back, and Archer settled into the Bentley's passenger seat. She rummaged around in the glove box until she found a Sinatra CD, and as we drove toward the city, we listened to the Chairman of the Board do what no one else has ever done as well.

The "small dinner" turned out to be, like many things Russian, deliberately misstated. The line of cars outside my grandfather's former home paralyzed traffic for blocks, and as we waited our turn at the valet, we watched the arriving guests disembark under the brightly lit portico. Not surprisingly, most were members of the new Russian elite—young politicians, oligarchs and wealthy ex-pats hovered over by bodyguards and sporting arm decorations of overdressed, overly obvious women.

"Nice-looking crowd," mused Archer. "Sort of a thug and moll ball."

Just then, one of London's leading bookmakers got out of a vintage Rolls with a tall, trashy-looking brunette wearing way too much makeup, several million dollars' worth of diamonds and, of all things, a tiara.

"Oh, look," said Archer, "the queen. Jesus, if Rudolfo were here, he'd ask for his dress back."

When we finally made our way up the red carpeted stairs, past the guards and into the home's foyer, the place was full, and the guests were milling about to background music provided by a string quartet.

Many in the crowd recognized one or both of us, but no one approached. "Ever get tired of being resented by every woman in the room?" I asked.

"Never. But it pisses the hell out of me when they give equal time to my date."

"I was thinking the same thing."

She elbowed me and hit my bad rib. Time to put away the rapier wit.

My grandfather had built and disposed of the mansion long before I was born, so I'd never been inside. I'd heard, however, that the Yugoslavs had replaced the original décor with Rococo Extreme. Serbin evidently liked the look, because there was enough gilt on the mirrors, murals on the ceilings and overblown chandeliers to satisfy even the most subtlety-challenged Parisian pretender.

But what the place gave away in ostentation, it more than compensated for in art. I remember Bert's telling me that Russian painting takes some getting used to. That Nikitin, Levitskii, and, later, Briullov were so heavy-handed that their work feels like it's being sledgehammered through your eyeballs. In his opinion, only Vrubel and the lone, consensus female master, Bashkirtseva, possessed as fine a hand as any of the more well-known Western Europeans.

However, as ponderous as the majority of Serbin's paintings were, and as unsophisticated a viewer as I am, the cumulative effect was nothing short of august. More interesting was how, since Russian law explicitly prohibited the export of any artwork older than fifty years, the colonel had managed to assemble a collection rivaling the Hermitage's.

The tuxedoed and gowned guests were ushering themselves along the walls, commenting on the masterpieces while pairs of white-coated, white-gloved waiters pushed vodka and caviar carts among them. The decanters were set in hollowed-out blocks of ice marked with small labels. I ordered two glasses of Siberia, which the server made great theatre out of pouring into silver-stemmed Operetta flutes. I passed on the cut-crystal bowl of caviar also imbedded in ice, but Archer wolfed down several toast points heaped with Beluga. "No lunch," she said with her mouth full. "Why not you?"

"It would feel like I was cheating on Wandie."

"How very droll. I must be in England."

We were in a drawing room admiring a Bakst canvas when an accented voice behind us said, "It's a fake."

We turned to find Konstantin Serbin smiling at us. "Not

one of Tiziano's. My insurer introduced me to this fellow. I'm fascinated at the services you capitalists dream up." He extended his hand. "I'm delighted to meet you, Mr. Black. It's always a pleasure to make the acquaintance of a fellow soldier."

He was smooth in a Moscow sort of way. Tanned and expertly tailored in a suit cut to complement his thick chest and five-foot-seven height. His speech was also impeccable and his manners perfect, but there was the split-second hesitation of an autodidact as he ran through his mental checklist.

"My congratulations on your successful departure from the Watergate. The note was a particularly nice touch . . . not to mention a bit awkward, since I'd asked a favor of an old friend."

I bowed ever so slightly. "Glad to be of service."

"I was much more disappointed to learn that Mr. Bruzzi is no longer with us. I'm told it was his heart."

"You were misinformed. His heart was the last to go."

He allowed himself a moment, discarded what he'd intended to say and turned to Archer. "I'm sure you've been told this many times, Ms.Cayne, but your photographs do not do you justice."

She took his hand. "Neither do yours, Konstantin. You're much shorter."

I saw his eyes harden. "Now I understand why one of my fellow citizens decided to retire you." Without warning, Serbin reached up and pushed Archer's hair away from her bad eye. "Russian men are not so amused."

The motion had been so sudden that she went rigid. I didn't. I clamped my hand down on his wrist and pulled him toward me. He stumbled slightly, and I felt his powerful frame tense as we locked eyes. I knew my size was of no consequence. The only issue was whether he was prepared to let me break his arm when he made his move. We stood that way for an uncomfortable moment, then he relaxed. I waited just slightly longer and released my grip.

He turned to Archer and smiled tightly. "Excuse my manners, Ms. Cayne. It is sometimes easier to take off the uniform than the privilege."

"Oh, do please call me Archer. After one murders a family member, I think first names should be *de rigueur,* don't you?"

Serbin allowed himself a smile. "What I think, *Ms. Cayne,* is that if you keep score only by clever remarks, you're not really in the game."

He and Archer held each other's eyes, then he turned back to me. "I'm told my home used to be your grandfather's. Why don't I give you a short tour?"

The three of us walked while the colonel pointed out the finer points of Yugoslav interior design and commented on his paintings. As we progressed, my initial impression of his collection changed. Comparing it to the Hermitage implied differences. In Serbin's case, some of what used to hang in St. Petersburg now hung in Belgravia. As Bert Rixon would be the first to tell you, I'm no one's art muse, so if I recognized them, a slug could have.

Half an hour later, we found ourselves on a stairway leading to the third floor. At the top, a pair of thickly built Mongolian security men in too-tight suits parted to let us pass. We turned right and walked to the end of the hallway, where an ornately carved black ironwood door added an impression of security and menace to the already heavy décor. Serbin took out a skeleton key and inserted it into the old lock. The click of the dead bolt was loud, and the door creaked open, very Vincent Price-like. I felt Archer's hand go into mine.

The colonel entered and was swallowed by the dark. Seconds later, the soft radiance of museum-quality lighting revealed a thick-carpeted, mahogany-paneled gallery. "I believe," said Serbin, "this is what you came to see."

I knew it was going to be the Tretiakov Collection, but there was nothing familiar about how being physically in its presence affected me. Often, when someone's death touches us, we try to imagine his last moments. Though I had never known any of these men, as I came face-to-face with their paintings, I could suddenly see each one seated before his canvas, feel his final rush of creativity. I watched his hand execute his last stroke and put down his brush. Saw him look over his shoulder one last time as he was led away to have his unique light extinguished forever.

And then I understood. Kim was in that room with me, and she was revealing what I would never have been able to see for myself. I can't explain how I knew, but I knew.

Not all of the paintings were masterpieces. As talented as these painters had been, they had become dissidents first and artists second. But each, even the lesser works, radiated an unmistakable energy and life.

I felt Archer let go of my hand. She followed the paintings around the room. I glanced at Serbin. He stifled a yawn. He'd already grown indifferent. It was a familiar affliction. People who acquire simply because they can, or to keep others from having something, lack a basic building block of humanity. A core. The colonel appreciated nothing. A priceless diamond or a rusty car had the same meaning. If someone else wanted it, all that mattered was that he had it, and they didn't.

Archer stood in front of *Offering of the Babushkas*. At four feet square, it was larger than the others, and now exquisitely framed and perfectly lighted, its detail came fully to life, colors surging off the canvas. Most haunting was the stricken look on the face of Illya's mother. It had been present in the photograph, of course, but now if you looked closely, her lip even seemed to tremble.

As Archer stared at the painting, Serbin said to her, "Pavlova Mikhailovna Orlov. Royally born, then married a Jew. Who can understand the foolishness of women who bring dishonor to themselves and suffering to their children?"

I braced myself for what was coming, but Archer surprised me. "Have you ever loved anyone, Colonel? Besides yourself, that is?"

Serbin seemed amused. "I love as all Russian men do, with passion . . . and frequently."

"That is not what I meant."

He looked at her with a cold smile. "It is exactly what *I* meant, Ms. Cayne. The difference is that I am never given over to things I do not control."

A faint chime rang somewhere in the hall, and the colonel clapped his hands once as if placing a final punctuation on the exchange. "If we're finished here, let us join my other guests."

As we returned downstairs, Konstantin Serbin was enveloped by people vying for his attention. Before he was swept away, he instructed one of his security people to escort us to dinner.

"Thank you, but we're leaving," I said.

Archer interrupted, "No, we're not."

"Excellent," said Serbin. "We'll chat again later. I'll be most interested to hear what you think of the entertainment. It's something particularly fascinating."

When he was gone, Archer looked at me. "Can you feel the evil in this place? It's like decay, clinging to everything. I can even taste it."

I put my hands on either side of her face. She tried to pull away, but I wouldn't let her. "I know what you're thinking, but this is out of your league."

"Killing a president was supposed to be out of Oswald's league."

"Yes, but he had an unsuspecting target. This one bites, and usually first. I'd stop you before he had to." I reached down and took her clutch purse. She held on at first, then let go. I opened the bag and found what I expected—the small, beat-up handgun Guinevere keeps in a drawer next to the stove. I shook my head. "I've seen her breaking walnuts with this. I'm not even sure it fires."

"It does," she said. "A little to the left and not very far, but that won't matter if it's jammed in his gut."

I shook my head, slipped the gun in my jacket pocket, then handed her back her purse. "So what's it going to be?"

"Well, I didn't get all trussed up for some maitre d' with a bad hairpiece. And I haven't met the queen yet." We started walking, and she added, "Besides, you didn't check me for poison."

The grand hall had been set with long tables heaped with seafood delicacies from around the world. Every conceivable shellfish, sushi, salmon and roe was represented, accented by trays of layered accoutrements more sculpture than cuisine. Along the four walls, wide carving stations offered mountainous cuts of meat and game, and wandering among the crowd were servers in full Cossack regalia wielding swords of Russian shish kabob.

To keep Givenchy, Dior and Rudolfo free of splashing sauces and purees, each guest had been assigned a white-coated attendant to walk ahead and heap designated food onto oversized white china plates emblazoned with Serbin's Cyrillic monogram, KC. After a few moments of watching the milling horde Belushi themselves through the buffet, Archer remarked none too quietly, "Pearls before swine."

We passed on the attendants and handled our own plates. Sufficiently loaded down with gourmet excess and glasses of Chateau Margaux 2000, we gravitated to the library and seated ourselves with a pair of vacuous Czech sisters displaying multiple facial piercings and no discernable English skills. Accompanying them were a former nuclear missile commander from Vladivostok and a biological weapons scientist once employed by the KGB's Research Institute. I knew the institute because it had been a Delta target in the event of U.S. land operations against the Soviets. Small talk was not this group's forte, so Archer and I listened as the Russians debated the merits of blowing up cities versus depopulating them. It didn't take a scorecard to realize neither was retired.

When we excused ourselves for coffee, Archer looked at me with the kind of horror you sometimes see in rookie cops after their first gruesome homicide. "Did I miss something? Maybe a late Halloween?"

"Your stomach's full now, so why don't we make a quiet exit."

"Jesus Christ, I can't get away from this place fast enough. Promise me we'll take a shower as soon as we get home."

Suddenly, without warning, the lights went out. There were some nervous whispers, and I thought there had been a power failure. I remembered the direction of the front door and took Archer's arm. Frankly, it was a fitting end to the evening.

I was stopped by the sound of distant drums. Faint, then louder as they seemed to be approaching from all directions. Then, almost directly over me, a dark figure dropped on a wire from the ceiling. There was a burst of fire, and four flaming sabers appeared in his hands. The crowd gasped . . . then started applauding as the man began juggling the swords, throwing them higher with each catch.

From the illumination of the flames, I could see he was dressed head to foot in a black body stocking. Only his eyes and hands remained uncovered, and though he was slenderly built, his forearms and biceps rippled through the fabric.

The audience was mesmerized, Archer included. I scanned the entrances to the room and saw more body-stockinged figures coming from all directions, the ones in the lead pounding on some kind of tribal drums strapped over their shoulders. Behind them came bearers, carrying long coffin-shaped boxes high over their heads. Abruptly, half a dozen of the shapes—women, from their movement—raced forward and lit torches from the juggler's fire, then ran back to their processions.

The room danced in light, and the boxes became more visible. They were bronze with two long poles attached at the top for transport. The drums got louder, and the room began to reverberate. The crowd parted to let the columns through, then closed in tight around them.

Now able to see the front door, I noticed that the Mongolian security men who had been on duty when we arrived were gone. In their place were more body-stocking-clad figures.

I reached forward and grabbed Archer's arm. She let out a sharp cry. "That hurts."

I didn't have time for explanations. I wrenched her backward, and she came stumbling toward me. "Take off your shoes," I said.

"What? What for?"

I put my arm around her waist and picked her up, knocking her shoes off with my foot. Then I dropped her, grabbed her hand and ran toward the grand staircase.

"Goddamn, Rail, those fucking shoes cost more than I made on my last job."

"They made your feet look big. Now shut up and run."

An adrenaline rage kicked in, and she would have passed me on the landing if I hadn't had hold of her.

The security we had seen on the third floor earlier was also now gone, and we continued up one more floor to what had been my grandfather's private living space. The access gates I remembered from the photographs in my father's office had been taken down, replaced by a bust of Lenin opposite one of Yeltsin. But which way was the master bedroom? I gambled and plunged down the hallway to my left.

Just then, I heard automatic gunfire slamming into the ceiling and walls downstairs. Screams erupted and running feet hit the stairway. There were more gunshots, and bodies fell.

Archer stopped. "My God, what's happening?"

"What part of 'shut up and run' don't you understand?"

Then a chandelier fell somewhere . . . a woman's scream began and ended . . . and Archer got back with the program. I got lucky. The room I was looking for had been turned into an overdone study, but I recognized the walk-in marble fireplace from the twin carved elephants holding up the mantel. Apparently, someone had decided my grandfather's Indian proclivities went well with Louis XIV. I pulled Archer inside and locked the door.

She was on the edge of hysteria, only a few seconds from losing it. I needed her lucid and mobile, and I had no time to talk her down, so I pulled her close and covered her mouth with my palm while I clasped her nose with my thumb and forefinger. In her hyperventilated state, she went into oxygen deficit almost immediately, and her eyes began to bulge. Fear of suffocation gets the brain's attention over everything else, and she locked eyes with me and began pounding on my chest and kicking me with her bare feet. But I held my hand in place until I felt her starting to go out.

As soon as I let her breathe again, she started coughing and swearing and took a wild swing at me. "Welcome back," I said as I grabbed her fist. "Now pay attention, we've only got a few minutes before they begin sweeping the place."

"How are we going to get out of here?" Her voice was trembling, but she was focused on the right question.

I walked to the large bay window along the back wall. "When my grandfather was a kid, he had to jump three stories to escape a boarding school fire. He lived the rest of his life in mortal fear of burning to death." I pointed outside. "The first private residence fire escape in Belgravia."

The window was painted shut, so I grabbed a $100,000 chair and threw it through the glass. My adrenaline must have been pumping as well, because it went far enough to hit the next building. I went out first and was reaching up to help Archer when she suddenly froze, a look of stark terror on her face. I turned. Standing on the first steel landing below us were two body-stocking figures aiming Kalashnikovs directly at our faces.

One motioned me to join him, and as I complied, his partner retreated down a few steps out of range. These were pros, so I complied slowly and without comment.

As soon as we were both on the landing, the man with the rifle quickly climbed past me and was in the house in seconds. The remaining gunman indicated I was to do the same.

* * *

Archer and I walked down the grand staircase ahead of the gunmen. As we made the last turn, I put my arm around her. I had a pretty good idea what we were going to see, and I didn't know how she'd react.

The lights were back on, and there were two men's bodies on the stairs, badly mangled after being shot from behind with 7.62 rounds. I couldn't be sure, but one looked like the bookmaker. The fallen chandelier had spread glass in a wide circle across the inlaid marble floor, and Archer sucked in her breath and leaned into me when she saw the pair of shapely legs sticking out from under it, one foot still wearing a high heel.

Other corpses weren't immediately apparent, but the scene in front of us was its own spectacle. The hundred or so partiers had been made to lie facedown and were spread across the wide foyer and into the grand hall. Dozens of black body-stockinged men with assault rifles walked among them, kicking anyone who moved. Some of the women were crying, a few of the men too.

Four men stood over Konstantin Serbin. He turned his head slightly, and we made eye contact. Then one of the intruders hit him with a rifle, and he looked away.

It was then that I smelled gasoline and saw figures taking ten-liter cans out of one of the coffin-shaped boxes and lining them against a wall. That made my decision easy. I'd rather be shot.

I was about to whisper to Archer that we were going to run for it when a man in a white dinner jacket bolted to his feet and rushed one of the intruders. He managed to wrestle the man's rifle away before he was cut down in a hail of bullets. A second burst then cut down the guard who had allowed his weapon to be taken.

Everyone was distracted, and I squeezed Archer's hand, hoping she'd understand. She squeezed back, and I nodded toward the front door. It was still twenty feet away over broken glass with a pair of armed men guarding it. But it was now or never.

I slipped my hand into my jacket pocket and gripped Guinevere's tiny gun. It was worthless, but it made me feel like I wasn't completely naked. As every nerve ending poised to signal its corresponding muscle, the barrel of a Kalashnikov suddenly jammed into the back of Archer's neck so hard, it almost knocked her down. At the same time, an accented voice inches from my right ear hissed, "Don't."

I turned and saw another body-stockinged man step directly in front of me. He gestured to the guards standing at the front door, and one of them inserted a key, turned it and pushed the heavy steel frame outward. I eased my hand out of my pocket. Had the voice come a hundredth of a second later, we would have died against the glass.

The man led us outside. The air was cool, and there was a misty fog blanketing the city. It was so quiet I could hear a train leaving Victoria Station. I looked for traffic, but the street was empty. Someone had made sure there would be no surprises.

I felt Archer limping, looked down and saw the blood prints from the glass-cut soles of her bare feet. And then my car appeared. It was double-parked with its lights out and its motor running. I turned, half-expecting to catch a rifle butt to the face, but instead, the man who was escorting us pointed for his partner to return to the house.

I opened the car and got Archer inside. I tried to bandage one of her feet with my handkerchief, but it was beyond inadequate. She'd have to make do until we got back to Strathmoor Hall. I stood and closed her door.

The body-stockinged man had pulled his hood off, and I could now see his face. He was handsome and dark-haired and of indeterminate ethnicity. His eyes, however, were blue, which didn't fit the accent. And then I remembered I had seen people with this characteristic before.

"I know you, don't I?" I said.

He smiled. "I used to call you Mister." He extended his hand. "Nice to see you again, Sergeant Black."

I took his hand. His grip was warm and firm. No nervousness at all.

"May I ask?" I said.

"Colonel Serbin headed the Soviet pacification program in my country. The Americans had brought us food and books for our schools. Colonel Serbin had a different approach. He would position his tanks around a village, then open fire with incendiary shells. It was quite effective. Ashes are very peaceful." He paused. "If I close my eyes, I can still hear the screams."

"I'm sorry."

"Don't be. Every person with me lost somebody. Tonight our dead will finally sleep."

"Then I really am sorry . . . sorry that it had to be you."

I thought for a moment he was going to embrace me, but he changed his mind and extended his hand again. I put my left hand over our grip, and he did the same. Then he turned and walked back toward the house.

I got in the Bentley, half-expecting to find Archer in shock and needing a hospital. Instead, she reached over and took my hand. I put the car in gear. When we reached the front of my grandfather's former home, muzzle flashes were visible through the white-draped windows, and there was a sudden rush of flame inside the front door.

Archer put down her window, stuck her head into the cold and yelled, "For the record, Colonel, the entertainment was fucking grand. Just fucking grand."

Epilogue

It was December on Dove Way, but the night was warm, so I'd cracked the French doors in the bedroom. I looked at the clock on the nightstand. 3:47.

Since I live near the end of the street, it isn't unusual for someone to use the apron in front of my gates to turn around, but the car out there now had been sitting with its lights on and engine running for a couple of minutes.

I got out of bed, slipped on a bathrobe and walked out onto the balcony. The front gate obscured all but a pair of unidentifiable taillights. Then a man stepped into view and lit a cigarette. Manarca.

I went back inside and hit a button that opened the gates. Archer lay sprawled across the sheets, sound asleep. Her half-packed luggage was strewn around the room. Rudolfo had called from Rome and said he needed her—desperately. His modeling coordinator was completely incompetent, and the Milan show was approaching. He wanted her to stay at least a year.

Then Jannicke had dropped in unexpectedly and asked if

she'd consider doing a photo shoot in Norway. Top money and a guaranteed cover of *Elle*. I knew Archer wanted me to try to stop her, but even if I'd been able to, I wouldn't have. She wasn't finished with that life yet, and in truth, I wasn't finished with mine.

We'd gone to the cemetery the previous afternoon so she could say good-bye to Kim. Unlike the downpour when we buried her, it was a perfect Southern California day, and the celebrity-obsessed were meandering the grounds, including a dozen or so lined up to make rubbings of Marilyn's marker.

Archer brought along a HUG ME—I'M LONELY cactus, and after setting it on Kim's grave, she asked me to say a few words. It's not my line of work, but I gave it some thought, then said, "If it's true we enter the next life cleansed of the past, then no one deserves it more. Good luck, Kim. We both would have liked to have known you better."

"Amen," said Archer.

Suddenly, I felt somebody at my elbow. It was an attractive young lady, not long out of her teens, dressed in jeans and a skimpy UCLA T-shirt. She had an expensive camera draped around her neck. "This somebody famous?" she asked.

I looked at her. "No."

"Good, all the other kids have done stars until I want to puke." She regarded Kim's marker for a moment. "Cool poem," she said. "Mind if I take a picture?"

"I think my sister would approve," Archer said.

The girl focused and snapped off a couple of shots. When she finished, she said, "Kinda young. How'd she die?"

"She was murdered," I answered.

"No shit. By who?"

It should have been an easy question, but it wasn't. And while I thought about it, Archer answered. "By life."

The girl looked at us and seemed about to say something else when another young lady with a camera came trotting up, out of breath. "Hey, Angela, Soledad just told me that little girl from *Poltergeist* is buried here. You know, the one who yelled, 'They're heeeere.' Her older sister in the movie too. Jesus, how weird is that? You know where they are?"

Angela rolled her eyes at us as if to say, see what I mean. "Sure, Sheila."

We watched them walk away, and Archer said, "At least Kim won't suffer from a shortage of laughs." Then she slipped her hand into mine, and we headed back to the car.

Downstairs, Mallory had the house decorated for the holidays, once again putting Macy's to shame. He got more out of control every year, but he always pushed it through by telling me that the party for Sister Vonetta and her students couldn't be the same ol', same ol'. Really?

Somewhere in the east wing, he'd be sleeping to an old movie. Growing up with a father mostly gone, his mother had put him to bed with the television on when she went to work, and he'd been so terrified that he pretended the voices belonged to angels. Now he can't sleep without them. We'd head down to the boat Christmas Eve and stay through New Year's. This would be Bert's last of both, and the plan was heavy on everything, especially the laughs.

I opened the front door and saw Manarca resting casually against the fender of a Pontiac Grand Prix with a nice set of rims. Not police issue. Since he didn't look like he wanted to come in, I went out.

"You didn't ring, Detective," I said.

He looked at me and smiled. "Now that I've had time to check you out, I didn't figure I had to. Looks like I was right, doesn't it, *Sergeant*?" He leaned on the last word longer than he had to.

He offered me a cigarette, and I took it. We smoked in silence for a while, then he opened the passenger door of the Grand Prix, reached in and came out with a clear plastic evidence envelope. Inside was a scorched, but legible, sheet of paper. The outdoor lighting provided enough illumination to see the twenty or so names on it and, about halfway down, to make out mine and Archer's. Konstantin Serbin's guest list.

"Recognize it?" Manarca asked.

"Should I?"

"There are four more pages, if you need them. One hundred and two people." He paused. "Everybody dead." He looked at me. "Well, almost everybody."

"I get on a lot of lists. Occupational hazard."

He laughed, but not with much mirth. "Some guy in London with a name like a bank merger sent this. Asked me to look you up. Mention that they worry a lot."

"You can tell him I'm fine."

Manarca wasn't finished. "I checked with a friend over at Homeland Security. National Security type. Didn't even have to call me back. Knew you right off. Said you were in the UK at the time. And that just before that you'd been in Corsica when some shit went down. Corsica? Isn't that where that prick Dante was from?"

"Late prick," I said.

"Fuckin' shame. Now, how about putting away the tango shoes and telling me how come people on both sides of the Atlantic seem to be keeping track of you?"

"How about telling me why an LAPD detective cares."

"That's the same thing my friend in Homeland Security asked. Told him I didn't. I was just handling some bullshit assignment for the chief."

"That true?"

"Yep, but I'm a naturally curious guy. Occupational hazard."

I looked at him for a couple of seconds, then smiled. "I think maybe somebody thought they saw Paris." He didn't laugh this time, so I added, "Happens. Even to professionals."

Manarca hesitated, then nodded. "Ain't that the truth." He took back his list, got in the Pontiac and started it up. Just before he pulled away, he rolled down the window. "Hey, I almost forgot. Your buddy in London said to mention the name Bibiana. Let you know she opened a gallery in Dubai."

Dubai. Made sense. Follow the money. I didn't offer a comment, and Manarca rolled up his window. I watched him drive through the gates then went back inside.

I went to the bar and poured two fingers of the Bowmore 40 that had just arrived. The warmth of the fine single malt felt good. I opened a drawer. The key was where it should have been.

I made my way to a door just off the study—the room that had so aroused Kim's curiosity that she'd gone outside to look. I inserted the key into the substantial dead bolt, stepped into the darkness and closed the door behind me, standing still for a moment to let my eyes adjust.

As always, the plantation shutters were closed, but the full moon bathed them in enough light to give shape to the larger pieces in the room. I noticed the faint odor of furniture polish. Mallory again. Always one step ahead. Everything else was the same as I'd left it more than a year ago.

I walked to the center of the room, careful to avoid bumping into the ottoman I had kicked several times in the past, and reached for the matches that should have been there. They were, but they'd gotten pushed a few inches to the left. I struck one and lit the single white candle.

I sat down and pushed the cover off the keyboard. I started to play, but the notes were hollow, uninspired. I got up, crossed the room and touched a switch. While the turntable came to life, and the stylus fell silently into the first groove, I eased into a large leather chair.

My mother's words and Sanrevelle's voice filled the room. . . .

The snowflakes of midnight drift gently to ground,
Painting streetlights and rooftops without making a sound.
I sit here alone in this world turned to art.

Christmas always breaks my heart.
Caressing your picture by the glow of the fire.
A last look between us, a smile of desire.
Wrapped up in your bathrobe, trying to find,
A kiss still in hiding; a touch left behind.

A house full of memories; songs full of lies.
Champagne in a teacup; tears in my eyes.

You went on the wind, without a last kiss;
I reach out to catch you, but I always miss;
You slipped out of my life like a dream in the dark.
Christmas always breaks my heart.

I turn in the night, and you're not there to hold.
When I need you most, your side of the bed is cold,
You promised me that we'd never part.
Christmas always breaks my heart,
Christmas always breaks my heart.

The cards are unopened, tucked away in a drawer,
Poems filled with verses I can't feel anymore.
Pretty pictures and words that good people send.
Prayers for a heart that won't ever mend.

I'm trying to be brave, like you taught me to;
Trying to be strong, for the friends
(the friends) that we knew.

But deep in my soul, there's a place that's still true,
Where my life has meaning, because once I had you.

You went on the wind, without a last kiss;
I reach out to catch you, but I always miss;
You slipped out of my life like a dream in the dark.
Christmas always breaks my heart.

I turn in the night, and you're not there to hold.
When I need you most, your side of the bed is cold,
You promised me that we'd never part.
Christmas always breaks my heart,
Christmas always breaks my heart.

Acknowledgments

This book would not exist—or it would have someone else's name on it—if it were not for the talented writer, director, art lover and collector, Nick Meyer, whom I tried to convince to write it, and who told me to write it myself. What I think he actually said was, "Leave me alone already." Thanks, Nick.

I would also like to thank my wife, Sandra, for reading my ramblings and telling me where I wasn't funny or clever or insightful or particularly literate. And for occasionally pointing out where I was. My sons, Andrew and Trevor, for their unfailing support. And my late boxer, Annie, for sleeping on my feet while I typed and eating the things on my plate I wouldn't.

I am also grateful to my sister, Marsha Russell, the extremely gifted designer, from whom I appropriated some of the more tasteful design elements in the story, and her husband, Lee Tawes, for his unwavering support. And to my brother-in-law, Scott Ricketts, for making sure I never ran out of pasta sauce or laughs.

Every first novel needs a fan in the right place at the right time. Mine was Doug Grad at HarperCollins. My sincerest gratitude to him. And to the person at HC who had the power of the pen to say yes, Liate Stehlik . . . thank you, Liate, very, very much. To my editor, Matt Harper, who fielded the unenviable task of dealing with an aggressive, often wrong Hollywood hardhead, a thank-you isn't nearly enough, but thank you, Matt.

During this adventure, I was fortunate enough to meet Lisa Erbach Vance, my literary agent at Aaron Priest. Every ship needs a calm voice at the helm and a steady hand on the tiller. Thank you, Captain Vance, from your unruly crew of one.

Warm thanks to: Homer Hickam for putting his own heavy workload aside and reading my manuscript; my friends and fellow writers, Joe Stinson, Dennis Hackin and John Mullins for slogging through early drafts; fellow author and friend U.S. District Court Judge James Zagel, who somehow found time between gavel raps to read and give comments; and two of the best people—and producers—in Hollywood, Stephanie Austin and Walter Coblenz, for their kind words and unfailing encouragement.

I would also like to give special thanks to my terrific attorney and friend, Jay Coggan; to my always supportive Hollywood agents, Tony Etz and Matthew Snyder at CAA; to my Mississippi attorney, friend and covert writer, Ned Currie; and to the brilliant composers, Chris Lang and Cesar Benitez, who set music to "Christmas Always Breaks My Heart," and to Benny Faccone, who made magic with the track.

To Clive Cussler and Gayle Lynds, I am still overwhelmed by your praise. Thank you again.

For twenty-five years, my friend and business partner, Bob Turner, has never failed to be there for me. I have no idea what he thought of the book, because no one can tell what Bob really thinks about anything, but he read every word and let me know where I was right and where I wasn't. And that's all one can ask for.

I also owe a great debt to Frank Yablans and the late Norman Weitman for taking a chance on a wet-behind-everything college kid and bringing him into Paramount Pictures. And to Robert Evans for making the movies I get to put on my resumé.

Lastly, I would like to thank the person who inspired me to write in the first place. She died before I could invite her to Hollywood and take her and her tall collars, flashy skirts, hoop earrings and French chanteuse hairstyle onto a studio lot, then to Spago for dinner. Betty Ruth VerBeck didn't look, talk or act like a steel town, high school English teacher. She twirled like a dancer when she read poetry, swooned over her desk when she loved an essay and laughed so loud when she was happy that you could hear her in the gym three stories down. But she sent this sixteen-year-old kid home every day with his mind racing with possibilities. Sleep in peace, Miss VerBeck.

Neil Russell
2010